THE PROMETHEUS ENGINE

BOOK FOUR OF THE FOREVER AVALON SERIES

Mark Piggott

Curious Corvid
PUBLISHING

The Prometheus Engine by Mark Piggott

© 2024, Mark Piggott

All rights reserved.

Published in the United States by
Curious Corvid Publishing, LLC, Ohio.

No part of this publication may be reproduced, stored in a retrieval system, stored in a database and / or published in any form or by any means, electronic, mechanical, photocopying, recording or otherwise, without the prior written permission of the publisher, except as permitted by U.S. copyright law.

Cover Art by Emily's World of Design
Formatted by Ravven White
Interior Art by Dennis Saputra

ISBN: 978-1-959860-53-2
Hardcover: 978-1-959860-52-5

Printed in the United States of America

Curious Corvid Publishing, LLC
PO Box 204
Geneva, OH 44041

This is a work of fiction. Unless otherwise indicated, all the names, characters, businesses, places, events and incidents in this book are either the product of the author's imagination or used in a fictitious manner. Any resemblance to actual persons, living or dead, or actual events is purely coincidental.

www.curiouscorvidpublishing.com

TO MOM AND DAD, GONE BUT NOT FORGOTTEN.

THANK YOU FOR SUPPORTING MY JOURNEY AS AN AUTHOR.

PROLOGUE
MACHINATIONS BENEATH CASTLE PENDRAGON

Pendragon filled the grand halls with hope, justice, and honor. For more than 3,000 years, the descendants of King Arthur and Queen Guinevere made their home in Castle Pendragon, one that the people of Avalon could aspire to. However, such was not the case anymore.

Terror, oppression, and hopelessness now spilled out of Castle Pendragon under the auspices of the new King of Avalon—Mordred, the bastard son of King Arthur. After three millennia, the "immortal child" finally achieved his goal…To reign on the throne of Avalon.

Curly blonde hair, a beautiful face, and youthful grace made him appear as a young man, but in reality, he was one of Avalon's oldest beings. The gift of immortality imbued on him by his mother, the sorceress

Morgana le Fay, kept him immortalized, handsome, and practically untouchable. After the day known as "Avalon's Reclamation", he assumed the throne with relative ease.

Five years have passed since Avalon suddenly returned to the real world, faced the loss of magic, and survived an invasion by the modern technological might of the United States and Russia. However, that victory came at a high price. Through the efforts of the Gil-Gamesh, Lord Bryan MoonDrake, Champion and Knight Eternal of Avalon—along with great sacrifice by the elves of Alfheimer—Avalon disappeared once again from the real world, hidden away behind a magical barrier that separated the two.

Avalon had been torn asunder, shattered from one giant landmass into an archipelago of islands. At this moment of weakness, Mordred usurped the throne from King Bowen Pendragon, Avalon's reigning ruler. King Bowen had recently assumed the throne after the death of his mother, Queen Cadhla, murdered at the hands of Morgana le Fay. With an army of undead wraith knights at his command, it was child's play for Mordred to seize the granite throne and become King of Avalon.

Mordred celebrated his glorious ascension as he walked down the stairs and into the depths of Castle Pendragon. He achieved something no one thought he ever could. He was the undisputed ruler of Avalon, something he had longed for all his life. The immortal king had a bounce in his step and a smile on his handsome, boyish face.

He could barely contain his giddiness. His dream of total domination over Avalon was within his grasp. The only thing that stood in his way were the children of the Gil-Gamesh, Lord Bryan MoonDrake: Hunter,

Rose, and Ashley. Since their father's death during Avalon's Reclamation, these three had resisted Mordred's reign at every turn.

Even though they were Outlanders—people from the outside world—they inherited their father's powerful magic. Mordred and his allies tried to blame Avalon's destruction on their father, but it did not sway everyone. Many rallied to their side in an all-out rebellion against Mordred, but that would soon change.

This was the reason for Mordred's happiness. He had been waiting for this day for over five years, and the anticipation was unbearable. The winding staircase took Mordred deeper and deeper underground. Though the original halls beneath Castle Pendragon went deep in the earth, Mordred dug down even deeper to ensure his pet project's secrecy.

He stepped up to a large steel door, void of any handle, hinge, or doorknob. He placed his hand on the door and said, "*Apertus!*" The door slowly lowered to the floor as a wash of hot air escaped past him before Mordred stepped inside.

The room was filled with grinding gears, clanging metal, and burning fires. Gnomes worked tirelessly at their tasks within the dank chamber, unaware of Mordred's presence. Though relatively small, gnomes were meticulous, inventive, greedy, cunning, and ruthless. Their dynamic nature made them the best workers money could buy. Gnomes were shorter than dwarves, most under three feet tall, with large, bulbous heads and slim bodies. Their tiny hands allowed them to perform precision work, particularly in building small instruments and machines. Though the laws of magic that governed Avalon didn't allow for many mechanical and electrical devices to operate, gnomes got around this by using magic to power them.

The gnomes were all working on a giant engine of sorts. It towered more than twenty feet tall and nearly forty feet wide. Though the engine was silent, the work was intense. A small army of workers painstakingly calibrated each gear, pipe, and valve. Gnomes covered the machine—on ladders and scaffolding or dangling from harnesses suspended from the ceiling—like busy bees working in a hive. A large crystal mounted on the engine resembled a weathervane perched on a rooftop. It was a marvel that somebody could build such a device on Avalon, but this was no ordinary engine.

Mordred gazed at the craftsmanship of their work as he reveled in the potential fruition of their labor. He stared at the engine longingly until the gnome leader noticed him there.

Master Tinker Edwyn Broadfoot stood less than three feet tall, his bulbous head covered with a leather skullcap as wisps of hair stuck out from underneath it. A pair of thick goggles covered his eyes, affixed with varied magnification lenses. Around his waist hung a utility belt with various tools dangling from it. Edwyn carried a massive iron wrench, which he used as a walking stick and a weapon.

The little gnome bowed to the king. "Your Majesty," he murmured with respect and fear. "We're about ready to begin."

"Excellent, Master Tinker. Are you sure it will work?" Mordred asked.

"Who can say, Your Excellency, I've never built anything like this before," Edwyn responded. "The plans you provided were incomplete and difficult to translate, so I had to improvise and interpret its designs myself.

Ancient Atlantian, by all accounts, is a dead language, but they were way ahead of their time. By my calculations, it should work."

"I have faith in your abilities, Master Tinker. You have not failed me yet," he implied with a resounding vote of confidence. "Just don't start now!" he added grimly.

Edwyn swallowed hard, fully knowing what King Mordred had done to those who had failed him. "No, milord," he muttered. Edwyn placed two fingers in his mouth and whistled loudly to the other workers. With a wave of his hand, they moved quickly off the engine and down to the floor.

Edwyn walked to the table where a beaker of bubbling red liquid sat. He carefully picked up the glass container with a set of metal tongs and carefully carried it over to the engine. One of his assistants opened a cap to one of the pipes and placed a funnel. He stepped back as Edwyn slowly poured the liquid into the machine.

Once all the liquid was in, he replaced the cap and shouted, "Start her up!" Gnomes pushed and pulled on levers to the rear of the massive engine, forcing the liquid into the machine, while others began to turn the engine's enormous crankshaft. The engine sputtered and coughed as if trying to come to life.

"Now!" Edwyn yelled. Another gnome pointed a metal staff at the crystal on top of the engine. "*Magis Fulger!*" he chanted. The crystal sparked when the lightning bolt leaped from the staff to the crystal. The machine growled with the sudden surge of electricity as the gears slowly moved independently.

Edwyn carefully watched the gauge as he turned the crank slowly, increasing the power coursing through the engine. "40%, 50%, 60% ..." he shouted as the pressure began to build inside the magical engine, but then the smile on his face soured. "45%, 30%, 25% ..." That was the last number he got out before the engine stalled. Gears seized, and smoke billowed out of every pipe as the engine died as quickly as it came to life.

Master Tinker let out an audible sigh. That was not the result he expected, and he tried to think of what to say to King Mordred to stem his obvious disappointment. "Well, that was a good first run," he crowed with as much enthusiasm as he could muster. "We got nearly 62% efficiency before—"

"*Suffocatio!*" Mordred chanted as crimson bands of magical energy erupted from his fingertips and wrapped around Edwyn's throat. The gnome grasped onto the magic energy bands as he struggled to breathe. "Tell me again, Master Tinker Broadfoot, how confident are you of your work?"

"Please, Your Majesty," he pleaded with every breath he could muster. "I will get it working. I need a little more time!"

Mordred thought about it momentarily before waving his hand and releasing him. The crimson bands dissipated as Edwyn dropped hard onto the floor. Two other gnomes helped him to his feet while Edwyn coughed violently, trying to force air into his lungs. "The engine is perfect, Your Majesty. I need a proper alchemist to decipher the formula," he begged. "We gnomes do not know how to mix such complex ingredients."

Mordred's frustration boiled over as he grabbed one of the gnomes helping Edwyn and hurled him across the room. The tiny creature's head exploded when he hit the wall, spraying blood and gray matter all around to the disgust and fear of the other gnomes.

"Come now, Your Majesty," came a voice from the doorway. "You must not take your aggression out on these helpless creatures."

Mordred turned and smiled at a vision of rare beauty and evil as dark as his black heart. Lady Mavis Payne was the newest member of Mordred's court. The raven-haired woman entered the room, and all eyes turned to watch her. Her delicate pale skin and ruby-red lips demonstrated the lengths she went to make herself attractive to both men and women. Her scarlet gown was quite revealing as she showed no modesty regarding her body.

"Though limited in many ways, they are the only ones who can help you get this infernal contraption working," she added with a hint of wit and sarcasm.

"Tell me, Lady Mavis, what do I need to accomplish my goal?" Mordred asked.

Lady Mavis strolled up to the dead gnome and crouched down. She ran her long nails through the blood, tissue, and brains, trying to divine any signs of the future. Her precognitive powers were what brought her to Mordred's attention. Her devastating beauty made her practically irresistible, even to one as reviled as the son of Morgana le Fay. The words she whispered into the King's ear made everyone fear her, something she aspired to do.

"You are very close to achieving your goal, milord," she started to say as she continued to pick through the blood and body parts, much to the chagrin of the other gnomes. "A proper alchemist will complete the task at hand."

"I already know that, Mavis, but unfortunately, all of the best alchemists are locked away in Strongürd Keep, out of my reach," Mordred shouted angrily as he turned his back on her. "Tell me something I don't know!"

Mavis picked up a piece of the dead gnome's brain between her fingernails and stared at it intensely. "The one you seek is practically within your grasp—" she said as she dropped it to the floor. "They are a friend of your enemy, Your Majesty." Mordred was curious as he turned around and smiled at Lady Mavis.

"A friend of the Gil-Gamesh?" he asked. "Tell me, my darling Mavis, who is this alchemist, and where can I find them?"

CHAPTER 1
SEARCHING FOR AN ALCHEMIST

The *Weathered Wren* sat on the edge of the dark and deadly woods known as Blackbriar Forest on the outskirts of King's Crossing. Once, it was a bustling tavern filled with travelers, locals, and assorted adventurers daring to enter the foreboding brush to hunt goblins and the like. Unfortunately, the inn had not been as busy lately. Since the reclamation, the *Weathered Wren* had become nothing more than a local watering hole.

The tavern sat along the Vanir Road—once the main thoroughfare across Avalon—but fewer travelers had stopped by the inn since the reclamation. Mordred taxed all travel across Avalon, and many were unwilling to pay his outrageous tariffs. His way of controlling the populace was relegating them to stay on their islands, where magistrates loyal to the king kept the masses subdued through fear and subjugation.

The mood in the *Weathered Wren* was somber and quiet. The usual boisterous music, the regaling of tales of adventure, laughter, and lovemaking, was long absent. Instead, very few people were at the bar or tables, mulling their discontent quietly into their pints of ale. Sam Perrywinkle stood behind the bar, cleaning the mugs for the second time that day, as he looked out in disgust as his business crumbled around him.

His thinning hair had receded even further these past five years. Most of his staff left to find better-paying work in one of the big cities, the only place in the islands of Avalon where you could make money in these harsh times. He managed to run the *Weathered Wren* between his wife and children as best as possible.

Suddenly, the door burst open, and four of King Mordred's Adalwulf Guard stormed in. Meaning "Noble Wolf"—but rather far from it—the Adalwulf Guard was the secret security force for King Mordred. Every island in the Avalon archipelago had a contingent of these guardsmen, spying on locals while upholding Mordred's laws.

Cutthroats and brigands comprised the Adalwulf Guard—most having previously been imprisoned under the Pendragon rule. Their unique deception, theft, and murder skills made them prime candidates.

The men wore purple and gold tunics over their armor, embellished with Mordred's Coat of Arms—a winged lion holding an eye with a crossed sword and lightning bolt in the iris. A buckler shaped like a wolf's head held their cloaks in place. They all carried swords, daggers, and axes that hung in plain sight around their waists.

As they walked into the tavern, Sam recognized the leader immediately. Cayden Devlin was a tall, burly man. His beard was a mat of thick red hair like the rest of his body, hiding his yellow, stained teeth and numerous facial scars. His bloodshot eyes were large and protruding beyond the norm, making him appear like he was always staring. He used his size and appearance to his advantage, intimidating others to do his bidding.

Cayden was a well-known hooligan, locked away at Devil's Point Prison on more than one occasion. That made him a perfect fit for Mordred's Adalwulf Guard.

The few people in the tavern scattered as the reprobates stepped up to the bar. Cayden looked around the room and could not help himself as he laughed in Sam's face.

"What's going on here, Perrywinkle?" he boasted. "I thought the *Weathered Wren* was supposed to be the best pub in Avalon. I see an empty bar filled with a bunch of local degenerates who couldn't pour piss out of a boot with the directions written on the heel."

Sam ignored the sarcasm as he leaned on the bar. "Is there something I can do for you, Cayden Devlin? Do you want a drink or need a room for the night?"

"Drinks, absolutely," Cayden said. "We've had a long ride from Albarossa to Steinfisk, and we are thirsty men."

Sam quickly began to pour ale from the casks behind the bar, sliding them down one at a time to each one. Cayden took the pint and gulped it down heartily. Sam started to move away from the bar to find something to keep him busy away from these thugs, but Cayden grabbed him by the arm before he could leave.

"Not just yet, Perrywinkle," he fumed as he tightened his grip on Sam's arm. "According to our records, you haven't paid your taxes to King Mordred this quarter."

"That's rubbish," he snapped back. "The tax collector was here last week, and I paid it all, down to the last fin. Just ask your man there," Sam pointed to one member of the Adalwulf Guard. "He was here when I paid!"

The guardsman took another swig of his ale. "I don't remember being here last week," he lied as he continued to drink. "You must be thinking about last quarter."

"You are a lying sack of—" Sam threatened, but not before Cayden drew his dagger and stuck it under Sam's chin.

"Threatening an official of King Mordred, are we, Sam?" he warned. "I'll have to add that to the charge of unpaid taxes unless you want to recompense us, and maybe, just maybe, we'll forget the whole thing."

Sweat beaded across Sam's forehead as he desperately feared for his life. "I don't have that much money; I paid all I had last week," he pleaded.

"Well then, I guess it's the irons for you," Cayden admonished. "Look at it this way; you'll lose some weight sweating your ass off in the mines of *Ür Tár*. It might do you some good, eh?"

The rest of the Adalwulf Guard joined Cayden in the joke as they finished their ale. "Lock him in irons. He can walk to Steinfisk. That'll also be some good exercise for you, eh Sam?"

They all started laughing again as the guard locked heavy chains around his hands and feet. His wife and children could do nothing but watch as tears rolled down their cheeks. Sam struggled against the heavy chains, so one of the guards smacked him in the head with the blunted end of his ax handle to get him in line. Blood trickled down his forehead across his brow from the blow.

"Don't do that, you idiot," Cayden scolded. "If you knock him out, you'll carry him all the way there yourself."

Two guards held Sam up while the other finished locking the shackles on him. Meanwhile, Cayden jumped behind the bar to find Sam's cashbox. He dumped it out on the counter, but there were only a couple of silver duckets and some copper fins, hardly anything worth stealing.

"Dammit all, Sam, there's hardly enough here to pay for our drinks," he mocked as he pocketed the coins. Suddenly, a sword appeared out of nowhere, pressed sharply under his chin. A hooded stranger jumped into action to subdue the Adalwulf leader.

"If you want to leave here alive, I suggest you return the money and release Sam," the stranger demanded.

"Are you threatening me, boy? Do you know who I am?" Cayden barked in anger.

"I do," he answered. "And do you know who I am?" The stranger pulled back his hood to reveal himself. The people in the room gasped with a collective shock to see Sir Hunter MoonDrake, the Gil-Gamesh of Avalon.

His light brown hair flowed down to his shoulders. His neatly trimmed beard and bright green eyes showed his youth, yet seemed to convey the spirit and determination of the ages as the Knight Eternal of Avalon.

The mantle of Gil-Gamesh was passed down from generation to generation through the descendants of Sir Percival Peredyr as the protector of the people of Avalon. Hunter assumed the role when Mordred and his allies killed his father, Lord Bryan MoonDrake, during Avalon's Reclamation.

He kept his sword leveled at Cayden's throat. His blade, the *Edenstar*, was the sword of the first High King of the Elves, given to Hunter by Merlin the Magician. The long sword shimmered like starlight, from the blade down to the eight-pointed star that formed the guard.

The guards gasped at the sight of Avalon's champion, intimidated by his presence. However, Cayden kept his cool under pressure. "Well, well, well ... It's the Gil-Gamesh himself," Cayden cajoled. "I'd put that sword away before you get yourself killed. In case you hadn't noticed, you're outnumbered."

Hunter smirked a devilish grin, something his father was well known for. Some called it arrogance, but he saw it as confidence. "Are you sure about that?"

From out of the shadows, Elven warriors jumped into action, keeping their longbows drawn and disarming the remaining members of the Adalwulf Guard while freeing Sam from captivity. These were members of the *Hildrägo Boquè*, an elite corps of Elven fighters loyal to the Gil-Gamesh. They wielded leaf-shaped long swords and elaborate longbows, traditional weapons for the elves, keeping them trained on the Adalwulf Guard.

"Care to reevaluate your situation?" Hunter crowed.

Cayden grew angry, and in one swift motion, he drew his sword and knocked the *Edenstar* away. He rolled across the bar and landed in front of Hunter, ready to fight. The *Hîldrägo Boquè* moved in to restrain him, but the Gil-Gamesh waved them off. Hunter knew this was a matter of honor and reputation, something he constantly needed to prove on Avalon.

"I reckon bringing you down will move me up in the King's eyes," Cayden boasted.

"Anyone can exalt themselves in a world where they think they are the center of the universe," Hunter explained. "The hard part is making the rest of the world believe you!"

Cayden scowled at Hunter's insult. He lunged at the Gil-Gamesh, swinging wildly without rhyme or reason. Hunter parried his attacks before pushing Cayden back. He lunged at the Gil-Gamesh again, but when Hunter tried to block him, Cayden drew a dagger with his free hand and slashed him in the arm. Fortunately, the blade cut his leather coat, not the chainmail underneath.

Cayden smiled as he cackled like a hyena, thinking he got the best of the young Gil-Gamesh. "Give it up, boy. You're out of your league."

"Think so? Let's have another go, then," Hunter exclaimed as he held up the *Edenstar* horizontally. Without saying a word, the sword glowed softly before the blade shifted form. The hilt extended another six inches while another blade formed on the opposite side of the extended handle, creating a double-sided lance. The power of the *Edenstar* was child's play in the hands of a master alchemist like the Gil-Gamesh. His prowess allowed him to shape the magical sword into any weapon he could imagine. It was a deadly combination against any foe.

Cayden's expression went blank when he saw this display of power, but he was undeterred in his quest to bring in the young hero. He swung his sword hard and fast repeatedly. Hunter blocked each blow while spinning the *Edenstar* rapidly in his hand. He spun it like a buzzsaw, chopping through the air. This time, he cut Cayden on the hand holding the dagger, causing him to drop the weapon. Then, two slashes across his thighs brought Cayden to his knees.

Hunter then leveled the Edenstar across his throat. All the brigand could do was drop his sword in defeat. "Now, unlock Sam and return the money you stole," he demanded, his voice nearly breathless from their battle.

"OK, boys, let him go," he gruffed. The Adalwulf Guard released Sam from his shackles. He was helped to a chair by his wife and son.

Hunter lowered his sword and stepped back from Cayden. "Next time you pass through King's Crossing, I suggest you stay clear of the *Weathered Wren*. This establishment—this town—is now off-limits to you."

"All righty then, Gil-Gamesh. We'll leave quietly," Cayden acknowledged as he gingerly rose to his feet. "But you remember this, hero; you can't always be everywhere! We'll be back, and then we'll burn this rundown tavern to the ground, along with the rest of the town!"

Hunter's mood turned sour with Cayden's threat. As he turned to leave, the Gil-Gamesh grabbed him by the collar and dragged him back onto the bar. He kept his blade leveled across Cayden's throat as he drew his GunStar. The magical weapon looked like a flintlock pistol made of brass and wood, covered in mystical runes. It could shoot alchemical shells that exploded with various spells, from fireballs to dragon nails.

He pointed his GunStar at Cayden's right hand and fired, spraying a freezing mist that engulfed it. The brute screamed as he clutched his hand until it crumbled into icy pieces.

Hunter quickly holstered his first GunStar and drew the second one from his other leg. He pointed it at Cayden's remaining hand as fear filled the brigand, causing him to scream and beg for mercy.

"No, please, Gil-Gamesh, don't—" he started to plead before Hunter smacked him in the head with the butt of his weapon.

"Shut up, Cayden, and listen carefully," Hunter crowed. "This town is under my protection. If you or any of the Adalwulf Guard come back here, I will find out about it, and then you will lose more than a hand!"

Hunter slowly shifted his aim from Cayden's hand down to his groin to make his point. "Am I making myself clear?" he sassed. Cayden nodded repeatedly, biting his tongue so as not to anger the Gil-Gamesh any further. Hunter released his grip on Cayden but kept his sword, and GunStar, trained on him as his men helped him up and out of the tavern as quickly as possible.

Hunter sheathed his weapons as the elves tended to Sam's injuries. "Are you OK, Sam?" he asked with concern for his injured friend.

Sam took several deep breaths, trying to shake the cobwebs out of his head. One of the elves grabbed a bar towel and held it on Sam's head to stem the bleeding. "I think so, Sir Hunter," he mumbled. "Thank you, Gil-Gamesh, but I'm afraid you've only delayed the inevitable."

"What do you mean, Sam?" Hunter asked, confused by his response.

"I've heard what happens to people who help or are helped by you," he groaned. "They either end up in prison or dead. Please understand that I mean no disrespect. It just doesn't seem worth fighting back against King Mordred."

Hunter sighed loudly. He knew how hard it's been to gain people's trust across Avalon. As much as they wanted his help, they feared Mordred and his allies more. "I understand, Sam, but we don't abandon our friends. I swear we will free Avalon from his reign, but we can't do it alone. I need you, Sam, and I will ensure they never threaten you again."

Sam looked at him, confused. The door burst open just then, and young Peter McMillan walked in. When Hunter's father first met the farm boy from King's Crossing, he was only a child. Peter joined Lord MoonDrake's crew on his flagship when he was old enough.

Sam had not seen Peter in quite a while. He worked in the *Weathered Wren's* stables for extra money, but the curly-haired boy was gone. Now, a young man, strong and fearless, stood before him.

Peter immediately went to Sam to greet his old boss. "Peter?" Sam cried as tears of joy flowed from his eyes. "I can't believe it. Look how you've grown."

"I owe it all to the Gil-Gamesh, Sam," Peter replied as he hugged his old boss. "But I'm back now and here to help protect my home and family."

"Peter's going to be staying here, Sam," Hunter explained. "If there's any trouble, Peter will let us know. As I said, Sam, we don't abandon our friends."

Sam felt a wave rush over him as tears continued to warm his eyes. He felt relieved knowing that his tavern and his family were safe. "Thank you, thank you both!" he stammered.

The Gil-Gamesh knelt beside him and put his hand on Sam's shoulder. "That's all right, Sam, but I need your help now."

A look of bewilderment came across Sam's face. "What can I do to help you, Gil-Gamesh?"

"I was told you were the last person to see my friend, Oliver Beasley. I need to find him, Sam. Do you know where he is?"

CHAPTER 2
RESCUE FROM THE MINES OF ÜR TÁR

The Fenris Mountains were the most extensive mountain range in all of Avalon. They stretched from Steinfisk in the East to The Gilded Halls of the Dwarves in the West. After Avalon's Reclamation, the Fenris Mountains became Fenris Island, one of the largest islands in the Archipelago of Avalon.

For thousands of years, the Gilded Halls were once the mystical island's shining gem. The wealth that poured out of the ancient caverns—gold, gemstones, and other precious minerals—helped shape New Camelot into a thriving capital. The port city of Dvallin was nestled beneath the Majesty of Hursag, the legendary mountain home of the dwarves, along the Trieste River's shores. It was the heart of commerce in the east of Avalon. Ships would arrive by sea and air to exchange goods while transporting the mines' riches throughout Avalon.

Today, the Gilded Halls were nothing more than a slave pit for the machinations of King Mordred. A mine where slave labor tried to retrieve the wealth of a nation from a watery grave. Those who spoke out against his rule or opposed him in any way were sent here to work in the mines of *Úr Tár*. It was known as the *Mine of Drowned Tears* out of respect to all the dwarves thought to have drowned when the Gilded Halls flooded during Avalon's Reclamation.

Dwarf Lord Sempir Dwallis had ruled the mine with an iron fist for over five years. After the apparent death and disappearance of Lord Dinius Oddbottom and most of the dwarves who resided there, Dwallis moved in with his Iron Mount mercenaries. Even that had been no easy task. The earthquake that ripped Avalon apart buried the Gilded Halls' entrance under tons of rock, while seawater filled the lower hall from the foundation's cracks and holes.

Dwallis had wanted to be Lord and Master of the Gilded Halls, but now he was a warden to a slave pit that was always damp and muddy. In addition, the Iron Mount Dwarves were not miners. They were considered by many as mercenaries for hire. These dwarves sold their expertise to the highest bidder, making weapons for anyone who could pay the price.

Sempir was taller than most of his kin, almost four-and-a-half feet tall. His rust-colored, unkempt beard and hair, combined with his general scruffy appearance, were generally accepted by dwarves from the Iron Mount. They believed their disheveled appearance showed their hard work ethic while creating powerful weapons and armor for battle.

With the abundance of slave labor provided to him by King Mordred, Dwallis could get back into the dwarves' stronghold. The process, however, was slow. As one level cleared, the prisoners pumped out more water. The enslaved prisoners worked night and day as their dwarf masters punished them relentlessly to make them work harder and faster.

Now, their efforts were keeping the water at bay. If the pumping stopped, they would flood again. The only way for them to descend into the mine was through devices the gnome tinkers called "diving bells." Two men sat inside the bell-shaped craft and operated mechanical arms to dig for the riches. High above, prisoners worked bellows that provided air circulation and winches that raised and lowered them into the mine. The process was slow and tedious, but it was the only way to clear the mines.

The dwarves preferred to let the humans take risks while watching over their slave labor force like rigid taskmasters. They rebuilt the port city of Dvallin into a new home for themselves, a prison to keep their captive labor force confined. The mine operated day and night, with little to no rest for the prisoners and plenty of rest and drinking for the slave drivers. This horror was just one example of the new Avalon under King Mordred.

Time virtually stood still inside the mines. The day turned to night without anyone noticing. Rock bearers carried heavy loads of ore as they cleared the passages to access the fabled city and its riches below.

Oliver Beasley wheezed with each breath as he worked with four others on the pumps, keeping the water at bay. He focused on the repetitive routine to get him through the grueling hours.

His round-rimmed glasses, repaired often since his internment in the mines, were fogged due to the excess moisture. His body had weaned from his former husky physique to a thin shadow of his former self. His clothes were covered in mud, soaked through and through.

Ollie was not used to this type of labor. As a Silver Sage Alchemist, he owned one of New Camelot's most prestigious shops. He was well known for providing the best elixirs, potions, and reagents for any ailment, disease, or injury. More recently, he was better known for his work with Sir Hunter MoonDrake to create and improve the alchemical "spellshots" for cannons, Lancers, and GunStars.

They designed these weapons so any magical novice could be on equal footing with any mage or wizard in a fight. Ollie turned Hunter's ideas into reality, creating new weapons for the Knights of Avalon, and that's how he ended up in the mines of *Ür Tár*.

Though he cut off all contact with the Gil-Gamesh after Avalon's Reclamation, they considered him a potential spy for the renegade knight and his forces. Eventually, he knew they would imprison him on whatever charge they wanted. He tried to escape Mordred's wrath, but it finally caught up with him.

Ollie didn't blame Sir Hunter for his predicament. Even though he cut all ties with the Gil-Gamesh, he knew that guilt by association was always a possibility.

Suddenly, the other pump man collapsed from exhaustion, falling lifeless to the muddy ground. One of the dwarf taskmasters immediately walked over and kicked the fallen man in the stomach.

"Get up, lazy bum!" he shouted as he kicked him again, but the dying man simply wheezed and groaned his last breath. The dwarf grabbed him by the face, moving it from side to side until he was sure he was dead.

"You two," he called out to two rock bearers. "Carry this carcass out of here!" The two men dropped their loads and picked up the dead man, trying to respect the fallen prisoner. "You!" he shouted at another. "Take his place on the pumps!"

"I'll do it, Master Dwarf!" shouted a different bearer. The man looked like he had just arrived in *Ür Tár*. His clothes were barely torn or dirty. His body was muscular, not lean, and his hair was short, neat, and not unkempt like the others.

He jumped on the handle and joined the others in the pumping motion. Ollie noticed that he kept staring at him but ignored it and continued working the pump.

"Ollie Beasley?" the stranger asked. "Are you Ollie Beasley?"

Ollie just ignored him and kept pumping. "Dammit, are you Ollie Beasley, or aren't you?" the stranger prodded him again.

"You best keep to the pump, newbie," Ollie replied sternly. "They don't like it when we talk amongst ourselves. All you'll do is earn us all a beating."

The stranger quieted down when one of the dwarf taskmasters walked by. Once he was out of earshot, the stranger leaned in again to speak. "Look, I just need to know if you're Oliver Beasley?" he whispered.

Ollie hated his persistence but knew it might be the only way to shut him up. "Who wants to know?" he asked.

"My name is Andrew St. Johns, and I have a message for Ollie Beasley from Sir Hunter MoonDrake!"

All three men operating the pump stopped and looked at Andrew in shock. They knew of him, husband to the Gil-Gamesh's sister, Ashley, the *Sorceress Magnate,* and heir of Merlin the Magician. He was also instrumental in the design of the Lancers, another magical weapon that used Ollie's spellshots.

Ollie looked around to see if any guards were near as he continued to pump. "What on earth are you doing here?" Ollie inquired. "Did you get captured? Do they know who you are?"

"That's not important," Andrew explained. "I'm here to get you out."

"In case you hadn't noticed, we're hundreds of feet underground, surrounded by dwarf mercenaries," Ollie remarked.

"That's why we need a diversion. Reach into my front pocket. You'll find everything you need to make your 'Nitro-9' explosive," Andrew said. Ollie kept pumping with one hand while he reached into Andrew's pocket. His arm disappeared up to his elbow until he pulled out a large bag filled with bottles and jars filled with the ingredients.

"How?" Ollie started to ask before Andrew cut him off.

"It helps when your wife is a powerful sorceress," he interjected. "We'll keep pumping while you mix things."

Ollie sat beside the pump and immediately combined the ingredients for one of his best creations. Ace, an old friend of his, taught him this explosive formula. Nitro-9 was known to be unstable, which made it so destructive. It took Ollie less than an hour to complete his task. In a small bowl, he had made his Nitro-9, a clear liquid that looked relatively innocuous but was quite deadly.

"OK, now what?" he asked.

"We wait for the signal," Andrew replied.

"What signal?" Ollie started to say until the sound of horns bellowing and bells ringing echoed from high above the cavern. The dwarf guards quickly ran by them, heading up towards the entrance of the mines.

"It's time to go! You two, get any man who can fight and bring them to me," Andrew ordered the other prisoners. They took off as Andrew reached into his bottomless pants pocket, pulled out a Lancer, and handed it to Ollie with a bag of spellshots. The Lancer resembled an over/under shotgun with blades running along the top of both barrels, covered in magical runes.

Andrew then pulled out a pair of hand axes. The two axes had a pike on top of the ax and a hook curved down behind the ax head. They were *Rota* and *Myst*, formidable weapons in the hands of someone like Andrew.

"Let's go. We need to place the explosive at a weak spot on the cavern wall, and I think I know just where to put it," he exclaimed as he guided Ollie to a spot in the tunnel below. The dwarves heavily reinforced this section of the mine with wooden shores and beams. You could see where water was trying to seep in through the rock as it slowly dripped down the wall.

Ollie immediately went to work placing the explosive while Andrew watched for any guards. "How are you going to set it off?" he asked.

"With this," Ollie replied, holding a small stone wrapped in parchment. "It's white phosphorus. Hunter re-engineered it with a slow burn," he explained. "Once I unwrap it and set it in the Nitro-9, we'll have about ten minutes before it explodes."

"That should be just enough time to get to the staircase," Andrew responded as several prisoners approached him. Once again, he reached into the unknown depths of his pants pockets and pulled out various swords and axes, passing them out to the men.

"Fight your way to the outside," he yelled to them. "There will be transport waiting for you once you get there. Those who can't fight, help whomever you can to the surface. We're all getting out of here together."

The men and women roared together in approval as they ran toward the entrance. Andrew turned back to Ollie. "Now!" he said as the alchemist unwrapped the white phosphorus and placed it on a thin piece of parchment floating in the Nitro-9. The liquid bubbled around it, increasing in intensity with each passing second as the white phosphorus sparked to life.

"Let's go!" Andrew shouted as the two men followed the others toward the entrance of *Ür Tár*. The armed prisoners engaged the few remaining dwarves, but their weakened state made them easy targets.

Andrew threw his ax at one dwarf, cleaving his head in two. As he charged forward to engage another, Ollie stopped and fired his Lancer. Three thorny projectiles erupted from the weapon, wrapping the dwarves with constricting vines on impact. Andrew retrieved his ax from the dead dwarf as they ran up the winding staircase.

When they finally reached the top, Ollie realized how big of a rescue effort this was. The fighting raged throughout the city of Dvallin. Shield Maidens—the remaining warrior caste of Avalon after the decimation of the Knights of the Round Table—and the *Hîldrägo Boquè*—Elven warriors known as the 'Army of 10,000 Years'—were waging war against the Iron Mount dwarves. Hundreds were fighting the mercenaries while they evacuated the prisoners as quickly as possible.

Between their flying airships, dragons, and magical portals, the forces of the Gil-Gamesh were coming at them with full force. Andrew and Ollie stayed at the entrance to the mines, moving people along as quickly as possible.

"How much longer?" Andrew asked the alchemist.

"Any minute now, but why pick that section of the mine to set off the explosive?" Ollie inquired.

"I overheard some of the guards saying that behind that wall was a downward tunnel leading directly to the ocean," he exclaimed. "That'll keep the mine flooded, so they'll never be able to return to it again. Mordred's lost *Ür Tár* forever!"

The ground rumbled beneath their feet as they felt the explosion deep within the mines. Standing at the entrance, Andrew and Ollie could hear rushing water, growing louder and louder as it arose from the depths below.

"Step aside!" Andrew shouted. "Move!" He motioned for everyone to clear away from the opening before grabbing Ollie and keeping him close. Like a geyser, water sprayed out from the entrance, washing away all those in its wake. After the water subsided, the geyser became a waterfall, flowing down the city's steps.

Andrew scoured the battlefield around him, looking for Hunter and a possible escape route for Ollie. Suddenly, in a flash of light, his wife

Ashley appeared beside him, draped in a flowing royal magenta robe embroidered with magical runes around the cuffs and front clasps. Her head was cloaked in a shadowy hood bearing the same embroidery. Only her glowing eyes, burning with the fire of magic, could be seen beneath its brow. She held the Staff of Merlin, a twisted wooden rod of Wych Elm with three branches at the top, resembling a trident. They were each embedded with rose, smoky, and white quartz crystals. The crystals glowed softly as magical energy hovered between them.

She reached out and hugged her husband tightly, grateful that he survived his ordeal in the mines of *Ür Tár*. "Are you hurt, darling?" she asked, her voice fraught with worry.

"I'm fine, Ash," he replied. "Take Ollie and get him out of here. I'm going to find Hunter."

Before he could leave, one of the Iron Mount Dwarves surprised them as he leaped from his hiding place above the mine entrance. He raised his sword above his head, screaming as he swung down at them. Andrew raised his axes to block him.

"Duratus!" Ashley chanted as she raised her staff. The magical energy flowed between the crystals and wrapped around the attacking dwarf. He hung there, frozen in mid-air with a confused look. In a single motion, Ashley swung her staff out toward the water. The dwarf screamed as he was hurled thousands of feet through the air until he splashed into the river.

"Thanks, babe," he said with a peck on her cheek before Andrew raced toward the heart of the fighting, leaving Ollie and Ashley behind.

"Hunter's with Eileanora, down by the square!" she shouted. "Be careful, sweetheart!" Andrew waved back at her, acknowledging her advice. Ashley muttered something to herself, but Ollie couldn't quite make out what she said.

"Did you say something, Miss Ashley?" he asked.

"No, Oliver, just muttering to myself about my bull-headed husband," she said. "He's going to get himself killed sooner or later, and he doesn't seem to care."

"Oh, I'm sure you're wrong, Miss Ashley," Ollie said to comfort her. "He has much to prove to himself and your siblings."

"He has nothing to prove to me," Ashley snapped back. Her rash outburst took Ollie by surprise. Ashley realized her rude behavior immediately. "I'm sorry, Ollie. I didn't mean to snap at you. These are trying times for all of us."

Ollie smiled and nodded his head. Ashley took him by the arm and teleported them both to safety in a flash. All the while, Andrew rushed through the fighting masses. The shield maidens and the Hîldrägo Boquè fought valiantly against the Iron Mount Dwarves. Though they were outnumbered two-to-one, they prevailed in the battle. Although, that never really mattered to them.

The shield maidens and the Hîldrägo Boquè were selected and trained from birth. Their fighting skills were unsurpassed in all of Avalon. No matter what the weapon, they were the masters of combat. Their devotion to the fighting arts was a duty to them and a calling, almost religious. When they fought together, they acted like the Spartans of ancient Greece or the Samurai from Japan.

Luckily for Andrew, he had the good fortune to train with them daily, honing his skills as a fighter, though it wasn't all training. Rota and Myst were formidable weapons in the right hands. Their magic lay within the relationship with their wielder. Only someone with a strong heart and purpose could wield them like their Valkyrie namesakes. Andrew was just such a man.

The two axes sang as he fought his way down to the square. Flesh and blood met strength and steel as the fury of Rota and Myst cut them down. He did not relish killing in combat, but the ends justified the means to him. His purpose was to help his family reclaim their birthright and restore balance to Avalon. Nothing else mattered.

Within minutes, he reached the square of the port city of Dvallin. At the heart of the battle, he watched as Hunter stood toe-to-toe with Sempir Dwallis. With the Edenstar in one hand and a GunStar in the other, he fought against Dwallis' massive double-bladed battle ax. Though formidable as a fighter, the Gil-Gamesh could not get through Dwallis' defenses.

He used the long handle of his battle ax to keep Hunter just out of reach. Additionally, Dwallis used the ax's broad head as a shield to block magical attacks from Hunter's GunStar.

Hunter spied Andrew out of the corner of his eye and saw a perfect opening for a double-team on the dwarf leader. "Andy ... *Karate Kid*!" he shouted. Though no one else understood what that meant, Andrew understood it perfectly. The vague movie reference told him precisely what Hunter wanted him to do.

He slid low and used the hook on his ax to grab the dwarf's leg and twist it from under him, using his momentum to "sweep the leg" out from under him. Dwallis spun around, turning in the air before crashing to the ground. Andrew swung back with his other ax and jammed the pike on the top of the ax into Dwallis' shoulder, pinning him to the ground.

The dwarf screamed in pain, but not before Hunter spun his sword around and plunged it into his other shoulder, causing him further agony. "It's over, Dwallis," Hunter announced. "Order your men to surrender, and I'll spare you."

Sempir Dwallis thought momentarily as he realized the severity of the situation. He had no choice but to submit. "*Beyonte' Gru!*" he shouted in dwarvish. "*Beyonte' Gru!*" As they relayed the order across the city, the dwarves ceased fighting. Within minutes, the battle was over as quickly as it began.

Hunter and Andrew withdrew their weapons, freeing Dwallis. Two other dwarves quickly moved in to help him to his feet. "Ür Tár is lost. We breached the lower walls, and the entire mine is underwater," Hunter explained. "Now, order your men to drop their weapons, and I will allow you to board your ships and leave in peace."

Dwallis lowered his gaze and sighed as he winced in pain. "Drop your weapons, lads," he started to say grudgingly. "We're leaving!"

"No!" shouted one of the dwarves defiantly. "We are Dwarves of the Iron Mount. We do not surrender, especially to elvish scum and females. We—"

Before he could say another word, a spike struck the back of his head and reached through his forehead. He stuttered and stumbled as the blood trickled down his face. As he fell to the ground, his attacker stepped up from behind. She was an elf dressed in green, black, and brown leather armor covered in mithril scales that resemble leaves. Her long black hair was pulled back into a ponytail and braided neatly down her back just past her lower torso. At the end of the braid was an ornate metal spike, still impaled in the head of the fallen dwarf. She held a beautiful Elven long sword, Fire Dance, that burned with a blue flame. She was Eileanora, better known as the *Dubh Bhean*, The Dark Lady, the Assassin of the Elves, and Commander of the Hîldrägo Boquè.

With a twist of her head, she pulled the spike out of the fallen dwarf. The other dwarves were shocked, wrought with fear at the sight of her. They immediately dropped their weapons and started to walk down toward the piers. The shield maidens and Hîldrägo Boquè formed a corridor to ensure their compliance as they trotted past, their heads hung in shame.

Hunter walked over to Eileanora as he sheathed his sword. "I think they got the point," he joked with a smile and a laugh. As usual, Eileanora kept a grim, emotionless expression on her face.

"Is everything a joke to you, Gil-Gamesh?" she asked.

"Only the funny things," Hunter retorted. Eileanora tried to maintain her composure, but she found, as of late, that he knew just what to say to get past her defenses. She smiled and started to chuckle but quickly caught herself and regained her composure.

Hunter smiled and chuckled under his breath. In the past five years, he had gotten to know Eileanora very well, learning that underneath all the death and darkness surrounding her, there was an outgoing, wonderful person.

"Did you secure Mr. Beasley, Andrew?" Eileanora asked.

"Ashley's got him," Andrew replied. "I think you can chalk this one up as a success, Hunter."

Suddenly, a ghostly howl echoed between the mountains. Everyone knew that sound and what it meant. Their emotions quickly went from pleasant to terror. "I don't think we can chalk this one up just yet, Andy," Hunter exclaimed as he drew his sword. "Eileanora, find Rhona and tell her to keep the dwarves moving to their ships. We don't want them to take advantage of the situation."

Eileanora took off to find General Rhona McLoughlin, Commander of the Shield Maidens of Avalon. She advised the Gil-Gamesh on battle strategies while commanding the Holy Order of Shield Maidens in the fight against Mordred's forces.

The ghostly howl echoed again, growing louder and louder. Hunter looked into the sky as he put his fingers in his mouth and whistled loudly. A giant dragon flew down toward them. Its purple scales glistened with a gold tint in the sunlight, like the knight's bright green armor on its back.

The dragon was Dee Dee, short for Desdemonia. Riding on her was Hunter's sister, Rose, his shield maiden. She wore the legendary armor of Bredbeddle, the Green Knight. The armor and shield made Rose practically invulnerable to harm, but her skill as a dragon rider made her an invaluable asset. Dee Dee bonded with Rose long ago, making the two practically inseparable.

"They're coming, little brother," she started to say as she raised her visor. "We need to get out of here now."

"We need time to evacuate the prisoners and get these dwarves out of here," he argued. "Tell Edan to fire up some 'Angels Tears' to slow them down."

Rose nodded her head as she spurred Dee Dee back into the air. "Eileanora, can you and Ashley open a direct portal to Alfheimer? It might speed up the evacuation process."

"That's a dangerous proposition, Hunter," she exclaimed. "Doing so would bypass the barrier that protects the ancient city. While the portal is open, Alfheimer will be exposed."

"It's a chance we have to take. Otherwise, we might abandon all these people to the wraiths," Hunter implored. Eileanora reluctantly agreed with his assessment. Before Hunter said another word, Ashley teleported beside them, startling the Gil-Gamesh.

"You've gotta stop doing that, sis," he groaned.

"Sorry, Hunter, it comes with the job description," she retorted. "Where do you want to establish the link?"

"Down there, near the slave quarters," he directed her. "That's where all the prisoners are gathering together. Eileanora, take some *Hildrägo Boquè* with you to protect the portal on both sides."

Eileanora shouted orders as the *Hildrägo Boquè* quickly followed her and Ashley as they made their way toward the prisoners. The shrieks echoed off the canyon walls louder as Hunter and Andrew focused on the sky.

"Here they come," Andrew remarked.

They were hard to see as they flew. Their ghostly visage blended into the blue sky like clouds in the air, but their form was unmistakable—a spectral knight with a floating head enveloped in a fire-like glow. They were the Wraith Legion of Purgatory, fallen knights bound to serve the heavenly host to prevent the demons of Hell from accessing our world. However, the legion now had a new commander, Abdel Ben Faust.

He rode a black stallion, a Nightmare steed, galloping through the air on the flames of hellfire that emanated from its hooves. The eyes of the Nightmare burned with the same hellfire that coursed through its body. Faust looked like a man, but his true heritage was easy to spot. His skin had a reddish-brown hue. His long black hair and Fu Manchu mustache hid slightly pointed ears, and a goatee of twisted, black horns protruded from his chin. From his left temple, a scar was visible across his nose to his right cheek, a small reminder of being cut from his mother's womb because of his unwanted birth.

In his hand was a broadsword, more than four feet long, yet he skillfully wielded it with one hand. The sword had a jagged edge on one side. The runes glowed as steam shrouded the sword as if the blade's heat superheated the surrounding. It whistled in the air as he flew across the sky. The sword was *Deathsong*, a cursed blade that only he could wield.

On his chest armor was a heart-shaped gemstone. It pulsed with the same beat as his own wicked heart. Inside the gem, the image of an angel was visible, fighting against its unnatural imprisonment. This heartstone was how Faust controlled the Wraith Legion. As long as he possessed it, the legion was his to command.

He fought hard against the Gil-Gamesh and his siblings since he killed their father, Lord Bryan MoonDrake. However, he could not capture or kill these children for all the power given to him by Mordred. Every encounter with them fueled his burning hatred more and more.

As Faust and his Wraith Legion charged down toward Dvallin, the sound of cannons firing overtook the ghostly howl of the phantoms. Above the town, a pirate ship floated effortlessly in the air. Unlike the other airships of Avalon, this one had no wings and what appeared to be torn and tattered sails in the rigging. The skull and crossbones flag flew effortlessly from the mainmast, but this one had a snake wrapped around the bones under the skull and its head coming out of one of the skull's eyes.

The *Black Adder*, the ghost ship of Avalon, attacked the oncoming horde. Under the command of Rose's husband, the Pirate King Edan O'Brien, the ship's cannons fired at the legion. The batteries used a similar compliment of spellshots, like GunStars, but far deadlier. These rounds soared through the air until they exploded in a starburst, sending multiple streams out like glowing rain from heaven.

The "Angel Tears" released a volley of pure starlight, powerful enough to disrupt the connection in a wraith heartstone, releasing its spirit from its ghostly shell. The wraiths scattered to avoid the deadly rays, but it was hard to outrun a thousand falling stars.

In a final blinding flash, they exploded, stunning everyone around them temporarily. When their eyes cleared, Faust and the wraiths were all gone. Hunter and Andrew scanned the skies, from horizon to horizon, looking for any sign of their adversaries.

"It can't be that easy," Andrew exclaimed with relief. Just then, the ground beneath them began to rumble. They looked out across the river as the water started to boil.

"It's not," Hunter cried out. "They dove under the river!" He jumped up to where everyone could see him. "Fall back to your evacuation points! The wraiths are beneath us!"

The shield maidens and *Hîldrägo Boquè* followed his orders and began to head toward their evacuation points while keeping a watchful eye on the ground and water. Wraiths emerged beneath their feet, rising from the ground like ghostly apparitions.

The only way to defeat a wraith was to shatter its heartstone, something the shield maidens and *Hîldrägo Boquè* had ample training in. For these spirits, though, one blow from their phantom blades meant instant death for mortals. It also provided an almost instant replenishment for the Wraith Legion as most of the fallen warriors killed by wraiths immediately joined their ranks.

Hunter and Andrew fought back-to-back, moving through Dvallin as they dispatched wraiths as fast as possible. The two men had fought in numerous battles over the past five years, familiar with each other's fighting styles during combat. Hunter used his alchemy to transform *Edenstar* from a long sword to a duel-bladed lance. In this form, he could strike and block the wraith attacks instantly. Andrew swung *Rota* and *Myst* like a conductor at the symphony. He utilized the multiple edges on his ax's head—the ax, pike, and hook—to bring down as many phantoms as possible.

Suddenly, both men were thrown to the ground as flaming hooves struck them out of nowhere. Faust's Nightmare knocked them down, appearing behind them through a "demon hole"—a magical gift of Faust's half-demon heritage that allowed him to move around in a puff of fire and brimstone.

Hunter leaped to his feet as he drew his GunStar from its holster on his thigh. He fired a bolo spellshot at Faust. The magical spell exploded from his weapon, creating two metal balls connected by an iron chain. They flew toward Faust to entangle the half-demon in iron, thus preventing him from using his demon holes. However, anticipating the ploy, Faust sliced the bolo chain with the burning edge of *Deathsong*.

"You didn't think I'd fall for that trick again, did you, Gil-Gamesh?" he boasted.

"Of course not," Hunter cajoled. "That was just the distraction."

Suddenly, Andy brought *Myst* down and chopped through his boot, lopping off a couple of toes. Faust screamed in pain, but he acted fast to a vulnerable Andrew. He kicked him in the head with his other foot, knocking Andrew to the ground. His head bounced off a rock, knocking him unconscious.

Hunter reacted as he spun the *Edenstar* in his hand and lunged toward Faust. The blade spun through the air, slicing at the half-demon at a furious pace. He cut little nicks in Faust's flesh and armor, not inflicting much damage but annoying nonetheless. It was like being bitten by hundreds of mosquitos.

Faust had enough and did something unexpected. He grabbed the *Edenstar* with his open hand, holding the blade back. Faust sneered at him, relishing in his feat of strength over the Gil-Gamesh.

"Surprised? Well, you shouldn't be. After all, you did this to me!" Faust sneered as the blade cut through his gauntlet and exposed his bare hand. Then Hunter saw what he meant.

His hand resembled a demon's claw, covered in scales and bony spikes. His nails were razor-sharp, like the claws of a dragon. After the Gil-Gamesh had lopped his hand off at King Mordred's coronation, it regenerated into this abomination thanks to Mordred's dark magic.

Hunter laughed under his breath as he pushed against Faust. "It must be hard to shop for gauntlets?" he joked. "You can never find just one, can you?"

"Joke all you like, Gil-Gamesh, but this ends now!"

"You're right," Hunter said as he transformed *Edenstar* into a long sword, releasing it from his grip. Faust tumbled forward as Hunter lifted his elbow and slammed it into his chin. A little disoriented, he stumbled back as Hunter backed away to protect Andy.

"That's right, Gil-Gamesh," he sneered. "Cower away!"

"I'm not cowering Faust," Hunter snarked back. "I'm getting out of the line of fire."

Faust's expression changed as a shadow fell across him. He quickly realized what the Gil-Gamesh meant as he looked up. Dee Dee swooped down as Rose jumped in front of Hunter and Andrew, shielding them as the dragon blasted Faust with dragonfire. The flames didn't bother a half-demon; instead, they burned away his clothes and some of his armor. The explosive impact stunned Faust.

Once Faust regained his senses, he opened his eyes to see a green shield aimed at him. The massive shield, adorned with a tree that formed a mask-like face with thorny branches growing out like hair, knocked him across the square into one of the buildings. He slumped to the ground, groggy, as he shook his head repeatedly to clear his senses.

Faust began to focus his eyes, watching as the Gil-Gamesh picked up Andrew and laid him across the back of the dragon with Rose. Hunter jumped behind her as Dee Dee leaped into the air, flying off with the other airships. *Ūr Tár* and the city of Dvallin fell silent.

Faust brought himself to one knee, quite gingerly, as he tried to stand. A hand reached out for his, offering some assistance. Faust snarled. He saw it as a weakness but took Artūras Blackstone's hand anyway.

Blackstone was King Mordred's Minister of Magic, an advisor to the crown. His robes were large and billowy, giving a false impression of his size and stature. Dark runes covered his body, both as tattoos and brands. They were a compilation of protection wards designed to deflect certain spells and curses aimed at him. He was bald except for a long ponytail hanging down his back. His face was dark and careworn, a reflection of his tortured soul.

"Are you injured, General?" he asked as he pulled Faust up.

"Only my pride," Faust scoffed as he spat blood from his mouth. "That damn bitch and her dragon knocked me down. One of these days, I will peel that armor off her flesh. Let's see how tough she is then."

"Once we get the engine working, nothing will stand in King Mordred's way, including the MoonDrake children," Blackstone remarked. Faust's curiosity peaked when he heard Blackstone's remark.

"So, did it work? Did our spy get through to Alfheimer?"

"Yes, indeed. Everything went just as Lady Mavis foretold," Blackstone said as the mountain rumbled. The two looked up toward the entrance to *Ür Tár*. More geysers erupted from the mountainside as the water pressure built up from the depths of the mine.

"*Ür Tár* is gone," Faust replied. "That's a heavy price for one alchemist."

Blackstone smiled ever so slyly. "That, my dear Abdel Ben Faust, is the price we must pay to end the line of Pendragon once and for all."

THE PROMETHEUS ENGINE · MARK PIGGOTT

CHAPTER 3
THE REFUGE OF ALFHEIMER

Alfheimer was once called the "Shining City" of Avalon. It glowed from the magic emanating from the city and the elves. As New Camelot was the seat of power on Avalon, Alfheimer was considered its heart. But after Avalon's Reclamation, the city lost its luster. The "Shining City" was no more.

Most of Alfheimer lay in ruin, as it was the epicenter of the earthquake that splintered Avalon. The city became an island, surrounded by mountains on all sides and nestled in a small valley. The sheer cliffs outside made it impossible to enter the city even from above. The dragons protected that realm.

Floating in the sky above Alfheimer was the island of Emmyr, home of Avalon's dragons. It floated effortlessly in the air due to the concentration of magic from its inhabitants. Dragons were a primary source of magic on Avalon. It seeped into every rock and every tree, causing it to levitate high above Alfheimer.

Emmyr was home to Lord Bryan MoonDrake and his family. He discovered ships built from the trees harvested on Emmyr were lighter than air and could fly easily, so he made the dragon isle his home. Port Charles was named after a dear friend who died protecting his home. Emmyr was once the center of commerce on Avalon. Airships flew in and out of the city, bringing goods and other merchandise to Avalon's four corners.

Today, Port Charles was a ghost town. The dragon king, Gamorg, decreed that the island was now off-limits to the people of Avalon. Though a strong ally of Lord MoonDrake, he couldn't risk endangering the dragons from future harm. Some dragons like Dee Dee continued to assist Lord MoonDrake's children. Gamorg tried to remain neutral in this conflict but would not allow Mordred to attack his family and friends. Emmyr floated above Alfheimer as a warning to stay away.

Alfheimer was now a refuge for those fleeing Mordred's reign. Together with the Gil-Gamesh and his siblings, the shield maidens and the Elves of Alfheimer fought against Mordred's tyranny and oppression. The city flourished again, but this time for Avalon, including humans, elves, centaurs, and other races put out by his evil reign.

The Hall of Freyr was the center of power in Alfheimer. The city council met to discuss any issues among the people living there. At the same time, Hunter, his siblings, and their military advisors met to plan strategies. Inside the great hall, mosaics portrayed the elves' history, from their creation by Bryr and Begguila to the death of Lord Baldrid at the hands of Morgana le Fay and the sacrifice of the elves at the *Oriĕntür*.

Hunter and Rose walked quickly through the hall, politely nodding to the people scattered around the room. They rushed toward the back as they were already late for the meeting.

"Where's Ashley?" Hunter asked.

"She's with Andy in the hospital," Rose replied. "She won't be here while he's unconscious."

"She can't blame herself," Hunter noted. "Faust took him completely by surprise. That was a hard hit for anyone."

"Yeah, well, you know how protective she is of Andy, especially when he gets reckless."

Hunter stopped suddenly and faced his sister, angry at her callous remarks. "Andy's not reckless, Rose," he snapped. "He's a knight, like me. Andy wants people like you and Ashley to stop treating him like a novice. He may not have our abilities, but he's still a formidable warrior."

Rose thought about it for a moment and realized her mistake. "You're right, little brother," she began. "We need to respect his prowess. He's earned it."

Hunter caught himself and sighed. He knew he shouldn't have snapped at her. "Sorry, Rose, the whole situation has me on edge," Hunter apologized as they continued walking toward the other end of the hall. "Ollie's been through Hell and back just because he's my friend. I thought he went off the grid for his protection to keep Mordred from finding him. If I had known sooner that he was in *Ür Tár*, I would have—"

Rose laughed, interrupting him quite rudely. "What's so funny?" Hunter asked.

"You sound just like Dad," Rose said. "He was constantly second-guessing himself, thinking he had to be one step ahead of the enemy. Being the Gil-Gamesh doesn't make you omnipotent, Hunter. After all, you're only human."

Hunter laughed, conceding her point about being fallible, though he appreciated the comparison to his father. "I miss him," he said quietly. "Especially at times like this. I wish I could call on him for advice like he used to get from the spirits of the past Gil-Gamesh's."

"You will, little brother, once we get his swords back, but right now, we're late!" They hurried off to what was affectionately known as the "War Room." The MoonDrake siblings often called it "The Death Star"—a vague movie reference that made them laugh whenever someone else called it that.

Inside, there was a long table displaying a three-dimensional map of the archipelago. Each island was outlined and represented by the flag of those in control. Purple flags bearing the coat of arms of Mordred—a winged lion holding an eye etched with a sword and lightning bolt in the iris—were controlled by the king's forces. While blue flags with the MoonDrake coat of arms—a flying dragon with a moon wrapped in its tail over two crossed swords—were islands loyal to the Gil-Gamesh and his allies.

Surrounding the table, waiting patiently, were the other leaders of the resistance. Captain Edan O'Brien looked like his moniker, The Pirate King. Though weathered from years of battle, his face was still young and boyish. A Napoleon-style captain's hat was adorned with the skull and crossbones on his head. His coat was flowing and regal, with ruffles around the cuffs and collar. He wore a steel breastplate under his jacket with a leather belt across his chest. His sword, *Crossbones*, hung from the belt.

The blade had been passed down through the generations from the first Pirate King of Avalon, Captain Henry Avery. Edan won the sword in combat when he defeated the previous Pirate King, John Avery.

General Rhona McLoughlin lived up to her name as the Shield Maidens of Avalon commander. She resembled the Valkyrie of legend, standing nearly six feet tall, muscular, and beautiful, with long blonde hair braided under her winged helm. Her armor was chain mail with plate adornments, demonstrating the shield maiden's devotion to the old ways. Across her back was slung a massive two-handed sword, *Brisingr*. This legendary sword was considered a Valkyrie's sword, and only a female warrior could wield it.

Eileanora was there, as was Dame Sarafina, Headmistress of the Shield Maidens and stepsister to the MoonDrake siblings. Sarafina was adopted and raised by Lord MoonDrake when he first arrived on Avalon. Though once married and forced to leave the order, she returned to take charge of the warrior's training regimen. She had to temper her role as Head of the Order and mother to her children. Her beauty shone through her long blonde hair and cold, steel eyes. Her armor was like Rhona's, apart from her flowing, fur-lined coat. Embroidered with the signets of every headmistress who led the Covenant of the Shield Maidens, the train grew with each generation that took up the mantle.

Lastly, there was Henri Beauchamp, former Chancellor of Emmyr. Henri was a meticulous administrator from one of the few French families on Avalon. His reputation as an efficient organizer and an outlandish dresser was apparent by his flowing frock coat, a wide-brimmed hat, and neatly waxed mustache. He looked more like a character from *The Three Musketeers* than a distinguished member of the court of Avalon.

Hunter and Rose approached the table and glanced at the ever-changing landscape. "How many did we rescue from *Ùr Tár*?" he asked.

"Nearly a thousand prisoners, Gil-Gamesh," Eileanora stated. "Most of them are suffering from malnutrition and dehydration. The hospital is at capacity, including some of our own wounded."

"And what are our casualties?"

"Minor, for the most part," she answered. "About twenty shield maidens and several *Hildrägo Boquè* fell in battle, adding more to the ranks of the Wraith Legion. We had a dozen or so injured, but not severely."

"What will we do with the prisoners once they've recovered?" Rose interrupted.

"*Le plus* 'high profile' prisoners will remain with us," Henri replied. "It is too dangerous to let them return to their homes. I will contact our *confidents* across Avalon to take the rest in."

"At least *Ùr Tár* is closed for good," Edan interjected. "That's one less prison for Mordred."

"That may be, Edan, but if he continues to add to the ranks of the Wraith Legion, none of it matters," Sarafina snapped back. "If we can't find a way to break Faust's control, we'll never make any headway against Mordred."

"Sarafina's right. For everyone we rescue, for every island we wrest control from his rule, Mordred still holds the upper hand," Hunter explained. "Until we find a way to break Faust's bond with the heavenly host locked in his heartstone, our gains mean nothing.

"Not to mention, we have no idea what this 'Prometheus Engine' is that Mordred's rumored to be building. The description from our spy in New Camelot was vague, at best. All we have to go on is a name," he concluded.

"I have someone here who might be able to help you with that," came a voice from behind as Lady Stephanie MoonDrake helped Ollie into the room. Everyone politely bowed to the mother of the MoonDrake children and widow of Lord Bryan MoonDrake. They treated her with the utmost grace and reverence.

Her bright auburn hair, starting to gray at the temples, was braided neatly around her head. Her face appeared ageless, as her beauty glowed like the morning sun. Her dress was a long, flowing blue gown with silver embroidery, a colorful symbol of the house of MoonDrake and the life she had stepped into since she arrived on Avalon with her children more than twenty years ago.

"Oliver insisted on coming to see you as soon as possible, Hunter," she added. Hunter reached out to his friend and took him in his arms, hugging him tightly.

"I'm so sorry, Ollie," he started to apologize. "If I had known sooner that you were in that awful place, I would have—"

"You don't owe me an apology, Hunter," he interrupted the Gil-Gamesh. "Sooner or later, they would have found some reason to lock me up. I'm just glad that you came looking for me when you did. Thank you, my frien, but I must ask, why were you looking for me?"

"We got word that Mordred has been scouring Avalon for alchemists, and you were on top of his list. They probably didn't realize that you had been sent to *Ür Tár*," Hunter explained. "He's got Master Tinker Broadfoot and his gnomes building something called the 'Prometheus Engine.' Do you have any idea what it is?"

"The Prometheus Engine? Are you kidding me? He's trying to build that?" Ollie exclaimed.

"Yes, but what is it?" Hunter begged.

"Oh, come on, Hunter, you've heard of it from the history of alchemy: The Lathe of Hephaestus, the Apparatus of Jannes, Archimedes' Magical Wheel," he explained. "These were some of the first machines designed by sorcerers and alchemists."

"But machines won't work on Avalon," Sarafina queried.

"These are not normal machines, Dame Sarafina. They don't run on fuel or electricity like Outlander machines but magic."

"For what?" Eileanora asked. "What do they do?"

"That's just it; no one knows for sure," Ollie said. "The machines are legendary, but what they can do has been lost over time. They're nothing but fairy tales that have always been a part of the alchemist lore. Some legends say the Prometheus Engine could replicate any substance imaginable. It could weave elements which bind the universe together, creating the 'God Spark' as it were."

A hush fell across the room as everyone tried to imagine the power Mordred could wield if he got this machine working. "But there's never been a blueprint or drawing of any kind for a machine like this," Ollie concluded. "As I said, it's a myth."

"In my experience, there is always some truth behind every myth. We need to find out as much as possible about this Prometheus Engine," Hunter declared.

"Perhaps Ollie can work with Ashley in Merlin's library," Lady Stephanie suggested. "I'm sure those two can scour the stacks for something related to this machine."

"Merlin's library? That's here?" Ollie wondered with wild amusement.

Hunter laughed at his friend's sense of wonder. He knew Ollie would like his time here. "Mom, can you please take him to Ashley and tell her what we're looking for? It might give her a needed distraction while Andy is recovering."

"Of course, sweetheart," she said, accentuating the 'sweetheart' which caused some in the room to chuckle. No matter what, Hunter was her baby boy, and she would always speak to him as a loving mother, not a knight. Lady Stephanie took Ollie by the arm again and led him out of the room.

"As for the rest of us, we need to regroup and coalesce our forces and see if anyone else might know something about this machine," Hunter said. "Rose, you and Edan, go visit Barbarossa and see if your little band of cutthroats have any new information for us. Meanwhile, Eileanora and I will head to Strongürd Keep, check in with Jean-Claude Baptiste, and see what the Wizard's Council may know about this Prometheus Engine."

"And what about me, Gil-Gamesh?" Rhona asked.

"I have a special assignment for you, Rhona. I need you to deliver a message for me to Lord Tomas Elderson of Eldonshire," Hunter remarked. "He owes me a favor, and I'm calling it in."

"Is that a wise decision, Sir Hunter?" Eileanora inquired. "He did join Mordred's coup willingly. I doubt he would honor any debt he may owe you."

"Trust me, Eileanora, Tomas may have sided with Mordred, but the man I know is one who always repays his debts," Hunter explained. "And he owes me big time. I know Rhona can deliver my message without any issues."

"I have some friends in Eldonshire who can help," Rhona stated. "The Swann sisters live there. They're former shield maidens who decided to live the rest of their life peacefully farming the land."

"Former shield maidens? Do you think they'll help?" Hunter asked.

"Of course they will, Gil-Gamesh," she retorted sternly. "The Oath of the Shield Maidens extends beyond death. It is an unbreakable bond."

Hunter chagrined. He knew he shouldn't have questioned her about shield maidens' loyalties, even former ones. "My apologies, Rhona. I didn't mean to offend the Order. Nowadays, it's hard to tell your friends from your enemies."

"It's quite all right, Sir Hunter," Rhona said with a curious grin. "I know you, so I'm rather forgiving. The Swann sisters, however, may not be."

As she turned away to prepare for her journey to Eldonshire, Hunter got a lump in his throat and swallowed hard. He should have known better than to irritate a shield maiden.

Sarafina giggled at Hunter's discomfort for his slight but decided to be a good stepsister and ease his mind. "I wouldn't worry too much, Hunter. I'm sure the Swanns haven't swung anything heavier than a scythe or an ax since they retired," she joked.

Hunter glared at her, knowing full well she was ribbing him. "That's what I'm afraid of," he replied. "We better get going, Eileanora. I'll tell Captain Hawke to get *Avenger* ready to fly."

Before Eileanora could say another word, Sarfina jumped in. "As father so famously reminded me, little brother, you have some other duties to attend to first," she interjected. "Your son is waiting patiently to see you."

Hunter sighed, cursing under his breath at his ignorance. As usual, he got so wrapped up in his responsibilities as Gil-Gamesh that he forgot an essential thing in his life—his son, Bowen. "Thanks, Sarafina," he remarked as he hugged her, kissing her cheek. "Eileanora, will you please see that Captain Hawke is ready to get underway?"

"Of course, Gil-Gamesh," she replied with a bow as she left. Hunter headed off with Sarafina to find his son.

Bowen Pendragon was the rightful heir to the throne of Avalon. Years ago, while Hunter was in New Camelot, training to be a Knight of Avalon, he fell in love with Her Royal Highness, Queen Cadhla Pendragon. They met rather innocuously when Hunter explored some of the secret passages in the castle and mistakenly found his way into the Queen's private quarters. Instead of being upset with him, she invited him in to get to know him better.

They would spend hours talking about the outside world, music, art, and family. Over time, the friendship blossomed into something more, and they fell in love. To keep their relationship a secret, Cahdla would use her innate magical talent as an illusionist to alter her appearance so that she could meet Hunter at the local taverns around New Camelot. To the rest of the people, Hunter got a reputation as a "Casanova," dining and drinking with a different girl every night. However, it was only ever Cahdla.

When Cahdla learned she was pregnant with his child, the two were secretly married, and Hunter became the Queen's Consort. When he became a Knight of the Round Table, they promoted Hunter to Master-at-Arms. It was during that time that he developed the GunStars. It was also when Bowen was born.

They kept their relationship a secret, even after Morgana le Fay killed Queen Cahdla and King Bowen assumed Avalon's throne. Hunter and his parents felt it would raise suspicions, leading people to believe that the Gil-Gamesh was trying to place his heir on the throne. It was not until after the coup that Mordred revealed Bowen's parentage.

Bowen was only twelve years old. He wanted to prove himself worthy of his father, mother, and grandfather. His determination was unmatched by his desire to reclaim the throne of Avalon. He had a powerful combination of his mother's heart and his father's spirit.

Hunter found Bowen where he usually was—the training field. The shield maidens and *Hildrägo Boquè* worked tirelessly to keep their fighting skills honed. Bowen had the best teachers in all of Avalon to instruct him in the art of warfare. From archery and spears to swords and axes, they gave the young king the necessary tools to fight.

Elves and shield maidens filled the field, conducting hand-to-hand combat, close-quarter drills, and archery practice. Most regiments required blunted or wooden weapons, but they treated all training as if it were the real thing. Battle scars were not only badges of honor but a reminder of what not to do in a fight.

Brigette, one of the senior trainers, engaged Bowen in close-quarters combat. From the look, it appeared to be a complete mismatch. Brigette was nearly six feet tall, her red hair braided neatly around her head. She wore an eyepatch over her left eye, hiding an old wound that never properly healed. Her armor was ring mail with a leather baltea hanging around her waist.

Bowen, on the other hand, was just five feet tall. The chain mail armor he wore hung on him like a baggy shirt. It was held on him by plate mail pauldrons and vambraces. He had the same youthful, handsome features as his father, though everyone said he had his mother's blue eyes. Sandy brown hair framed his face, but he wore no helmet, something Hunter disapproved of entirely.

"I thought we agreed he would wear a helmet in practice?" Hunter asked Sarafina.

"We did, but he refuses to wear it," she retorted. "He says it limits his field of vision."

"Oh, come on, even shield maidens wear helmets into battle. He could be seriously injured."

"Maybe you should tell him that. He needs to hear it from his father. No one else can seem to say no to him. After all, he is the King."

"Let me talk to Toledo first," Hunter said. "Maybe he can forge something practical that we'll both be happy with."

"Oh, I think he'll be changing his mind before that," Sarafina said. "That's why I assigned Brigette to spar with him today."

Hunter was confused as the two continued to watch the sparring session. While Brigette carried a long sword and shield, Bowen opted for two blades, a family tradition. For centuries, the Gil-Gamesh wielded *Twilight* and *Dusk*, the Twin Swords of the Dragon Moon, forged from *Excalibur's* broken pieces. Morgana le Fay and the Dark Tides had destroyed those swords. His father took the shattered pieces to the Lady of the Lake. She took the broken pieces and made *Excalibur* whole once again. With that, the King gave the Gil-Gamesh the Twin Swords of the Dragon Knight—identical to the original—forged from Orichalcum and enchanted with two powerful dragon stones.

Abdel Ben Faust had stolen these swords after he murdered Hunter's father at Avalon's Reclamation. Nevertheless, Bowen hoped to wield them someday, so he always practiced with two.

The combatants circled each other, looking for the right opening. Brigette lunged at Bowen, but he quickly swatted her attack away. Brigette used the momentum of his repose to spin counterclockwise and smack him, somewhat unexpectedly, in the side of his head with her shield.

Brigette knocked Bowen to the ground hard. He gingerly sat up, still dizzy from the blow. Brigette impatiently waited for him to get to his feet.

"There are no rest periods in battle, Your Majesty," she scolded him. "On your feet, sire, and back to the ready!"

Hunter didn't like the tone she was taking with the boy king. He wanted to jump in, but Sarafina held him back.

"Wait, Hunter," she whispered. "Let's see how he responds."

Hunter bided his time as he watched his son slowly get up. Bowen shook his head a few times to clear the cobwebs before he took his fighting stance. "Ready!" he announced.

Brigette didn't hesitate and started on the offensive. She swung her sword repeatedly at him, making him defend rather than attack. When he tried to lunge at her with both blades, she smacked his swords away and slammed her shield into him again. This time, Bowen flew backward more than twenty feet before hitting the ground.

Brigette walked over to him and offered her hand. He reluctantly took it as she helped him to his feet. "That is why we wear helmets, Your Majesty," she explained. "My first blow made you dizzy, and you could not recover before my second strike. You cannot block every attack, so what you wear to protect yourself needs to be an equal part of your defense."

"I see what you mean, Lady Brigette. Thank you for pointing that out to me, although I wish you had done it less painfully." Bowen shook his head again and yawned as he tried to pop his ears.

"If I did, Your Majesty would have never learned the lesson," she said sternly yet courteously. It was then that Brigette noticed Hunter and Sarafina watching them. "I see we had an audience for our duel, and your father looks none too pleased."

"He's just over-protective of me, that's all," Bowen replied as he picked up his swords. The two walked over to Hunter and Sarafina. They bowed respectfully to the King before Hunter reached out and hugged his son.

"Are you hurt, Your Majesty?" Hunter asked as he examined Bowen's head for bumps, bruises, and cuts.

"I'm fine, Gil-Gamesh. Brigette was teaching me a valuable lesson about defense," Bowen said bravely. "I think it is time for me to wear a helmet."

"I think so, too," Hunter said as he touched Bowen's shoulder. "For now, let's see Doctor Bonapat and make sure you're OK."

"No, I'm alright, father. Besides, the hospital has its hands full with all the prisoners injured from your raid at *Ür Tár*."

Hunter was proud of his son's spirit and determination yet worried about his health and well-being. He gave in to the King's wishes but with a slight caveat.

"Well then, how about you let Nona look at you instead? OK?" Hunter asked. Bowen sighed. He knew that Lady Stephanie was a little more problematic than his father, but there was no way to avoid it. He nodded his head as Hunter led him away to find his Nona.

Sarafina and Brigette watched as father and son left the training field. "I understand that Sir Hunter wants to protect his son, but he needs to let him take his lumps as any young boy would at this stage of their training," Brigette remarked. "Ultimately, it'll make the King skittish in combat."

"He's just cautious, Brigette," Sarafina inferred. "He doesn't want any harm to come to His Majesty before he assumes his rightful place back on the Granite Throne."

"With respect, Dame Sarafina, I don't remember your father asking us to take it easy on you, nor Sir Hunter, when he was training to be a knight."

Sarafina glared at Brigette for bringing Lord MoonDrake into the conversation in such a way, but she consented because, deep down, she knew Brigette was right.

"Those were different times, Brigette," she snapped back. "Avalon's Reclamation and Mordred's ascension to the throne has made us a little more protective of the king. You may think my father wasn't overly protective because he hid it so well. He wanted us to grow up independently, but he had a guiding and protective hand in everything. Even today, he still influences every decision I make as the headmistress of the Order of the Shield Maidens."

"Speaking of which, we desperately need to replenish our ranks," Brigette interrupted. "I suggest we look at the prisoners to see if any would like to join the Dragon Guard or us."

"I doubt any of them would be willing to put themselves through the rigors of our training after the pain and anguish they've been exposed to."

"You'd be surprised, Dame Sarafina," Brigette charged. "The hardships of a prison break some but strengthen others to a resolve stronger than steel. Some of them will thirst for a little revenge against Mordred."

Sarafina couldn't deny the logic in Brigette's argument. "Very well, Brigette, see to it."

With a courteous bow, Brigette left Sarafina and headed toward the hospital. Sarafina stared out across the training field, watching the form and function of her warriors. She suddenly felt something tug at her coat. She looked down and smiled at seeing her son, Thomas, and her daughter, Meriel.

Thomas was a handsome little eight-year-old with golden blonde hair and freckles. He looked like his father, Nevan. His smile was bright and cheerful as he held his sister's hand. Meriel was the cutest little five-year-old girl you'd ever seen. Her blue eyes sparkled with a look of innocence—her strawberry blonde hair curled against her head, framing a smile that exuded joy and laughter.

"What are you two doing here?" she asked as she knelt and kissed her children. "I thought you were doing your studies with Miss Sophie."

"Miss Sophie had to go help the doctor in the hospital," Thomas said, enunciating each word slowly. "We came up here to be with you, Mama!"

Sarafina smiled and hugged her children tightly. As much as she loved being a shield maiden, she loved being a mother even more. It was rare for a woman who became part of the Order to be both, but Sarafina was the exception.

She was shield maiden to Lord MoonDrake until she fell in love and married Sir Nevan Forest, the Captain of the Dragon Guard. Nevan was killed during the resurrection of Morgana le Fay. Afterward, she assumed the mantle of Headmistress of the Covenant of the Shield Maidens. It allowed her to train the next generation of women warriors while letting her raise her children.

"Well, why don't we go under the shade and find you two something to eat while Mama finishes up here?" She took them by the hand and walked with them to a canopy set up for her. Under cover of a billowing white tent, two young servant girls stood patiently, waiting to serve the headmistress. These initiates into the Covenant of the Shield Maidens recently joined the Order. Part of their training included performing menial tasks in service to the senior members of the Order, something all the sisters did at one time or another.

The servants brought the children a plate of assorted fruits, cheeses, and a goblet of wine for Sarafina. "Thank you, Analisa," she complimented as she took the goblet. When their fingers touched, Sarafina instantly saw flashes of a vision. She watched as the Lady of the Lake, the Covenant of the Shield Maidens' patron saint, struggled against heavy chains. She cried out and quivered in anguish as she strained beneath their weight. The chains glowed in unnatural energy with every move she made. The emotional torture felt honest to Sarafina.

"Sarafina," she whispered as the agony she was experiencing came through in her voice. "Help me!"

"Mistress?" Analisa said, snapping Sarafina out of her trance. "Are you all right?"

Sarafina composed herself, momentarily breathless as the vision had startled her. "I'm fine, Analisa, perfectly fine."

The servant girl curtseyed as Sarafina took a sip of wine to calm her nerves before turning her attention back to the training field. She tried to focus on the activities, but her mind wandered back to the vision. She could feel the pain and suffering of the Lady of the Lake. She tried to remember more, but the sight and sounds of her children distracted her. They ate the fruit and cheese while the servant girls played with them.

She lived for her children and the Order, but these visions showed her that something more was afoot—something that could change her destiny and perhaps the fate of Avalon.

CHAPTER 4
THE WRATH OF MORDRED

The King had very little patience for failure. Mordred sat back on the granite throne and rubbed the throbbing pain pulsating in his forehead as he listened to the pleadings of Dwarf Lord Sempir Dwallis. The dwarf tried his best to explain how the prisoners' loss and the flooding of *Ūr Tár* were not his faults. Abdel Ben Faust and Artūras Blackstone stood off with Lady Mavis, listening to him drone on and on about the incident at the mines. While he continued his rant, the only one in the room with the worst headache than the king was Magister Ulric Ocwyn.

He stood next to the granite throne and sighed, rolling his eyes as he looked away from the sniveling dwarf. Ocwyn's appearance was as regal and distinguished as his role as advisor to the King. His robes were royal purple with gold embroidery. Beneath his robes, he wore a green tunic, the only color he could wear besides Mordred's colors. He tightly grasped a staff of gold and precious gems with an orb of black marble. His long black hair flowed neatly around his bald head, draped down to the middle of his back.

Ocwyn had a long history of service to the crown. As the former Chamberlain to King Bowen, he made a "deal with the devil" to save the boy king. He agreed to be one of his advisors if Mordred promised that neither he nor his servants would ever kill Bowen. He loved Bowen so much that he consecrated his pact with Mordred. As long as he remained loyal to Mordred, the boy remained safe.

"I did all that I could, Your Majesty," Dwallis continued to plead. "We fought against the Gil-Gamesh's forces to hold them back until General Faust arrived with the Wraith Legion. We held our ground until—" He paused momentarily to gather his thoughts. "Until—"

"Until he gave you a choice to leave in peace or die fighting," Ocwyn interrupted. "Is that all it took for you to surrender *Ür Tár* and all its riches to a watery grave?"

"*Ür Tár* was always a lost cause," Sempir snapped back at Ocwyn. "I had to do what I could to save my people."

"Your people?" Mordred interrupted. "Your people!" He quickly rose to his feet and stepped off the throne toward Sempir. "The only reason your people live is that I allow it. Your people are supposed to be the best warriors money can buy, yet you failed to stop the shield maidens and *Hîldrägo Boquè* from freeing the prisoners. So, not only are the mines gone, but so are the prisoners who were mining them."

Sempir swallowed hard as fear swelled up inside him. "You once told me that your people were not miners, like your cousins of the Gilded Halls," Mordred continued criticizing him. "Well, now you will learn to be miners. You and your Iron Mount Dwarves will return to *Ür Tár* and provide me the riches so I can continue to wage war against the Gil-Gamesh and his forces and rebuild Avalon."

"But Your Majesty, you cannot expect—" Sempir started to say before Mordred slapped him across the face to silence him. Two Iron Mount Dwarves stepped up to defend their leader, but Faust's burning blade held them back.

"Oh yes, you will, Sempir," Mordred indicated as he spun around and returned to his seat on the granite throne. "You will mine *Ür Tár* for me, or you and your dwarves can serve as part of the Wraith Legion. The choice is yours. Now, get out of my sight!" he demanded, and with a wave of his hand, two guards jabbed at the dwarves with massive glaives, threatening them to leave the throne room immediately. These were the king's guard, the *Cosc Fháil*, or Forbidden Guard. They wore black plate mail armor with flowing tunics and capes adorned with the purple and gold heraldry of King Mordred.

Of all King Mordred's minions, these were the finest and most brutal warriors imaginable. Although fierce war masks hid their identities, the *Cosc Fháil* were personally trained by Abdel Ben Faust and bound to King Mordred physically and spiritually. Should Mordred be attacked or injured, the *Cosc Fháil* would protect the king and give him their life force to renew and heal any injuries. They were the ultimate bodyguards to ensure Mordred remained on the throne of Avalon.

"Magister, assign some of the Adalwulf Guard to keep an eye on the dwarves at *Ūr Tár*," Mordred commanded. "If they begin to waiver in their new positions, they need to be eliminated before they become a threat."

"It will be done, Your Majesty," Ocwyn said with a courteous bow.

"If there is nothing else, Magister, I want to rejuvenate. These proceedings have drained me," Mordred stated as he rose to his feet to leave.

"There is one more thing, sire," Ocwyn started to say, irritating Mordred. "Guildmaster Keane Foley is here to see you. He would not tell me what it was about, and I hesitated to bring him into the throne room to discuss the matter with you openly. He is waiting in your chambers."

Mordred sighed, visibly upset at the delay in his relaxation. "Very well, Magister," Mordred huffed, pulling his cape tightly around him. "General!" he commanded, and Faust immediately followed behind the King.

As the two of them left the throne room, Blackstone stepped up to Ocwyn, confused by his actions. "This is a mistake, Ocwyn," he insinuated. "Why should the King be made to meet with common thieves like Foley? You're turning the King into a common beggar."

"You forget your place, brother," Ocwyn snapped back at him. "Matters of the court are my responsibility, not yours." Though the two men were brothers, they followed different paths. Ocwyn worked his way through the oligarchy to become Magister to King Mordred. Artūras dabbled in the dark arts, shunned by his family and the wizarding community until the return of Mordred.

"We are trying to ingratiate the King to the people of Avalon," Ocwyn explained. "How would it look if word got out that the Master of the Thieves Guild was meeting with the King in the throne room? Such talk could potentially tear down all we have built here. It's bad enough that the Adalwulf Guard terrorizes the populace regularly."

"Fear helps keep the people in line, submissive and compliant," Blackstone argued.

"It also takes away the one thing people yearn for—freedom! The desire for freedom creates longing, which leads to dissent and chaos. We should tread lightly here, brother, so support and loyalty to the crown do not waiver."

"So long as your support and loyalty to the King do not, dear brother," Blackstone chided Ocwyn. The Magister squeezed his hand around his staff tightly as he tried to restrain himself. His anger toward Artūras seethed from within, but the one thing Ocwyn had learned in the past five years was control and composure.

"My loyalty has never wavered to the King nor Avalon, Artūras, a fact I'm sure your spies have reported," Ocwyn remarked. "We all serve the King in our ways. I suggest you worry about your duties and leave the court matters to me, brother."

As the Magister walked away, Lady Mavis strutted toward Blackstone. She hung back, listening to their entire conversation, awaiting the right time to interject herself into the fray.

"I see you continue to badger your brother, Minister of Magic," she quipped. "You are wasting valuable time and resources. I will discern any deception from Magister Ocwyn toward King Mordred. You need not fear your brother. I will know if he falters."

"As impressive as your foresight is, Lady Mavis, I know my doting brother better than any of you. He will turn on King Mordred, and soon, very soon."

"And if he doesn't? What then?" she asked. "All the paranoia and distrust on display makes you look weak in the King's eyes. Your ridicule will lead to exile from New Camelot."

Artūras glared at Lady Mavis, visibly shaken by her prophetic vision. "You have foreseen this?" he questioned, his voice quivering with fear. He knew how accurate Mavis' visions were.

"I have, and that is why you must be stealthier in your pursuits," Mavis explained as she ran her hand across his back, teasing Artūras. "If you were not so outward in your efforts, Magister Ocwyn may relax and lower his guard so we may discover his true intentions."

Artūras considered what Lady Mavis said, and a devious smile gleamed across his face. "Thank you for your counsel, Lady Mavis. I will do just that." He bowed, and she curtseyed as the two left the throne room, arm-in-arm, happy in their alliance.

Keane Foley waited patiently for his audience with the king. He sat quietly, balancing a dagger on the tip of his finger. He liked to check the precise balance of his blades daily, ensuring their handling and accuracy.

Only his piercing violet eyes were visible from underneath his shrouded hood. He wore what appeared to be a loose-fitting robe and trousers, but that was quite deceiving. Underneath it was fine leather armor fitted to his body, providing protection and maneuverability, a necessity for a thief.

Unlike Keane's quiet demeanor, his brother Pert was impatient, pacing frantically around the room. His clothes and appearance were similar to his brother's, except his robes were dark red. The color of the robes indicated their rank within the Thieves Guild. Only the Guildmaster wore black. Pert's dark red robes identified him as a Shadowfoot, second-in-command to his brother. As he watched him pace, Keane started to tire of his brother's impatience.

"Sit down, Pert, before you wear a hole in the King's rug," Keane chided his brother. Pert didn't listen and continued his pace.

"We shouldn't be here, Keane," he replied. "We're thieves, not palace guards or knights. It's unnatural, and you know it."

"I do, but we must see the King about this, Pert. We—" Keane started to say until he was interrupted. The door to the king's chambers swung open, and Mordred entered with Faust close behind. Keane jumped to his feet and stood next to Pert. The two men bowed as the king passed by, not acknowledging their presence.

He poured himself a goblet of wine, taking a drink as he ignored the two thieves in his chambers. "Why are you here, Guildmaster Foley?" Mordred asked as he continued to drink, not bothering to look at them.

Keane became nervous as his eyes moved between the king and Faust. The half-demon looked at them with a sour grimace, his hand on his sword hilt, making both thieves nervous.

"Forgive the intrusion, Your Majesty, but my guild has issues with the Adalwulf Guard," he stammered. "They are coming into my guilds and taxing us forty percent on what we steal. That is not what we agreed to, sire. The agreement was—"

"Remove your hoods," Mordred interrupted. The king's request took the two thieves by surprise.

"Your Majesty?" Keane asked. Mordred finally turned around and looked directly at the two.

"Remove your hoods, now," he said again. "I will not be addressed by a pair of eyes from the dark."

Both Keane and Pert were apprehensive about removing their hoods. Outside the guild, anonymity was a thieves' best defense. The king patiently waited while Faust gritted his teeth at them.

Keane realized they had no choice. With a nod of his head, the two men pulled back their hoods and lowered their scarves. Keane's face was long and thin, his hair pulled back in a ponytail. A scar was visible under his left that extended down his face and throat.

Pert had a gruff exterior compared to his brother. His face was full, covered by a thin beard, and his hair hung loosely. Like Keane, he too had a scar, but his went up into his eyebrow.

"As I was saying, sire, the Adalwulf Guard is overtaxing my guilds in every city," Keane continued. "They are pocketing the extra tax money themselves, of that I'm sure."

"Why are you bothering the king with these petty squabbles?" Faust interjected. "You should address your concerns to Magister Ocwyn or Captain Grisgutt, not the king."

"I wasn't speaking to you, General Faust," Keane snapped back. "As Guildmaster, I am equal to one of the Lords of Avalon. I can speak directly to the king, not one of his lackeys."

Faust started to draw his sword, but King Mordred raised his hand to stop him. Faust snarled and obeyed the king, sheathing his sword.

"Very well, Guildmaster Foley; I will speak to Captain Grisgutt about the taxes on the guilds," Mordred said in a calm, steady voice.

Keane smiled, happy that the king saw things his way. "Thank you, Your Majesty," he said. "That is all I wanted." The two thieves bowed politely and started to leave.

"I am still speaking," Mordred interjected before they could take another step. "I will tell Captain Grisgutt to order the Adalwulf Guard that taxes on the guilds are now seventy percent."

"But, Your Majesty, that's outrageous," Pert insisted.

"King Mordred, you're unreasonable. That's not what we agreed to," Keane added. Before he could say another word, Faust drew his blade and decapitated Pert in one swift stroke. He swung the sword toward Keane, but the thief quickly drew a dagger and blocked his attack. Faust struggled against him, amazed that a mere dagger held back his cursed sword.

"Faust!" The general hesitated momentarily to the king's command before he released his blade from Foley, lowering it to his side but not sheathing the sword.

Foley stared at the head of his deceased brother as his grief turned to anger. There was no blood as Faust's blade seared the wound. His body twitched uncontrollably, the last flickers of life fading from his corpse.

Foley turned his attention to the king, but his anger turned to fear as he stared into the darkness within Mordred's eyes. Nothing was behind them—a lifeless pit of darkness that tore through his heart.

"This is the price you pay for insubordination and disobedience to your King, Guildmaster Foley," Mordred started to say as his voice grew louder with each word. "I will not be bartered like a butcher at the market! I am your King!

"Your brother forfeited his life when he raised his voice to me," he continued as he stepped toward Keane. "I will not kill you because I don't want the entire thieves' guild against me. So you will pay for your obedience in taxes, seventy percent of which you will pay to the Adalwulf Guard. Any thief that doesn't will be killed on sight. Are we clear on this, Guildmaster Foley?" Mordred concluded as he stared a hole through Keane.

He swallowed hard as his eyes wandered between the king, Faust, and his dead brother. "I understand, Your Majesty," he complied.

"Good, now get out of my sight. I never want to see your face again," Mordred said as he turned away while taking another sip of wine.

Foley lifted his brother across his shoulder, hoisting him in one hand while carrying his head in the other. He started to leave but then stopped and directed his attention toward Faust.

"This isn't over, half-demon," he cursed. "When next we meet, I will cut out that black rock you call a heart and feed it to the dogs."

Faust said nothing. He growled at Foley, gritting his teeth at him. Keane left the king's chambers, letting the door slam behind him.

"You should have let me kill them both, my king," Faust grumbled as he sheathed his sword. "He will become a thorn in your side, you'll see."

"Foley and all his thieves will die soon enough, General," Mordred replied. "In the meantime, while we collect taxes from the populace, we'll also collect taxes on what the thieves steal from them. Ultimately, I will give you the pleasure of killing Keane Foley when his usefulness ends."

Faust relished the thought of killing this common thief who dared to stand up to half-demon. The last thing he needed was rumors circulating that a simple thief with a dagger bested Avalon's best swordsman.

CHAPTER 5
THE PIRATE HAVEN OF BARBAROSSA

Barbarossa was a place of legend and intrigue even before Avalon's Reclamation, and today, its reputation remained equally mysterious. Since the first pirates arrived more than 1,500 years ago, they have gone from privateers on the seas to marauders in the sky. They have always been ruthless, cunning, and feared by all who encountered them.

Their home was an island cove shrouded by an impossible mist as the ocean seemed to protect Barbarossa from outsiders. According to legend, the first Pirate King, Captain Henry Avery, fell in love and married the sea nymph Calypso when he arrived on Avalon. To demonstrate her love for him, she shrouded the entrance to this cove in a perpetual mist. No spell can dispel her magic, and only a skilled pirate knowledgeable of the pathway could navigate past the jagged rock formations into the hidden cove. The pirates built the town on a mishmash of wood pilings, old ships, and abandoned buildings from various seaside communities. There were always sounds of laughter and music, debauchery, and violence throughout Barbarossa. One thing that remained true was that pirates knew how to have a good time.

Since the reclamation, some of them had returned to their fleet of corsairs, sailing between the islands of the archipelago of Avalon. With the dragon isle of Emmyr—the source of the wood for flying ships—off-limits, there were fewer airships capable of soaring through the skies of Avalon. The sea was the only option for these buccaneers, a change relished by many.

Barbarossa itself changed, too. The pirate sanctuary was no longer a refuge from the Gil-Gamesh and the Knights of the Round Table. It was a second home for those leading the rebellion against Mordred.

Pirates loved one thing above treasure, and that was freedom. King Mordred's rule turned the usually ruthless scourges into relentless privateers, providing aid, supplies, and protection to the outlying islands—at a nominal fee.

With the Gil-Gamesh's brother-in-law assuming the Pirate King's mantle, they brokered a deal with the illusive buccaneers. They could attack, pillage, and steal whatever they wanted from King Mordred and his Lords of Avalon. In return, they supported the Gil-Gamesh and his allies in their efforts against the ageless king. Of course, Edan did something else that no Pirate King had ever done—he bought their loyalty.

skulls motif. A traditional sea captain's bicorne hat adorned his head, except for the large griffon feather protruding from the band.

"Ladies and Gentlemen, pirates one and all!" Edan trumpeted, bringing the hall to a low silence. "I bring you the bounty from the mines of *Ür Tár* and, with it, the return of our captured brethren!"

Behind him, crew members from the *Black Adder* were each carrying a large chest, a massive haul overflowing with riches. A rag-tag group of buccaneers followed them in. The prisoners rescued from the *Ür Tár* prison break were greeted with a hero's welcome. The crowd erupted in cheers and toasts as their former shipmates were welcomed back into the fold with drinks, food, and long-overdue companionship. Others congratulated Captain O'Brien on his victory, savoring the bounty of gold, jewels, and precious metals.

Rose and Caesar San Martine, the first mate on the *Black Adder*, were behind the entourage. Rose wore her green armored breastplate, with her shield slung across her back, but a comfortable skirt flowed to the floor instead of armored leggings. She dressed her part as the "Dragon Queen" to her husband's Pirate King.

Ceasar, a muscular, handsome black man towered over her, nearly seven feet tall. Various tattoos covered his body—a time capsule of his life from childhood to today—so everyone knew his life story no matter where he went. He always wanted to be unforgettable.

Caesar was brought onto the *Black Adder* when Edan first came to Barbarossa to assume the Pirate King's mantle. He wanted someone on his ship that other pirates respected, a way to curry favor and get them to fall in line. Caesar was an honorable man who lived his life by the pirate code. He was proud to take his place as the right hand of the Pirate King.

"The captain is relishing in his victory, my lady," Caesar noted. "He is working very hard to cement his position as Pirate King every time he returns to Barbarossa."

"He is at that, Caesar, though I wish he wouldn't be so flamboyant," Rose replied. "He's getting more and more like Chancellor Beauchamp. It's embarrassing."

"You would rather he go back into his shell and be the timid little boy he once was?"

"No, of course not. I wish he weren't so eccentric," Rose sighed. "I sometimes miss the quiet, reserved man who fawned over me behind my father's back."

"That man is still in there, Lady Rose," Caesar interjected. "I know this from my many conversations with the captain. He wears two masks, like an actor on the stage."

Rose continued to be impressed with Caesar. His eloquent speech was a part of his personality rarely seen in Barbarossa. Most people just saw the mountain of a man, the warrior of the sea, and not the gentle soul he was inside.

"You damn braggart!" a voice shouted across the room at Edan. A group of pirates stormed toward them, led by Fergus Darrow, known to all as the "Red-Faced Scotsman." His hair and beard were a dark auburn, flowing about his head, braided with iron spikes hanging at the ends. He wore a tartan kilt with a thick leather strap across his bare upper body. On his back was a Scottish Claymore, nearly five feet in length.

He stepped up, toe-to-toe, with the Pirate King, gritting his yellow, crooked teeth. "You won't be buying me or my crew like a whore on the street, little boy," he growled at him. "All your bounty does is dig us into a deeper hole against King Mordred, one that we'll never get out of!"

Edan did not back down from the outward challenge. He stood his ground and stared him down. "The only one digging a hole is you, Fergus," Edan said. "You seem concerned about your place in the kingdom of Avalon. As far as I know, no pirate has ever declared their loyalty to the King."

"You know nothing of pirate history, pretender," Fergus snapped back. "You're nothing but a whelp, married to one of the Gil-Gamesh's whore daughters, playing pirate for fun."

Rose almost leaped toward Fergus for his insult, but Caesar held her back. "The captain will deal with this, Lady Rose," he said. "To be the Pirate King, he must take all challenges alone." Rose understood and waited for Edan to act.

Edan slowly stepped forward until he was face to face with Fergus. "If you want to challenge me, old man, declare your challenge and draw your weapon."

Fergus stepped back and motioned to his men to spread out. Edan did the same as he drew his sword, *Crossbones*. Fergus reached for his Claymore and unsheathed his sword, but the ceilings in *Mad Mollies* were a bit low in places, and his blade stuck into a crossbeam as soon as he drew it out.

Edan took advantage of the delay and kicked Fergus in the groin. The pirate dropped to his knees, grabbing onto himself as he tried not to cry.

His mood quickly changed when Edan laid his sword across Fergus' neck. He stammered a soft-spoken plea as the sharp steel caressed his throat.

"You bastard, you cheated me of my rightful challenge!" Fergus grumbled.

"By the Pirate Code, once you drew your sword, the challenge commenced," Edan interjected. "I can't help it if your blade got stuck in the rafters. Perhaps you shouldn't try to overcompensate for things with such a long sword."

The pirates laughed at Edan's joke, except for Fergus, who remained under Edan's sword. "Now, you have a choice, Fergus," Edan crowed over his competitor. "You can swear fealty and loyalty to the Pirate King, or I can kill you and confiscate your ship and crew as reparations for your slight against me."

Everyone in the tavern went silent, with a few whispers echoing around the room, wagering how Fergus would respond. Even Rose watched in awe of her husband. She could not believe how quickly Edan handled the challenge from Fergus.

It didn't take the Scotsman long to nod his head in agreement. "I swear by the broken bones of Davey Jones, I do pledge my blood, my breath, my pieces of eight, to the Pirate King!" he said, in a slightly disgruntled tone, under his breath.

Edan nodded his head as he stepped back and sheathed his sword. He reached down to help Fergus to his feet. "Mollie! A round of rum for the crew of the *Clan Macleod*!" The cheers went up in the tavern as the music and bawdry antics resumed. Most of Fergus' crew nodded and saluted to the Pirate King, affirming their captain's loyalty.

As Fergus turned away, he encountered Rose. Without warning, she grabbed him by the groin, holding him tight and causing Fergus more pain.

"You may have pledged your loyalty to my husband, Fergus Darrow, but if you ever call me a whore again, I'll feed these to my dragon for a snack," she said as she tightened her grip. Fergus couldn't move, but the pain showed clearly on his face, his voice breathless.

"Yes ... yes, milady, I'm sorry. It'll never happen again!" Fergus stammered as an apology. Rose let go and stormed away. Edan and Caesar pitied the poor man as he slowly limped away, wanting to put distance between him and the Dragon Queen.

Edan joined his wife at their private table in the tavern. The secluded booth was near the back of the bar, allowing them to sit with their backs to the wall so anyone approaching would have to face them. The table had a wooden stall and partially opened velvet curtains, giving the Pirate King some privacy. Caesar took his post at the front of the table. Anyone wishing to speak to Edan or Rose must first have his approval.

Mollie brought pints of her best ale and a platter of fruit, bread, meat, and cheese. Her hair was as bright as sunlight, her skin as smooth as the inside of an oyster shell. She wore a tight-fitting bodice that left nothing to the imagination. Around her neck, a string of black pearls nestled seductively in her ample cleavage. Molly was never seen without them, fueling rumors and speculation that the pearls were the source of her longevity.

"Mollie, please see to the treasure distribution," Edan commanded.

"Don't you worry none about it, Captain O'Brien. I'll take care of it personally," she said with a slight cockney accent. "They won't leave here without a little gold in their pockets tonight."

"Minus your usual cut, right, Mollie?" Rose insinuated. Mollie smiled wickedly and winked at Rose before returning to running the tavern. "That woman is more of a cutthroat than most men here."

"She is that, but in all fairness, Mollie keeps the rest of them in line that way," Edan remarked as he took a swig of ale. "Pirates come and go, but Mollie is always here. She's an institution in Barbarossa." Rose acquiesced to her husband's logic as she joined him in drinking the frothy ale.

"Speaking of institutions," Edan paused before turning to his wife. "You could've put Fergus in the 'locker' with that grip you had on him."

"You've never complained about my grip," she joked as she drank more ale.

"I'm serious, Rose. I'm trying to keep these buccaneers on our side, not Mordred's."

Rose knew where he was going with this, which upset her, but she knew not to make a scene here. "When someone calls your wife a whore, your response should be to defend her, my dear Pirate King. Since you didn't do that, I took it upon myself."

"Fergus had already consented to me. That should have been—" he started to say.

"He pledged his loyalty to you, Edan, not me!" she interrupted. "I have my reputation to consider."

"As do I, Rose," Edan retorted back at her. "There are hundreds of pirates here whom I am trying to keep from joining forces with King Mordred and his allies. The only way to do that is through bribery, cunning, and guile. Unlike tonight, I must sometimes use force to coerce their obedience. When Fergus swore loyalty to me, everyone here knew from that point on, any insult or threat to you or me was punishable by death, as written in the pirate code."

"It's not enough, Edan," she snapped back at him. "These people still see me as my father's little girl, someone who didn't earn my position, or for that matter, even this armor!"

Before she could say another word, Edan leaned in and kissed her, abruptly ending the argument. Rose kissed him back and held him close. When he finally released her, her face brightened with a smile.

"I hate it when you end an argument like that," she scolded him before punching him in the arm.

"Well, it's the only way I can win one. Besides, you have nothing to prove to me. I know how strong you are. You are your father's daughter, and that's all that matters."

Rose kissed him again, wrapping her arms around him and holding him tight. Since her father's death, they have gotten close these past five years. She would not have made it through those difficult times without him.

"Ahem!" came a voice from behind the curtain. Caesar stood patiently, not wanting to interrupt them. "Begging your pardon, Captain, but someone here has information from New Camelot."

Edan nodded his head as Rose moved over slightly. Caesar brought in a gaunt, young sailor. He looked like a boy, not even eighteen years old. His face was smooth and handsome, not scarred and grizzled like other pirates. His light brown hair was dirty and neglected, held back by a bandana tied across his forehead. His clothes hung loosely on his body. Edan knew by looking at him that he was probably a cabin boy, a memory of his start on an airship. He remembered all the tiresome chores and duties, trying to earn his way through the ranks.

"This is Roy Gillibrand from the *Black Manta*," Caesar introduced the young man as he shoved him into the chair across from Edan and Rose. "They just arrived from a supply run to New Camelot."

"All right, Roy, if Caesar let you back here, you must have something good, so let's hear it."

"Yes, sir—" he stammered, nervous about being in the presence of the Pirate King. "Well, sir, my brother, you see, is part of the Thieves Guild in Dunwitty, but I ran into him in New Camelot. I was surprised to see him there since he never leaves home.

"You see, me mum ain't doing too well, and Georgie is the only one left to take care of her, and she's got so much on her plate in the guild there," he continued, but his rambling confused Rose.

"Wait a minute; your mother is in the thieves' guild?"

"Yes, ma'am, she's the guildmaster in Dunwitty," he answered quite serenely. Rose and Edan laughed at his revelation but quieted down to hear more.

"Please continue and get to the point," Edan demanded. Caesar slapped the young boy on the back of the head, insinuating he was taking too long to explain his story.

"Yes, sir. Georgie told me that the Thieves' Guild is in an uproar. That half-demon, Faust killed Pert Foley."

That bit of information caught both of their attention. "Pert Foley? Who is he?" Rose asked. Before Roy could answer, Edan jumped in.

"He's the Shadowfoot, second-in-command to Guildmaster Keane Foley. Are you sure about this, Roy?"

"Oh, yes, sir, Georgie said he did it right in front of Guildmaster Foley and King Mordred," Roy explained. "They were trying to get the King to reduce the guild taxes, seeing how the Adalwulf were lining their pockets with extra tax money. It seems Mordred took their demands as an insult, then Faust killed Pert, and the king raised the guild taxes to seventy percent."

"Seventy percent? No wonder the guilds are in a panic," Rose exclaimed.

"Yes, ma'am. They're emptying the guilds, sending all the thieves into hiding until Guildmaster Foley can think of a plan. Georgie's scared for me Mum; she's not a young woman anymore."

As disreputable as his family may be, Edan still recognized the importance of family, even to thieves and brigands like these. He reached into his pocket and pulled out a gold coin. Unlike the gold talons that bore Mordred's face, this coin had the Pirate King's emblem—a skull and crossbones with a serpent woven through it. He tossed the coin across the table to Roy.

"Give that to Mollie, Roy. She'll make sure you're taken care of tonight," Edan said with a smile, imagining what pleasures awaited the young buccaneer. Anyone who passed those coins received a night in Mad Mollies that they would never forget.

Roy picked up the coin, almost giddy with anticipation. "Thank you, sir—thank you very much," he cried out in excitement. He nodded, saluted quickly, and practically ran out, leaving Edan and Rose to discuss what he had told them.

"What do you think? Maybe this is the break we've been waiting for to get deep into Mordred's plans," Edan remarked.

"I don't follow you?"

"'The enemy of my enemy is my friend,' Lady Rose," Caesar explained. "If we can get to Guildmaster Foley, he may be convinced to become an ally against Mordred's reign."

"Foley? He sided against Avalon with Morgana le Fay. Why should we care about his little band of cutthroats and assassins? They deserve what they—" Rose said before realizing that she was talking about some of the people in the room, even Caesar. "I didn't mean you, Caesar."

"It is alright, Lady Rose. As pirates, we know our place in the world. It is as Poseidon deems," he said. "With your permission, Captain, I will get the ship ready to sail. I know you will want to return to Aflheimer soon."

"There's no need for that, Caesar," Rose interrupted. "The crew deserves some downtime, as does its Captain." She took Edan by the hand and pulled him away from the table. "You, my husband, need to help me out of my armor. It's been too long!"

As Rose dragged Edan off to their private room at *Mad Mollies*, Caesar decided to go and find some companionship for himself. Eyes carefully observed their every move from a prime viewing spot above the main floor, especially one pair of eyes. Sitting alone at a small table, Jason Hawke closely watched the Pirate King. He took another swig of rum from his bottle. Although the alcohol blurred his vision constantly, his drive kept him focused.

Jason was Jasper Hawke's twin brother. At one time, he was a welcomed friend on the floating island of Emmyr, working side-by-side with Lord Bryan MoonDrake in building the shipyard, piers, and warehouses once used on the dragon isle. It was his overindulgence in alcohol that drove him away from his family, his friends, and his life.

Jason came to Barbarossa to join the pirates, fight against the Gil-Gamesh, and earn glory and riches. He was on his way to captaining his first ship when Captain John Avery, the former Pirate King, sided with Morgana le Fay and lost his title to someone like Edan.

He hated Edan the most. First, he became captain of the Gil-Gamesh's flagship, the *Morningstar*; then, he took command of the *Avenger*. Now, this pissant of a man was the Pirate King. The anger boiled up inside Jason as he continued to guzzle his rum.

No matter what he did, Jason could not escape from the things in his past that reminded him of his failures, and he hated that. He drank some more as he contemplated what to do and how to get revenge. For now, he would sit, drink, watch, and wait.

CHAPTER 6
AMBUSH AT STRONGÜRD KEEP

Hunter leaned across the rail as he looked out from the bow of the *Avenger*. He stared through the clouds at the vast ocean that rolled beneath him. His hair fluttered in the breeze as Hunter heaved a visible sigh as if something was wrong. His mind was so focused on the seas below him that he didn't hear someone calling his name.

A hand gently touched his shoulder, bringing him back to reality. He turned to see Eileanora staring at him with an unusual, worried look. "Hunter, didn't you hear me calling for you?"

"I'm sorry, Elle," he apologized. "I was letting my mind wander." He turned back to stare again at the ocean below. "My Dad used to tell me that staring into the ocean was like staring into a blue abyss. Sailors can get lost when it's all you see for days."

Eileanora stepped to the rail beside him and looked down at the rolling seas. "It's just water, Hunter."

"It used to be more than that," he replied. "This used to be the Stoney Meadows, rolling hills of tall grass and huge rocks spread out for miles. You couldn't farm it, so it was perfect for shepherds to bring their cattle, sheep, and goats into the meadows to graze." Eleanora recalled the open field of giant boulders and tall grass from her journeys across Avalon.

"I remember once after the Queen knighted me, my father took me across Avalon, sort of my own 'Grand Tour' as it were," Hunter continued. "We spent a month, just the two of us, crisscrossing Avalon, from Emmyr to Togo, Candletop to Devil's Point. He wanted me to see every town, village, and city so I would never forget my responsibility as a knight."

He spun around and leaned against the rail, recalling another particular time. "When Queen Cadhla traveled across Avalon, I would accompany her as a part of her guard, of course. We would look out from the bridge of her airship and marvel at Avalon. I would point out things my father showed me, something her father never did with her. She loved learning these little details about Avalon that she never knew before," he concluded. "And now, it's all gone ... disappeared beneath the waves."

Eileanora saw lines of frustration burrowed on his face. After five years of fighting Mordred's forces, the walls Hunter placed around himself started to crumble. "You don't talk about Queen Cadhla much. Why is that, if you don't mind my asking?"

Hunter glared at Eileanora, a little perturbed by such a forward question, but then he realized she was right. He never really did talk about

Cadhla, and for as much time as Hunter spent with Eileanora, she knew him better than anyone else—even better than his sisters sometimes.

"I guess it's because I hold my memories of her close to my heart. She was my first love, like how you were with Eonis," he smirked.

Eileanora blushed at the name of her first love. She even laughed a little. She appeared surprised at how Hunter knew exactly what to say to get to her. "You're right. I don't talk about Eonis that much," she replied. "It's a little different for me, however. I have thousands of years of memories of Eonis to reflect on. It's hard to pick just one to talk about."

"You must have one memory that sticks out?" Hunter inquired.

Eileanora thought about it momentarily until one moment stuck out. "There was this one time," she began as a smile slowly formed. "I had just returned from a mission, a not-so-successful one. I was frustrated and tired. I think the word you would use is grumpy."

"Yes, I've seen you quite grumpy before," Hunter remarked.

"Point taken," she interrupted. "I just wanted to be alone and meditate, but Eonis wouldn't let me. He took me down to the unicorn grotto. An opening lay at the back of the cavern, just big enough to squeeze through. It led to this pool. The water there is warm, crystal clear, and so inviting. We stripped down and—"

"Wait a minute, stripped down? You went skinny dipping?" Hunter exclaimed with glee.

"Skinny dipping?" she wondered, unfamiliar with the phrase.

"It's a human term. It means swimming without any clothes on."

"Well, of course, how else would one go swimming?" she remarked. Hunter chuckled again, but this time, his humor irritated Eileanora. "What in Freyr's name is so funny, may I ask?"

"I'm trying very hard not to picture you or Eonis naked?" he laughed.

"You've seen me naked before—after that mud bath fighting off the Brood at Innisfree," she reminded him. "We both stripped down to wash off the muddy mess in Lough Gill."

"Yes, I remember that. I also remember how embarrassing it was for me."

"Why is it that human men find it so embarrassing to be naked around women?" Eileanora asked, quite confused. "We elves find it quite natural."

"Yes, well, when elves are as attractive as you, it's hard not to be—" he started to say before he realized he might have said too much. The shocked look on Eileanora's face proved that. She blushed like a teenage schoolgirl. "You were saying how Eonis took you to the pool?" Hunter blurted out to get the conversation back on track.

Eileanora quickly came to her senses after Hunter's shocking confession. "Yes, the water just seemed to wash my frustrations away. It was just perfect. That pool was somewhere we would go alone, away from the prying eyes of Lord Baldrid, Lady Lyllodoria, and others."

"That's funny. It was the same for Cadhla and me," Hunter interjected. "Whenever we would go out to the tavern—with her identity hidden by her illusions—it was just us, hiding in plain sight, having the time of our life. She liked being out amongst the people, like that. It made her feel normal and not royal."

In the end, his voice grew quiet and sad. It warmed her heart to hear Hunter talk this way. Thrust into the role of Gil-Gamesh, Hunter matured rather quickly. The weight of responsibility lay heavy on him, except at times like this.

"As for the changing landscape, Hunter, you must not dwell on the past," Eileanora added. "What happened to Avalon happened. We must move forward and focus on the mission, depose Mordred and his allies, and restore King Bowen to the throne."

"I know. Every time we seem to be making progress against Mordred, he takes two more steps ahead of us."

"Yes, but we should—" Eileanora started to say until her voice trailed off as something caught her attention. In the crow's nest, one of the *Hildrägo Boquè* signaled her through gestures and hand signals. The meaning behind these elaborate gestures was only known to the elves, although Hunter was beginning to learn them.

"What is it?" he asked as he tried to interpret the motions.

"Five dreadnaughts are closing in from the Southeast," Eileanora said. "One of them is the *Hood's Revenge*."

Hunter grimaced at that name. It was the flagship of Jaeger Nottingham, the Earl of Nottinghamshire. Jaeger was, to many, a bully who used his size and strength to intimidate people. Hunter used to be Jaeger's favorite target when they trained as knights in New Camelot. "Captain Hawke, battle stations!" he shouted.

"Aye, sir! Battle stations!" Captain Jasper Hawke commanded as he relayed the order. "All hands to your stations! Let's go, men! Move along quickly now!"

A drummer beat a repetitive tune as the *Avenger's* men and women ran to their stations, climbing into the sails and handling the guns below deck. The gun ports opened on both sides of the ship as the twelve cannons were moved into position. Like the GunStars, sailors loaded the batteries with alchemical shells, providing various magical attacks from within their arsenal. The Gil-Gamesh stepped onto the bridge and began formulating a plan.

"Eileanora, move the *Hîldrägo Boquè* topside. Tell them to target anyone at the helm or in the sails of the enemy ships. We need to keep them off-balance," Hunter charged. Eileanora started shouting orders in elvish to the other members of the *Hîldrägo Boquè* and signaling the ones already at the top of the mast.

"Captain Hawke, how much further until we reach Strongürd Keep?" Hunter asked. Captain Hawke looked down at his charts and made a quick calculation.

"About twenty miles, give-or-take, Gil-Gamesh, but there's not enough wind for us to pick up enough speed to outrun the dreadnaughts."

"Put up every piece of cloth we got, from the handkerchiefs to the bedsheets," Hunter exclaimed. "If we can get in range of Strongürd Keep, they'll be able to help us push back against the dreadnaught's attack."

Captain Hawke started to relay orders to his sailmaster while Hunter focused on defense. "Falchone!" Hunter shouted. "Have the gunner's alternate loads of dragonfire and dragon nails! Raise the gun's elevation fifteen degrees to target the sails and masts." As the first mate relayed the orders, Eileanora walked over to Hunter, concerned about his plan.

"Hunter, why are we running? We should take the fight to them."

"Normally, I'd agree with you, Elle, but not this time. Not with Jaeger leading the hunting party," he explained. "Ever since we crashed Mordred's coronation, the Duke of Nottinghamshire has made me his personal vendetta. I heard he promised Mordred to bring me before him for execution personally."

"All the more reason to fight him, here and now!"

"My father had me read *The Art of War* by Sun Tzu when I became a knight. There's this one quote that always sticks with me. He said, 'He will win who knows when to fight and when not to fight.' This is one of those times. Besides, bringing five dreadnaughts to intercept us either means we're onto something about this Prometheus Engine, or they're desperate to end the resistance."

"I don't follow? Why do you think that?" Eileanora inquired.

"With *Ür Tár* sealed up, they've got a limited supply of lodestones," he explained. "Pretty soon, they won't be able to fly those dreadnaughts anymore, and the skies over Avalon will be ours again, but, at the same time, the more of our ships they take out, the less we'll have to travel across Avalon and fight against Mordred. It's a double-edged sword."

Eileanora smiled with pride. She had watched Hunter grow into the role of Gil-Gamesh over the past five years. He was more like his father all the time. "We are here for you, Gil-Gamesh, and we'll die fighting if we have to, you know that."

"Let's hope it doesn't come to that, Eileanora. Besides, we won't do King Bowen or anyone else in Avalon any good if we die here today. We're no match for those dreadnaughts on our own. Our best recourse is to get to Strongürd Keep as fast as possible."

Hunter reached into his cloak, into one of the many pockets lining the inside. The Cloak of Thieves once belonged to his father, a prize he won by defeating the former Thieves' Guildmaster, Nigel Foley—father of Keane Foley. Besides granting the wearer near-perfect invisibility, it had dozens of pockets that opened into a magical dimension. It allowed the wearer to carry thousands of items inside a simple cloak.

Shaped like a trumpet, he pulled out a small silver horn with a corkscrew curl. From the mouthpiece to the opening, it was covered in runes, some with distinct wind and lightning patterns. The Horn of the Zephyr was a gift from Pasha Bataar of the Jotunn to his father.

"Pasha Bataar gave this to my dad after the battle with Morgana le Fay. He didn't know when he would ever use it. I think that the time is now," he said as he pursed his lips in preparation.

"Tell everyone in the riggings to hang on!" he shouted. Everyone above grabbed onto ropes, riggings, and the masts as tight as they could. Hunter blew the horn. It thundered with a resounding echo, like a thunderstorm bouncing off a mountainside. After all that, nothing happened. There was only silence.

"Well, that was anti-climactic," Hunter gruffed.

"Wait for it," Eileanora chimed in, smiling gleefully. She knew that powerful magic needed time to build up momentum. The wind started to howl, slowly building up like a train rushing toward them. Suddenly, the sails filled with hurricane-force winds propelled the *Avenger* faster through the air.

"That worked quite handily," Hawke laughed as he grasped tightly to the helm, steering the *Avenger* through the rush.

"Yeah, a little too well!" Hunter glanced back over the rail as the five dreadnaughts came into view. They were flying in a "V" formation, with *Hood's Revenge* in the lead. The dreadnaughts were massive warships covered in metal plating and armed with over thirty cannons and other weaponry.

Dwarf lodestones inside the gnome-built engines powered the ship's unique flying ability. The lodestones were highly magnetic, and the engines used magic to control and extend the magnetic field to the armored hulls of the dreadnaughts. It made these monstrous war machines fly.

The dreadnaughts were closing in fast on the *Avenger*. Eileanora feared that the Gil-Gamesh might have miscalculated. "They will be on top of us any minute," she observed.

Hunter smirked that devilish grin his father made quite famous. "Have the gunners aim the cannons forty-five degrees aft. Tell them to stand by to fire on my command," he directed. The orders were relayed below to the gun crews, patiently waiting for the command to be given.

Eileanora suddenly realized what he was doing. "You were planning this all along, weren't you?"

"Sun Tzu said, 'Do not engage an enemy more powerful than you, and if it's unavoidable, then make sure you engage it on your terms, not your enemy's terms,'" he explained. "If we make them push their ships harder, they'll expend energy faster and drop out of the sky."

"I really must read this Sun Tzu. He sounds like an excellent tactician," Eileanora complimented.

Suddenly, a loud boom came from behind them. Hunter and Eileanora turned to see two large metal projectiles on the end of chains fired at them from the lead dreadnaught. The giant arrows pierced the back of the *Avenger*, allowing the hooks to lock onto the hull, securing the airship to *Hood's Revenge*.

The *Avenger* lurched forward, bringing its momentum to a standstill and causing everyone to grab onto something quickly so as not to fall. The airship slowed dramatically as it dragged the massive dreadnaught through the air. "If that thing drops out of the sky, it'll bring us down!" Captain Hawke observed.

Hunter knew they had to act fast to separate the two ships as winches on the *Hood's Revenge* kicked in and began pulling the *Avenger* toward it. He drew his GunStars and loaded them. "Eileanora!" he said. Instinctively, she drew her sword, ready for action.

Hunter leaned over the back rail and aimed his GunStars at the two chains. "Tell everyone to hold fast!" he shouted, warning the crew of what would come. He fired his weapons, projecting an explosion of frost. The swirling vapors of frigid air froze everything it touched. A layer of ice covered the metal chain as the spellshot reduced the temperature to sub-zero.

In an instant, Eileanora leaped over the rail and landed, surefooted, on one of the spears. She swung *Fire Dance* at the chain. The heat of the burning blade reacted with the frozen metal, causing it to shatter. With the skills of an acrobat, Eileanora backflipped onto the remaining spear and swung at that chain, separating it before she tumbled back onto the bridge.

As she landed on her feet, the *Avenger* lurched free as it surged forward. Hunter marveled as the abilities of this fierce elf warrior continued to amaze him. They said nothing—a passing glance, a smile, and a nod of respect between warriors. They had fought side-by-side for five years and knew each other's fighting styles, anticipating each other's moves. There was an unspoken trust between them, which never exceeded their mutual appreciation for each other as warriors and friends.

"What the hell is that?" Hawke observed as he glanced back at *Hood's Revenge*. His revelation caused everyone to turn and stare in disbelief. Two doors opened beneath the bow ornament as the muzzle of a cannon came into sight. This was no ordinary cannon. It was three times the standard size and extended nearly ten feet from the bow. This monster-sized gun possessed immeasurable power.

The positioning of the cannon made Hunter realize they were not aiming at the stern of the *Avenger* but rather the mast and sails. "Get down from the rigging!" he screamed. "Everyone, clear the topsail now!"

Sailors and elves scrambled to clear the topmast and sail riggings quickly. Some jumped to the deck below, others slid down ropes as fast as they could, but it was too late.

The massive cannon fired, leaving a sonic boom in its wake. The recoil almost stopped *Hood's Revenge* in mid-air. A blazing fireball rolled toward the *Avenger*, causing death and destruction to everything in its path. As the sails, masts, and riggings disintegrated. Those caught in the topmast were either burned alive or jumped over the side to save themselves from being burned alive.

Fiery embers drifted down on the wings and deck, causing small fires to ignite. Captain Hawke struggled to maintain control of his ship while his crew attempted to douse the flames. "She's not responding, Gil-Gamesh! We're going down!"

"Then dive, Jasper! Dive as steep and as fast as you can!" Hunter commanded. Hawke seemed confused at first, staring at Hunter in disbelief. Then, in a moment of clarity, he knew precisely what the Gil-Gamesh wanted him to do.

"Can you do it?" Hunter asked.

"Against those *churls*? Just watch me!" Hawke said with a grin. "All hands, hold fast, and prepare to dive!"

The remaining crew grabbed onto each other and the injured. Hunter wrapped his arm around Eileanora, pulling her tight against him without thinking. She was surprised by his bold actions but felt comforted in his arms. Hawke pushed the ship's wheel forward, causing the *Avenger* to dive straight toward the ocean below.

"Another one of your Sun Tzu strategies?" Eileanora asked as the wind whipped by her head.

"Nope, this one is a gut check!"

"Gut check?" Eileanora asked.

"Those ships are big and heavy," Hunter started to explain. "If we get them to dive after us, they shouldn't be able to turn in time before crashing into the ocean."

"Will we?"

Hunter shrugged his shoulders. He knew the odds were against them, with no sails and burning wings and deck, but it was their only choice. Captain Hawke looked down at the ocean, mumbling as he calculated the remaining distance before reaching the water's surface. The dreadnaughts pursued the *Avenger* with an increased tenacity as they fired their cannons recklessly. Thankfully, their wild shots were off-kilter due to their tight formation and increased speed, but Jasper had counted on it.

"Falchone! Stand by to fire a broadside, port side!" he charged. The first mate nodded as he struggled to relay the message to the gunners. Captain Hawke knew he had one chance to pull this off.

"Brace yourselves!" he shouted as he executed his maneuver. Hawke pulled the *Avenger* out of the dive and swung the ship hard to the left as the hull skidded across the waves. "Fire!" he screamed. The guns fired a barrage of dragon fire—a stream of fiery plasma that burned anything it touched—and dragon nails—a blast of a thousand nails that could pierce anything. The combination of the alchemical shells pierced through the iron hulls, flooding the enemy ship with dragonfire inside and out.

Hood's Revenge and the two lead ships could make the turn, and they took the brunt of the attack. The dreadnaughts settled on the water, their ships burning and splintered. The other two, however, were not as lucky. The blast from the *Avenger's* cannons blinded them to the distance from the water. They crashed head-on into the waves, crushing the ships and all their crew.

The *Avenger* dropped down, dead in the water. Without sails, they were unable to move anywhere. The three remaining dreadnaughts were burning but still maneuverable in the ocean. Hunter watched as they found themselves surrounded, each ship positioned out of range of the *Avenger's* guns.

"I don't see any way out of this," Eileanora surmised. "They can maneuver, but we can't. There's not much we can do."

Whatever wealth he garnered, Edan shared it with all the pirates of Barbarossa.

At the heart of this makeshift city was a town hall in the form of a tavern. *Mad Mollies* was known as the rowdiest tavern in Avalon for a good reason. Entering its doors was like a game of Russian Roulette—one never knew whether they would live or die. It was also one of the largest taverns on Avalon and capable of serving the hundreds of pirates who called it home.

The tavern owner, Mollie McBride, was a voluptuous woman with loose morals but very high standards. She was considered by many to be the official/unofficial mayor of Barbarossa. Rumors swirled about her age and lineage. She was thought to be the long-lost daughter of the original Pirate King, or so the story goes, and her extended life was due to Calypso's magical origins. Still, everyone knew never to ask Mollie about either. It was a sure way to end up beaten, bloodied, and banned from her establishment.

At the heart of the tavern was the best-kept secret in Avalon. *Mad Mollies* had a distillery and brewery on-site and were known for their delicious libations, from whiskey, rum, grog, and ale. The ceiling rose more than seventy feet high, five stories from floor to rooftop, with enough tables, chairs, and bars to seat hundreds of patrons. It took an army of barmaids, cooks, musicians, prostitutes, and assorted servants to satisfy the rabble in Barbarossa.

The doors swung open, and Edan strutted in, dressed in his best with a grin from ear to ear. He wore a long, flowing black coat with an elaborate, fluffy white brocade and gold embroidery with his snakes and

"On the contrary, Elle, there is," Hunter shot back. "I need your best archer."

"Feredir!" she shouted, signaling one of the *Hildrägo Boquè* to come over. Hunter recognized him from the beach defense during the Outlander War.

"What's your plan, Gil-Gamesh?" Eileanora asked.

"I want to get Jaeger mad," Hunter explained. "When he gets mad, he's reckless, which may give us the opening we need."

Feredir stepped forward and bowed politely to the Gil-Gamesh. His green eyes glowed from behind the delicate helm he wore. Hunter pulled out a five-inch glass lens from his pocket, another artifact passed down from his father. *"Video Visum!"* he chanted, causing the lens to zoom in and out until it came into focus.

"Can you spot Jaeger Nottingham on the *Hood's Revenge*? He's probably the biggest man there."

Feredir looked carefully across the water to the massive dreadnaught. "Yes, I see him near the bow."

Hunter adjusted his view to zoom in on Jaeger. "There he is, and he's wearing that tiny helmet on top of his head!" Hunter noted. He spotted the hulking brute, nearly seven feet tall and covered in scale mail armor. Jaeger carried a large mace in one hand, swinging it about while barking orders.

On top of his head was a domed helmet. It rested behind his ears, causing them to protrude awkwardly from his head. Jaeger strived to protect his head but not limit his field of vision.

"Do me a favor, Feredir, pin his ears back for me."

The elf grinned like a sly fox. He understood what Hunter wanted him to do. He nocked an arrow and took careful aim, taking a moment to gauge the wind speed, direction, and the current on the sea.

He fired, and the arrow sailed through the air, striking Jaeger's ear and ripping through it. The Lord of Avalon dropped his mace and grabbed his ear as he screamed in pain. Everyone on the *Avenger* could hear his guttural screams of agony. He clutched the side of his head where the arrow protruded from his ear as blood poured out from the wound.

Hunter chuckled at his nemesis' anguish. "Great shot, Feredir! That did the trick!" Hunter exclaimed. "Falchone! Tell the gunners to reload and prepare to fire!"

The crew quickly moved to reload the cannons, putting their faith in the Gil-Gamesh. Many of these men were older and more experienced than Hunter. His father trained them, so their respect for him was passed on to his son. Hunter earned even more respect in the past five years by fighting by their side.

Just as Hunter predicted, Jaeger's injury caused him to react rashly. He stormed onto the bridge and shoved the helmsman aside. Taking the wheel, he recklessly steered the *Hood's Revenge* toward the *Avenger* on a collision course.

"He's relentless. I'll give him that," Eileanora observed.

"Yeah, he's a real pain in the ass," Hunter replied as he ran over to the gunners. "We'll only get one shot at this! Stand by to fire!"

The gunners waited patiently, their fingers wrapped tightly around the lanyards. With the pull of a string, the hammer would strike the cannon. Unlike traditional batteries—using flint to ignite gunpowder—the hammer's magical runes would strike the cannon's runes, igniting its charge.

Hood's Revenge crashed through the waves, aiming straight for the center of the *Avenger*. Hunter tried to gauge the distance as the dreadnaught closed in. "Fire!" he shouted. The guns exploded with the second volley of dragon fire and dragon nails. The blowback from the broadside nearly lifted the *Hood's Revenge* out of the water, stopping its forward momentum. Unfortunately, that's all it did.

The only visible damage was minor in scale—severed lines, injured sailors, and burning sails. Much to Hunter's dismay, the rest of the ship remained intact.

The door on the bow of the *Hood's Revenge* opened as they rolled out the massive cannon again. At this range, there would be nothing left of the *Avenger*. Hunter looked over at Eileanora and Captain Hawke. The expressions on their faces said it all. This could be the end.

As the cannon fired its final blow, a voice from above cried out, "*Acheron Draconis!*" A giant dragon of pure magical energy formed before the *Avenger*. "*Defendo!*" the voice cried out as the magical dragon folded its wings in front like a shield, deflecting the cannon fire and saving the *Avenger*.

At first, Hunter thought it was his father, back from the dead, coming to save him. To his surprise, he saw a young wizard wrapped in a flowing white robe hovering above him. Flashes of a shimmering scale mail caught Hunter's attention, as fiery red as the man's ponytail. A thin beard covered his face. Within his grasp was a double-bladed spear with a pike on one end and a dragon's head on the other. Embedded in the spear was a dragon stone, glowing with magical power that held the two ends together.

"*Pugillo Aquas!*" Another voice cried out as a fist of water rose from the sea and crashed into one of the other dreadnaughts. Hunter caught the image of a beautiful mermaid with flowing blonde hair perched on the crest of a wave from the corner of his eye. Hues of pink and blue reflected off her tail in the ocean spray as it slapped against the water. Her torso was protected by armor encrusted with seashells, barnacles, and coral that amplified her feminine form. A trident of gold and coral was her weapon of choice.

"*Daemonium Accersi!*" shouted a third mage joining the battle. He sat on a cloud of smoke, wearing a simple black robe covered in gold runes. His long, black hair fell across his shoulders and down his back. Dark spectacles rested on the rim of his nose and hid his eyes. He waved a black onyx wand, creating a magic portal of brimstone as a flying demon erupted into the skies. The horned beast resembled a giant squid with bat wings and razor-sharp talons on its tentacles. It landed on the last remaining dreadnaught, devouring sailors and destroying the rigging.

All three were Magus, the battle wizards of Strongürd Keep. While older wizards researched and studied magic, these mages used their power to protect the tower. With Avalon under Mordred's rule, they were hard-pressed to keep the enemy at bay.

"The Magus? Thank goodness. We must be closer to Strongürd than we thought," Jasper surmised. "That headwind you whipped up sure did the trick."

"Yeah, I guess it did," Hunter stammered as he stared intently at the Magus wielding the same magic his father did. "See if they can get us to Strongürd, Eileanora. I'm going to check on our wounded."

Hunter left the bridge in a huff, leaving Eileanora and Captain Hawke to wonder about his state of mind. "He's distracted by that young Dragonmage," Eileanora noted. "His father still lays heavy on his mind."

"If you were in his position, wouldn't it bother you?" Jasper retorted. "There aren't too many Dragonmage's in Avalon. The fact that this Magus is wielding such power is like someone stepping on his father's grave."

"It doesn't matter what type of magic he wields. What matters is the fight against Mordred," she snapped back. "And in this fight, we need all the help we can get."

The elf stormed off the bridge angrily, frustrated at the human emotions wasted on such petty insignificance. It was something she could never understand about mortals. For thousands of years, her contact with them was limited. Fighting alongside the Gil-Gamesh had been a new experience, unlocking emotions she thought she had hidden away.

"*Dubh Bhean!*" The voice startled her, breaking her concentration. Eileanora turned to see Falchone, the first mate on the *Avenger*. The sailor saluted the elf commander, something Eileanora despised, scoffing at the human courtesies. His gray hair and beard showed his age, but he was known to be as strong as any man on the ship.

"Falchone, I've asked you not to call me that," she scolded him. "What is it?"

"Begging your pardon, miss, but I wanted to let you know that we're rigging up for a tow by the Magus. It may be a bumpy ride until we reach Strongürd."

"Thank you, Falchone. What about the *Hood's Revenge*?"

"Oh, they're running home with their tail between their legs, miss," Falchone joked as he pointed over the rail. Eileanora turned to see the dreadnaught turning away, picking up survivors of the destroyed ships as they headed back to New Camelot. "I don't think we'll have to worry about that lot anytime soon."

Eileanora simply nodded as Falchone saluted again before he walked away. She stared across the rail at the retreating dreadnaught, trying to control her emotions and bring them into perspective. She said a silent prayer for guidance from Freyr to ease her heart.

Below decks, Hunter took stock of the injured and tried his best to reassure his tired and battered crew. He was personally invested in each one of them. By now, he knew their names and life story, a trait he had learned from his father. Identifying with these warriors on their level made him a better leader and endeared the sailors to him.

Tending to the wounded was Julianna Bonapat. Her smooth black skin and long gray dreadlocks were testimony to the effectiveness of the alchemy beauty products she developed over the years. Her brilliant smile and optimistic attitude showed everywhere she went, no matter how dire the situation was. After meeting and marrying her husband, Alain Bonapat, they worked as a team to provide medical services to the Gil-Gamesh, his family, and the refugees in Alfheimer. Alain was an Outlander—a doctor from Haiti— bringing his knowledge of traditional medicine to Avalon. With Julianna's help, he learned to combine his conventional medical expertise with her alchemy to create a new form of magical therapy.

"How's the crew, Julianna?" Hunter asked as he surveyed the injured men and women under his command.

"Pretty beaten up, Gil-Gamesh," she answered. "Six dead, nine severely wounded, about a dozen or so with broken bones, bruises, cuts, and scrapes. They would be better cared for if Alain was here."

"Nonsense, you're doing fine, Julianna, though I'm sorry to force you into this. I know you were tagging along to pick up supplies from Master Ostanes. I appreciate everything you're doing for the crew."

"I serve at the pleasure of the Gil-Gamesh," she said with a slight bow and a smile, mimicking her husband's affection for the MoonDrake family.

Hunter returned the bow with respect. "Well, I'll let you get back to work. Thanks again," he said as he turned and walked away. He knew being the Gil-Gamesh came with all the respect afforded to his father, but he was uneasy with the honor, unlike his father. After all this time, Hunter still struggled with the weight of the mantle, but he knew he must carry on for the sake of his family and friends. It was his burden to carry.

CHAPTER 7
THE SECRETS OF MORDRED REVEALED

Mordred reveled in his life as King. It was everything he dreamed it would be. Servants waited on him, hand and foot, with anything and everything his heart desired. Even with news from the ongoing rebellion by the MoonDrake siblings filling his day, he always took time for leisure.

In a secret cave beneath New Camelot, there was a pool of crystal clear water. It was a secret known only to the Pendragon family, and for a good reason. The Spring of *Manannán mac Lir*, the Celtic Water God, was born from these same waters. In return, the spring had supernatural qualities to heal wounds, strengthen muscles, and give long life to anyone who bathed in it.

Although protection spells ensured his survival, he was still vulnerable to other magic and weapons. Bathing in the magical spring, Mordred sought to augment his ageless beauty. He lounged at the edge, soothed by its healing properties and comforted in his immortality.

He closed his eyes and cleared his mind, enjoying this moment of solitude, until… "May I join you, Your Majesty?" said a sultry voice. Mordred opened his eyes and smiled at seeing Lady Mavis standing before him. She wore a simple red silk robe over her subtle figure. Her raven black hair hung effortlessly across her shoulders and down her back.

"Of course, Mavis," he cooed. "Please do— "

"Thank you, Your Grace," she said as she stepped up to the water's edge and dropped her robe, revealing herself entirely to the King. She stepped slowly into the pool, using every step to entice and delight her monarch. "I heard you speak of the amazing properties of this spring, and I just had to experience it for myself, if that's alright?"

"Yes, my dear, it's wonderful, but tell me, how did you find me here?" Mordred inquired.

Mavis chuckled as she swam over to Mordred. "Come now, Your Majesty, a woman needs to have some secrets," she joked. Her humor disappeared when Mordred grabbed her by the throat, choking the life out of her. Mavis smacked at his hands in vain, desperately trying to free herself.

"Not from me, Mavis, my dear! Never from me," he scolded her. "Now, how did you find this place?"

Mavis tried to catch her breath as she tried to speak through his powerful grip. "I overheard you and Magister Ocwyn talking about its location," she said, gasping for air. "I would never come here on my own, milord. Only with you, I swear… Only with you!"

Mavis pleaded for her life until she was about to pass out. Mordred finally released her as she frantically gripped the side of the pool to avoid sinking beneath its waters. "I don't like skulkers or spies, Mavis darling. The next time you have a question, simply ask me."

Mavis coughed violently as her breathing slowly returned to normal. "Of course, Your Majesty, please forgive me," she gasped. Mordred retreated from her to the other side of the pool, outstretching his arms across the edge.

"Now, tell me about our spy in Alfheimer. Have they gotten any closer to the alchemist?" Mordred asked.

"I haven't heard anything new, Your Majesty," she replied, carefully guarding her words not to anger the King again. "It is hard to communicate inside Alfheimer with all the magical wards placed around it by the elves."

"Then how will you know when the deed is done, my dear Mavis?" Mordred inquired with evident frustration.

"Blackstone has assured me that we will be able to extract the alchemist immediately," she said cautiously, redirecting his attention away from her. "You need not worry yourself over this matter, sire. We have it well in hand."

"Your foresight is one thing, Mavis, but I need assurances," Mordred complained. "Every day, the Gil-Gamesh and his sisters draw more allies to their cause. The people fear me, hoping those three succeed in putting that brat Bowen back on the throne."

"All signs point to success once the gnomes complete the Prometheus Engine," she insisted. "Once you have the power of your infernal machine at your command, nothing will stop your reign."

Mavis slowly started to move toward Mordred. She spoke seductively, tempering her words as to entice the King. "Your greatness has been assured. You will rule Avalon forever, and I will be by your side, Your Majesty."

She wrapped her arms around Mordred's neck and kissed him passionately. Mordred returned her kiss, succumbing to his lustful nature as he ravaged Mavis' body. She smiled, loving the unbridled passion Mordred lavished over her, but he was more calculating than she knew.

He felt so alive making love to this beautiful woman in a sacred pool of eternal life. Mordred enjoyed being with Mavis, but contrary to her belief, it was never about her controlling him. He would never let any woman control him again—not Mavis, his mother, or anyone else. Mordred was in command of his destiny and would use anyone to achieve those goals.

Strongürd Keep was the home of the Wizard's Council of Avalon. The tower stood more than 1,200 feet tall. Although the structure resembled a smooth cylinder, it had windows, patios, and balconies disguised and hidden by the powerful magic contained within. The keep stood alone on a small island, protected by mystic wards, magical creatures, and the Magus. Mordred's forces had yet to penetrate or even damage Strongürd Keep.

Once moored next to the keep, the *Avenger* crew carried off the wounded and started to repair the damaged ship. While Julianna assisted the clerics with the injured, Hunter and Eileanora headed into the keep to speak with Grandmaster Jean-Claude Baptiste.

"Gil-Gamesh!" Jasper shouted as he ran over to stop them. "Milord, we can use our spare to replace the mainmast, but we have no spares for the foremast or the mizzen."

"Send word to Alfheimer and have them bring you what you need, then contact Edan and my sister in Barbarossa to get here as soon as possible," Hunter charged. "Do whatever you must to keep the *Avenger* flying, Jasper."

"I will not fail, Sir Hunter, nor will the crew. You have my word!"

"Gil-Gamesh!" another voice interrupted. Briskly walking toward them, tapping a crooked, wooden staff repetitively, was Chancellor Ilan Talbot, the Minister of Magic for Strongürd Keep. His regal purple robe hung heavy with an embroidered golden weave that overstated his elevated position. Thinning strands of white hair sparsely covered his balding head, too afraid to shave them for fear of death as foretold by a fortune teller eons ago.

"Gil-Gamesh, thank the gods that you are safe. When our outward guard spotted your peril, I sent the Magus to your aid."

"We are grateful for your assistance, Chancellor Talbot," Eileanora interrupted, "but we must see Grandmaster Baptiste as soon as possible."

"Yes, yes, of course, and he asked me to bring you to him. Please, follow me!"

He escorted the two travelers inside the tower. Even though Hunter had been there many times before, it still amazed him. The center of the building was hollow, except a spiral staircase winding its way up the inside of the structure. Giant statues of famous sorcerers and magical creatures supported the stairs from top to bottom. Each level of the keep contained various rooms, from magical libraries and conjuring rooms to living quarters and meditation chambers. In some places, bridges crisscrossed the tower, connecting one side to the other. Using various magical items and spells, Wizards and familiars floated and flew around the interior to conduct their daily business.

On the far side of the first level, a giant birdcage on a chain acted as an elevator. This made moving about the keep easier thanks to the magic-powered mechanism, avoiding all the flying traffic overhead. The three entered the elevator, where a tiny gnome sat in a hanging chair, waiting by the controls. A cigar stub hung out of his mouth as he chewed and smoked it relentlessly. His tiny body and large head made him appear out of place, but he seemed pretty happy in his work.

"Where to minister?" the little gnome asked as he drew a long puff on his cigar and blew the smoke out.

"The Grandmaster's office, if you please, Filbert," Talbot replied as he waved the toxic fumes out of the air. "And put out that disgusting cigar. I told you about smoking while on the job."

"Yeah, but I tend to ignore the advice I don't agree with," he cracked back sarcastically. Hunter and Eileanora chuckled under their breath as they stepped inside. Filbert switched some buttons and pulled the lever as the door closed. The elevator shuttered before it slowly began to rise in the air.

As they rode up the elevator, Eileanora looked at Hunter and saw that he was still bothered by the earlier events. "Chancellor Talbot, could you tell me about the DragonMage Magus who rescued us earlier? Who is he?"

"Oh, you mean Lothar Durandes," Talbot began. "He came here more than twenty years ago to study magic. The poor boy had a rather dubious upbringing, orphaned quite young. However, your father saw something special in him. He brought Lothar here, and after spending time with Lord MoonDrake, he decided to study to become a DragonMage."

"My father never mentioned him," Hunter interjected.

"No? Well, he mentioned something about not wanting to show favoritism with Lothar over your particular choice of magical studies," Talbot surmised.

"What do you mean?" Hunter inquired.

"Well, your father said he wanted you to have the option to pick whatever magical field you wanted and not be obligated to follow him as a DragonMage. He feared you might be intimidated if you learned about Magus Durandes."

Hunter smiled and chuckled under his breath, confusing Chancellor Talbot and Eileanora. "Is something funny, Sir Hunter?" Talbot wondered.

"No, not really. It's just that no matter where I go, I learn something new about my Dad. It's like getting to know him all over again. I want to meet this Magus Lothar Durandes, Chancellor Talbot. I would like to know more about his time with my father. Perhaps you could arrange an introduction for me?"

"Of course, Gil-Gamesh, it would be a pleasure," Talbot said as the elevator stopped. "But that will have to come later. Grandmaster Baptiste insisted on seeing you immediately."

The elevator lurched to a stop near the top of the keep. As the doors opened, Talbot led them toward the opposite side of the tower. Many of the wizards and apprentices bowed in respect as they walked by.

"Sir Hunter!" a familiar voice called out. Hunter turned to see Master Cyril Ostanes step out of his laboratory door. The head of the House of Alchemy wore simple red robes with a dirty leather apron, muddled from all his hard work. Pinned to it was a chain of rings, each in a different metal. The chain represented the ladder alchemists climbed to earn their rank. Master Ostanes was an Adamantine Star, the highest level in alchemy. Flecks of silver highlighted his black hair, pulled back into a tight bun to not interfere with his work.

He cleaned his hands with a rag as Hunter bowed respectfully before his superior. "Forgive me, Master Ostanes, but I have urgent business with Grandmaster Baptiste. I promise to stop by and see you later."

"Just make sure you do," Cyril told him.

Hunter thought momentarily before realizing why Master Ostanes wanted to see him. "Is it done?" he asked excitedly as he reached out and grabbed his shoulders. Cyril grinned from ear to ear, giving Hunter his answer.

"It is, but first, go see Grandmaster Baptiste. I'll speak to you afterward."

Hunter was elated as Talbot led them away toward the office of Grandmaster Jan Claude Baptiste, supreme leader of the Wizard's Council of Avalon. They stopped in front of an enormous alabaster door, gilded with gold and silver inlays depicting *Yggdrasil*, the mythical tree that connects all life in the universe. The branches reached high, caressing the stars while its roots beckoned to the world below. Chancellor Talbot stopped and tapped his staff on the door three times.

"*Luce Stellarum, Stella Splendida!*" he said. The stars on the door glowed softly. The grinding of gears followed a loud click as the doors slowly opened. Inside was a massive room filled with bookcases, magical artifacts, and various arcane components. At the far end of the room, a desk sat with papers and scrolls scattered about the top. A scrying pool rested on a pedestal in the corner, glowing softly with magical energy.

Hovering above the pool, staring into its magical abyss, were Grandmaster Jean-Claude Baptiste and Master Vilnius Maximillion, the head of the House of Divination. Dressed in flowing, regal robes of blue and gold embroidered in black, Baptiste reflected his title as Grandmaster and his allegiance to the House of Necromancy. The runes etched on his robes were actual protection spells against the dead. His bald head was adorned with metal piercings on his ears, nose, and chin.

Master Vilnius wore blue and white robes with silver embroidery. Each mystical rune represented the timeline from the first Master of Divination to the present. A floppy hat with a large feather perched on the brim hung off to one side of his head. His long black mustache, flecked with streaks of gray, reached down to his belt. He stared intently into the glowing water of the scrying pool. The light from within reflected his eyes as if mesmerized by the swirling liquid.

Hunter and Eileanora bowed respectfully to the supreme leader of the Wizard's Council before the Gil-Gamesh reached out to shake his hand. "Thank you for seeing us, Grandmaster Baptiste."

"Please, Hunter, call me Jean-Claude. I have known you for so long, and using such formalities between friends doesn't seem right."

Hunter chuckled under his breath, remembering how his father always said the people of Avalon were formal upfront but preferred casual conversation. "OK, Jean-Claude."

"Eileanora, always a pleasure," Grandmaster Baptiste said with a nod as Eileanora bowed. As Avalon's leader of the remaining elves, she consistently maintained courtesy and respect.

"Have you found anything more on the Prometheus Engine?" she asked, getting down to business.

"Yes, but we also discovered something even more dire," Jean-Claude started. "We think we know why Avalon tore apart after the *Øriĕntür*."

"What do you mean? I thought it was the backlash from the incomplete spell since Eileanora and the other members of the *Hîldrägo Boquè* left during the final part?" Hunter inquired.

"As did we, but Master Vilnius has discovered another possibility. The Lady of the Lake is missing."

The words shocked both Hunter and Eileanora. "Missing? What do you mean? How can she be gone?" Eileanora countered with amazement.

"The Lady of the Lake is the central magical force that binds all Avalon together. Her magic is vital to our existence, but Master Vilnius cannot sense her presence anywhere."

"No, no, nothing," Vilnius groaned. "I should be able to sense her, but there is nothing on any part of Avalon or in the waters surrounding our home. All I see is pain—unbearable binding pain!"

"But, I don't understand. What does this have to do with Avalon's Reclamation?" Eileanora asked.

"When the *Oriëntür* was almost complete, the spell of first magic spread the energy across Avalon to reform the barrier and hide us from the outside world," Jean-Claude explained. "When Merlin did this more than three thousand years ago, the Lady of the Lake captured the magical energy and bound it to Avalon, but this didn't happen during the *Oriëntür*. The magic reverberated repeatedly—through the land, sea, and sky—until Avalon was torn apart and the barrier reformed. That's what transformed Avalon from one island into thousands of islands, but that's not the worst of it."

"What could be worse?" Hunter exclaimed.

"Without the Lady of the Lake, Avalon will slowly deteriorate until it falls completely into the sea. The destruction will continue until there is nothing left of our home."

Hunter and Eileanora were stunned into silence. "How long do we have?" Eileanora asked.

"Years, maybe a couple of decades. We don't know for certain."

The longer they listened to Jean-Claude, Hunter grew increasingly angry. "And the only one capable of doing something like this was Mordred! That bastard will destroy Avalon and all we hold dear to massage his ego. Plus, without the aid of the Lady of the Lake, we cannot retrieve *Excalibur* for King Bowen either."

"Is she dead or just missing?" Eileanora inquired.

"No, she's not dead," Vilnius interrupted. "If she were, I would know. I can sense faint traces of her magical aura, but not enough to locate her. They are hiding her from my sight."

"What can we do, Jean-Claude?" Hunter asked.

"The only way of finding her is through the last person who had direct contact with her, but alas, that may be impossible."

"My father met her when he returned the shards of *Twilight* and *Dusk*, and she reformed *Excalibur*," Hunter said.

"Lord MoonDrake met with the Lady of the Lake but did not touch her," Jean-Claude explained. "I am referring to the only man ever to touch the Lady Viviane."

"And who is that?" Eileanora interjected.

"His Royal Highness, King Arthur Pendragon—"

The name of the first King of Britain and Avalon took Hunter by surprise. He received the sword *Excalibur* from the Lady of the Lake and was known to have spoken with her frequently when Merlin was unavailable to advise him.

"When Arthur died, the Lady of the Lake carried him to his final resting place. It should be relatively easy to use a spell of necromancy to speak with the spirit of the King, but first, we must discover the whereabouts of his grave."

"You mean, you don't know?" Hunter asked.

"No, only the family Pendragon was given that knowledge. Your son, King Bowen, might know, but I'm not sure he ever received that information. The only other person who might know is—"

"Magister Ulric Ocwyn," Hunter stated. "He was Chamberlain to Bowen, so he had access to everything the King knew."

"Which brings me to the Prometheus Engine," Jean-Claude interrupted. "All we know of this machine is what legend tells us. The only time they built the Prometheus Engine in recorded history was shortly before Atlantis sank. The power generated by this device was so uncontrollable that it destroyed an entire island.

"There was a second attempt when Morgana le Fay tried to build this infernal machine. She was secretly building it in a cave deep beneath Mount Badon, but her machinations were interrupted by King Arthur and the Knights of the Round Table.

"When the King learned what the device was and what it was capable of doing, he ordered the machine destroyed along with every scroll and every book that contained references to the Prometheus Engine, or so the story goes.

"Even Merlin removed all references to the Prometheus Engine," he continued. "Your sister confirmed that when we made our discovery. She has been going through all the alchemy texts with your friend Oliver Beasley and found every chapter ripped out that even mentioned the engine."

"But like the 'dreamweaver' spell used on Lord MoonDrake by Kraven Darkholm, something must have survived its destruction," Eileanora interjected. "That's how Mordred was able to build it."

"So, we need to find the grave of King Arthur to commune with his spirit to locate the Lady of the Lake and learn more about the Prometheus

Engine. Wonderful! Do you have any good news for me?" Hunter asked, frustrated at yet another set of nearly impossible tasks.

"Yes, as a matter of fact, I do," Grandmaster Baptiste said. "A number of our Magus have expressed interest in joining the resistance. We hope you'll take them with you and accept them into your ranks."

"Don't you need them here?"

"We have more than enough strong Magus and other more powerful sorcerers to keep the forces of Mordred away. Their prowess will show Avalon that the Wizard's Council stands against Mordred and his reign."

"They will be a force to be reckoned with and a welcomed addition to our ranks," Eileanora cried gleefully. "Thank you, Grandmaster Baptiste!"

"We all do what we can in service to the true King of Avalon," Jean-Claude said with a smile. "Besides, I hoped that Ashley would allow them to access Merlin's library. She's been hesitant to share the knowledge within its walls, and I was hoping that the presence of other wizards might change her mind."

"I'm sorry about that, Jean-Claude. Ashley can be very protective of Merlin's library. She won't even let me in there without her tagging along. She fears powerful magic falling into the wrong hands, but you may be on the right track. Having other wizards around to speak with might make her feel more comfortable and let her open up. I don't understand half the things she says sometimes, and Rose is more interested in dragons than magic."

"Well, I would appreciate any help you can give expanding their magical knowledge. It would benefit both the resistance and the Wizard's

Council," Jean-Claude concluded. "In the meantime, you and your crew will be our welcome guests until you can complete repairs to the *Avenger*."

"Thank you, Grandmaster Baptiste. We are in your debt."

"Now, go see Master Ostanes," Jean-Claude added. "I understand he has a special gift for you."

Hunter shrieked joyfully, like a child at Christmas, as he took off toward Master Ostanes' alchemy lab. Eileanora shook her head in embarrassment as she followed Hunter at a distance. Once inside, Eileanora was shocked at what she saw in the lab.

Hunter was there with Cyril, petting a dog. Hunter acted like a lovesick child, stroking and cooing over the animal. The dog resembled a Siberian Husky but with solid wolf-like characteristics. His fur, white and gray with black highlights, accentuated his deep blue eyes.

Hunter saw Eileanora at the door. She could hear the excitement in his voice as his eyes sparkled. "Isn't he beautiful?" he bragged.

"He is, but did you need an alchemist to get you a pet?"

"He's not just a pet, Eileanora. He's the Gil-Gamesh's familiar," Cyril retorted.

"His familiar? But I thought familiars were chosen for you by—" she started to say before Master Ostanes interrupted her.

"That may be for wizards, but alchemists create their familiars. Hunter did the preliminary work, but he asked me to keep an eye on his maturation while he attended to his duties as Gil-Gamesh."

"So then, he's not an ordinary dog," she inquired.

"Oh no, Boots is a special breed of chimera, the first of his kind," Hunter explained. "I did a lot of research before I crafted the perfect familiar for me."

"Boots?"

"Yeah, Boots. Because his paws are black, it looks like he's wearing boots," Hunter said as he pointed out the unusual coloring on the dog's paws.

"And what do you mean a special breed of chimera? A chimera combines different animals into one creature," Eileanora asked quizzically. "Boots is just a dog."

"Oh no, he's more than that. He's special. Watch closely," Hunter said as he stepped away from his familiar. "*Ursa!*" At Hunter's command, the dog's form began to change. Its muscles bulged, claws and teeth grew, and hair changed color. In an instant, the dog transformed into a large black bear. It stood up, reaching over ten feet tall on its hind legs and weighing nearly a ton. The bear dropped back on all fours as the floor creaked under its incredible weight. It gave off such a roar that the sound echoed throughout the keep.

"That's unbelievable!" Eileanora exclaimed.

"Oh, you ain't seen nothing yet!" Hunter crowed. "*Draco!*" The chimera shifted again, from a bear to a silver-scaled dragon, but not a winged dragon like those on Avalon. It resembled a Komodo dragon, with a long flickering tongue, sharp teeth, deadly claws, and more than twelve feet in length. It made no sound except an occasional hiss as its tongue flicked in and out of its mouth.

"*Feles!*" Hunter's next command changed the chimera into a huge snow leopard. The beast growled as it swung its large, fluffy tail around. The creature rubbed its head on Hunter like a cat, as if looking for some attention.

"*Aquila!*" His next command caused the leopard to leap into the air and become a black eagle perched on Hunter's extended arm. The bird spread its wings, displaying its massive wingspan. "*Canis!*" Hunter said as his last command transformed the bird into a dog, leaping mid-transformation to the floor before sitting at Hunter's side.

"Amazing," Eileanora said with an astonished look on her face. "I didn't know that was possible."

"To be honest, neither did I," Cyril interjected, "but Hunter came up with some radical yet brilliant theories that he put to the test, and the results are nothing short of magnificent. You have taken alchemy to a whole new level, my boy."

Master Ostanes reached into his pocket and pulled out a silver ring before he handed it to Hunter. "Here you go, lad, you've earned it. You're now a Silver Sage Alchemist!"

Hunter was amazed at the praise. He took the ring and stared at it momentarily before he bowed to his master. Hunter opened his coat and attached the ring to the chain clipped on the inside. It was the fifth ring on his alchemy ladder.

Eileanora went to shake his hand and congratulate him, but her emotions overwhelmed her, so she hugged him instead. It took a moment before she realized what she had done and jumped back, embarrassed.

"Forgive me, Gil-Gamesh. I let my emotions get the best of me. Congratulations on your achievement," she said, her face blushing red.

"Thank you, Elle, but there's no need to apologize. I think hanging around us is starting to rub off on you. My family are big huggers." The two laughed at his poor attempt at humor, but they both knew there was something there, just like before on the *Avenger*. They recognized it as an undeniable attraction but put it aside as a mere flight of fancy.

The moment was interrupted when Boots jumped up, barking at the two of them. Hunter let loose, giving some love to his new familiar. Eileanora was a little more tentative but reluctantly gave in and patted the dog gently.

CHAPTER 8
SPIES IN ELDONSHIRE

The wealthiest farmland in all of Avalon stretched across the fields of Eldonshire. Acres of luscious wheat, corn, potatoes, and other fresh fruits and vegetables filled the terrain. Cattle, sheep, and other livestock grazed about the fields and meadows. This simple life made Eldonshire one of the wealthiest provinces in Avalon.

The Lord of Eldonshire shared the harvest profits in the past, but times had changed. Lord Tomas Elderson, the youngest of the new Lords of Avalon, took part in the ascension of Mordred. He joined in the villainous plot to overthrow King Bowen. Like the other young Lords, Tomas formed a "Fatal Bond" with Mordred—a magical pact that required the user to complete a specific task or die. Ultimately, he killed his parents to save his life and become the new Lord of Eldonshire.

Under Lord Tomas Elderson, Eldonshire resembled a "work farm" like the farmland where the "proletariat" worked in the old Soviet Union. The people worked the fields from sunrise to sunset, toiling night and day to keep up with the demand for food across the archipelago.

Mordred forced Eldonshire to ship their crops and livestock across the seas, making spoilage an issue. Without the speed of the Gil-Gamesh's airships and King Mordred forcing the ships of Nottinghamshire to focus on war instead of commerce, the fields of Eldonshire were toiled nearly year-round with little to no profit. Whatever profit there was stayed in the coffers of Lord Tomas and, in return, King Mordred.

The young Lord of Avalon accompanied the Adalwulf Guard to inspect the fields and check the upcoming harvest. Mordred insisted on keeping Adalwulf close to Lord Tomas since he considered him weak and unreliable. The Adalwulf was there to ensure he complied with Mordred's wishes.

The last five years were not kind to Lord Tomas. His mind and body had grown frail as the years passed. Although he was a grown man, nearly thirty, his physique resembled that of a teenage boy. He had handsome features, but his face was gaunt, and his hair was short and thinning. He wore light regal clothing, and a simple dagger hung around his waist. He had no training in fighting and was not strong enough to wear armor.

As they rode through the various farms of Eldonshire, the people bowed politely to Lord Tomas. Those who refused to show respect usually found themselves subject to unannounced visits by the Adalwulf Guard.

The last stop on their tour was the farm belonging to the former shield maidens, the Swann sisters, Astrid and Sigrid. Though the identical twin sisters were well past their prime—nearly 105 years of age—they were both still healthy and active.

As they approached the farm, the sisters stood by the well, drawing water for those who worked the land with them. Their silver hair shone brightly in the midday sun. Years of battle and hard life had taken a toll on their once beautiful skin. Wrinkles formed deep furrows into the leathery texture of their faces and accentuated the battle scars left behind.

Astrid had lost her left leg and Sigrid her right arm during a mission to the goblin caves more than forty years ago. Both sisters became trapped under tons of rubble when the cave collapsed. It was after that they retired from the battlefield and returned to their family farm in Eldonshire.

The two bowed politely to Lord Tomas, ignoring the Adalwulf Guard completely. "Good afternoon, Lord Tomas. What can we do for you?" Astrid asked.

"We're here to check on your progress with the upcoming harvest," said Armin Heydrich, Lord Marshal of the Adalwulf Guard in Eldonshire. Behind his neatly trimmed blonde hair and clean-cut appearance laid the mind of a sociopath. He took pleasure in slowly killing people for information, savoring every moment. It was these qualities that earned Heydrich his position.

"I wasn't speaking to you. I was speaking to Lord Tomas," Astrid snapped back at him. The Lord Marshal was about to give her a scolding reprimand, but Lord Tomas raised his hand to stop him.

"It's important we get the next harvest on time, Ms. Astrid," Tomas inferred. "I just wanted to check on your progress."

"You have nothing to fear, milord. We will have the crops as promised," Astrid said. "However, we are having some problems with this potato harvest. The new crossbreed spuds are not growing as quickly as we expected.

"I was wondering if you could advise us on these difficulties," she continued. "I remember how much you studied cross-breeding and thought you could give Sigrid and me some insight. We have some of the first batches in the barn for you to inspect."

Lord Tomas loved the science behind farming, so he was anxious to look over the specimens. As he started to dismount, Heydrich raised his hand to stop him. "Milord, I don't think it's wise for you to do this," he said. "After all, these ladies are former shield maidens, sworn enemies of King Mordred."

Before Astrid could say anything, Lord Tomas put a slight stiffness in his spine and stood up to the Lord Marshal. "The Swann sisters have been friends of my family for generations. I trust them implicitly."

Astrid smiled at the courage of Lord Tomas to stand up to Heydrich. There may be hope for him yet. "I realize this sort of thing doesn't interest you, Lord Marshal, so you and your men are welcome to help yourself to some of our honey mead. I just put some fresh jugs on the table under the shade."

The rest of the Adalwulf Guard quickly dismounted and rushed for a refreshing break after a day of riding around Eldonshire. Heydrich closely observed as Astrid walked with Lord Tomas to the large barn. He sneered at them with disdain. He didn't trust the Swann sisters but had no power to overrule Lord Tomas.

The barn was dimly lit, except for some lanterns over a table. Sigrid stood by the counter, where a group of potato plants were laid out, each with a different shape and size. Tomas carefully inspected the potatoes while Astrid hung back by the barn door, watching the activities of the Adalwulf Guard.

Tomas picked up each one of the spuds and examined them closely. "I see what you mean, Sigrid. I think the problem is overbreeding. You can breed a good variety for about two years, but after that—"

Tomas stopped mid-sentence when he realized a scythe was resting under his chin. He dropped the potatoes as his hands trembled with fear. Sigrid kept the blade firmly against his throat.

"Don't call out to your guard, Lord Tomas, or I may have to cut your throat," she insisted. Tomas shook his head, utterly compliant to her demands. "I am not going to kill you, milord," she continued. "There's someone here who wants to speak with you."

Sigrid lowered her blade and nodded to the shadows across the room. Tomas turned to see General Rhona McLoughlin approaching him, towering over the Lord of Avalon. Her tunic bore the House of Pendragon's colors—red and gold—proclaiming the shield maiden's allegiance.

When Lord Tomas saw the General of the Shield Maidens, his heart started beating faster as fear filled his mind. Rhona stepped forward slowly so as not to make the young man overreact. "Lord Tomas Elderson, I bring a message from Sir Hunter MoonDrake, the Gil-Gamesh," she said as she reached into a small pouch. Rhona pulled out a broken sword piece about three inches long and two inches wide. She held it out to Tomas.

The frightened Lord was surprised to see the relic. His mind raced back to more than ten years ago to a more joyful time. He was out and about with Sir Hunter in the streets of New Camelot, celebrating his knighthood, when brigands suddenly accosted them. Hunter, being the more experienced knight, held them off, but when one of the thugs lunged at Tomas, Hunter stepped in and took the blow for him. The sword snapped, lodging a piece in Hunter's shoulder. After it was removed, Tomas gave Hunter the broken fragment and told him to return it whenever he needed a favor.

He reached out, his finger shaking with anticipation, as he picked up the piece. "What does he want?" he asked.

"The exact location of the Prometheus Engine."

He dropped the shard back in her hand when he heard that name. "Are you insane? The only reason I know that name is from the rumors I've heard in New Camelot. King Mordred guards his secrets well. If I ask anyone about that, it'll mean my death."

"We can arrange for that right now," Sigrid said, raising her scythe ready to strike. Rhona held up her hand to stop the elder shield maiden.

"You have a debt to pay, Lord Tomas, and this is what the Gil-Gamesh requires," she said stoically. "The Prometheus Engine threatens all of us, including you. We need to destroy this machine, no matter what the cost."

"Even if that cost is my own life? No, thank you," Tomas snapped back. "You can threaten me all you want, shield maiden. I have nothing left in me that isn't already dead."

"Death is irrelevant, my young lord," Sigrid inferred. "What about the people of Eldonshire? Did you think about them when you killed your mother and father? Lord and Lady Elderson were the kindest souls to walk on this Earth. They deserved better than to be killed like lambs to the slaughter. You have no honor, Lord Tomas Elderson. You—"

Rhona touched Sigrid on the shoulder to comfort her friend. She then turned to Tomas and reached out, holding the broken sword piece. "Are you a man who repays his debt, or are you the weak fool who threw in with Mordred and killed his parents to save his skin?"

Tomas thought about it once again before he reluctantly picked up the shard. "Tell Hunter that this makes us even," Tomas said sternly. "I never want any further contact with him again."

"If ever you meet the Gil-Gamesh again, I assure you, it will be the last time. When you have the information, let Sigrid and Astrid know. They will relay it to me."

Rhona said nothing more as Lord Tomas turned away to leave. He paused at the door momentarily before looking back at the Swann sisters. "And Sigrid, I want you and Astrid gone after this harvest. You are no longer welcome in Eldonshire."

Lord Tomas left the barn in a huff. He said nothing to the Adalwulf Guard as they mounted their horses and left the farm. Heydrich stared at the barn door, trying to calculate what went on to sour Tomas' mood as he mounted his horse and followed close behind. Once they departed, Rhona stepped out with the Swann sisters.

"Damn, brat! We should have killed him after the reclamation," Astrid said. "Our family has farmed this land since we came to Avalon. Now, we are homeless."

"I'm so sorry, sisters. I didn't mean to cost you your home," Rhona said.

"No need to apologize, general. We prepared for this," Sigrid replied. "We still have some time before we'll need to leave."

"Do you know where you'll go?" Rhona asked. "You have your place with us in Alfheimer. Our new shield maidens could use experienced warriors like yourselves as their teachers."

"That time is past, general," Sigrid interjected. "We are farmers now, not warriors."

"You will always be warriors to the Covenant of Shield Maidens, but I understand." Rhona thought about it for a minute before an idea came to her. "There is a small farming town, King's Crossing, on the border of Blackbriar Forest. We recently liberated it from the Adalwulf Guard. The young man we put there could use your help to keep things under control."

"That sounds like a good place to start again," Astrid added as the two sisters walked away to resume their work. Rhona strolled toward the house to get back undercover. Her ride back to Alfheimer would be there at midnight to pick her up, but none of that set her mind at ease.

Lord Tomas might get them the information on the Prometheus Engine, but destroying it was another matter altogether. *What could Mordred be thinking? What does the Prometheus Engine do? And how do you destroy something that you know nothing about?*

The questions continued to vex her thoughts, but the answers would have to wait for now. The secret of the Prometheus Engine would be revealed in time.

As the days passed, repairs went ahead as scheduled on the *Avenger*. Jasper was true to his word and did all he could to keep the airship flying. Without access to the floating island of Emmyr, their supplies were limited, but none of that mattered. Jasper knew how vital the *Avenger* was to the Gil-Gamesh, and he had to keep it airborne. It was his father's legacy. He had already lost so much: His home on Emmyr, his father's swords, and his one true love. Besides his family, this ship was all he had left.

Hunter helped with the repair work as best as he could. He could have left the job to Captain Hawke and the crew, but his father taught him better than that—to lead by example—and that's what he was doing. Bare-chested and covered in sweat, Hunter stood side-by-side with the crew.

Sailors were lined up on either side of the ship, holding fast to ropes that wound through several pulleys up to the top riggings. Attached to them was a massive replacement main mast. "Heave! Heave!" Hunter shouted as they strained and struggled under the weight to get it into position. With the arduous task completed, it was now up to the ship's carpenter and sailing master to secure it.

When they completed the work, the men gave a rousing "Huzza!" Hunter joined in the celebration as they cracked open a keg of grog, lifting a mug and toasting to his men. "To the *Avenger*! Long may she sail!" he shouted as they all clanked mugs and drank heartily to a job well done.

As Hunter drank the bubbly liquid, he spied Chancellor Talbot heading toward them, with Eileanora and a group of wizards following close behind. He recognized a few of them as the Magus who saved them from Mordred's forces before they arrived. He finished his drink, then toweled the sweat off his face and body as he strolled down the gangplank to greet them. The group bowed respectfully to the Gil-Gamesh.

"Good afternoon, Chancellor Talbot," he replied with a courteous bow. "What can I do for you?"

"Ah yes, Sir Hunter. Allow me to introduce the Magus who have requested to join you." The first Magus that stepped forward was the DragonMage.

"Lothar Durandes, Gil-Gamesh, DragonMage of Avalon. It is an honor to meet you finally," he said as he extended his hand to Hunter.

"The honor is mine, Lothar," Hunter said. "I've heard very little about you, especially since my father never told me anything about personally training you."

"I apologize if it seems suspicious to you, but your father requested I keep it discreet," Lothar explained. "He was truly a great man. He taught me everything I know about being a DragonMage."

"I would like to hear more about that," Hunter replied. Lothar nodded and smiled as he stepped back. Then, the beautiful blonde came into view and laid her hands lovingly on Hunter's bare chest.

"I am Luna Kjær, Sir Hunter. It is indeed a pleasure to meet you," she said as she got very close to the Gil-Gamesh. Hunter turned red as she leaned in.

"Yes, hello, Luna," he stuttered. "You're a mermaid from Tirulia, aren't you?"

"Why yes, I'm glad you remembered," she said, swooning over Hunter. "I'm an Aquamancer—a sea witch if you like—but I'm a different person both in and out of the water. Perhaps we can get together later, and I can show just how unique I am."

The female Magus ran her fingers across his bare chest quite invitingly. Hunter swallowed hard, enjoying her attention until he spied Eileanora. If looks could kill, Hunter would be a dead man right now. He had not known the dark elf to be the jealous type.

"Yes, thank you. I look forward to that," he stammered as he stepped aside.

"Salutations, Gil-Gamesh. I'm Ermo Melchom, demonologist extraordinaire," the next one said with an over-extended bow while reaching out to Hunter with his free hand. "My demons are at your service."

"Thank you, Ermo. I want to pick your brain on better ways to fight the wraiths," Hunter replied.

"Happy to oblige, milord. Happy to oblige!" he exclaimed before stepping back. The other two were similar in appearance, almost twins. They were both bald and wore long blue robes, though one was a man and the other a woman. Their ethnicity was that of Hispanic descent. Each one carried a metal staff—the man's was iron, while the woman's staff was silver. They wore ornate jewelry closely resembling their staff's design.

"Gil-Gamesh, this is Isaiah and Isabella Varela," Chancellor Talbot introduced. "Isaiah is a Ferromancer, while his sister Isabella is a Runeweaver."

"OK, Chancellor, you've got me there. What are a Ferromancer and a Runeweaver? I've never heard of that magic discipline before."

"My magic allows me to control and contort metal, Gil-Gamesh," Isaiah interrupted before Chancellor Talbot could answer. "It's like your alchemy but a bit more sophisticated."

Hunter took his little dig in stride. He knew there was a sense of pride between the different classes of mages, each one thinking they were superior to the next. "And you, Isabella? What's a Runeweaver?"

"I cast spells like any other wizards, but I weave my magic instead of casting it," she explained. "Weaving the runes allows me to cast spells twice the power of a regular mage. I can also unweave a spell, negating its effects, although that is a little tougher."

"Her magic leaves her defenseless while she weaves," Isaiah interjected. "So, it's my job to protect my sister while she spins her magic."

"That's quite impressive, the both of you," Hunter added. "It'll be interesting trying to strategize how to use your talent to the best of your abilities."

The last Magus was a tall, muscular man with dark, red-brown hair. He was very rough-looking, wearing a simple long coat of brown wolf's fur over leather pants. He carried no staff, wand, or ornamentation except a pentagram pendant carved in a moonstone. He towered over Hunter as he stood with his arms crossed and a slight scowl on his face.

"I'm Conner Iain Collins, Gil-Gamesh, at your service," he said with a sarcastic salute. His thick Irish accent was quite distinctive. "I'm one of the *Faoladh*." Hunter's mind buzzed with the stories he had heard about the *Faoladh*. The mystery and intrigue surrounding Conner's character piqued his curiosity.

"The *Faoladh*—the guardians of children and travelers—an Irish werewolf." Hunter heard that name before, but only in stories.

"*Maith thú*! I am also a druid," he added. "Tell me, how do you know of me and my kind?"

"When I first arrived on Avalon, our housemaid told me bedtime stories of the *Faoladh*. She used to say to me not to be afraid of dark creatures, like the Banshees and *Abhartach* that haunt the forests, because the *Faoladh* would be there to protect me."

Conner smiled, something he rarely did. "You had an excellent teacher, Gil-Gamesh, a true *Cailin*. I would love to meet her someday." He finally reached out and offered his hand. Hunter took it, glad he could break the ice with him.

"Thank you all for joining us in our fight against Mordred. We'll get you settled in once we return to Alfheimer. In the meantime, please ask Eileanora, Captain Hawke, or the crew any questions. We hope to return to Alfheimer in a few days, so make any necessary preparations.

"Now, if you'll excuse me, I need to get cleaned up," Hunter said as he excused himself and started walking toward the keep.

"My, he is a fascinating man," Luna observed. "I can't wait to get to know him better." Her comment caught the attention of Eileanora, who stormed off toward the *Avenger*.

"I'd rein it in if I were you, Luna," Ermo said. "That she-elf will filet you for Sunday dinner if you're not careful."

"He's right, *Merrow*," Conner interjected, using the Gaelic word for mermaid. "The *Dubh Bhean* is not known for her forgiving nature."

"Well, as far as I can see, they're not exclusive to each other," Luna said slyly. "That means he's fair game."

Out of nowhere, an arrow struck the ground near Luna, startling her and the other Magus. When they looked up, no one could see who fired it. A chill ran down Luna's spine, causing the others to chuckle at her obvious distress.

"I wouldn't be too sure of that," Isabella joked.

Dinner at Strongürd Keep was an over-the-top extravaganza every night. Due to their busy lifestyle and in-depth magical studies, most mages ate lightly during the day. So, dinner was a feast of food, drink, fun, and relaxation. The wizards, sorcerers, and others filled the dining room tables, eating the finest delicacies imaginable.

The newest initiates to the Wizard's Council took turns in the kitchen, preparing and serving food at these nightly feasts. Some initiates carried trays of food and drink around the dining hall, offering succulent appetizers and tantalizing cocktails. The mood was cheerful and uplifting, with a carefree attitude.

However, this time was not just for eating. It was also a time for discussions and arguments on all topics, ranging from philosophy to politics. There continued to be a divide among the Wizard's Council regarding whether they should recognize Mordred as King of Avalon.

While most were against Mordred and the new Lords of Avalon, some couldn't abide by Bowen as King either.

Hunter did his best to stay out of the politics of Strongürd Keep since most conversations revolved around him. He sat back quietly, enjoying his dinner with Master Ostanes, Julianna, and some of the other alchemists. As much as he would have enjoyed dining with Grandmaster Baptiste, the head table was no place for the Gil-Gamesh.

Many of the other masters tried desperately to bend the ear of Grandmaster Baptiste. They wanted the king's power, influence, and status. The wizards were considered by New Camelot as rebels and traitors, along with the Gil-Gamesh and the rest of the resistance. Although it gave them a certain level of autonomy and freedom to do whatever they wanted, the price of that freedom was isolation.

Hunter looked over at Jean-Claude and didn't like what he saw. Two different mages distracted the Grandmaster from enjoying his meal with their constant whispers in his ear. "I don't envy him. Jean-Claude should consider eating his dinner in his room on occasion."

"Unfortunately, that's against protocol," Cyril interjected. "It's a shame, in any case. Those idiots just don't understand what's happening outside these walls."

"They want to rail against the resistance, yet I doubt any of them have seen the devastation caused by Mordred," Julianna added.

"That's why he just sits there and lets them talk," Cyril said. "He'd instead talk his ear off instead of joining Mordred directly. They may not like you, Gil-Gamesh, nor the resistance, but they're loyal to the Wizard's

Council. They wouldn't do anything that would dishonor the Grandmaster or Strongürd Keep.

"Speaking of the council, when will you return to the keep and take my place, Julianna?" Cyril asked. "I'm getting too old for this place. I want to retire to an easier life."

"If you want me back in this hellhole, you need to convince my husband first, then Lady Stephanie, the Gil-Gamesh, and his sisters," she joked.

"Seriously? At least think about it, would you please? It's not every day an Atlantian alchemist becomes the Master of Alchemy. You're wasting your talent on healing elixirs and beauty products. Hunter, talk to her, will you please?" Cyril implored.

"Sorry, Master Ostanes, but anyone who gets on my Mom's bad side will find their picture on the back of a milk carton," he laughed as he clinked his goblet with Julianna as the two shared a private joke.

"By the way, Julianna," Cyril interjected. "I know Hunter's been looking for any information on the Prometheus Engine. Why don't you tell him what you know? After all, it is your heritage."

Julianna took another sip of wine, giving Master Ostanes a sideways glance. "I don't know much about it," she answered bluntly. "My knowledge about the engine comes from bedtime stories my mother and grandmother told me. I never knew the difference between the truth or what was made up to scare me from asking more questions about it. In a family of alchemists, the Prometheus Engine was a forbidden subject."

"That's alright, Julianna. Allain told me the subject was off-limits, so I never bothered to ask," Hunter explained. "If you knew anything substantial, you'd tell me." Hunter spied something out of the ordinary across the room as he poured himself some more wine.

The DragonMage Lothar Durandes sat alone, reading while casually eating his dinner. He kept his nose in his book, oblivious to the others engaged in a heated conversation.

"Excuse me a moment, would you?" Hunter said as he started walking toward Lothar.

It was relatively easy for him to maneuver through the room. Most of the wizards considered him a novice, unlike his father, so they practically ignored him. None of that bothered Hunter. He did not become an alchemist to curry their favor.

As he approached Lothar, the Magus did not even notice him. "Excuse me, Lothar, may I join you?" Lothar finally looked up from his book, surprised to see the Gil-Gamesh standing before him.

"Sir Hunter... Yes, of course, please, sit down!" he exclaimed as he closed the book before setting it down.

"That must be an excellent book if you can ignore everything going on here," Hunter remarked as he sat down.

"It's a book your father recommended for me to read. I finally found a copy of *'To Kill a Mockingbird'* outside New Camelot."

Hunter was surprised to hear the title of the book. "Why did he recommend that book to you?"

"He said it would show me what injustice looked like," Lothar said. "I'm finding it quite insightful in that area and more."

Hunter paused momentarily before coming to the real reason he wanted to speak to the DragonMage. "I just wanted to let you know,

Lothar, that I don't hold anything against you," he began. "It was my father's decision not to tell me about you, and I don't have any reason to resent you for it. It's just the way my father was, secretive and dismissive."

"I appreciate you telling me that, Gil-Gamesh. There were many times I wanted to tell you," he started to say as he poured some wine for Hunter, offering him a goblet. "I've seen you around the keep numerous times, but I didn't think it was the right moment to tell you. I knew you would find out and seek me out sooner or later."

"Well, believe me, I'm glad you were there to help us against Jaeger," Hunter said with relief. "That hothead has been a royal pain in my ass since the first day I met him."

The two laughed, but then Hunter became quite serious. "The truth is, I wanted to ask why you chose to be a DragonMage. Something specific had to make you choose this path besides my father."

"There is, but it's not what you think," Lothar replied. "It wasn't your father, but rather, it was mine. You see, my father was a dragon poacher."

When Hunter heard those words, it shocked him to the core. Growing up on Emmyr, he learned to love and respect dragons, and dragon poaching was the equivalent of animal cruelty on Avalon. Poachers captured dragons as babies and grew them in captivity before killing them to harvest dragon stones—ingots of pure magical energy.

"He tried to get me to follow in his footsteps, but I wouldn't," he continued. "Anytime I went near them, I would comfort the dragons, give them extra food, whatever I could do to ease their pain in captivity. It finally reached the point where my father wouldn't let me work with him anymore. He knew that I didn't have the stomach for it.

"Then, one night, I woke up to this terrible howling sound. It was coming from the cave where my father kept the dragons captive. I ran out to see what was going on. My father and the others tried to regain control of a dragon that had gotten loose from its bonds. They used magical chains to bind the dragons and keep them submissive, but that night, one of the new dragons got loose before they could tie it down.

"They were fighting with it, trying desperately to recapture it. It wouldn't produce a dragon stone worth selling if it died too young. When I arrived outside the entrance, the dragon flew near the ceiling with one leg chain still on. Its frantic movements made it nearly impossible to wrangle."

Hunter could feel the anger swelling inside him. He refused to understand how the son of a dragon poacher could become a DragonMage, but he was willing to give him the benefit of the doubt and hear him out.

"So, what happened next?" Hunter asked as he took another drink from his wine goblet.

"That's when your father showed up," Lothar continued. "I heard the roar of a dragon, and when I looked up in the sky, I saw him. I'll never forget it for as long as I live. It was a full moon, big and bright in the night sky. There must have been a thousand dragons up there. It looked like they were flying back to Avalon from the moon."

"They were—" Hunter interrupted. "It was a 'Dragon Moon.' The legends say that's when the dragons fly to the moon and back to replenish their magical power. I saw one on the first night I arrived on Avalon."

"Yes, well, it's rather frightening for a young child to see for the first time," Lothar continued. "Especially when all those dragons are flying straight for you. I hid behind some rocks as Lord MoonDrake landed with several large dragons. He rushed in and quickly subdued my father and his partners."

"You didn't try to warn them?" Hunter asked. Lothar chuckled as he poured himself some more wine.

"No, I didn't. I loved my father, but I knew what he did was wrong. Besides, he was no match for the Gil-Gamesh. Anyway, your father did quick work on them. Surprisingly, he subdued them without killing them. The dragons kept them cornered while Lord MoonDrake tried to free the young ones from captivity, but he couldn't find a way to break the enchanted chains.

"I went over and showed him how to remove them, which didn't sit well with my father. After that night, he never spoke to me again, not until the day he died in prison," he concluded.

A moment of silence hung in the air between them. Hunter felt sorry for him, but Lothar continued the story after finishing his wine.

"After the local magistrates showed up to take them into custody, the Gil-Gamesh spoke to me. He said the captive dragons told him how I helped them, comforted them, and kept them well-fed. He thanked me for helping his friends.

"To this day, I still don't understand it," Lothar continued. "I never told anyone that my father was a dragon poacher. I even helped him from time to time. Why would they thank me?"

"Because you showed them kindness," Hunter interjected. "While your father and his associates used and abused them, you showed them compassion. Dragons always remember those who treat them with respect."

Lothar was relieved to hear Hunter say that. "Anyway, one of the captive dragons died before it could return to Emmyr. Your father gave me the dragon stone made from that dragon's death. He told me that someday, I would understand why he gave it to me. I knew what he meant when I first came to Strongürd Keep. The dragon stone showed me my purpose and my future."

Lothar motioned with his hand and summoned his staff—a split spearhead set with a single dragon stone that held the two blades together. "This is *Jormugand*, named after the legendary dragon of Ragnarok."

"And that's the dragon stone?" Hunter asked. Lothar nodded his head.

"When it was time for me to pick my discipline, I chose to be a DragonMage. I guess it's a penance, of sorts, for me to reclaim my family name. Your father agreed to be my mentor, and I was humbled and honored. It was then that he told me the truth."

"The truth? The truth about what?" Hunter asked.

"On that day in the cave, when he handed me the dragon stone, he saw our future through his 'dragon sight' ability. He knew that this was the path I was supposed to be on and that he would be a part of it. He even helped me forge *Jormugand* and fuse it with the dragon stone.

"Lord MoonDrake was more of a father to me than my own, so in a sense, I guess that makes us brothers," Lothar said as he stood to leave. "I will fight and, if necessary, die by your side, Gil-Gamesh—to the bitter end."

He held out his hand to Hunter. The Gil-Gamesh put his goblet down and stood as he took Lothar's hand. "Anyone who stands against the reign of Mordred will forever be my friend and ally. I'm honored to call you brother. We are, after all, both sons of the Gil-Gamesh."

The two men stood there, holding in the emotion of the moment when Hunter spied something behind Lothar. His sister Rose and Captain O'Brien entered the dining hall, looking around for Hunter. When she finally spotted him, Rose waved frantically to get her brother's attention.

"Why don't you let me introduce you to my sister, Rose," Hunter said. "I think you two will have a lot to talk about."

CHAPTER 9
THE BARONESS AND THE DUKE

Jaeger Nottingham screamed in pain. The archer who shot him not only cut off half his ear, but the arrow became wedged in the back of his head and fractured his skull. The doctor on board the *Hood's Revenge* had died in battle, and his assistant was not as competent. His treatment of the Lord of Avalon caused Jaeger to squirm on the table.

"Please, milord, hold still," the assistant physician pleaded. "If I don't remove the arrow and heal this wound properly, it could get infected or worse."

"This is the third time you've tried to remove it, you idiot! How many times is it going to take you to do it?" Jaeger shouted.

"I'm sorry, milord, I'm doing my best," he apologized. "It's difficult to do this in the rough seas. It would be easier if we were flying again."

"If we could fly, we would already be in Nottinghamshire, where a competent surgeon could heal me. Stop your whining and get it done before I put an arrow in YOUR head!"

Jaeger took another big swig of whisky from the bottle. He gripped it tightly in his hand, chugging the amber liquid. Once he finished his drink, he turned his head sideways to expose the wound to the doctor. With his one free hand, he gripped tightly onto the table.

"Hold him!" the assistant physician commanded the other men. They held down his legs and body as tight as they could as the doctor continued his work. Just as he was about to start, the door to Jaeger's cabin swung open. In walked a woman of incredible beauty and strength known to all. Her long blonde hair flowed about her head and neck, framing her face underneath a helm shaped like a dragon skull with actual dragon horns and teeth. Though battle-worn and tattooed with Nordic runes, her face was beautiful and fierce. Her Northern heritage clearly showed through her attire, which consisted of leather armor with overlapping metal rings, vambraces, and leggings of leather and steel. Around her waist hung an *Ulfberht*, a traditional Viking sword.

Baroness Brigida Olafdotter of the Northlands reclaimed her legacy after Avalon's Reclamation sent her simple fishing village into the sea. She focused her anger for the Gil-Gamesh onto her people, turning them from successful fishers into invaders from the sea, reclaiming their Viking heritage. She once loved Hunter, but after she discovered his affair with Queen Cadhla, it turned her bitter and cold. She even started hunting down the dragons to spite Hunter and his family.

Under her rule, the Vikings of the Northlands conquered the towns, villages, and islands near her homeland, giving them total dominance of the region. Even the Gil-Gamesh and his resistance failed to make a dent in her area of influence. Once she got a foothold, her passion and drive turned the conquered people against Hunter and his sisters. She was the perfect tool for Mordred's reign.

Brigida removed her helmet and handed it to one of her Vikings as she pushed past Jaeger's men to see what had happened. "What happened, Jaeger? Who did this?"

"Who do you think?" he answered as he downed some more whisky. "I had that brat cornered and dead in the water just off Strongürd Keep when the damn Magus attacked. I was the only one to get away."

"Who shot you? Hunter?"

"An Elven arrow injured him, Baroness," the doctor interrupted. "There's an arrowhead embedded in his skull. I have been unsuccessful in removing it."

Brigida looked carefully at the wound. "Do you have any lodestones left?" she asked.

"If I did, don't you think I'd be flying?" Jaeger snapped back. "The battle knocked our engine off its mounting."

"Hamund! Go down to their engine room and find me a lodestone!" she ordered. The Viking saluted her by slamming his fist over his heart and bowing his head. He took off immediately for the lower decks.

"What the hell are you trying to do, Bree?" Jaeger screamed as he tried to sit up. Brigida stopped him and gently pushed him back on the table.

"I'm trying to save your life, you *mikill uxi!*" she argued with the "stupid ox," as she called him in their ancient tongue. "I can't heal the wound with that piece of metal still inside you."

"No, I mean, what are you doing here? I didn't send any messages for help?"

Brigida paused for a moment before answering. "I received word that the *Avenger* crashed on Strongürd Keep," she started to say. "I needed to know if he was dead or alive."

"See, you still care for the runt, don't you?" Jaeger replied. Before he could say another word, Brigida grabbed him by the face and kissed Jaeger, which surprised him and the others.

"That *forræder* is dead to me,' she said, using the Viking word for traitor. "I just want to ensure that there is nothing left of him or his *motbydelig* family on Avalon. To create our new world with King Mordred, we must wipe Hunter and the rest of his ilk from this world.

"Of all the Lords of Avalon, you are the only one with the strength and determination to fight the Gil-Gamesh and his sisters, and for that, I am forever grateful," she concluded, with a small peck on his lips. As she did, Hamund stormed in with a lodestone in hand.

"Now, lie down and let me help you," Brigida said as she helped Jaeger. He took one last swig of whiskey before turning his head to expose the wound.

"Hold him!" she commanded. Her men surrounded the table and held Jaeger in place.

"What are you going to do?" Jaeger asked, gritting his teeth.

"The lodestone acts like a magnet," she explained. "Instead of pulling our iron ships through the air, I'm going to pull the arrow out of your head. I've found this to be the best way to remove those damn Elven arrowheads."

She held the lodestone a few inches above his wound. "Now, this is going to hurt... *Attrahunt!*" Brigida poured her magic into the lodestone as the rock began to glow. Jaeger screamed as he felt the arrowhead moving around inside his skull. It slowly eased to the surface until it finally popped out and stuck to the lodestone.

Brigida handed the stone to one of her men. "Get me some healing salve," she dictated. Jaeger's assistant doctor gave her a small jar and a cloth. She carefully applied the salve to the wound and bandaged it.

"You should rest now, Jaeger. In a few hours, you'll be back on your feet. Hamund, you and Arne help Duke Nottingham to his cabin. Olav, tell the *Skuld* to tow the *Hood's Revenge* to New Camelot as quickly as possible."

"Don't worry about me," Jaeger said through gritted teeth. "You need to get to Strongürd Keep and finish that brat."

"The Gil-Gamesh will keep for another time," Brigida said sternly. "We need you and the *Hood's Revenge* at full strength to defeat him." With a simple nod, the Vikings followed her orders and escorted Duke Nottingham out of the room to rest. Brigida left to take command of the *Hood's Revenge*.

"Baroness Olafdotter, a word, please!" the assistant doctor called out. Brigida stopped and turned toward him, a scowl firmly on her face. "May

I ask how you knew to use the lodestone to pull out the arrowhead? It seems to be such an unorthodox way of removing it."

"Unorthodox? Really? And how reliable was your method of removing it?" she growled back at him. "You just gouged out his head to remove one simple arrowhead. Your incompetence could have killed the Duke."

The doctor, dumbfounded by her accusation, was at a complete loss for words. "Baroness, I assure you, I was doing everything possible to save Duke Nottingham. I—"

"You were doing nothing but trying to save your skin," she interrupted. "Consider yourself sacked. Your services are no longer required."

"Now see here, milady, I—" Before he could say another word, Brigida drew her sword and decapitated the man in one swift motion. His head rolled across the floor as his body dropped, shaking violently until the last of his life faded away.

She flicked her sword in the air, flinging the blood from her blade before she sheathed it. She left the body where it lay and headed topside. As soon as she stepped out on the deck, Olaf returned.

"Baroness, we have begun towing the ship. The captain of the *Skuld* says we should be at New Camelot the day after tomorrow."

"Good, thank you, Olaf," she replied as she walked toward the bow to inspect the lines herself.

"Also, milady, our scouts have reported that the *Black Adder* arrived at Strongürd Keep and departed shortly after," he continued as he followed close behind her. "But the *Avenger* remains there."

Brigida said nothing. She carefully inspected the tow lines as if she were ignoring his report. "Shall I order the scouts to follow the *Black Adder* or stay at Strongürd until the *Avenger* leaves?" Olaf further inquired.

"Neither Olaf. It's more than likely that the Gil-Gamesh is on the *Black Adder*, heading back for Alfheimer. Our scout ships are no match for that pirate ship. It would be a waste of time for them. The *Avenger* is probably waiting for replacement parts before it returns to Alfheimer."

Brigda gripped the rail tightly, staring into the open sea as bile filled her throat. "We'll wait until the *Avenger* leaves Alfheimer again," she concluded. "I want to watch Hunter die by my hand. I want his bastard son there as life leaves his body and his blood soaks into the ground like rain after a storm. They need to know the depths of pain his family has inflicted on me... on all of us."

"You want to do what? Are you out of your mind?" Rose screamed at Hunter. In the captain's cabin of the *Black Adder*, a war was brewing between brother and sister. Eileanora and Edan could only watch and stay out of their way, something everyone learned to do over the years regarding the MoonDrake family.

"You're not seeing the big picture, sis. You've got to think it through," Hunter calmly replied as he tried to put Rose at ease. "This could benefit us in the long run."

"You're talking about aligning with thieves, the most untrustworthy, ruthless individuals on Avalon. What am I missing here?" she continued to shriek.

"Rose, you need to calm down and listen to Hunter," Edan interjected as he stepped forward. "After all, we're the ones who brought him the information about the Thieves Guild." Rose turned and glared at her husband for siding with her brother. Edan could feel the daggers from her stare stabbing into him. He quietly stopped talking before Elieanora grabbed him and pulled him back.

"Sis, if we can secure Keane Foley and the Thieves Guild on our side, it'll provide us with a network of spies across every corner of Avalon. This, coupled with the additional manpower, could be a game-changer should the need arise," Hunter explained, emphasizing the strategic advantage.

"But you can't trust them," she interjected. "These are the same cutthroats that sided with Morgana le Fay. You expect them to side with us over Mordred?"

"After Mordred killed Foley's brother and his second-in-command? Yes, I do!"

"I have to agree with the Gil-Gamesh's assessment, Lady Rose," Eileanora added. "This may be a prime opportunity for us to gain an ally and an intelligence network."

"And you think we can trust them?" Rose asked.

"Oh no, absolutely not, but it's a chance we have to take," Eileanora explained. "We have a good foothold on Avalon, but Mordred's forces still outnumber us. We need all the help we can get."

Rose thought about it before she realized that maybe, just maybe, they made sense. "So, how do we contact Foley? He's disappeared now that the entire Adalwulf Guard is trying to run him down."

"Elle, would you please contact Mrs. Thurgoode and see if she can make inquiries about Foley's whereabouts? Once we get that information, I'll contact him."

"And what are you going to say to him?" Eileanora asked.

"I'm going to make him an offer he can't refuse!" Hunter said, making his best impression of Vito Corleone from *The Godfather*, complete with a raspy voice and exaggerated hand gesture.

"Can you please be serious for once in your life, Hunter?" Eileanora snapped.

Hunter noticed the anger in Eileanora's eyes, a sign that he might have crossed a line. "I'm sorry, Elle, I don't mean to joke all the time. It's just my way of coping with the gravity of our situation," he explained, sensing the tension between them.

"My dad was so stoic and serious all the time. I couldn't help but be a jokester. I guess it's my way of dealing with the situation without falling into a deep depression," he concluded. Eileanora had never heard Hunter talk so openly about his feelings. Now, she felt wrong for calling him out for his humor.

"Yes, well, it's understandable, but we need to be cautious," she inferred. "I don't want to risk Mrs. Thurgoode exposing herself."

"You worry too much about her, Eileanora," Rose interjected. "I doubt a soul out there could stop 'Mrs. T' from doing her job."

"In any case, we'll be back in Alfheimer by dawn," Edan added. "That'll give us time to plan our next step accordingly, but for now, please excuse me. I've got a ship to run."

Edan tipped his hat to Hunter and Eileanora before kissing Rose and leaving the cabin. "I will go and contact Mrs. Thurgoode with her next assignment," Eileanora said as she bowed politely before leaving. Hunter and Rose stood in silence. Rose looked at her brother's face and saw something she had never seen before.

"What are you thinking about, Hunter?"

"I was just wondering what Dad would do in this particular situation. Honestly, I'm flying by the seat of my pants."

"Normally, he would turn to Ocwyn or Archie for advice," Rose responded. "But, I guess we don't have that option now, do we?"

"No, but it's like Dad said before he died—the three of us are stronger together," Hunter said. "We need to talk to Ashley about all of this. She may have some insight into the Lady of the Lake and King Arthur's tomb."

"Why didn't you ask Master Maximillion to investigate it back at Strongürd Keep?"

"Because I don't trust most of the wizards there," Hunter replied vehemently. "They may not want to side with Mordred, but they don't want to help us out either. Those wizards have their own agenda. I don't know what it is yet, but we will soon enough."

"You don't suspect Grandmaster Baptiste, do you?" Rose asked.

"No, of course not. The Grandmaster is loyal as the day is long, but I think he's trying to help us weed out the spies."

"That's why you brought the Magus with us," Rose surmised. "You want to see if any of them are feeding information to the council."

"We might not have Dad's friends, but we have each other," Hunter said, emphasizing the importance of their family unity. The two smiled and laughed as if they could feel their father right there, reinforcing their strong bond.

"I hate to spoil the moment, Hunter, but I am worried about Ashley," Rose said. "She is becoming more and more distant from us. She spends more time in that library than with her husband."

"I know, but there's no talking to her either. She won't leave that damn library unless it's for a mission."

"Well, if we're going to get anywhere with her, you know what we gotta do?" Rose inferred.

"Yep, ask mom to talk to her!" Hunter replied with a devilish smirk.

CHAPTER 10
THE SORCERESS MAGNATE OF AVALON

Merlin's library was no ordinary place because, in reality, it didn't exist. The library was a book of all the magic the great wizard collected over thousands of years. Merlin hid the book for centuries, but it was accessible to those deemed worthy by Merlin. You could enter the library via a spiritual transfer through magic called the Thaumaturge Effect. A magical conduit, such as the Staff of Merlin, allowed the spirit of individuals to gain entry to the library. As his apprentice and heir, Ashley was such a person. She was now the *Sorceress Magnate* of Avalon.

The library appeared to be the size of a small mansion. The interior stood over a hundred feet tall, with five levels of bookshelves filled with every book imaginable on the arcane arts. Staircases spiraled to each one, and hanging ladders glided back and forth across the bookcases for easy access. Massive chandeliers hung from the ceiling to illuminate even the darkest recesses of the great hall. The only furniture was a couple of comfy chairs, a small table, and a sofa next to a roaring fireplace. However, the library's display cases, paintings, and sculptures added to Merlin's massive collection of magical writings and artifacts.

Ashley didn't bother to use the chairs. She hovered above the floor, sitting with her legs crossed. Her robe flowed around her and barely touched the ground. She had one book in her hand while another floated before her. She stared intently at the pages, flipping through them without touching the paper.

Lady Stephanie appeared from around the corner, carrying a tea tray. Even though the library only existed on a magical plain, spending time here taxed the body, mind, and spirit. Drinking and eating items made here replenished magical energy as if you were consuming them in the real world.

Stephanie set the tray down and started pouring the tea. "Ashley, I made tea for you and Oliver. You two have been in here for hours."

Ashley ignored her mother and continued to read. That irritated Stephanie even more. "Ashley, did you hear what I said?"

"Uh-huh..." Ashley murmured as she flipped another page.

"Ashley Summer St. Johns!" Stephanie shouted in a firm, motherly voice, calling her daughter by her first, middle, and last name. Ashley immediately knew she was in trouble and looked up from her book.

"You're acting rude, young lady," Stephanie started to say as she continued to pour the tea. "You know how much I hate it when you do that. I swear you're just like your father at times."

Ashley smirked at the comparison. "I guess I'll take that as a compliment," she joked.

"Don't get smart with me, young lady," Stephanie snapped back at her. "That wasn't meant to be a compliment."

"Oh, come on, Mom. I'm sorry, OK? I am trying to isolate a locator spell to help us find the Twin Swords of the Dragon Knight," she explained. "Faust has incredible layers of magical protection that keep his vault from my foresight. It's frustrating."

"About as frustrating as a daughter who neglects her own family to pursue said spell," Stephanie zinged back at her.

"Why do you do that, mother?" Ashley asked. "Why do you have to bring up my shortcomings to make a point?"

"I am pointing it out to you because that's what mothers do when their children grow up," Stephanie explained as she set out the teacups. "All a parent can do is point out the error of their ways. You must decide what you do with that information and make an informed decision on your own. Hopefully, it will be the right one." Stephanie could see Ashley listening to her advice, which made her soften her harsh tone.

"You'll understand that better when you're a mother yourself," she concluded. "Now, sit down and drink your tea before it gets cold. Where is Oliver? I thought he was in here with you?"

Ashley closed her books and floated down, putting her feet on the ground. As she sat down, the books were lowered to the table. "Oliver left to get something to eat and sleep," Ashley said. "His inability to find further information on the Prometheus Engine is as frustrating as my search for Faust's vault."

Stephanie handed Ashley tea before picking up her own and nestling into the oversized chair. "You should follow his example and step away for a while yourself. It might do you good to come back with a fresh perspective."

"But it's not my perspective that you're after. Is it, mother? You're concerned about Andy and me," Ashley fired back.

Stephanie was not surprised that Ashley saw her right through. After all, she took after her mother in more ways than one. "Yes, you're right. I am concerned about you and Andy. You spend more time here than you do in the real world. Andy throws himself into his work as a weaponsmith and his training as a knight. You only want to spend time with him out on some mission or when he's injured. There is more to marriage than that, Ashley, and you must spend equal time between being a sorceress and a wife."

Ashely kept her head down, her eyes staring at the floor. She didn't want to look her mother in the eye because, deep down, Ashley knew she was right, but not for the reasons she knew.

"How did you do it, Mom?" she asked before she raised her head and looked at her. "How did you make Dad take time between being the Gil-Gamesh and your husband?"

"With carefully spoken words backed up by years of experience," Stephanie replied with a smile. "Your father was very driven, just like you, and I had to constantly remind him to be more than the Gil-Gamesh—to be a father to his children and a husband to me."

"That's just it, mom. You reminded Dad of his responsibilities outside of being the Gil-Gamesh, but Andy is not you," she started to say. "To be perfectly honest, I'm not the problem; he is. Andy is determined, so much more than me. I keep to myself in this library because my husband is obsessed with wanting to protect me. He'd rather improve and upgrade the GunStars or Lancers than sit down for dinner together."

"I don't understand," Stephanie started to say, confused by her daughter's confession. "Andy can be a little protective sometimes, but why does he feel this overwhelming need to defend you? You're more than capable of taking care of yourself."

"It's not just me he's trying to protect," she began. Ashley paused and took a deep breath as she set her teacup down and stood back up. She took off a ring from her right hand, and suddenly, the illusion faded as her figure began to change from a thin, young lady to a pregnant woman.

Stephanie was shocked as she got up to help her daughter. "Ashley, what on earth... Why didn't you tell me? How far along are you?"

"About seven months," she said as her mother helped her sit back on the sofa. "Julianna's been looking after me. I knew Allain would tell you, so I asked for her confidentiality."

"My God, that's the one thing I hate about this place—too many damn secrets!" Stephanie cursed. "Things would be much easier if we all just talked to each other."

"I'm fine, mom. Really, I am perfectly fine, and the babies are too."

Ashley's answer caught Stephanie off guard. "Wait, you said babies?"

Ashley nodded her head and smiled. "I'm having twins," she said as tears rose in her eyes, emotion getting the better of her. "Julianna said it's common for a sorceress to have multiple births, something to do with the abundance of magic in our body."

Stephanie hugged her daughter as they both cried tears of joy. "But why didn't you tell me?" Stephanie insisted. "I understand not telling Hunter or Rose, but to keep this from me?"

"I didn't want to worry you, Mom, because I knew you would," Ashley said. "I have to be able to support Hunter and Rose in everything they do, and I don't want to be a burden. We already have so much on our plate in our fight against Mordred."

"Ashley, you are not a burden," Stephanie said as she cradled her daughter's face. "The birth of a baby is the kind of miracle that brings joy into lives, so two will bring twice as much."

Ashley felt relieved by her mother's kind words as if she had lifted a weight off her shoulders. "Now, when Hunter and Rose arrive, we'll pull them aside with Sarafina and Andy so that you can tell them the good news," Stephanie concluded.

"They're not going to be happy that I hid this from them," Ashley retorted.

"At first, but then they will be thrilled. I know they will," she replied. "I think Julianna is going to have a bigger problem. She has to tell Allain what she's been hiding from him."

The two women laughed and hugged, relishing the moment as a mother passed the torch of motherhood to her daughter. "Have you and Andy decided on names yet?" Stephanie asked.

"No, not yet. Julianna can't determine if it's boys or girls or one of each. We'll wait until they're born to give them names. So, for now—" Ashley paused as she placed the ring back on her finger, reactivating her illusion. "I'll keep my secret hidden from everyone."

Stephanie smiled proudly. All she could do was hide her concern for Ashley and her unborn children. As idyllic as her life has been here on Avalon, the dangers of this world persisted against her family. All Stephanie could do was stand by her children and pray for a quick end to this conflict. She clung to her faith, as she always did whenever needed. It's what kept her going through these dark times.

On Avalon, South Essex was a city of artisans where wealthy men and women lived a life of luxury. The finest artisans in all mediums—wood, metalwork, or canvas—and exceptional tailors, tinkers, and tradesmen practiced their professions here. It was a town full of the finest shops outside of New Camelot. As one of the largest islands within the Archipelago of Avalon, people crowded the streets for a chance at wealth.

Merchants and artisans, con artists and thieves, worked in unison on the streets and in the shops to barter and steal whatever they could. The chaos within the city was created by the Earl of South Essex, Finnick Devereaux, to keep the people in line. Fighting amongst themselves took away from what Mordred had done to the rest of Avalon. Besides, it appealed to the wealthy nobles of Avalon and kept them in lockstep with the regime. As long as they had the comforts of wealth about them, it all but assured their allegiance to Mordred.

Amid all this conflict, South Essex became a perfect hiding place for the Guildmaster of the Thieves Guild. With the constant barrage of disputes, robberies, and brawls, the Adalwulf Guard was kept busy, so they had little time to search for him or his thieves.

The Thieves Guild kept themselves hidden from the rest of the world deep underground through a series of tunnels and catacombs. Their underground hideout had food, water, and other distractions to keep them safely absconded from prying eyes.

Keane Foley sat back in his chair, feet propped up on a table, as he picked at his fingernails with a dagger. Across from him, impatiently pacing, was his daughter Regan. Her steady tempo started to wear a path on the stone floor. She was a fair-haired girl who hid her beauty behind leather armor, a scarf, and a hood. Her piercing green eyes were bloodshot from lack of sleep and overwhelming anger and fear.

Ever since her father told her about Mordred's decree and her uncle's death, Regan found herself thrust into the role of the Shadowfoot and the guild forced into hiding. Regan was a storm of unbridled rage, with the Adalwulf Guard looking for any chance to arrest or kill the Thieves Guild members.

"What are we doing here, father?" she screamed. "This waiting around is absolute madness!"

"It's necessary, Regan, and you know it. Until we finish the new safehouses, we're stuck down here," Keane calmly replied while he manicured his nails. "King Mordred has already culled half our number. We can't afford to lose anymore."

"If we're down here hiding, we're not stealing anything either," she argued. "Pretty soon, we're going to run through our supplies, not to mention our gold reserve. What are we going to do then?"

Keane huffed as he sheathed his blade. "Regan, do you have to be so dramatic? We have all our available resources committed to building the new safehouses. I've got Skell and Brom working with splinter teams to hit a few high-profile targets so that we can keep ourselves afloat. Now stop worrying... God, you are like your mother that way!"

Regan drew her dagger, spun around, and threw it at her father. Keane caught the blade with ease, inches from his face. He glared at his daughter before his smile broke through the tension. "You almost had me that time!" Keane said with a grin. "Your timing is almost perfect—*almost*!"

He threw the dagger back at Regan. She caught it in mid-air as well. "I told you not to mention her around me! Are you deliberately trying to piss me off?" Regan snapped back as she threw the dagger at him once again.

Keane caught the dagger before immediately throwing it back at her. "Now, now, Regan, we talked about this. You need to get past your 'mommy' issues."

Regan caught the dagger and flung it back as her apparent anger started to show. "I don't have 'mommy' issues! Why do you keep saying that?"

"Because it makes you angry, and that shows weakness. If you don't get past it, you'll always be vulnerable to enemies to exploit!" Keane said as he caught the dagger and flung it back at her again, but this time, it stopped mid-air between them.

The two thieves looked in awe and curiosity at the floating dagger. "You know, I used to play catch with my Dad," came a voice out of nowhere, until Gil-Gamesh pulled back the hood of his cloak, and the invisibility spell faded. "But, I must admit, your version is much more intimidating."

Keane and Regan immediately drew daggers and took defensive stances. "Hold on, hold on!" Hunter said, raising his hands after he set the blade down on the table. "I'm not here to fight. I'm here to talk!"

"You have a funny way of showing that, Gil-Gamesh, sneaking into my guild using my father's cloak," Keane growled, drawing a second dagger into his free hand.

"I wouldn't do that if I were you," Hunter advised. "You might upset him."

"Upset who?" Keane inquired until a shadow rose over him. He turned around to see a bear standing behind him. The bear roared, revealing his protective nature as Keane stepped before his daughter.

"Don't worry. Boots won't harm either of you as long as you don't do anything to me," Hunter said as he pulled out a chair and sat at the table. "As I said, I only want to talk."

Keane and Regan paused momentarily before looking at each other, conferring through a simple nod. Keane sheathed his daggers and sat across from Hunter while Regan stood behind him, her arms crossed with two blades held firm in her grip. She stared at Hunter with intense scrutiny.

"What about your pet?" she asked. "I thought your family liked dragons, not bears?"

"Oh, Boots isn't an ordinary bear," Hunter replied. "He's my familiar. *Canis!*" Boots' form began to shift as the beast transformed from a bear to a dog. He sat next to Hunter and barked as Hunter petted his head gently.

"Nice pet, though I doubt you came down here to show off your skills as an alchemist," Keane retorted. "What do you want?"

"I heard you were having a little trouble with King Mordred. I came here to offer you my help," Hunter said.

"Your help?" Regan snapped back. "Why in the world would you help us?"

"An ancient proverb once said, 'The enemy of my enemy is my friend!'" Hunter replied. "We both want Abdel Ben Faust dead and King Mordred off the throne. I'd say we have a lot in common."

"I will take care of Faust in my own time. I don't need your help to kill him," Keane screamed as he slammed his fist into the table.

"You're probably right. I've never heard of anyone holding off that cursed sword of his with a dagger before. That's quite impressive. Be that as it may, Mordred is a different story. You can't take him down on your own, and I can't do it without the Twin Swords of the Dragon Knight, *Twilight* and *Dusk*," Hunter said.

"And Faust has them locked away, doesn't he? But that still doesn't explain why you need my help?"

"It's simple. I need your help in finding Faust's vault. You are the 'eyes and ears' behind every dark alley, every shadow, and every backroom in Avalon. Once we find it, you can have anything and everything in it, except for my father's swords. That should fetch a pretty hefty price.

"As for what's in it for you... Well, here is something I owe you," Hunter continued as he took off his cloak and laid it across the table. The move surprised Keane as he picked up his family's mantle—the Cloak of Thieves that once belonged to his father, Nigel Foley. Hunter's father took the magical cloak as a trophy when he beat him in combat.

"Why? Why would you give this back to me?" Keane asked.

"Because I know what it's like to lose something that once belonged to a father," Hunter explained. "Magical items like these are the heritage of our families. I wanted to return this to you as a sign of mutual respect, shall we say."

"So, this is my payment? What about the rest of the guild?" Keane asked. "My thieves don't work for free."

"I'll offer them the same thing I did the Pirates of Barbarossa. You can steal whatever you want from those who side with Mordred. Just leave the people be."

"What happens after you depose Mordred and put your little bastard back on the throne?" Regan joked before Keane elbowed her to shut her up.

"Don't believe everything you hear about King Bowen," Hunter said. "He is no bastard. I was Royal Consort to Queen Cadhla, but that's beside the point. We'll deal with what comes next when that time comes.

"Right now, we can help each other in more ways than one," Hunter concluded. "You can provide us with intel from all the major cities, and we can provide you with protection from the Adalwulf Guard and the wraiths."

"How can you protect me and my guild?" Keane asked.

Hunter grinned a devilish smirk as he reached into his pocket and pulled out an opal, almost three inches in diameter. "Did you know I've been here for more than two hours? While I wandered about, I placed these at various points throughout the guild."

He tossed the stone to Keane, who caught it and looked over the gem. Most experienced thieves can appraise gems in an instant. Keane knew this opal was priceless in more ways than one.

"Is this an oracle gem?" he asked.

"It is," Hunter stated. "My sister, Ashley, walked with me and determined the right points to place the stones to set up a magical protection network around your guild. You don't need to worry about moving or setting up new safehouses. Not even that witch, Mavis, could divine your location down here. You're perfectly safe."

"Your sister, the apprentice of Merlin?" Regan asked as she swallowed hard.

"She's not an apprentice anymore. She's the *Sorceress Magnate*," Hunter replied. "She's waiting for me at the entrance of the guild. She wanted to come with and protect me, but I told her I wanted this to be a one-on-one between us."

"You know, there's a pretty hefty price on your head," Keane said with a sly smile. "What's stopping me from turning you into Mordred and collecting on it? That'll put me and my guild back in his good graces."

Boots growled at the thieves, but Hunter patted his head to calm down. "If you were going to do that, why have this conversation? That proves that you're interested in my proposal."

"But why?" Keane asked. "Why would you do this?"

"We both need friends, allies if you want, against Mordred. The longer he stays in power, Avalon will be in ever-growing danger. We will slowly begin to disappear until it fades away into nothingness."

Keane heard those words and knew there was more than Hunter was telling him. "What aren't you telling us?"

Hunter took a deep breath. He preferred not to lay all his cards on the table, but it may help push the thieves over to his side. "The Lady of the Lake is missing," Hunter started to say. That revelation alone startled them. Even cutthroats like them knew of her importance in the magic of Avalon. "The only one who could have taken her is Mordred. Without her, the magic that binds us together will slowly fade, and Avalon will slowly fall into the sea. It'll take years, but it will happen. It's just a matter of time."

Both Keane and Regan were shocked. They knew Mordred was depraved and despicable, but to kidnap the Lady of the Lake was unheard of, even for thieves. Keane carefully thought about everything that the Gil-Gamesh told them.

"I need time to confer with the other guilds to gain a consensus of my thieves. I'll tell you my answer by the end of the week," he said. Hunter simply nodded his head and stood to leave. "Regan will escort you out since you'll be without the benefit of the cloak."

Hunter stood up and extended his hand to Keane. The guildmaster paused before he stood up and shook his hand. "Thank you for listening to me," Hunter said. "Even if you don't join us, the cloak and oracle stones here are yours. At least this place will be safe for you."

Keane nodded as he motioned for Regan to escort Hunter out of the guild. She sheathed her daggers and walked briskly toward Hunter. "Follow me," she said in a huff. Hunter followed her closely, and Boots kept close to the Gil-Gamesh.

They walked through the many passageways of the underground guild. Seeing the Gil-Gamesh with the Shadowfoot caught much attention, but no one moved against him. If Regan was with him, he was there with the permission of the guildmaster.

Regan was silent the entire time, making Hunter somewhat uneasy and curious. "Are you always this talkative, or should I consider myself lucky?" he asked sarcastically.

"You're lucky I didn't rip your insides out when you revealed yourself," Regan snapped back.

"Well, if I knew the Guildmaster had such a beautiful second-in-command, I would have shown my face a lot sooner," he said coyly, trying to sweet-talk his way past her defenses, but it did not work on her.

Regan immediately drew one of her daggers as she spun around and placed it under his chin. "I'm also his daughter, so don't try your 'pillow talk' with me, *Casanova*. I know about your reputation, so your words mean nothing to me."

Hunter touched the dagger's tip and slowly pushed it away. "As I said before, don't believe everything you hear," he said with a smile, leaning in close. "Besides, if this were pillow talk, we wouldn't be doing much talking right now."

Regan blushed as she stepped back, but she stopped suddenly when she bumped into something. She turned around to see the Staff of Merlin poking her in the back. Ashley stared her down as she kept her eyes locked on Regan.

"I suggest you put away your dagger unless you want to take these negotiations to another level," the sorceress said firmly to intimidate the thief. Regan immediately lowered her dagger and sheathed it.

Hunter walked casually over to his sister. "Thank you for the escort, Regan Foley. I'm looking forward to our next meeting." The two turned and walked away, exiting the guild. Regan stood there captivated in the moment, her heart fluttering, but she wasn't sure if it was from the Gil-Gamesh or his sorceress sister.

Hunter smirked as they walked down the tunnel. Ashley laughed at her brother's obvious glee. "You get off on this whole *'Casanova'* thing, don't you?" she asked.

"When it helps, I do. Besides, she is kinda cute," Hunter said. Ashley shook her head before smacking him.

"Keep it in your pants, will you please?" she scolded as she opened a portal that took them back to Alfheimer.

CHAPTER 11
PRAYERS FOR THE LADY OF THE LAKE

The Shield Maidens of Avalon kept a constant vigil over Alfheimer, ever watchful for any enemies that dared to attack the ancient city. They formed the foundation for Avalon's new army, replacing the Knights of the Round Table after their demise during Avalon's Reclamation. Although they didn't have the knights' numbers, their ranks had slowly increased in the past five years.

With every victory over Mordred's forces and every island reclaimed under King Bowen's banner, more able, young, talented women flocked to join the legendary ranks of the shield maidens. While some joined the Gil-Gamesh's personal army, the Dragon Guard, others committed to the order.

They had gone from soldiers under the direction of the Knights of the Round Table to warriors on par with the knights. Every victory cemented their legacy, and yet, they found themselves lost.

News that the Lady of the Lake was missing reached Alfheimer in the following weeks. Upon hearing this revelation, the sisters found themselves distraught. All considered their patron saint to be the first shield maiden—she who armed King Arthur with the holy sword Excalibur. Her disappearance brought down their morale and left a hole in their hearts.

Since Avalon's Reclamation destroyed their convent, the order built a new one in Alfheimer. It was simply called the Temple of Our Lady. Inside this holy church, the pews were continuously filled with shield maidens praying for God's guidance and their safe return to Avalon.

Their pleas for divine intervention filled the air with great sadness and trepidation. The maidens could not help themselves. The sorrow inside the chapel grew with each passing minute as maidens visited day and night. Their prayers, songs, and adoration were non-stop, a constant reminder of their despair and the void left by the Lady of the Lake's disappearance.

Sarafina watched from the back, feeling completely helpless. As the Headmistress of the Shield Maidens, Dame Sarafina was both the head of their order and its spiritual leader. Her heart was also troubled about the Lady of the Lake's disappearance, and in that despair, she was unsure how to comfort them. She was having a crisis of faith, something she'd never dealt with before, a feeling of helplessness that threatened to overwhelm her.

"Are you troubled, Dame Sarafina?" came a voice from behind. She turned to see General McLoughlin, her arms crossed, standing at the entrance without her sword. Weapons were forbidden in the chapel, as it was considered an abomination to bring blood and battle into a place of love and forgiveness.

The tension between them was palpable, a silent battle of wills that threatened to disrupt this solemn moment. "Yes, General, I am troubled," she started. "My warriors are lost, and I have no words to comfort them. All I can do is guide them through their training or send them out on missions and try to push them past their grief. It seems heartless and cruel, like a taskmaster's whip, but I don't know any other way."

"You cannot be the taskmaster and the confessional priest, Sarafina," Rhona advised. "You must choose the path to put them on. As headmistress, you must be steadfast and strong, whichever you decide."

"But which path do I choose?" Sarafina cried. "It's a difficult choice I'm not prepared to make."

"As the former headmistress, the only advice I can give you is to believe in yourself, the divine maiden, and trust in God," Rhona comforted her. "Without our faith, we have nothing. You must give that hope to your sisters in the order."

As she looked across the chapel, Sarafina pondered on her words, watching the shield maidens postulate themselves before God. "It is hard for me to give hope while visions of despair torment my dreams."

"What do you mean? Have you been having visions?"

Sarafina took a deep breath. She kept her visions a secret, but it seemed this was the right opportunity to tell someone about them. "I see the Lady of the Lake wrapped in heavy chains. Her movement causes them to burn, bringing her unbearable pain."

A tear ran down her cheek. "I can't divine where she is. All I can do is share in the pain and suffering that torments her," Sarafina cried as she wiped the tears from her eyes.

Rhona stared in disbelief at what Sarafina told her, realizing it was more than bad dreams. She wrapped her arms around her protégé to comfort her. "It's alright, Sarafina. Believe it or not, it's a divine prophecy that these visions have appeared to you."

"Hear me, my sisters!" she shouted to the assembled. They all turned away from their prayers to listen to the general. "Our headmistress, Dame Sarafina, has been given the sight to our beloved Lady! She sees her suffering, locked in chains by her captors! She suffers as our sainted Lady suffers; she feels the pain our precious Lady endures! It's the sign we have been praying for because now we know she lives! We must help her—help them both—so our sainted Lady will be found and returned to us!"

The shield maidens rejoiced at the news as they all surrounded Sarafina for a chance to touch, bless, and give her their love and support. Instantly, their spirits were lifted, and their hearts rejoiced at the news. The Lady of the Lake was alive and reaching out to the order through the headmistress.

"Do not despair because of your visions, Sarafina," Rhona said to comfort her. "Your sisters are here for you, but we must tell the Gil-Gamesh and the others about the visions. It may help us in finding our sainted Lady."

Sarafina wiped the tears from her eyes as she left the temple with Rhona. The other shield maidens continued to reach out to touch the headmistress, hoping to give her comfort and receive a blessing in return. Once they departed the temple, the women resumed their prayers, but faith and love filled the air instead of fear and despair.

"What? Are you sure about that?" Ashley asked in utter shock. Sarafina's revelation was eye-opening to everyone gathered in the war room. The entire MoonDrake family was there with Rhona and Eileanora, except for King Bowen. "When did you start having these visions?"

"A few months ago," Sarafina explained. "It mostly happens in my sleep, but more so whenever I touch any of my warriors. The visions are brief, only for a moment, so it's hard to remember details."

"The Lady of the Lake must be reaching out through her connection with the shield maidens," Ashley said. "But, what are those chains? How can they be holding her captive?"

"They sound like the Chains of Tartarus," Eileanora interjected. "Legends say these were chains forged by Hephaestus to bind the Titans in Tartarus by turning their power back against them. The harder they struggle, the weaker they become."

"I'm amazed that she's even able to reach out," Hunter assessed. "It must be unbearable for her."

"At least we know she's alive, but what can we do? We still have no idea where they're holding her prisoner," Rose said.

"It may be possible to use Sarafina as a 'divining rod' of a sort," Ashley surmised. "We must commune with King Arthur to learn more about the Prometheus Engine. If we use Sarafina and Arthur's spirit together, we should be able to pinpoint her location. I'll need to confer with Grandmaster Baptiste, but it's our best chance to find her."

"And have we heard back from the Swann sisters yet?" Hunter asked Rhona.

"Yes, but I'm afraid it's not good news," Rhona began. "According to the sisters, Lord Tomas informed them that the Prometheus Engine is underneath Castle Pendragon. Mordred ordered them to dig a few new lower levels beneath the castle so those accursed gnomes could build his engine. That was all they could find out before Lord Tomas kicked them out of Eldonshire."

"What do you mean? Why were they kicked out?" Hunter asked.

"My apologies, Gil-Gamesh, I forgot to mention this earlier," Rhona explained. "After I gave the sword piece to Lord Tomas, he told the sisters they had to leave Eldonshire after the last harvest. I found them a new home in King's Crossing. They're helping Peter on his family farm and providing extra insurance that the Adalwulf Guard will stay out of there."

Hunter was upset at hearing this news, seething with anger. He paused for a minute to calm down before responding. "Damn him," Hunter said in a low voice through gritted teeth as he slammed his fist on the table. "I didn't think he would stoop this low. He has completely succumbed to Mordred's influence, hasn't he?"

"Don't let him get the best of you, Hunter," Ashley interjected. "Save that anger for another time. We'll deal with Tomas soon enough."

Hunter agreed with his sister's wisdom. He knew this was not the time to focus on the Lord of Eldonshire. His time would come.

"So, now that we know where the Prometheus Engine is, we must figure out how to destroy it. To do that, we need to find where they buried King Arthur," Rose added. "What has King Bowen said about that?"

"No one has asked the King yet," Bowen said as he walked in with his grandmother, Lady Stephanie. Everyone stopped and bowed in respect for him. Even though most were his family, he was treated with respect and honor due to his nobility. "What is it you need to know?"

"We need to know where they buried King Arthur, Your Majesty," Hunter inferred. "The Wizard's Council told us that only members of the House of Pendragon know of its location. Did Queen Cadhla pass this onto you before—" Hunter paused, not wanting to bring up painful memories for him and Bowen. "—before your mother died."

"Yes, father, she did, but I don't think it'll help us," Bowen started to say. "He was buried in the outside world, in a place called Glastonbury in Somerset, England."

"Glastonbury? But legends say the Lady of the Lake brought him to Avalon after Mordred killed him," Andrew inquired. "Why would he be buried in England?"

"My mother told me that the Lady of the Lake decided to leave King Arthur in the outside world so that no one on Avalon, especially Morgana le Fay, could use his remains for their evil purposes," Bowen explained. "His body was entrusted to monks to bury him there. After Guinevere died, she too was taken to Glastonbury and buried with the King."

"What? How is that possible? Queen Guinevere was the first ruler of Avalon. How can she be buried with King Arthur?" Sarafina asked.

"I'm sorry, father, but I don't know. Chamberlain Ocwyn never explained how she was taken to the outside world. He said he would show me one day, but until then, it was a secret."

"You mean there's been a way between Avalon and the outside world all this time?" Ashley asked. "Why didn't anybody tell us about it?"

"I've found that Avalon and its people love secrets," Lady Stephanie interjected. "The people here are experts at keeping them, especially Ocwyn."

"So, the only man who knows how to get from here to the outside world is in the one place we don't dare go?" Rose said. "Wait a minute, Hunter, I thought you explored all the secret passages in the castle when you were a squire there. Don't you know how to get in undetected?"

"Not really," he explained. "I explored the secret passages within the castle, but I don't know any that'll get you into the castle."

"So, we must find a way to get back to the outside world, but we don't know how to get into Castle Pendragon to discover it," Edan added.

"Oh, there's a way," came a voice from the shadows. He peeled back his hood to dispel the invisibility, revealing Keane Foley, Guildmaster of the Thieves Guild. Everyone drew their weapon and took a defensive stance, except for Hunter, who just grinned.

"It's about time you showed up," Hunter said sarcastically, "I was beginning to think you turned me down."

"Yeah, well, it was difficult convincing my guild to join your little resistance, but when I explained to them it was either that or be hunted down by the Adalwulf Guard, they finally relented."

"How in the world did you get on Alfheimer?" Eileanora asked. "No one may enter without my permission."

"It's one of the unique properties of the Cloak of Thieves that the former Gil-Gamesh wasn't aware of, Lady Eileanora," Foley explained. "While wearing it, I can bypass any magical detection or protection. With this on, I can walk virtually anywhere."

Eileanora grimaced at the thought of this thief walking right into Alfheimer. "I told you this was a bad idea," she scolded Hunter.

"If I remember correctly, you're among the few who agreed with my plan," Hunter retorted.

"That was before I knew his cloak could penetrate Alfheimer," Eileanora snapped at him.

"Relax, *Dubh Bhean*, I'm here as an ally, not an enemy," Keane said. Hunter motioned for everyone to relax their weapons. Slowly but surely, everyone did as the Gil-Gamesh asked.

"Besides that," Keane continued, "if you need to get into Castle Pendragon, I know every secret passage in and out of that place. I checked them out before Mordred put a price on my head in case I ever needed to get back in there."

"Can you get me to Ocwyn?" Hunter asked. Keane smiled back at him. Hunter was beginning to like this alliance more and more.

"The front door of his office or inside his bedroom? Take your pick."

"Well then, let's get started," Hunter said gleefully. "OK, so here's the plan. Foley will get us in to see Ocwyn. Once we find out how to get to the outside world, Ashley and I will take King Bowen and Sarafina to find Arthur's grave. Andrew, you, and Eileanora will come along to protect the portal, ensuring we get back. General, I will need you, Rose, and Edan to create a couple of diversions to keep Mordred and his Lords of Avalon busy while we slip in."

"Excuse me, Gil-Gamesh, but are you sure it's safe to take the King to New Camelot?" Rhona asked. "If Mordred gets his hands on him—"

"He won't do anything to harm me, General," Bowen interrupted. "It's the only way to keep Magister Ocwyn loyal to him. Besides, you can't commune with King Arthur without me. I have to go."

"I am aware of that fact, Your Majesty. I just want to express my concern for your safety," she said with a bow.

"Your concern is admirable, General, but this is something I must do," Bowen said. Hunter couldn't help but be proud of his son. Each day, he grew in strength, wisdom, and maturity and acted more like a king.

"OK, Keane, we'll meet you at the *Grinning Toad* tavern in a week," Hunter said. "From there, you'll take us into Castle Pendragon. Sound good?"

"Not a problem, Gil-Gamesh, that is, if you keep your end of the bargain," Foley said as he stepped up, staring Hunter in the face. "I need the rest of the Oracle stones you promised me for my guilds in New Camelot, Nottinghamshire, and Steinfisk."

"Absolutely. Ashley, can you please help our guest," Hunter asked his sister. "Send one of the Magus along to help him properly place the stones."

"Yes, of course, Hunter," Ashley said, slightly hesitant. "Please, follow me, Mr. Foley."

Keane bowed politely to the king before leaving with Ashley. Eileanora followed close behind, keeping a close eye on Keane. The others kept a close watch as he went. "I don't like it, Hunter," Rose said. "I don't trust him."

"Oh, I know, and he probably doesn't trust us either," Hunter replied. "But I would rather have him fight with us than against us. Besides, if I know Ashley and Eileanora, they're already working out ways to detect that cloak of his."

"You're becoming more and more like your father, Hunter," Stephanie complimented her son. "But don't get too cocky, young man. Arrogance will be your downfall. You must know when to act and when not to take chances. You, young man, still have a lot to learn. You're not there yet."

"For now, I'll get His Majesty ready to travel. I know you still have some planning, so we'll leave you to it." Stephanie left it at that and walked away with King Bowen. Everyone was in awe of Lady Stephanie's prowess as an advisor and mentor to her children.

"That woman could talk down an insane man from jumping off the edge of a cliff," Rhona said. "Dear God, what a queen she would make."

"She already is one, at least to us," Hunter added. "Now, about those diversions. Edan, I want you, Rose, and some of your pirates to raid the shipyards in Nottinghamshire. See if you can get your hands on a couple of their warships. Tell the pirates we'll split the ships stolen, 50/50. That should be incentive enough for them to take part."

"Indeed, it will, Gil-Gamesh. Excuse me while I put things in motion," Edan said with a tip of his hat as he departed.

"Now, Rhona, how about we take back a big part of Avalon for the King?" Hunter added.

Rhona liked this direction—a challenge for the shield maidens to prove their metal in battle. "What do you have in mind, Gil-Gamesh?"

"Eldonshire..." Hunter said. "I want it!"

CHAPTER 12
THE ROUND TABLE AND THE WAY TO STONEHENGE

Mordred stood on his balcony, sipped his wine, and looked across New Camelot. Castle Pendragon sat at the center, raised high above with the city sprawling before him. From here, Mordred could see and hear everything: The ships coming into the port from around the archipelago, the hustle and bustle of the merchants, and the songs and merriment from the homes and taverns. He hated it.

For over three thousand years, trapped in the dark abyss inside the Gil-Gamesh's sword, *Dusk*, the madness created by that eternal darkness nearly drove him insane. The endless void had stretched his mind to its limits. An average person would have succumbed to the emptiness, but not Mordred. He embraced it, forged the darkness into his soul, and strengthened his resolve.

He spent all that time in the dark void while the people of Avalon went on with their lives. They lived while he suffered, and he hated them for that. The King was without remorse, pity, or love for any of them. To him, the people of Avalon were cattle, and they were put on this world to serve him.

"Excuse me, Your Majesty," came a voice from behind. Mordred turned to see Magister Ocwyn standing behind him. Although an efficient administrator, he hated having Ocwyn around. He reminded Mordred of Avalon's past, especially with his ties to the MoonDrake family. Still, the binding spell he evoked with Ocwyn kept him loyal as a dog to the king.

"Yes, Magister, what is it?" Mordred asked as he took another sip of his wine, keeping his back to Ocwyn.

"Sire, some disturbing reports are coming out of Eldonshire. It seems—"

"Ocwyn, I don't care what those dirt farmers are doing on Eldonshire," Mordred interrupted. "That sniveling brat needs to learn to deal with problems himself."

"But, Your Majesty, the shield maidens are invading Eldonshire," Ocwyn said, interrupting the King. "The Adalwulf Guard has been overwhelmed. The reports are that the city has been lost, and they've captured Lord Tomas, but we haven't confirmed any of it yet."

Mordred said nothing. He stood there, letting his anger build inside until he exploded in rage. The King hurled his wine goblet, spilling wine everywhere as it rattled, bouncing across the balcony.

"Where are General Faust and the wraiths?" he screamed. "Why isn't the legion wiping out the shield maidens?"

"General Faust and most of the Wraith Legion are in Nottinghamshire," Ocwyn explained. "Pirates are raiding the shipyards there. General Faust thought it was best to take the Wraith Legion to try and stop them."

"I don't care about a few ships!" Mordred screamed. "If we lose Eldonshire, we lose the primary source of all the food in Avalon! Tell Faust to get the wraiths to Eldonshire immediately. Duke Nottingham will have to deal with the pirates on his own."

Mordred stormed away as Ocwyn followed close behind, trying to answer the King's orders while he continued to rant and rave. "What in the world are they thinking? Why are they invading Eldonshire?"

"Strategically, Your Majesty, it was inevitable," Ocwyn interjected. "The Gil-Gamesh saw Lord Tomas as we saw him: weak and vulnerable. Most of our forces deployed to protect major sources of wealth—New Camelot and South Essex. Nottinghamshire and Steinfisk have capable fighting forces protecting them, leaving Eldonshire vulnerable. We should have anticipated this, sire."

"Yes, YOU should have," Mordred shouted. "Those children will not outdo me. Have we heard anything remotely optimistic about retrieving the alchemist from Alfheimer?"

"Lady Mavis and Minister Blackstone have not reported anything new to me," Ocwyn said. "I will ask them to provide you with an update immediately, Your Majesty."

"The only update I want from them is that the alchemist is in hand, and the engine is complete and working," Mordred snapped back. "Have

Artūras meet me in the throne room. I want to speak with Faust immediately!"

Ocwyn bowed and left the King's side to carry out his orders. He hurried to find Blackstone, knowing that delay would only further anger the King. He quickened his pace, looking in all the familiar places for Minister Blackstone. His zeal led him on a wild goose chase until he finally found him. The wizard casually strolled with Lady Mavis and overlooked Ocwyn's urgency as he stormed toward them.

"There you are, Blackstone," Ocwyn clamored. "The King needs you in the throne room immediately!"

"Hmm? Did you say something, Magister?" the upstart sorcerer replied rather rudely.

"Take the wax out of your ears and pay attention!" Ocwyn snapped back. "The Gil-Gamesh and the shield maidens are invading Eldonshire, the shipyards at Nottinghamshire are under attack by pirates, and the King is anxiously awaiting an update from you on the alchemist. I suggest you get your head out of your ass and get to the throne room... Now!"

Blackstone and Mavis were shocked to hear Ocwyn speak that way, but they knew he wouldn't be talking to them like that if the King's need wasn't great. "Very well, Magister, I will attend to the King," Blackstone said quietly yet humbly.

Both he and Lady Mavis bowed politely before heading to the throne room. Ocwyn felt a surge of confidence, standing up to those two. He felt proud of himself when he spied a maid carrying a tea tray in the corner of his eye. Usually, a simple maid would never have garnered his attention, but there was something different about her.

He followed close behind, but he kept his distance discreetly. It surprised him when the maid entered his quarters. It was nowhere near teatime, and he never ordered anything from the kitchen. *Who is the tea for, and WHO is in my room?* He waited for a few moments, but the maid never left. That irritated Ocwyn even more, thinking this servant was alone in his room doing who knows what.

He rushed over to the door and pushed it open violently. "Now see here, young lady, what do you think you're doing in my room?" he shouted, but when he looked around the room, it was empty. His personal belongings were just as he left them that morning. There was no sign of the maid.

Without warning, Ocwyn felt two blades glide across his throat, one from each side. He could not see them or their wielders. "Don't make a sound, Magister, or it'll be the last thing you do," said an invisible voice. "Now, close the door behind you and lock it."

Ocwyn did as he was told without hesitation. Once he locked the door, the invisibility spell in the room was dispelled, allowing Ocwyn to see who his captors were. Keane Foley and Eileanora were holding the daggers directed at Ocwyn. Across from him stood Ashley, Andrew, and Hunter.

"Ash, make sure no one can hear us," Hunter demanded.

Ashley held out her staff and touched the ceiling with the crystals embedded in the branches. "*Silentium!*" she chanted as a wave of energy cascaded across the room, sealing them within a barrier of silence.

Ocwyn was amazed they could sneak in, but he was curious why. "I'm impressed that you're able to pull off multiple attacks across Avalon and sneak into the castle simultaneously, Hunter," Ocwyn said. He slipped his finger behind the two blades and slowly eased them away from his throat. "Although I don't think your father would approve of the company you keep."

"You're one to talk," Hunter snapped back. "I'll take a thief like Foley over Mordred any day, no offense, Keane."

"None taken, Gil-Gamesh. The feeling is mutual," the master thief added.

"So, if the attacks on Eldonshire and Nottinghamshire are diversions, your real mission is here," Ocwyn surmised. "So, it begs the question, why?"

"We need your help, Chamberlain," said King Bowen, standing off to the side with Sarafina. Ocwyn failed to notice him until now. His eyes widened as he saw the boy king for the first time in several years. He marveled at how much Bowen had changed in five years, but then his joy turned to anger.

"What the hell are you thinking, bringing him here!" Ocwyn scolded Hunter. "Didn't I teach you anything? You've just given King Mordred the victory he's been waiting for, delivering Bowen right into his hands! Do you know what I sacrificed to—"

"What you sacrificed?" Hunter shouted, grabbing him by the collar of his robe. "How about what my father sacrificed? Or what Amelia sacrificed, too? They died protecting Bowen, protecting Avalon. You turned your back on everyone who trusted and cared about you, and for what? To join the bastard who ordered my father's death and tens of thousands during the reclamation."

"What are you talking about?" Ocwyn asked. Eileanora grabbed onto Hunter to separate them while Keane held Ocwyn back.

"It's the reason we're here, Chamberlain," Ashley interrupted as she stepped between them. "Mordred kidnapped the Lady of the Lake and imprisoned her in the Chains of Tartarus. Without the Lady, the binding spell had nothing to tie it together. That's why Avalon shattered in the reclamation." Ocwyn couldn't believe it. Deep down, he knew the depths of Mordred's evil intent but never thought he would go that far.

"We need to commune with the spirit of King Arthur to divine her location," Hunter added. "King Bowen told us you know a way to the outside world, to Glastonbury, where they buried Arthur."

Ocwyn paused to understand everything they told him, but he could sense something more. "Why else are you here? Looking for the Prometheus Engine, perhaps?"

Hunter was impressed. As always, Ocwyn was one step ahead of him. "And what do you know about the Prometheus Engine? What is Mordred building it for?"

Ocwyn thought for a moment. As much as he wanted to tell them about the spy on Alfheimer looking for an alchemist, he couldn't take the chance of betraying Mordred, causing him to break the pact and endangering King Bowen's life. "For that, I am in the dark as much as you are," Ocwyn said. "No matter what you think, the King does not share all his secrets with me. I know where it's located in the castle, but Mordred placed powerful spells on the door to keep people out. You won't get in there easily, not before every guard and wraith are on top of you."

Hunter thought about what he said, looking at Ashley as if to confer silently. "So, Ocwyn, so about this portal? Where is it, and how did they take Queen Guinevere to the outside world after she died? How do we get to Glastonbury?"

"The portal is accessible through the round table," Ocwyn explained. "Shortly after King Arthur died, Merlin enchanted the table to connect Avalon to the outside world through ley-lines, the streams of magical energy that spread around the world. Those lines converge at Stonehenge."

"There was no mention of this in Merlin's writings," Ashley argued.

"Of course not," Ocwyn continued. "After he created the link, Merlin erased his memory of doing it. The royal family passed the knowledge through the royal line but never intended to use it again."

"I don't understand. Why create a portal to the outside world if you're not supposed to use it?" Sarafina asked.

"The portal uses the magical energy of the ley-lines to enable it to work, but without an abundance of magic to replenish the energy, the connection has weakened over time," Ocwyn continued. "Also, there's a time limit. Once you use it, you only have until sunrise the next day to return to Avalon. Either way, there's a chance that going to the outside world could end up being a one-way trip."

"Well, we don't have a choice," Hunter said. "We can get to the round table from here without being seen. I know a shortcut through one of the hidden passages."

"And what about him?" Andrew asked. "What do we do about Ocwyn?"

"I'll keep an eye on him," Foley said. "I'll ensure he stays put while you're off to this Glastonbury place. We'll be waiting here until you get back."

"Are you mad? If I am gone for that long, it'll raise Mordred's suspicions, not to mention that of Blackstone or Lady Mavis," Ocwyn screamed. "Then you will be trapped in the outside world or captured, for that matter."

"Foley, you follow Ocwyn around with the Cloak of Thieves,' Hunter said. "That way, you can watch him without anyone seeing you. Plus, you can warn Eileanora and Andrew if he should betray us."

Foley gave Hunter a nod to acknowledge the plan. Hunter turned and stepped toward the back wall in Ocwyn's room. He pushed one brick in before pulling another next to it out. A small door opened on the other side of the room with a click and a mechanical whir. Eileanora looked down the dark passages with her elven eyesight to see if any threats awaited them.

"It's all clear, Gil-Gamesh," she assured as, one by one, they stepped inside. Hunter waited until everyone was in the passageway before he entered it himself.

"Hunter, don't do this," Ocwyn pleaded. "You and the others may not come back. Is that worth the risk?"

He paused before turning back to face his former tutor. "Unlike you, Ocwyn, I have faith that my family and friends will see me through this." Hunter remained stoic as he closed the door, leaving Ocwyn behind.

The hidden passageways within Castle Pendragon were cramped, dark, and smelled like an old, musty cellar. Eileanora led the way, her near-perfect vision keeping a close eye on the path ahead. Hunter gave her step-by-step instructions on where to go. Within minutes, another secret door slid open, and they exited.

The room was bare except for the legendary round table. The table was more than thirty feet in diameter, with a stone tabletop forming a four-foot ring. A rune identifying each of the original twelve Knights of the Round Table emblazoned each section. Before Mordred, the king used it for magical communication between him and the Lords of Avalon. Mordred felt it was beneath the king to talk to others like this, so he had the room sealed off.

"Ashley, can you cast a protection spell around the room? I wouldn't want someone walking by and finding us in here."

"No problem," Ashley said. She stepped over to the outside door and placed her staff on it. "*Praesidio!*" she chanted before a wave of magical energy cascaded around the room.

While Ashley set the protective wards in place, everyone else walked around the table, looking quite confused as they studied the runes written on the table and the floor. "So, does anyone know how to activate it?" Hunter asked.

"Now you ask that question?" Ashley snapped as she joined in the search. "However, if Merlin enchanted the table, he should have etched a teleportation spell somewhere on it." Ashley walked around the perimeter, examining every inch. She looked on the floor in the center area of the table when she finally spotted what she was looking for. "Hunter, we need to be surrounded by the table in the center."

Hunter helped the King and Sarafina over the table before he climbed over himself. Ashley kissed Andrew goodbye before he assisted her over the outer ring and into the center with the others.

"Be careful," Andrew said. "We'll be waiting for you until your return."

"I don't know how long we'll have, but I don't think it'll be more than a few hours," Hunter said. "Anything more than six hours, and we're probably not coming back."

"Don't say that, Hunter," Eileanora chimed in. "You have to return! You all have to come back!" Everyone was surprised to hear Eileanora talk that way. They listened to the concern in her voice, a side of her she rarely showed.

Hunter appreciated her thoughtfulness now more than ever. "Don't worry, Elle. No matter what, we'll find a way back. Just stay in here and keep quiet. I wouldn't want anything happening to you either." Hunter winked at Eileanora, causing the elf to blush at his forward remark. "Let's go, Ash!"

Ashley walked around the inner circle, interpreting the runes carved into the floor before casting her spell. "*Alium se Orbem Terrarum, se Interim,*" she chanted. "*Suscipe me In Quo Magica Coeperunt!*"

"*Another world, another time, take me back to where the magic began!*" the spell resonated as she repeated it in English. The runes around the tabletop and the center of the floor began to glow brighter and brighter. After two times around, Ashley stopped and raised her staff in the air, pulling the magic back into her.

"*Ianuae Magicae!*" she shouted the final part of the spell as the four of them brightly glowed until they disappeared. The room went quiet as the magic faded upon the spell's completion. Andrew and Eileanora looked around at the emptiness.

"Now comes the hard part," Andrew said, "waiting!"

CHAPTER 13
KING ARTHUR AND GLASTONBURY TOR

Moving between worlds was different from anything the Gil-Gamesh or the others had felt before. It caused nausea and dizziness as their bodies were stretched, sorted, and rearranged until they suddenly stopped. When they finally opened their eyes, the blurred vision and haziness slowly faded until they finally saw where they were.

The teleportation brought them to the ancient site of Stonehenge. Sitting on a hilltop in Wiltshire, England, the ring of standing stones stood its ground for over five thousand years. The massive stone circle stood nearly thirteen feet high, and each one weighed more than twenty-five tons. No one knew who built the ancient structure—early humans, druids, aliens, or perhaps Merlin himself. In any case, Stonehenge stood as a symbol of ancient man's power and knowledge of magic.

"Stonehenge? We're in Stonehenge!" Ashley observed. "It would make sense that this is where the spell would take us. Stonehenge lies on the strongest ley-line in the world."

Hunter glanced about to get his bearings. He looked west, watching the sun drop lower and lower into the sky. "It's sunset," he said. "We have less than twelve hours to get to Glastonbury and back... Wait a minute, will magic work here?"

"Yes, Hunter. The Staff of Merlin keeps us connected to the magic of Avalon," Ashley said. "As long as you're with me, we'll be alright."

"OK, so where is Glastonbury from here?" Sarafina asked. Both Hunter and Ashley looked at each other with a blank stare. "You mean, you don't know?"

"Well, we've never been here before," Hunter explained. "But it should be easy to find someone with a cellphone to give us directions."

"And a ride," Ashley added.

"Hey! What are you doing here?" shouted a voice from a distance. The group turned to see a uniformed officer running toward them with a flashlight. The man appeared slightly overweight, wearing a security officer's uniform.

The officer stopped short of the inner ring, trying to catch his breath until he finally looked up at them. "The park is closed. You'll have to leave here right now," he said until he looked at their strange clothes. "Christ, how many times do I have to tell you damn 'cosplayers' to stay away from here!" Hunter and Ashley chuckled at the comparison.

"I'll take care of this," Ashley assured as she stepped toward the officer. Her staff began to glow softly in the dying light of dusk. "*Leporem!*" she said as her eyes shone like the staff. The officer stared at her, his eyes glazed over, as the spell began to take effect.

"I was hoping you could help us," she started to say. "Can you tell me how far it is to Glastonbury?"

The officer glazed over his eyes, charmed by her spell. "It's about fifty miles west of here," he said, stumbling with his words. "The easiest way to get there is via A361!"

"And, do you have a vehicle we could borrow?" Ashley asked. The enchanted officer reached into his pockets and handed her his key chain.

"It's a Range Rover, parked behind the visitor center," he added. "Just leave the keys in the car. I'll get it when my shift ends."

"Excellent, we should be back before sunrise," Ashely said. "In the meantime, continue your rounds, but don't tell anyone about us."

"Of course, I won't tell anyone," he muttered as the officer turned and left them. After he was gone, Ashley tossed the keys to Hunter.

"Let's go," she said with a sly smile.

"I hate to tell you, sis, but I don't think we should go dressed like this," Hunter said. "If he thought we were cosplayers, imagine what people on the road would think."

"What's a cosplayer?" Sarafina asked. Ashley and Hunter laughed.

"Maybe later, Sarafina. That will take a little more time to explain," Hunter joked.

"In the meantime, I'll take care of our attire," Ashley said before holding her staff out again. "*Novum Vestimenta Sua!*" She cast her spell, causing their clothes to transform from medieval armor, tunics, and robes to modern, everyday clothes.

Hunter wore a button-down shirt and jeans, while Bowen looked like a modern boy in basketball shorts and a t-shirt. Ashley converted her magical robes into capri pants and a crop top.

"What on earth am I wearing?" exclaimed Sarafina. She was staring at her clothes—a short skirt with a loose-fitting top—pulling her skirt and top out to examine them more closely. "Why is my skirt so short? Do women dress like this here?"

"Usually, yeah," Hunter exclaimed. "Besides, it looks good on you, Sarafina, but I wouldn't hold your skirt up like that."

"Huh? Why not?"

"I think Ashley forgot to give you underwear," Hunter said, causing Sarafina to blush as she pulled her skirt down quickly. Then she saw Bowen, whose face was as red as hers.

"Oh, Your Majesty, please forgive me," she said, embarrassed as she turned angrily toward Ashley. "Ashley!"

Ashley held her hands up, laughing. "Sorry, Sarafina, it was an honest mistake. I keep forgetting that you don't normally wear—"

"Ashley, that's enough!" Sarafina shouted as she tried to shut her up before embarrassing her even more.

Hunter laughed as he escorted Bowen away from the situation. "Why don't we start heading down the hill while the girls sort this out? Come on, Bowen!"

"Father, I'm confused," Bowen muttered. "What... How..."

"Bowen, this is not the time or place for that talk yet," Hunter assured him. "How about you file that away for now? We'll talk about that when we get back to Avalon. OK?"

Bowen nodded as he tried to get past the embarrassment at what he saw, especially from his aunt. Once the girls were situated, they joined them at the visitor center parking lot. They found the Range Rover, but once Hunter opened the door, he saw a problem.

"Hey Ash, I don't know how to drive a stick shift," Hunter said.

"Relax, Hunter; Andy taught me how to drive a stick," she said as she snatched the keys back from her brother. However, she made the mistake of opening the passenger side door, which is usually the driver's side in the U.S. but not Great Britain.

"Uh, why's the steering wheel on the wrong side?" Ashley asked.

"This is England, dummy. They drive on the left, not on the right," Hunter explained. "Are you sure you're up to this?"

Ashley closed the passenger side door and walked around toward Hunter. "Can you think of a better way to get to Glastonbury? We can't teleport because we've never been there nor have a line of sight."

"And flying would be way too conspicuous," Hunter interrupted. "I guess we'll have to be fast learners. Shotgun!"

Ashley shook her head in disbelief. Her brother was always a jokester and knew what to say to cheer her up, no matter how dire the situation. As much as she hated his constant joking, there were times when it was just what she needed to hear.

The four climbed into the SUV and headed west toward their target—Glastonbury Tor. This site has known myth, mystery, and religious fervor for over two millennia. At one time, the sea washed right up to the foot of Glastonbury Tor, nearly encircling the cluster of hills. Although it was considered a peninsula, the Tor would have looked like an island from most angles of approach, hence its old Celtic name, *Ynys-witrin*, or the Island of Glass.

The only remaining structure at the top of Glastonbury Tor was St. Michael's Church, an open-roofed stone tower. Legends say the entrance to the underworld lay beneath this tower, but that's not where they were going. Next to Glastonbury Tor resided Glastonbury Abbey, the final resting place of King Arthur and Queen Guinevere.

"But I thought the graves were just a ruse, a show put on by the abbey monks to King Henry II?" Ashley asked.

"It was considered a ruse, but actually, it was all true," Bowen explained. "My mother told me that the Lady of the Lake swore the monks to secrecy, but they were honor-bound to God and King to tell the truth. So, they did, but no one believed them."

"And after all that, the monks were considered charlatans, and the whole thing was chalked up as an old-fashioned publicity stunt," Hunter interjected. "The truth is, Arthur and Guinevere were there all the time. It's said to be one of the top tourist destinations in Britain."

"It seems we're not the only ones headed for Glastonbury," Sarafina noticed as she pointed out the window. "Many of these motorized carriages are heading to the Tor too."

The traffic was getting heavier the closer they got to Glastonbury. Ashley then realized what was going on. "A music festival, it must be the Glastonbury Music Festival."

"A music festival?" Bowen asked.

"It's a big festival lasting five days," Ashley said. "Andrew and I were going to see it before we returned to Avalon. Some of the best bands in the world play at the festival."

"It sounds exciting," Sarafina added. "I wish we had time to listen to music."

"I don't think it's your kind of music, Sarafina," Hunter replied. "Here, maybe there's an example on the radio." Hunter turned on the car's radio and began looking for a station. He found one playing the *Foo Fighters*. The rock n' roll beat was an intense stream of rhythm, from the soaring guitars to the powerful drumbeat. Ashley and Hunter rocked their heads to the melodic beat, but Bowen and Sarafina looked at each other, confused.

"This is music?" Sarafina asked as she held her ears, cringing at what she thought was noise. Bowen was also plugging his ears with his fingers, shaking his head.

"Well, I guess it's an acquired taste," Hunter said as he turned down the radio. "Not something you'd hear in a local tavern back on Avalon, is it?"

"No, definitely not," Sarafina answered. "It sounds like a cat after its tail got caught under a rocking chair."

They rode on quietly for the next few miles. While a drive like this was regular for Ashley and Hunter, it was a new experience for Bowen and Sarafina. They looked out the window, eyeing the billboards, the road signs, and the countryside itself. This was an adventure into a new world, but it raised even more questions for them.

"Ashley, what is significant about this place, Glastonbury?" Sarafina asked. "What relationship does it have to Avalon?"

"Well, at one time, many people thought Glastonbury Tor was Avalon," Ashley replied. "Long ago, the sea was closer inland, and it made the hill look like an island, so many people thought it was Avalon or the entrance to Avalon." She loved to talk about ancient history to people. At times like this, she could tap into all her schooling and talk about the things she loved besides magic.

"Is that why people thought of Avalon as more of a legend than a real place?" Bowen interjected.

"Yes... Avalon, elves, dwarves, and dragons were considered myths after Avalon disappeared behind the barrier," Ashley said.

"I think that's what made the Outlander War so important to the people of the outside world," Hunter added. "It meant the stories were true."

"Why is that so important?" Sarafina inquired.

"Stories about myths and legends are part of our history," Ashley said. "Most of the time, you can just read about them or visit some ancient ruins that may or may not represent what they were. The good thing is that we know the truth.

"In Merlin's library, I found a notation he made about visiting the outside world around the 14th century," she continued. "He met a writer named Thomas Malory and sat down with him, spinning the tales of King Arthur, the Knights of the Round Table, and of course, he didn't leave himself out. That led Malory to publish '*Le Morte d'Arthur*' or King Arthur and the Legends of the Round Table. It was from that book that King Arthur's story came from."

"So, Merlin started the legends himself. Is that what you're saying, Ashley?" Hunter interrupted. "Geez, that old man had his hands in everything, didn't he?"

"More than he let on, that's for sure," Ashley replied. "I didn't know him very long, but Merlin was extraordinary. We owe him a lot more than we give him credit for."

"I think you're right, Aunt Ashley, and when I regain the throne, I will make sure he gets the recognition he deserves," Bowen said.

"I appreciate it, Your Majesty, but Merlin was never one for the limelight."

"Still, he does deserve recognition for his efforts. Maybe a statue or a monument in New Camelot," the King pondered.

"I think the pigeons would love it more than Merlin," Hunter joked. They all had a good laugh. It was the first time they felt relaxed in the past few weeks. It made the rest of the ride a lot easier.

Within an hour, they reached Glastonbury and worked their way to the abbey. The small town was busy as the music festival revilers filled the streets and the local pubs. They were a loud and raucous group of people, something they did have in common with the people in Avalon's taverns.

Hunter noticed a "No Parking" sign as they entered the abbey parking lot. "They must have done this to keep the festival-goers from using their parking lot," Hunter noticed as he exited the car. "I sure hope we don't get towed while exploring here."

"Towed father?" Bowen asked.

"It means the authorities take the car for being parked illegally," he explained.

"Don't worry, I can take care of that," Ashely said, looking around to see if anyone was watching. She waved her hand, and the staff appeared in it. "*Invisibus!*" she chanted as a wave of magical energy sparkled from the glowing crystals at the tips. Like glowing fairy dust, they enveloped the car until the vehicle disappeared.

The four of them went to the graveyard next to the abbey. There, they found a marker indicating the grave of King Arthur and Queen Guinevere. Ashley walked up to it and began to read it aloud:

"*In the year 1191, the bodies of King Arthur and his Queen were said to have been found on the south side of the Lady Chapel. On 19 April 1278, their remains were removed in the presence of King Edward I and Queen Eleanor to a black marble tomb on this site. This tomb survived until the dissolution of the abbey in 1539.*"

"Wait, does that mean they're not here? Then, where are they?" Hunter asked.

"I don't know. The only place I discovered in my research was here. I'm guessing that, since no one ever came back here since Merlin visited in the 1400s, no one ever thought they would move the tomb," Ashley explained.

"Since they found the graves in the Lady Chapel, maybe we should check there," Hunter interjected.

"Agreed, but this may help," Ashley said as she transformed into her magician's robes. She reached inside her robe and pulled out a golden skull hanging on the end of three chains. "The Talisman of Yahowah can detect spirits through the creation fire that's contained inside," Ashley explained. "Give me a moment."

Ashley began to chant in an ancient tongue unknown to even those who use magic daily. The eyes on the skull smoldered until flames flickered out of the openings in the eye sockets. The fire danced around the talisman as Ashley continued to chant. The fire flew away, leaving a trail toward the abbey's ruins.

"This way," Ashley said as she led them after the blazing trail. They made their way down into the Lady Chapel inside the old abbey. They had to be extremely careful as they entered the crumbling structure. Once inside, they watched the flames dancing over one corner of the chapel. Ashley knew they had finally found the last resting place of King Arthur.

"Let's get you three properly dressed to meet the King," Ashley said. "*Novum Vestimenta Sua!*" she cast, transforming their clothes back into medieval garments and armor.

"What do we need to do, Ashley?" Hunter asked.

"Bowen and Sarafina, place your hands on me and concentrate on the image you seek... King Arthur and the Lady of the Lake. That should open the door for us to commune with the spirits."

She extinguished the Talisman of Yahowah and put it away. Ashley reached into her robe again, but she pulled out an oil lamp hanging from a chain this time.

"*Saint Nicholas of Tolentino, light the lamps. Saint Christopher, light the lamps. With the Lord of the Heavenly Hosts' permission, we make a safe and sacred space that we may traffic with the honored dead. Beloved Saint Nicholas of Tolentino, shepherd my guides and helping spirits to this place so we may speak to our beloved King, Arthur Pendragon.*"

Ashley stood in silence as the lamp lit all on its own. The lamp grew brighter and brighter as wisps of light came from everywhere, filling the chapel with a beautiful glow of holy light. Like faeries on the moors, the lights danced around them until the spirit lights came together and began forming into the shape of a human being.

"Hey! What're doing down there?" shouted a voice from above. Hunter turned to see a security guard peering down at them. The guard started to make his way down into the abbey ruins.

"Keep going, Ashley. I'll take care of this," Hunter told his sister as he quickly moved to intercept the guard. He was an older man, probably in his fifties, stumbling about in the dark. His hat fell off his gray, balding head, and he dropped his flashlight as he struggled. Hunter quickly picked up the flashlight and returned it to the guard while pointing his GunStar at him. The terrified security guard took the flashlight as he raised his hands.

"Don't shoot, please. I only get paid a minimum wage!" he pleaded.

"I'm not going to shoot you if you listen to me carefully," Hunter commanded. "Now, stand over here and don't say another word. We'll be out of here soon enough."

"What the hell are you doing down here anyway?" the old man asked as he moved to where Hunter directed him.

"That's a little hard to explain," Hunter said.

"What kind of a gun is that? Are you funning with me, son?" the old man asked. Hunter pointed his GunStar at the wall and pulled the trigger. A billowing cloud of icy fog shot out, freezing the stone into solid ice. The security guard became completely terrified and raised his hands even higher.

"What's your name?" Hunter asked.

"It's Henry, Henry McLoughlin," he said, his voice quivering from fear.

Hunter laughed, hearing that his last name was the same as Rhona. "I know a six-foot, blonde amazon named McLoughlin. Any relation?" Hunter asked sarcastically.

"No, sir, well... maybe on my mother's side," Henry answered.

"Just relax, Henry. As I said, I'm not going to hurt you," Hunter said as he returned to the summoning. The spirit lights continued to form until they started to look more like two people.

"Who... What... What are you doing?" Henry stuttered.

"We're trying to reach the spirits of King Arthur and Queen Guinevere," Hunter told him, knowing that the truth may be hard to accept, but it was better than lying.

"King Arthur? Wait, are you from Avalon? That island that appeared and then disappeared?" Henry asked.

Hunter nodded his head. "Just stay back, Henry. It's a matter of life and death, OK?" The security guard fumbled with his flashlight, almost dropping it before turning it off.

When the summoning was complete, the spirits of King Arthur and Queen Guinevere hovered in the air before them. King Arthur was a handsome, regal man with flowing brown hair and a neatly trimmed beard. He wore a gleaming suit of full plate mail armor. A tunic bearing his coat of arms—three golden crowns emblazoned on blue—flowed across his chest. A regal red cape hung off his shoulders, and a golden crown sat on his head.

Queen Guinevere was as beautiful as the day she met the king. Her blonde hair was neatly pinned underneath a golden crown. She wore a flowing, white dress with golden embroidery. Across her chest, a red sash emblazoned with the Pendragon coat of arms hung from her shoulder to her waist.

The four of them immediately dropped to their knees, a gesture of profound reverence to the first monarchs of Avalon. They gazed at their subjects before looking at Henry. The security guard, caught by surprise, immediately followed suit, dropping to his knees like the others. He kept his head down, too afraid to look up.

"Arise and tell us your names," King Arthur commanded. Still in awe of the royal spirits before them, the four of them stood up one by one to introduce themselves, all except for Henry.

"Your Majesties, I am Ashley Drake-St. Johns, apprentice to Merlin the Magician, Sorceress Magnate of Avalon," Ashley started.

"Dame Sarafina Thomas, Your Majesties, Headmistress of the Holy Order of Shield Maidens."

"Sir Hunter MoonDrake, Your Majesties, Gil-Gamesh and Knight Eternal of Avalon," Hunter said. Bowen remained silent as he tried to collect himself. Hunter looked down at his son, who looked up at his father, unsure of himself. Hunter nodded his head and smiled, giving him some needed encouragement.

"Your Majesty, I am King Bowen Gregory Bartholomew Pendragon of Avalon," he said as he tried to stand tall before his ancestor.

King Arthur and Guinevere looked at the last one in the room with them, waiting for an answer. Henry continued to kneel, face down.

"Henry, stand up," Hunter whispered to him. The frightened security guard looked up at the glowing visages of Britain's ancient king and queen. He slowly got to his feet, still fumbling with his flashlight.

"I'm, uh, well, you see... I'm Henry McLoughlin, Your Majesties, Security Guard for the Glastonbury Abbey," he muttered.

"You're not from Avalon?" King Arthur asked.

Henry looked confused by his question. "Uh, well... No, I'm from Horrington, Your Majesty."

"I see. So, you must guard and protect this holy place?" Queen Guinevere asked. Henry nodded his head, completely lost for words. "Then you have our thanks and our gratitude, Henry McLoughlin. You may remain in our presence."

The praise from Queen Guinevere's spirit made Henry feel good, so he smiled and bowed his head again to the ancient monarchs.

"King Bowen Pendragon, it does gladden my heart to see that the line of Pendragon is secure, but it also bodes the question as to why you are here?" King Arthur asked.

Bowen took a deep breath before answering. "Your Majesties, I'm afraid I have come in dire times. Mordred has usurped the throne of Avalon."

They were utterly shocked to hear this news, though it was King Arthur who was seething with anger. "How is that possible, Gil-Gamesh?" Guinevere asked. "Your ancestor, Sir Percival, killed Mordred more than 3,000 years ago?"

"Not exactly, Your Highness," Hunter began. He explained everything about the return of Morgana le Fay and the Dark Tides, the destruction of the Twin Swords of the Dragon Moon, the reformation of Excalibur, Avalon's return to the outside world, and its reclamation.

They could see the anger rising in King Arthur. All he fought and died for had been lost to his bastard son. However, he remained stoic and steadfast. "This is troubling news, but I fail to see how we can help you, Sir Hunter?" he retorted.

"Mordred is trying to build something called the Prometheus Engine, Your Majesty," Bowen interjected. That name sent a shockwave through the monarchs.

"That is impossible!" King Arthur shouted. "I destroyed everything about that infernal device. Why Merlin himself burned countless pages from his library to rid the world of that knowledge."

"Nevertheless, Your Majesties, something about the machine survived, and Mordred found it," Hunter added. "He's attempting to build it, but we don't know what it is or can do."

"The Prometheus Engine was a machine designed by Atlantis' great alchemists," King Arthur began. "That infernal mechanism destroyed their island thousands of years ago. The engine is capable of creating Promethium."

"Promethium? I'm a Silver Sage Alchemist, Sire, and I've never heard of it," Hunter interjected.

"Nor would you," the king snapped back. "The knowledge of Promethium is dangerous for everyone involved. If Mordred makes one tiny mistake, it could destroy all of Avalon.

"You see, Promethium is from the beginning of creation, the 'Spark of Eternity' if you will," King Arthur continued. "In simplest terms,

Promethium is a material created from the beginning of the universe. It is the most potent element ever made.

"The great blacksmiths forged Promethium into the first magic items: The Golden Armor of the Lady of the Lake, the Aegis Shield, the spear Gungnir, even Excalibur itself," he concluded.

They were all stunned by this revelation. "My God, it would make Mordred invincible," Hunter exclaimed. "Nothing could stop him."

"The only good tidings I can give you is this... You need an Atlantian alchemist to decipher any of the instructions for the Prometheus Engine," King Arthur added. "Without one, recreating the formula to fuel the engine would be nearly impossible."

"Oh, my God!" Hunter exclaimed. "Julianna!"

"What?" Ashley asked. "What about Julianna?"

"Her family is of Atlantian descent," Hunter explained. "She's the alchemist they're after, not Ollie! If they can get to her, Mordred would be able to finish his damn machine."

"But they can't enter Alfheimer; there's no way to reach her unless—" Ashley pondered until Hunter interrupted her.

"Unless they placed a spy with the prisoners we liberated from *Ür Tár*," Hunter exclaimed. "We have to get home immediately!"

"Then you must make haste, Gil-Gamesh," Guinevere said. "You must protect the Atlantian and destroy that machine."

"Your Majesties, there's one more thing," Sarafina interjected as she stepped forward. "Before the reclamation, Mordred captured our Blessed Lady of the Lake. He imprisoned her in the Chains of Tartarus. However, we don't know where he has taken her. We were hoping—"

"We were hoping to use you and Sarafina as a beacon to try to find her, Your Grace," Ashley interjected. "She has been having visions of the Lady in utter agony." Once again, the news devastated the two spirits. The Lady of the Lake, the very soul of Avalon, was gone.

"I knew Mordred was capable of many things, but this is beyond the pale of his evil," King Arthur said. "Do what you must, sorceress. We have no objections."

Ashley motioned for Sarafina to step forward. She stepped up to the spirit of King Arthur and held out her hand. The King laid his hand on hers, and Ashley placed hers over the two of them. With her other hand, she raised her staff into the air.

"*Quaerite et Invenietis*... Viviane, Lady of the Lake!" she chanted. Her staff glowed as wisps of magical energy flowed around them like a swirling tornado. The magical vortex started to flow upward into the sky until it began to bend, heading toward the north.

"Where is that pointing to?" Hunter asked.

"It's heading north, toward Glastonbury Tor and the Tower of St. Michael," Henry commented as he strained to follow the magical trail.

"But why, father? Why is it pointing there?" Bowen asked.

"Well, you see, legend says that Glastonbury Tor is the entrance to the underworld," Henry said. When Hunter heard that, he knew where it was heading.

"To Purgatory," Hunter exclaimed. "Faust commands the Wraith Legion of Purgatory for Mordred. Since he controls them, it makes sense that he would hide the Lady of the Lake there as his prisoner."

"Yes! I see her!" Sarafina cried out. "She's in pain! So much pain!"

"Oh, my Lady!" King Arthur shouted. "What have they done to you?"

The image of the Lady of the Lake, wrapped in heavy chains, filled their minds and souls. They could see and feel her tortured existence, imprisoned in purgatory. As she struggled against the chains, it inflicted even more pain and suffering.

The spell ended, releasing the three of them from their visions. Even the spirit of King Arthur was disconcerted by the torment she endured. Hunter helped his sisters as they regained their composure.

"Damn him!" King Arthur shouted. "Damn you, Mordred, for this blasphemy!" Guinevere reached out to comfort him and quiet his rage. When he was right with himself, Guinevere turned her attention to Sarafina.

"Dame Sarafina, as patron of the Holy Order of Shield Maidens, I charge you with the task of returning our blessed Lady to Avalon," she said. "You are honor-bound to release our Sainted Lady from her captivity."

The images of the Lady of the Lake imprisoned in Purgatory hardened Sarafina's resolve. She placed her fist over her heart and bowed her head to Queen Guinevere. "I promise, Your Majesty, I will return the Sainted Lady to her rightful place in Avalon. *Dues Vult!*"

Her last words were the shield maidens' battle cry, meaning "God Wills It," accepting the command from her patron. "Your sword is my sword," Guinevere added. "Use it as a beacon to find your way across the Wretched Wasteland of Purgatory. It will lead you to the Sainted Lady."

Sarafina placed her hand on the hilt and drew her sword until the golden blade shone bright, even in the dim light. The grip resembled angel wings with a halo—as the guard—encircling it. The *Gilded Queen* was passed down through the millennia to all the Headmistresses of the Shield Maidens Order. It was the same sword Queen Guinevere used during her reign in Avalon.

"Take this with you as well, Headmistress," King Arthur said as he handed her a crystal orb. The ball flowed like water and glowed brightly from deep within. "When you find the Lady of the Lake, you will know what to do with it." Sarafina took the orb from the King and bowed.

"Thank you, Your Majesty. I will!"

The King turned his attention to King Bowen and the Gil-Gamesh. "Gil-Gamesh, I have one final charge for you," he started to say. "When you kill my bastard son, let him know that I will see him again, and we will battle once more, and he will die again and again by my hand."

The monarch's spirits began to fade as their time on this earthly plane ended. "May your journey's end be the start of a new beginning," King Arthur said. "Fare thee well, Bowen Pendragon, my great-grandson. For such a young boy, you already have the courage and the heart of a king.

"I look forward to the day when we meet again," he concluded as they all bowed one last time. Even Henry reciprocated as the ghostly visages of King Arthur and Queen Guinevere faded from sight. The Lady Chapel fell into darkness again, only lit by the magical light from Ashley's staff.

"Ashley, teleport us to Glastonbury Tor immediately. I must make haste to Purgatory!" Sarafina said.

"Wait, you're not going there alone," Hunter said. "We can find our way to Purgatory once we return to Avalon and assemble an assault team."

"No, Hunter, the entrance is here in Glastonbury. I must go now. This is my mission and mine alone," Sarafina asserted with unwavering determination. "Queen Guinevere entrusted me with this task, and I am bound to fulfill her command."

"No, I won't let you go in there alone," Hunter snapped back.

"This is not your decision to make, Gil-Gamesh. Brother or no brother, I must do this on my own," Sarafina said, fighting back.

"Ashley, tell her she can't do this," Hunter said, hoping his sister would help dissuade Sarafina from this suicide mission.

Ashley thought for a minute as she looked at both Hunter and Sarafina. She saw the resolve in Sarafina's eyes. "Sorry, Hunter, but she's right," Ashley concurred. "She has to do this, but when you find the Lady, find a way to let me know, and we'll send you some reinforcements."

Sarafina was glad to hear her sister's vote of confidence. She reached out and hugged her. Hunter reluctantly gave in and hugged Sarafina, too.

"All right, we'll get you there and back you up when you need it," Hunter said. "OK, Ash, teleport us to the tower."

Ashley raised her staff and was about to teleport them when she remembered that the security guard was still with them. "I'm sorry, Henry. Do you need me to teleport you out of the ruins?"

"Oh no, miss, I'll be just fine," he said. "I'm not really up for teleporting, not that I know what that is. I'll just climb out of here. Don't you worry none about me."

King Bowen walked over to Henry and reached into a small pouch on his belt, pulling out some gold coins. "Here, Master Henry, a reward for your service," he said, handing them to him. Henry looked at the gold coins in disbelief.

"Is this real gold?" he asked. Bowen just nodded his head. Henry was thrilled, thinking about how much money these coins would bring him.

"Thank you, thank you, uh... Your Majesty!" he exclaimed. "I can finally retire and take care of my wife. Thank you. Thank you very much!" He bowed to the boy king, which made Bowen very happy. Hunter reached out and shook his hand.

"I think it's best if you don't tell anyone about what you saw here tonight, OK, Henry?"

"Oh, don't you worry about that. I doubt anyone would believe me anyway!"

Hunter stepped back to rejoin the others. Ashley and Sarafina politely bowed to Henry as the sorceress raised her staff. "*Migro-transit Glastonbury Tor*!" she chanted as the four of them disappeared, leaving Henry a happy man in the dark.

CHAPTER 14
THE SPY IN ALFHEIMER

Inside Castle Pendragon, Andrew and Eileanora waited patiently but were very antsy. Andrew sat quietly, his feet propped up, staring at the center of the table, waiting for his wife and the others to return. Eileanora stood near the door, listening for anyone approaching the room.

"How long have they been gone?" Andrew asked.

"Four hours, twenty-nine minutes, and forty-five seconds," Eileanora replied. "Ten minutes since the last time you asked me."

"If I knew waiting would be like this, I would have gone with them instead," Andrew remarked.

"As would I, Andrew, but we must protect this portal until they return. Mordred could destroy the table, trapping them in the outside world forever."

"I know, I know, I just hate all this waiting—" Andrew started to say before Eileanora shushed him.

"Sh-hh... Someone's coming," she whispered. She leaned against the door to listen. She could hear tiny footsteps coming down the stairs just outside the door. At the same time, she overheard many grumblings from what sounded like a gnome. As she listened more closely, she recognized the voice from the hallway. "Broadfoot... Master Tinker Edwyn Broadfoot!"

She had pursued that lecherous little gnome before, and the fact that he got away from her repeatedly still irked Eileanora. No one escaped from the *Dubh Bhean*. She waited until he passed, and his voice began to fade.

"I need to follow him and see where he's going. Wait here," she said before searching through her pouch.

"Wait a minute, Eileanora, you can't go out there like this. That's not part of the plan!" Andrew argued with her as quietly as he could, but Eileanora was having none of it.

"He could lead us to the Prometheus Engine. I'm the only one with the stealth to do it," Eileanora declared, her determination shining through. "Stay here and keep an eye out. I shouldn't be too long."

She pulled out her chameleon stone and rubbed it between her fingers. The rainbow-colored rock was a smooth, shimmering jewel that shined even in the darkness. "*Mutátio e' Vanescet!*" She whispered to the stone as her body vanished. The light bent around her, granting near-flawless invisibility.

She snuck out the door, ensuring no one was around before she descended the stairs. Elves were relatively light on their feet, making them exceptional at stalking. Eileanora could hear Broadfoot still grumbling up ahead, stomping his little feet down the stairs.

"What the hell does he want from me? If I can't make it work, I can't make it work, but if I don't, he'll kill me like the others." The gnome's grumblings continued as Eileanora moved in closer. She stalked him down the stairs to a seamless iron door. She watched as the little gnome put his hand on the door and cast a spell to open it. As the door slid open, blue smoke poured out of the room.

Luckily for Master Tinker, his small stature kept him below the smoke. However, Eileanora caught the brunt of the noxious fumes. She knelt on the steps to try and catch her breath. The acrid smoke burned her lungs as she breathed it in. Eileanora swallowed hard, trying to stifle a cough tickling her throat. She knew she would never make it into the room as the smoke would reveal her form along with any coughing. The door stayed open to clear the smoke, so she got as close as possible to listen in. Eileanora could hear Edwyn shouting at one of the other gnomes.

"What the hell happened? Are you trying to kill us all?"

"I'm sorry, Master Tinker Broadfoot, I was trying a variation on the formula using red algae instead of brown. I thought that since they're common to the Cyprus region, maybe that's where we went wrong with our calculations."

"You idiot, how many times have I told you—" As Edwyn scolded his apprentice, Eileanora peered around the corner to see things for herself. She saw the massive Prometheus Engine—a complex assortment of pipes, boilers, gears, and gauges—being worked on religiously by the gnomes. Master Tinker Broadfoot was off to one side of the room with a few other gnomes standing next to a table filled with breakers, bottles, and flasks. The blue smoke billowed out of a large flask sitting over a flame.

"We're never going to get this right if we don't get that alchemist to help us," one of his assistants said. "When will that 'Beasley' fellow bring us the Atlantian from Alfheimer?"

Eileanora was shocked to hear them talk so casually about Hunter's friend Ollie that way. "How am I supposed to know," Edwyn replied. "Minister Blackstone doesn't tell me anything. They are waiting for Beasley to signal that he has the alchemist in hand. Once she's ours, we can get this baby working at 100%!"

Eileanora's shock turned to anger. Beasley was a spy for Mordred, and they were after another alchemist—an Atlantian—in Alfheimer, but the only other alchemist in the ancient city was Julianna. *Could she be an Atlantian?* Eileanora never spoke with her at length. She knew Hunter would be devastated when he learned about his friend's betrayal.

We must get back to Alfheimer immediately! Eileanora started to move back up the stairs but suddenly stopped. If she could destroy the plans, the formula, and the engine, here and now, it would save them the trouble of coming back to destroy it. Plus, these gnomes were not much of a challenge for her.

Eileanora slowly made her way into the room. She did not want to draw her sword immediately as *Fire Dance*'s blue flame would dispel her invisibility. She needed to get the lay of the land before she attacked, so she hugged the wall tightly. She moved next to the laboratory table near Master Tinker and his assistant. They had a variety of notes and plans scattered across the table. However, one page of ancient parchment caught her eye.

Discolored and deteriorating, she could not understand the language written on it. It had to be the Atlantian formula for the Prometheus Engine. Without it, Mordred would be unable to activate the power of the infernal machine.

She wrapped her hand around her sword hilt, ready to draw and strike swiftly. "Broadfoot! What the Hell is going on!" came a disembodied voice from the doorway. Eileanora turned to see Mordred, Blackstone, and Lady Mavis enter the room. Mordred was furious, and the other two were not very happy either. "There is smoke filling up every room of the castle!"

As much as she wanted to drive her sword through Mordred's black heart, she didn't know if it would work against the dark magic that protected him. She was also afraid that Blackstone or Lady Mavis might detect her presence.

"I'm sorry, Your Majesty, but my apprentice was attempting a variation of the formula, and I'm afraid it backfired on him," Edwyn explained. "I didn't know or approve of his little excursion."

Mordred fumed as the three covered their faces to try and filter out the noxious fumes. "I told you to stop any more attempts!" Mordred screamed as he grabbed the scroll with the formula. "Your continued failures will only cause damage to the engine or me! Now, clean this mess up!"

Mordred spun around and left as quickly as he arrived, as Blackstone followed behind. Lady Mavis paused momentarily, her lip quivering as if she could taste something in the air before she turned and followed the king.

As soon as they were gone, Eileanora decided it was best not to wait any longer and headed back toward the room with the round table. Hopefully, the Gil-Gamesh and the others had returned from the outside world, but she dreaded telling Hunter his best friend had betrayed him.

The tower of St. Michael was the lone structure at the top of the hill known as Glastonbury Tor. Built in the 15th century from local sandstone, it ascended 518 feet above sea level over what legends say was a labyrinth leading down to the underworld.

This story brought Gil-Gamesh and the others to the top of the hill. When they teleported into the open interior of the tower, it was empty. Ashley immediately began to look for signs of the entrance to the underworld. Lit by the glow of her staff, she examined every stone inside the tower.

"Sarafina, I don't mean to nag, but are you sure about this?" Hunter continued to plead with his adopted sister as he helped Ashley with her search. "Purgatory is full of wraiths and demons. It's suicide to go down there on your own."

"I know it is, brother, but I must do as my patron asked. Queen Guinevere was key to me going down there on my own. There must be a reason for that. Her faith is more than enough for me. I can, and I must rescue the Sainted Lady!"

"We know you can do it, Aunt Sarafina," King Bowen interjected. "We're just worried about your safety."

"Thank you, Your Majesty. Your concern is always appreciated. But this is something I must do on my own. Once I find the Lady of the Lake, I will contact you to help us escape to Avalon."

"Here it is!" Ashley shouted once she found a rune carved on a single stone on the floor of the tower. It looked like the letter "M" to anyone looking at it. "This is the Norse rune *Ehwaz*. It means transportation."

"What is a Viking rune doing in a Christian church?" Hunter asked.

"I found one here, Aunt Ashley," Bowen said, pointing to another rune carved on the floor. That one looked like the letter "R" to him. "I believe it's *Raidho*, meaning a journey."

"Excellent, Your Majesty," Ashley remarked. "Now, there should be one more to complete the spell—"

"I found it," Hunter exclaimed. "It looks like a 'Y' with a line through it... Like an upside-down peace sign."

"It's *Algiz*, but that means protection. What is that doing here?" Ashley asked.

"I believe it also means taboo, a warning," Sarafina said. "That must be the last one."

"Sarafina, you stand in the middle of the three runes," Ashley instructed. "Hunter, King Bowen, stand over the runes and repeat after me... *Aperiam in Porta Purgatory*!"

Before they started, Hunter approached his adopted sister and hugged her tightly. "We believe in you, Sarafina. Come back to us with the Sainted Lady!"

Tears welled up in their eyes as Hunter kissed her on the cheek. Ashley also hugged and kissed her sister before reaching inside her robe. "Here, take these with you," she said before Ashley pulled out a brown cloak and a simple leather sack. "This is the Cloak of the Hermit and the Cornucopia Sack. Merlin used them when he wandered around Avalon. The cloak doesn't grant you invisibility, but it affects the perception of others around you. The sack has an unlimited supply of bread and water. It's not much, but it'll keep you from starving to death down there."

Sarafina removed her headmistress coat, handing it to Hunter while she put on the cloak and slung the sack across her shoulder. "Thank you, Ashley. These will help me in my quest. I will find a way to signal you once I find the Sainted Lady."

"You better," Ashley said as they stepped away from her. Sarafina bowed to the King one last time. Bowen wanted to reach out and hug his aunt, but he knew he must maintain his composure. It was part of being a king.

The three began to chant, *"Aperiam in Porta Purgatory!"* As they chanted incessantly, the runes started to glow as the doorway opened. Magical lines connected the runes, formed a triangle, and then into a pentagram. The spell grew in strength as cascading energy surrounded Sarafina until she disappeared. Her journey into purgatory had begun.

Once the magic faded, sadness fell over the three of them. Hunter went over and comforted his son. "It's going to be alright, Bowen. Sarafina is strong. She'll return the Lady of the Lake, and we'll bring them home."

"It's not that, father. It's just so hard for me to see all of you—my family and friends—sacrificing so much for me, and all I can do is watch," Bowen remarked.

Hunter knelt next to him, putting himself at eye level with Bowen. "But that's not all you're doing, Bowen. You're more than that to all of us; you're the idea of what Avalon should be," Hunter explained. "Your grandfather once told me about the four tenets of a knight of Avalon—Faith, Family, King, and Country.

"He said, 'You must love, protect, and fight for God, your family, your king, and your country. If you cannot dedicate yourself to all four of these tenets, then you cannot be true to your heart, mind, and soul.' That's what it means to be a knight of Avalon."

"I don't understand what you're trying to tell me, Father."

"Your Majesty, YOU are one of those tenets. We fight because we believe in what you stand for... A free and peaceful Avalon. We can't achieve that goal without our King. So, we will stand and fight, no matter what the cost.

"We... No, I have faith in you, Bowen," Hunter concluded as he saw a smile come to his son's face. The boy-king understood what they expected of him and the task ahead.

"I understand, father. Thank you. I know what I have to do now." Bowen hugged his father, grateful for the words he needed to hear. Hunter was proud of his son, now more than ever. He was growing up to be the king that Avalon needed.

"I hate to break this up, but we need to get going," Ashley said. "We still have to drive back to Stonehenge."

The three started walking down the hill and back to the parking lot, where they had left the car. Ashley did not bother with the disguises this time. Fortunately, they blended in easily with all the revelers from the music festival, so nothing seemed out of place to the average onlooker.

The ride back was uneventful and quiet as the three tried to absorb everything they had learned from this trip and its meaning. "Hunter," Ashley started, "I've been thinking about this possible spy. Even if they could get Julianna, how would they get off Alfheimer with her?"

"I've been thinking about that, too," Hunter replied. "Eileanora and I discovered a small section on the north side, just outside the barrier. It's an outcropping of rocks you can get to if you jump from the shoreline—rock-to-rock-to-rock."

"OK, but who knows about it?" Ashley asked.

"Only me, Eileanora, Rhona, and I told Rose so she could have the dragons patrol it occasionally, and—" Hunter paused momentarily. Something terrible just crossed his mind. He tried to understand, but it was hard to comprehend.

"What is it, Hunter?" Ashley asked.

"Father, what's wrong?" Bowen interjected.

"Ollie, I also told Ollie about it, too," Hunter stuttered. "I was just thinking that if Ollie was never the intended target of Mordred, then why were we told they were looking for him? Unless—"

"Unless they wanted us to find him and bring him to Alfheimer because it was the only way to get him inside the barrier," Ashley interrupted. "Hunter, do you think Ollie could be the spy?"

"I wish he weren't, but it's the only thing that makes sense. With everything going on, no one in Alfheimer can stop him from taking Julianna."

"But Ollie? He's been your closest friend since you came to Avalon. Why would he do this?"

"I wish I knew, Ash. Jealousy, revenge, or maybe he's under Mavis' control, it doesn't matter. Friend or no friend, we must stop him from taking Julianna to Mordred."

"I just hope we're not too late," Ashley concluded.

Andrew kept a nervous watch outside the room. He had double the anxiety between Eileanora's search for the Prometheus Engine and waiting for Ashley and the others to return from the outside world. His wife told him not to let his nerves get the best of him, but he could not help it in such a situation. They were deep within enemy territory with an ever-changing exit strategy.

It made Andrew even more nervous when Mordred, Blackstone, and Lady Mavis stormed past, heading in the same direction as Eileanora. He knew that the *Dubh Bhean* could take care of herself, but he could not help but worry. No additional guards or wraiths passed by, so he knew everything was OK, at least for now.

Andrew heard a buzzing sound, like a machine starting up. He turned around to see the floor at the center of the round table begin to glow.

"Oh, thank God," he sighed as relief overcame him. The center glowed brighter and brighter until three figures began to emerge from the light. Seeing only three caused Andrew to become worried again. *Oh no, what happened?* he thought to himself.

Ashley, Hunter, and King Bowen stood in the circle when the magical light finally faded. They had made it back to Avalon, but that left Andrew confused. *What happened to Sarafina?*

Once the gateway closed, the three travelers shook out the cobwebs and cleared their heads from the interdimensional transport. Andrew rushed over and helped Ashley across the table, giving her a passionate hug and a kiss once she was in his arms again. He was thankful that his wife had made it back to him.

"Thank God you're safe, but where's Sarafina?" Andrew asked.

"We'll tell you about it on our way back to Alfheimer," Hunter said as he helped Bowen across the table. "Wait, where's Eileanora?"

"Following Edwyn Broadfoot," Andrew explained. "The little gnome walked past us, mumbling something about Mordred and the alchemist, so she followed him, hoping he'd lead her to the Prometheus Engine."

"Is she crazy? She can't go off half-cocked like that," Hunter argued. "Why didn't you stop her?"

"Hunter, in what universe do you think I could stop Eileanora?" Andrew snapped back.

"OK, point taken. How long has she been gone?" Hunter asked.

"About forty-five minutes, give or take. Shortly after she left, a noxious blue smoke drifted up the stairs from the lower dungeon. She must have found where they kept the engine, and then Mordred and his lackeys suddenly stormed past."

The fact that Mordred walked by caught them by surprise. "Wait; what?" Hunter started to ask, but then he heard someone outside the stairwell. Everyone quickly quieted down and listened as they got closer.

"Your Majesty, I think Master Tinker Broadfoot has outlived his usefulness," Blackstone said to the King.

"Do you know anyone else who could get the Prometheus Engine working, Minister?" Mordred asked, followed by silence from Blackstone. "I thought not. He will continue to be valuable until he gets the engine working. After that, we shall see.

"However, YOU will surely outlive YOUR usefulness if you don't bring me that damn alchemist from Alfheimer!" He stopped outside the door to discipline Blackstone. The Minister of Magic took the King at his word as he nervously tried to answer him.

"This is not an easy task, Your Highness. He recently learned of a breach in the shield that we can use to our advantage. With all the ongoing attacks, this is the perfect opportunity to grab the alchemist and bring her here." His explanation satisfied Mordred, but barely, as the king let him continue his rant.

"Lady Mavis and I are waiting patiently to hear something from Beasley," he concluded. Hearing that name confirmed Hunter's worst fear. His friend had betrayed him.

"If that woman isn't here by the end of the week, I'll send you down to purgatory to become the Lady of the Lake's new caretaker," Mordred retorted. "You can consider it a permanent reassignment!" The King spun on his heels, leaving them behind as his anger fumed. The two remained quiet until he was out of sight before speaking.

"We cannot fail at this, Lady Mavis, or it's our heads," Blackstone cried.

"Your head, Artūras, not mine," Mavis jested as she walked past him. "I convinced your man Beasley to betray his friend. The rest was up to you."

Blackstone huffed in disgust, grinding his teeth angrily as if King Mordred and Lady Mavis had cast him aside. He started to mumble to himself again as he stormed up the stairs. Hunter breathed a sigh of relief, thankful they were not discovered.

"What do we do now, father?" Bowen asked.

"We wait for Eileanora. She shouldn't be far behind if Mordred and the others have already left the lower dungeons."

"The longer we stay in one place, the more likely we'll be found," Andrew surmised.

"I don't care! We're not leaving here without her!"

"Your concern is appreciated, Gil-Gamesh, but unnecessary," a voice rang out behind them. Eileanora dispelled her invisibility as she entered the room. "I'm relieved to see you all made it back... Wait, where is Dame Sarafina?"

"On her way to purgatory to rescue the Lady of the Lake," Hunter added. "I'll explain details on the way back to Alfheimer, but we must get going now."

"Hunter, there's something you need to know first about your friend, Oliver Beasley," Eileanora said.

"I know, Elle. We figured it out after we talked to King Arthur. They're after Julianna. Ollie's the spy, though I don't know what could make him turn?"

"Oh, that was easy!" came a voice from the door as it swung open. Lady Mavis stood there as a contingent of the Adalwulf Guard stormed in, weapons drawn. Mavis grinned at the thought of her reward for bringing the Gil-Gamesh and his family to Mordred.

"I sensed your presence downstairs, Eileanora. I fear the *Dubh Bhean* is losing her touch," Mavis gloated.

"Why don't you come over here, Mavis, and I'll show you my touch!" Eileanora shouted.

"Do you think you and a few Adalwulf scumbags can stop us, Mavis?" Hunter wondered.

"Oh, we don't need to stop you, Gil-Gamesh. Any second now, the alarm will sound, and you will have no choice but to surrender, and you, dear Bowen, will make King Mordred very happy," Mavis said as she gloated. "You'll get to watch the execution of your family as you take your place at the side of His Majesty."

"I will never side with Mordred. I'd rather die!" Bowen screamed back at her.

"I've had enough of this!" Ashley snapped back as she slammed her staff to the ground. Without warning, a wave of magical energy cascaded out, slamming the Adalwulf Guard into the walls and ceiling. Mavis protected herself but was not fast enough to see Eileanora charging at her. Before she knew it, Mavis received a sharp blow to the head from the hilt of her blade, rendering her unconscious.

Hunter stepped over the unconscious guards next to Eileanora. "You left her alive? You have changed, Elle."

"Not at all, Gil-Gamesh. As much as I would love to rip her heart out, killing her might trigger a warning to Mordred and delay our escape. It was a practical decision."

"It was a smart decision on your part, Lady Eileanora," said Ocwyn as he moved down the stairs toward them. "Her death thrall would have reached the King almost immediately." As Ocwyn carefully stepped over the guards, Foley peeled back his cloak.

"I haven't been seen or heard the entire time I've been here," he snarked. "You're back but a few minutes, and everyone knows it. Damn bloody amateurs!"

"Very funny! Does anyone else know she discovered us?" Hunter asked.

"No, I think she was trying to take all the credit herself," Foley observed. "But, we need to leave now before more come running."

"Let's get back into the hidden passageways. We've got no time to waste," Hunter said.

"What about him?" Foley asked, pointing toward Ocwyn.

"Leave him alone. I'm sure he'll be able to talk his way out of this," Hunter quipped as everyone left Ocwyn behind without saying another word. Even King Bowen gave his former advisor a sad look as he left him behind. Ocwyn's heart sank when he realized that all was for naught. He had lost the boy king forever.

He heard a slight whimper as Lady Mavis was beginning to regain her senses. Ocwyn walked over and reached down to help her to her feet. "Take it slowly, milady. You've had a terrible blow to the head."

"What? No, where are they?" she cried, looking for the Gil-Gamesh, Bowen, and the others.

"Where is who, Lady Mavis?" Ocwyn queried. "I heard a loud noise from down here, and I found you and the Adalwulf Guard sprawled out. Who did this to you?"

"You know damn well who it was!" Mavis shouted, accusing Ocwyn. "The Gil-Gamesh and his brat were here? Where did they go?"

"I have no idea, Lady Mavis. As I said, I came down to find you unconscious. Since I haven't been down here in quite a while, I wasn't sure what I'd find."

"You're lying through your teeth, Magister!" she snapped at him, wagging her finger in his face. "When the king finds out—"

"When the king finds out that you tried to capture the Gil-Gamesh on your own and then let him escape—instead of alerting the guard—you will be the one who will have to answer to Mordred, Lady Mavis, not I," Ocwyn scoffed back at her. "I suggest you think about that before you accuse me of anything."

Mavis thought about it for a minute, and unfortunately, Ocwyn was right. Accusing him of something she has no proof of would only make her failure stand out even more. In the king's eyes, she would seem desperate. At this moment, Mavis would have to relent and bide her time.

"For now, I suggest you make sure these guards don't tell the king or anyone else their story about how you failed to capture the Gil-Gamesh. I'm sure you'll come up with something," Ocwyn imparted before he headed back up the stairs.

Mavis fumed with anger toward Ocwyn. She knew that one day, she would bring that pompous ass down. The more pressing matter was dealing with the Adalwulf Guard and making them forget what happened here. *A simple memory charm should do it. No one can resist me.*

She looked into the room with the round table and cautiously stepped inside. Curiosity got the best of her as she examined the table closely. *What were they doing in here?* She wondered curiously as the mystery deepened.

CHAPTER 15
THE ALCHEMIST AND THE ENGINE

Henri Beauchamp ran recklessly through the streets of Alfheimer, excusing himself and greeting people as politely as he could as he made his way to the hospital. It was unusual to everyone who saw him. He had received an urgent message from the Gil-Gamesh to find and protect Julianna Bonapat and arrest Oliver Beasley. Henri was shocked to learn the young alchemist was a spy for Mordred. He had always acted like a perfect gentleman and an excellent friend to Hunter.

In such a situation, Henri usually relied on the Dragon Guard or shield maidens to help him. But with the simultaneous campaigns and missions across Avalon, no one was readily available. Hunter was counting on Henri to complete this task, and he was never one to disappoint.

The hospital was always near capacity, with an influx of prisoners, refugees, and others escaping Mordred's reign. It had plenty of room to care for patients, provide privacy for examinations, conduct operations if necessary, and a suitable laboratory area for Julianna to work on medicines and other elixirs.

Henri charged into the hospital as he slowed down to catch his breath. He quickly scanned the area, searching for Julianna or Oliver among the patients and staff scattered about the courtyard and open rooms. He walked over to one of the many nurses assisting in the clinic.

"*Pardonne-moi madamoiselle*, where is Madame Julianna?" he asked.

"She's back in her laboratory with Mr. Beasley," the nurse answered politely. Henri rushed back towards the lab, worried that he was already too late.

Without knocking, Henri stormed into the room, where he was confronted with his worst fear. Oliver held a lifeless Julianna in his arms. He had a small bowl billowing green smoke under her head. Henri could see she was unconscious and immediately drew his rapier.

"Release her, *traitre!*" he threatened, "*ton complot diabolique* is over!"

"I'm sorry, Henri... Truly, I am, but I must do as my mistress commands." Oliver threw the bowl at Henri. With the speed of his blade, he slashed it in half with ease, causing the contents to disperse and fill the air. Henri coughed uncontrollably as the noxious fumes engulfed his head. When he finally opened his eyes again, Oliver and Julianna were gone.

Henri turned around to chase after them, but he was surprised to see Oliver standing right behind him. He held a GunStar and placed it directly over Henri's heart.

He whispered something as he pulled the trigger. A freezing mist exploded out of the barrel. At this close range, the frost had nowhere to go. Instead, it went straight through Henri's chest and froze his heart into a ball of ice. He dropped his sword and clutched his chest as he fell back. As the pain shot through him, his body convulsed uncontrollably as the blood flow suddenly stopped. It was sheer torture for Henri. He could do nothing but slowly die.

"*Pardonne-moi*, Gil-Gamesh," he gasped, struggling to regret his failure, "*Je t'ai échoué...*" The Frenchman's last sight was Oliver leaving with Julianna slumped over his shoulder. He feared nothing could stop Beasley from escaping with her.

"Henri!" He heard a voice calling his name. Henri barely opened his eyes to see Lady Stephanie running toward him. "Henri, what happened to you?" she said as she knelt beside him.

"*Pardon*, Madame Stephanie, but I could not stop him," he sputtered. "Beasley took Julianna—he is *le traître!*"

Stephanie could not believe it as she touched Henri's chest and felt the frozen mass beneath her fingertips. "Henri! Henri!" she shouted. "Don't you dare die on me, you... French fop! Don't you dare! We need you here with us! I need you, Henri!"

Henri smiled when he heard her say that to him. "It is nice to know you care for me, *chère Madame*," he gasped. "I always knew you did, *au revoir...*"

The cries of Lady Stephanie echoed around the hospital as others rushed over to help, but it was too late. Henri Beauchamp, another close friend of her late husband, died at the hands of one of Mordred's minions. She cried uncontrollably, but her tears turned to anger toward a man her family risked their lives to save. She looked around until she saw two shield maidens rushing in.

"Find Oliver Beasley!" she commanded. "Get everyone looking for him! He's a spy for Mordred! Hurry!"

No one hesitated at Lady Stephanie's orders. Immediately, they scoured the city looking for the traitor as word spread fast throughout Alfheimer of Henri's murder. Everyone started looking for Oliver in all the wrong places.

They thought he would slip out on one of the airships docked down by the warehouses. No one knew about the rock outcroppings in the north corner of Alfheimer. After Hunter told him about it, Oliver found the quickest, most straightforward way to get there without being detected. He practiced it for days, ensuring he could get there without raising any alarms.

Oliver carried Julianna on his shoulder as he crossed the rocks. Standing on the last one, he laid her down at his feet. Oliver reached into his pocket and pulled a jeweled locket on a gold chain. The locket had no clasp, just a tiny ruby stone inset on the front. Oliver kissed the ruby before he laid it in his open palm. He heard a faint "click" as it opened to reveal a picture of Lady Mavis hidden inside. Oliver brought it close to his lips and whispered into it, causing the locket to glow slightly. He clutched it in his hand, looking at the sky as if waiting for a sign or something to happen.

He smiled, thinking that he would see his love soon, but the roar of a dragon made his smile disappear.

"Oliver!" Rose shouted as she landed with Dee Dee near the shoreline. She returned to Alfheimer after their successful raid on the Nottinghamshire shipyards when she heard what had happened. She knew where Oliver was going.

The dragon roared again as they inched closer toward him. "Move away from Julianna, Ollie! It's over!"

"No! I won't! I must do this for milady!" he screamed at her.

"No, Ollie, you're wrong! Mavis seduced you with her magic. She made you turn against your friends!"

"No, you're wrong! She loves me!" Oliver shouted. "It's you and your family that abandoned me! You left me to rot in prison. I was beaten, tortured, and persecuted just for being Hunter's friend, but Lady Mavis took care of me! She healed me and brought me back from the brink. She loves me, and I will do anything for her."

Rose could not believe how obsessed Oliver was. He was so different from the man she knew as Hunter's best friend. She had no choice but to take him down. "You're out of your mind, Oliver. So, I'm going to knock some sense into it," she said as she patted Dee Dee on the side. The dragon instinctively knew what she wanted her to do.

Dee Dee spun around and whipped her tail at Oliver. It smacked him hard, throwing him off the rock and into the stone wall off the beachhead. Oliver dropped the locket on Julianna's unconscious body as the dragon tossed him aside. The jolt stunned him. He grasped his body in pain as he landed on his feet, leaning back against the wall.

Rose repositioned Dee Dee to face him. "Surrender, Ollie! Don't make me kill you!" she shouted. Before Oliver could say anything, a magical glow appeared over Julianna. Artūras Blackstone appeared out of nowhere, standing over her unconscious body. He quickly assessed the situation and acted fast. He smiled wickedly, reaching down to put his hand on Julianna.

"*Migro-transit, New Camelot!*" His chant activated as he quickly teleported away with his unconscious captive.

"No! Don't leave me here! I must return to my love!" Oliver shouted before they faded away. His despair turned to anger as he stared down Rose and Dee Dee, drawing his GunStar. "You! You ruined everything!"

He fired his weapon, sending a fireball at Dee Dee, but the dragon and Rose were immune to its effects. All he did was irritate Dee Dee and anger Rose for losing Julianna to Mordred.

"Burn him, girl!" she commanded. Dee Dee inhaled and breathed dragonfire at Oliver. He screamed in agony, engulfed in flames before falling away to nothing. All that remained was a burned shadow on the wall of rock.

Rose looked across the water but knew it was already too late. "Dammit!" she muttered under her breath. "Dammit all to Hell."

Two Adalwulf Guards carried the unconscious body of Julianna Bonapat. They brought her into the gnome's workshop, followed close behind by Blackstone. Mordred's Minister of Magic was as giddy as a child, overjoyed at his accomplishment.

The guards laid her down on the floor next to the laboratory table. Blackstone shooed the guards away as he knelt next to her. He placed his hand over her eyes. "*Evigilare Faciatis!*" A wave of luminescent, magical energy cascaded through her body. Julianna slowly regained consciousness. She raised herself on her elbows and rubbed her head to relieve the pain and fuzziness.

"What? Where am I?" she muttered, rubbing her eyes. When her vision finally cleared, a lump filled her throat, and fear raced down her spine. She saw gnomes standing around her, Adalwulf Guard and Artūras Blackstone. Her mind tried to recall everything that had happened to her.

She remembered working with Oliver when he placed a mixture of the Kava Kava plant, the Valerian flower, and lavender beside her. They used that combination to help the patients sleep at night, but he did something to the mixture, causing it to billow and smoke. Before she could do anything, she passed out. The next thing Julianna knew, she was here. *But where was it?*

She looked around the room, and that's when she saw the massive engine. Gnomes were scrambling around it like bees on a beehive. She instantly knew what it was, something from her childhood memories. Her parents would tell her stories to scare her from ever thinking about creating such a beast. It was the Prometheus Engine.

"Welcome to New Camelot, my dear Julianna Bonapat," Blackstone said, greeting her with a sly, monotone voice. "We've been waiting for you!"

Julianna slowly got to her feet, leaning on the table for support. She looked down at the ancient parchment and recognized the Atlantian language written across the pages. Her fears grew worse once she realized why she was there.

"We have a great need for your alchemical expertise and linguistic skill in ancient Atlantian," Blackstone continued as he tried to seduce her into cooperating.

"No!" Julianna muttered. "I won't help you! I'd rather die!"

"No, no, that won't do," Blackstone replied. "We know you may not care about your own life, but what about that of your husband?"

"What? What do you mean? What about Allain?"

"We knew that you would probably be unwilling to help us on your own, so Mr. Beasley had an idea on how to get your cooperation," Blackstone explained. "While you were away at Strongürd Keep, he gave your husband a uniquely engineered form of hemlock. He told me he used a specific inhibitor to slow down the symptoms of the deadly herb so that no one would know who poisoned him until it was too late."

Julianna stood there, stunned into silence. She knew that Oliver was quite capable of producing such a poison. Unless she knew which inhibitor he used, she could not know how long she had to administer an antidote before Allain succumbed to the poison. Hemlock was easy to cure but deadly if left to run its course.

"So, if you cooperate and provide us with the proper formula for the engine, we will gladly let you go so you can save your husband, but time is ticking, my dear," Blackstone concluded. Julianna tried to reason through everything Blackstone told her. She knew they would probably kill her, but she had to take a chance to save her husband.

"I want guarantees that I will be allowed to save my husband if I cooperate," Julianna insisted.

"Of course, I guarantee everything. You have my word," Blackstone coerced.

"No, not from you—from Mordred. I will do everything you ask as long as HE guarantees I can return to Alfheimer and save my husband."

Blackstone was infuriated that this woman would not take his word on this, and the last thing he wanted to do was disturb King Mordred with this matter. "You have my word, dear lady," came a voice from behind. They turned to see King Mordred and Lady Mavis entering the laboratory. Everyone bowed to their monarch, save for Julianna.

"You have my word as King of Avalon that you will be allowed to return to Alfheimer and save your husband as long as the formula you provide works in the engine."

Julianna looked Mordred straight in the eyes. She had no reason to trust him, yet deep down inside, she hoped he had some semblance of integrity. "Where are you getting your supplies from?" Julianna asked.

The King turned to Master Tinker Broadfoot, giving the little gnome a nod and a push to answer her question. "Uh, well, we've been sourcing through Schiff's Alchemy Shop."

"Schiff? No wonder you haven't got this thing working. That cheat waters down his elixirs and cuts his reagents with gypsum to make a bigger profit," Julianna explained. This news angered Mordred and Blackstone, who leered at the gnome for his incompetence.

"Is Maliofrich's still in business?" she asked.

"Uh, yeah, I believe it is," Edwyn answered.

"Then send someone there to pick up the ingredients," Julianna said as she started looking over the pages of Atlantian text. "It'll take me a couple of hours to decipher this, so have someone ready to go as soon as it's finished. Now, if you'll excuse me, I have work to do."

She turned away from her captors to concentrate on the work at hand. Mordred smiled as he stepped away, Mavis and Blackstone following the king. "What happened to the alchemist Beasley?" Mordred asked.

"When I arrived, he was fighting with the Gil-Gamesh's sister and her dragon," Blackstone explained. "We can assume he is no longer a viable asset."

"It's a shame. My charms so easily coerced the boy's heart," Mavis added. "Beasley could have accomplished much more for you, Your Majesty."

"He fulfilled his duties brilliantly, Lady Mavis," Mordred interjected. "Soon, the engine will be complete, and we will have the Promethium. We will be one step closer to total domination of Avalon and the end of the Gil-Gamesh and the Pendragon line forever!"

"And what about the attack on Eldonshire, Majesty? Lord Tomas is asking for reinforcements," Mavis inquired.

Mordred thought about it for a minute as he watched Julianna working diligently on deciphering the documents. "Let him be. We will take back Eldonshire soon enough. Besides, maybe this lesson will toughen that little brat up."

"Just out of curiosity, Your Majesty, will you allow her to return to Alfheimer when she completes the formula?" Blackstone asked.

"Of course, Artūras, I gave her my word. After all, she should be with the one she loves before they are utterly destroyed."

Etheldreda was the cultural center of Eldonshire. It was the smallest of Avalon's four major cities and the heart of agriculture for the entire archipelago. Many of the scattered islands had small farms. Still, much of the food that fed all of Avalon grew here—agriculture, livestock, feed, and grain production centered on the capital of Eldonshire, but Elethedra was burning.

War arrived in Eldonshire when the shield maidens laid siege on these lands. Their main objective was to eliminate the Adalwulf Guard and capture Lord Tomas. They did all they could to protect the farms, livestock, and people from harm. However, such was not the case for the retreating Adalwulf Guard. The cowards burned entire fields as they retreated from the shield maiden's offensive, hoping to give themselves a chance at escape.

As the shield maidens rounded up the Adalwulf Guard's remnants, they assisted the locals in putting out the fires and saving as many crops as possible. While they struggled to keep Eldonshire from burning away, the remaining Adalwulf blockaded themselves inside the Elderson castle, *Wohlstand*.

Wohlstand, which meant *prosperity*, was a castle of beauty and refinement. The Elderson family spent years collecting priceless art, tapestries, furniture, and trinkets to adorn the castle interior. Tomas often considered it a museum more than a home, but he kept it the same way. It reminded him of his past, something he destroyed to get here.

Lord Tomas was frantic, terrified at what was happening around him. "What are we going to do? They'll break through soon enough! Why haven't we received word from New Camelot? Surely, King Mordred wouldn't let Eldonshire fall to the Gil-Gamesh?"

"I don't know, milord. We received reports that the shipyards at Nottinghamshire were being attacked at the same time as Eldonshire," Lord Marshal Heydrich said as he placed his men defensively around the room. "If that's the case, the King probably decided ships were more important than cabbage."

"He may regret that when he's eating rotten vegetables and spoiled meat in a month or two," Tomas ranted. He cursed Mordred and others under his breath. It was not just that they considered him and the rest of Eldonshire second rate to Jaeger's shipyard, but to leave him to the Gil-Gamesh and the shield maidens showed how little they cared.

"How many men do you have left here with us, Heydrich? Is it enough to fend off a siege?" Tomas inquired.

"About fifty or so, placed at crucial access points around the castle, Lord Tomas," Heydrich relayed. "They won't be getting in here anytime soon, milord. We can hold them off until reinforcements arrive from Nottinghamshire and—"

Before he could finish his sentence, the main doors to the interior room exploded as a dragon-form of magical energy burst through. When the dust cleared, Lothar stood at the door with his dragon lance. As the Lord

Marshal and his Adalwulf Guard prepared for a counterattack, shield maidens stormed past the Magus.

"What are the Magus doing here?" Heydrich exclaimed. "They're supposed to be at Strongürd Keep, not with the Gil-Gamesh?" Before anyone could answer his question, the shield maidens charged.

The female furies fought with tremendous resolve, pushing back the ill-trained and ill-equipped warriors' feeble attempts. Lord Tomas cowered behind Heydrich, who was briefly able to hold them off. His skill with a saber was evident as he parried and thrust back against the onslaught to protect his charge.

A sudden sound frightened the pair. It was the howl of a wolf, like a chilling song that turned their blood into ice water. A massive werewolf leaped over the shield maidens from out of nowhere. It landed on Heydrich, knocking him and Tomas to the ground. The beast was huge—more than seven feet tall and over three hundred pounds—covered in reddish-brown fur, wearing only a pentagram around its neck. Conner Iain Collins let out a deafening howl, using his druidic magic to summon a pair of frost wolves by his side. The icy spirits sprinted through the castle, hunting down the other guards scattered about.

The feral beast growled as its massive weight held both men to the ground. The snarling lycanthrope bared its teeth, drool dripping from its fangs, and looked quite menacing to the two captives. As the shield maidens captured or killed the remaining Adalwulf Guard, the werewolf slowly backed off as Lord Marshal Heydrich and Lord Tomas were brought to their feet. General McLoughlin marched in as victor in this battle for Eldonshire.

Tomas was not happy to see her again. "Why are you doing this, General?" Tomas screamed as he struggled against the shield maidens holding him. "I kept my word and told you where the Prometheus Engine was. Isn't that enough? Why are you attacking me?"

Rhona waved off her warriors, holding the little noble back. She stepped up to Tomas, towering over him by more than two feet. "It wasn't my decision, Lord Tomas. It was the Gil-Gamesh's choice to invade Eldonshire," she explained, angering Tomas even more. "He felt that your information was less than forthcoming. Perhaps you should have considered that before exiling the Swann sisters from their family home."

Rhona turned to walk away, but then she remembered something. "By the way, Lord Tomas, you realize that you just admitted to helping Mordred's number one enemy in the presence of the Lord Marshal," she said with a wicked grin. Horrified, Tomas realized his mistake when he turned back to look at Heydrich. The Lord Marshal was seething and angry at the act of betrayal by Lord Tomas.

"You... You traitor!" Heydrich screamed as he freed himself from his captors, drew a hidden dagger, and lunged at Tomas. The noble closed his eyes and cowered under his arms to protect himself. He trembled, waiting for his death, when a sword rushed past him. Rhona swung at Heydrich, blocking his attack before spinning around, decapitating her foe. When Tomas opened his eyes, he saw Heydrich's lifeless body fall to the ground as blood dripped from the end of Rhona's blade.

She swung her sword to the side, flinging the blood off her steel before sheathing it. "I would say you owe me your life now, Lord Tomas, but to be honest, you have nothing that I need or want," she said as she turned and walked away. Tomas was left trembling, sad, and defeated, with nowhere to turn and no one to help him. He was truly alone.

The following day, the Lord of Eldonshire was found dead in his cell beneath the castle he had once called home. Tomas hung himself from the dungeon bars. He left a note for Sir Hunter apologizing for his betrayal and admitting his complicity in the murder of his parents. He also wrote an impromptu will, giving all the land to the people of Eldonshire, rescinding his title and lordship over them. His last act as their lord would be to ensure the people had control over themselves and the land they toiled on.

Hunter had Tomas buried with his family, though some argued against it. He did it as one final favor to the man he once called a friend. Now that they had won the battle and Eldonshire was in control of the Gil-Gasmesh and the shield maidens, Hunter and King Bowen had an idea that would surely sting Mordred right where it hurt the most—his pride. Mordred considered Tomas weak and unimportant. In the end, he died with dignity and honor.

CHAPTER 16
THE TRUE KING SPEAKS

King Mordred sat on the Granite Throne, as happy as he could be. Everything was finally falling into place. The engine was near completion, and he would soon have the last piece to complete victory over the Gil-Gamesh and his siblings. With the power of Promethium at his disposal, no one would stand in his way ever again.

Mordred slowly sipped on his wine as he chuckled under his breath. He was so happy, giddy even, unable to contain his emotions. It was all going as predicted. All of his preparations, his planning, reached its climax. He could see it all before him, and he loved it. He wanted to relish and enjoy every minute of this.

"Pardon me, Your Majesty," Ocwyn said, breaking the King out of his joyful exuberance. "I'm sorry for disturbing you, but Minister Blackstone wanted me to inform you that Ms. Bonapat has completed the first batch of elixir for the Prometheus Engine. They are running some tests to ensure the formula works properly, but he anticipates that the engine will begin production of Promethium within the next six hours."

"Excellent, Magister," Mordred crowed. "For that bit of news, you can interrupt me all you want." The King sipped his wine as Ocwyn politely bowed before turning to leave. "Come, Magister... Join me for a drink!"

"Thank you, but no, Your Majesty, I have other matters to attend to."

"Come now, Ocwyn. Surely, you wouldn't deny your King this simple request?" he mockingly said to his Magister. Ocwyn reconsidered the offer and returned to the King's side. The King motioned for the servant girl to step forward. She kept her head down while carrying a tray with a pitcher of wine and another goblet. She poured wine into Mordred's cup before filling the other one on the tray. She slowly stepped over to Ocwyn so as not to spill the wine and offered it to him.

Ocwyn picked up the goblet as the King shooed the servant away. He smiled like a sly fox as he gestured a victory toast to Ocwyn. "To the completion of the Prometheus Engine and the true beginning of the reign of Mordred!" Ocwyn raised the goblet so as not to insult the King.

Mordred greedily gulped his wine while Ocwyn sipped it slowly. He never enjoyed celebrating with the King, but he knew it was necessary for his part in Mordred's grand plan.

"Hear me, Avalon! Heed the words of the true King of Avalon!" a voice echoed through the air. The resounding words roared through the castle, causing Mordred to choke. He violently coughed as he threw the goblet down, ratting it across the floor.

"What is that?" Mordred screamed as he ran across the throne room to the outside. Ocwyn, as confused as the King, followed close behind, wondering who or what was blaring the announcement.

As they stepped outside, Lady Mavis, Abdel Ben Faust, and Adalwulf Guard members joined them. "Hear me, Avalon! Heed the words of the true King of Avalon!" the voice cried out again. They could hear the announcement booming across the sky, repeated frequently, but they did not know from whence it came.

"What sorcery is this?" the King asked.

"I don't know, Your Majesty," Mavis answered. "I've never known any magic that can cover all of Avalon."

"I do," Ocwyn interjected. "It's an ancient spell called 'World Speak,' or so I've heard. The first rulers of Avalon used it to speak to everyone across the island since the people scattered to the four corners."

"Let me guess, the apprentice of Merlin is casting that spell," Faust snarked back at Ocwyn.

"More than likely, yes, General Faust," Ocwyn remarked. "But I believe someone else will be speaking."

As if on cue, the announcement stopped, and an image of King Bowen appeared, projected across the sky so that every island in the archipelago of Avalon could see and hear him. Mordred turned red with rage at seeing the young upstart trying to usurp him.

"People of Avalon, I am King Bowen Gregory Bartholomew Pendragon, the rightful ruler of Avalon. I am here today to tell you the truth about the false king Mordred, how his lust for power destroyed our once beautiful home, and how he's attempting to do that again."

"Is there nothing we can do to stop this tomfoolery?" Mordred wailed.

"I'm afraid not, Your Majesty. The spell is too powerful," Ocwyn explained. "Besides that, the only way to stop it is at the source, and we know Alfheimer is off-limits to us." Mordred cringed at the inability to stop Bowen, which infuriated him even more.

"Recently, I communed with the spirit of our first ruler, my ancestor, King Arthur Pendragon," Bowen continued. "It was through that discussion that we confirmed our suspicions. Before the Elves of Alfheimer sacrificed themselves to save Avalon by performing the *Øriĕntür*, Mordred committed an unbelievable and unforgivable atrocity. He kidnapped and imprisoned the Lady of the Lake, the Sainted Lady, and protector of Avalon."

Most of the Adalwulf Guard standing outside with Mordred were shocked to hear the revelation, but none of those close to the King were surprised, not even Ocwyn.

"Without the Sainted Lady, the magic that restored the barrier protecting Avalon also caused its destruction, splitting our home into an archipelago of islands," Bowen continued. "It was Mordred's ruthless ambition that tore Avalon apart, not the actions of Lord MoonDrake, the Gil-Gamesh. Mordred and his allies lied to cover their complicity in destroying our homeland.

"And now, Mordred conspires to endanger Avalon again for his ambitions. Deep within the dungeons of Castle Pendragon, under the instruction of Master Tinker Edwyn Broadfoot, Mordred has a legion of gnomes building a device known as the Prometheus Engine. This unholy machine is the same instrument responsible for the destruction of the ancient city of Atlantis. Now, Mordred is trying to recreate this infernal mechanism without any care for the repercussions it may have on Avalon or its people.

"You may wonder why I am telling you all this. The reason is simple. It is time for the people to revolt against their oppressors. It is time to reclaim Avalon from Mordred and his allies, these so-called Lords of Avalon. Thanks to the Holy Order of the Shield Maidens, we have already taken back the land of Eldonshire. The people now control the rich farmland they toil for us all. Lord Tomas Elderson, fraught with grief over his involvement in Mordred's coup, decided death was better than living with the shame of his complicities. His last act as the lord was to return Eldonshire to the people, and for that, I have pardoned him for his crimes against Avalon."

As Bowen continued with his speech, Mordred's anger grew. In this singular moment, they were undoing everything he had accomplished in the past five years and impeding all that was still to come. "Your Highness," Faust said, breaking Mordred from his rage. "I can gather the wraith legion and attack Eldonshire. We will have it back in no time. I can promise you that."

Mordred thought about Faust's proposal, wondering if they should wait or try to reclaim Eldonshire, but then a guard attacked him. "Damn you! You did this!" shouted one of the Adalwulf Guard as he lunged at the King. He thrust a dagger towards Mordred's heart, but the vigilant ruler blocked it with his hand. The blade was embedded in his palm, and the blood dripped from his gaping wound.

Mavis pulled the King away as Faust drew his sword and struck the traitor, nearly slicing him in two. Faust stood between the King and the other Adalwulf, some of whom were unhappy with what they heard. As Mavis tended to Mordred's wound, the usurper listened to the last of Bowen's speech.

"So now, I ask you, my loyal subjects, to join our fight against Mordred. You now know the truth about the depravity and the selfish ambition of the son of Morgana le Fay. Help me, the Gil-Gamesh, and our allies to take back Avalon. If you need any assistance, we will always be here for you. Remember, if we come together as one, we can achieve anything.

"'One Land, One King!'" Bowen concluded by using a phrase made famous by King Arthur as a rallying cry for the people. As quickly as he appeared, he disappeared. Mordred stood holding his hand in pain as he looked into the eyes of the people around him. The servants, the courtiers, and the Adalwulf Guard looked at him with distrust and contempt. The love Mordred longed for as their King faded as quickly as it came.

"Lady Mavis, take the King inside so we can properly tend to his wound," Ocwyn ordered. Mavis did so without hesitation, taking the King by the arm while Mordred held his bleeding hand. "General Faust, I would suggest removing all the Adalwulf Guard from the castle for now. I believe we can trust the *Cosc Fháil* inside the throne room, but I would have your wraiths stand guard outside the castle for now," he suggested.

Faust nodded in agreement as he sheathed his sword to carry out his orders. Ocwyn quickly moved inside to tend to the King's injuries. He found Mordred in his private quarters with Mavis. She applied healing salve to the King's injured hand as Ocwyn stepped inside.

"Are you well, Your Majesty?" he asked.

"No, I am not, Magister, because I had a dagger plunged through my hand. That should be obvious."

"Unfortunately, I think you can expect more of the same. I have asked General Faust to replace the Adalwulf Guard around the castle with wraiths until we can ascertain the damage to the integrity of the Adalwulf."

"Integrity? I think that's rather obvious, Magister," Mordred screamed. "One of them blatantly attacked me! Can't you see that?"

"I do, Your Majesty, which begs the question... Was what he said true? Did you kidnap and imprison the Lady of the Lake?" Ocwyn asked. The silence hung in the air as Mordred and Ocwyn stared at each other.

"It would do no good to lie to you, Magister. Yes, I did kidnap Lady Viviane. Faust has her imprisoned with the Chains of Tartarus in Purgatory."

Ocwyn was not surprised by Mordred's admission, but it still angered him. "I see, and I suppose you never thought about the consequences of your actions, did you?" Ocwyn said as if to provoke the King.

"Watch your tongue, Magister," Mavis snapped back at him. "Do not forget to whom you are speaking!"

"This is exactly why I am speaking this way, Lady Mavis. I cannot advise the King if I don't know everything, and I would have advised against such folly. Did you know the repercussions of kidnapping the Lady of the Lake?"

"If you mean, did I know it would tear Avalon apart... No," Mordred fired back at Ocwyn. "I didn't think about it at the time. It was just another part of my plan."

"In any case, Your Majesty, your actions have some severe consequences. I suspect you will find that more of your subjects will turn against you like that man in the Adalwulf Guard. Although you have your supporters, many believe the Lady of the Lake to be the heart and soul of Avalon. They will believe that your actions have directly impacted us all," Ocwyn concluded.

Mordred thought about what his Magister said. "So, what would you recommend we do to combat this, Magister?"

"Since I know you won't release the Lady of the Lake, I suggest we find a way to let the people know that your actions were a part of your vision for the future of Avalon," Ocwyn said, trying to explain it without angering the King any further. But, before the King could respond, a knock rapped on the door. Before the King could grant permission to enter, the door burst open as Blackstone carried something carefully wrapped in silk.

"I apologize for barging in, Your Highness, but I couldn't wait," Blackstone said. "The test run was a complete success." He presented it to the King, who unwrapped it anxiously, like a kid on Christmas morning, to find a small lump of golden-hued metal. It was small, about the size of an apple, but quite heavy in hand.

Mordred picked it up. It was still slightly warm to the touch from its formation. His attitude changed, and his smile widened at the sight of this unusual metal. "Promethium, at last!" he softly spoke as he gazed lovingly at his prize.

"Well, Magister, I think we will have a demonstration that will, at long last, show the people that I have the divine right to rule," Mordred cajoled. "Blackstone, we need more of this immediately and a blacksmith."

Bowen slowly opened his eyes, adjusting to the dimly lit room. He took a deep breath and sighed, thankful he had gotten through his speech in one try. Bowen made his speech to Avalon from inside the Temple of Eternal Starlight. This sacred place flowed with magical energy, making it easy for Ashley to cast the "World Speak" spell.

The temple was an amphitheater with trees and intricate statues surrounding it at the top. Inside, the carved stone formed seats that descended into a small, circular platform at the base. A small stone pedestal was inlaid with silver, gold, and mithril at the center, forming an ornate basin. Bowen and Ashley stood across from each other at the pedestal as the magic faded slowly after the ceremony. The rest of the family and Eileanora sat around and watched the spectacle.

After Bowen caught his breath, Ashley nearly fainted and had to sit down. The spell took a toll on her, and being pregnant exacerbated her condition even more. Andy immediately stepped in to help her. "You shouldn't push yourself like this, Ashley. You don't know what it could do to the babies."

"I'll be fine, sweetheart," she answered as she grabbed her aching back with one hand and her belly with the other. "It would have been much worse if I tried to cast that spell anywhere but here."

"In any case, sis, I'm proud of you, both of you," Hunter said, turning to his son. "You gave quite a speech, Bowen, and you recited it perfectly."

"Nona helped me practice," Bowen replied with a smile.

"And you did it beautifully, Your Majesty," Lady Stephanie congratulated him, followed by a hug and a kiss.

"Nona, please, not in front of everyone," Bowen pleaded, causing everyone else to laugh.

"So, what now, Hunter? What's our next move?" Rose asked.

"We've got to secure Eldonshire as quickly as possible. Conner Iain Collins, the *Faoladh* Magus, used his druidic magic to create Oracle Towers to help keep the wraith legion out—"

"I meant about Julianna," Rose interrupted. "No offense, but we've got to go to New Camelot and get her back."

"I know, Rose, but things have changed," Hunter said, trying desperately to calm her down. Rose was always the brasher of the three of them. "According to Keane, all the hidden passageways have been sealed off, in and out of the castle. He's looking for another way inside, but that could take time."

"And the longer we wait, the more Promethium Mordred will acquire to do God knows what with," Rose shouted. "We can't let this go on, and you know it!"

"Oh, come on, Rose, we're doing everything we can," Ashley snapped back at her.

"How can you say that? After everything Julianna has done for us, you'll just leave her in Mordred's hands?" Rose inferred as her anger began to get the best of her, making her lash out at her siblings.

"That's enough, Rose," Lady Stephanie scolded her daughter. "None of this is helping Julianna!"

"Neither are we, Mom! The great Gil-Gamesh sits on his hands instead of fighting to get Julianna back!"

"No, I'm not, Rose. I'm doing exactly what he told me to do!" Hunter argued with her.

"Who? Who told you to do nothing?" Rose asked.

"I did!" came a voice from the top of the theater. Dr. Allain Bonapat walked down the steps to the center. His movements were slow and staggered. You could almost sense the sadness emanating from him as he walked down.

"When Mordred took Julianna, I knew I would never see her again. I told Hunter not to bother with a rescue. All it would do is get others killed unnecessarily."

"But why, Allain? She's your wife! Why are you giving up like that?" Rose asked incessantly.

"When we first heard that Mordred was building this Prometheus Engine, Julianna was scared, frightened right out of her mind," he began. "She recalled the stories that her parents and grandparents told her about the day Atlantis sank into the ocean, about how that machine killed her family, her people. She knew that if Mordred succeeded in getting that contraption working, it would wipe New Camelot off the map."

"Why didn't she tell us any of this?" Andrew interjected. "We've been looking for any information on the Prometheus Engine!"

"You have to understand that, to Julianna, this machine was the stuff of nightmares," Allain continued with stoic resolve. "When it came to her

Atlantian heritage, she was very private. Only a few people knew about it, and she kept it that way. She was afraid that—"

Allain started to stutter his words, unable to breathe. He collapsed, clutching his throat as he gasped for air. Hunter and the others rushed over to his side. Besides his inability to breathe, the veins in his neck began to bulge.

"What is it? What's happening to him?" Lady Stephanie cried.

"It's Hemlock poisoning," Hunter assessed. He quickly ripped Allain's shirt as he tried to help him breathe. "It's starting to restrict his airway, but I've never seen a case where Hemlock worked so fast. It's as if—"

Hunter paused for a minute. Something about this seemed familiar, as if someone told him about this before. "Eileanora, go to the hospital, in Julianna's lab, and bring me some Yarrow root, St. John's Wort, Valerian petals, and a mortar and pestle. Hurry!"

Eileanora took off as fast as her feet would carry her. "Rose, I need some water in a pitcher." Rose followed Eileanora, running as fast as she could.

"Hunter, what is it? What's happening?" Lady Stephanie asked.

"Ollie poisoned Allain with Hemlock laced with Feverfew to delay the onset of the symptoms," Hunter explained. "I need to give him the remedy within the next few minutes, or he'll die."

"But how do you know all this?" Ashley asked.

"Because Ollie told me about it," Hunter stated, shocking everyone around him. "When he started mentoring me, he taught me about poisons and antidotes. He said that some people would use Feverfew to delay the onset of certain toxins, like Hemlock. That way, an assassin could be miles away when the person finally succumbed to the poison. The bulging in his neck signifies that Ollie poisoned him that way.

"The only cure for it is Yarrow root, St. John's Wort, and Valerian petals," he concluded. "Ollie may have succumbed to Mavis' will, but deep down inside, he was doing things that he knew I could counteract."

"But why poison Doctor Bonapat? They already have Lady Julianna?" Bowen inquired.

"They needed something to convince her to cooperate," Hunter told him. "I'm sure they did this to persuade her to decipher the formula for the chance at healing Allain in time."

Within minutes, Rose arrived with a pitcher of water, followed by Eileanora with all the ingredients Hunter required. He poured the water into the vessel on the pedestal, which caught the *Dubh Bhean* off guard and irritated her.

"Hunter, you don't mean to use the *Şâæcró Labrɥumɲ* to mix the medicine?"

"I'm sorry, Elle, but I need to heat this quickly, and the magic within this pedestal can do it faster than a fire," Hunter explained as he quickly broke down each ingredient, crushing it in the mortar and pestle before putting it into the basin.

"Ashley, I need you to heat this slowly," Hunter instructed. Ashley started to stand up, with Andrew helping her gingerly, but Eileanora raised her hand to stop them.

"No, I will do it," Eileanora insisted. "Ashley is still drained from the 'World Speak' spell. Besides, I can infuse some healing magic with the remedy. That may aid in his recovery."

Hunter nodded as Eileanora stood next to the pedestal. She reached into her tunic and pulled out a wand. It was eight inches long, made from an Elder tree branch, with a green stone embedded in the wand's core.

"A wand?" Hunter asked. "I've never seen you use a wand before, Elle."

"It once belonged to Lady Lyllodoria," she said. "I found it when we were cataloging items left behind by my people after the Øriëntür. I didn't think she would mind if I kept it for times like this."

Hunter was impressed with her thinking. She was trying to get over her sordid past as the "Elven Assassin" of Alfheimer. She focused on other Elven magical arts and practices to bring her more in line with her fellow elves.

"*Calefâc Autëm!*" she chanted over the pedestal. The mithril bowl began to glow as the mixture slowly began to bubble up and boil, slow and steady. Hunter took the water pitcher Rose brought and scooped up the remedy.

He knelt next to Allain as Andy helped raise his head. "Here, Allain, drink this!" Hunter poured the remedy into his mouth. Allain spat some of it out as he gasped for air while trying to drink it. When Hunter thought Allain had enough, they laid him back down. He watched Allain and waited patiently to see if it worked. Within minutes, Allain started to breathe more manageable, and his pulse steadied as the veins in his neck and head slowly shrank down.

Everyone breathed a sigh of relief, happy that Allain was doing better. "Rose, can you please go over to the hospital and have them bring a stretcher to carry Allain? He needs his rest," Hunter asked. Rose took off to get some help in transporting Allain down to the hospital.

"Thanks for the assistance, Elle. I'm sorry if I crossed a line when using the sacred temple for some alchemical cooking," he apologized.

Eileanora laughed softly at Hunter's poor joke. "No apologies necessary, Gil-Gamesh. You saved the Doctor's life, and if anything, the Temple of Eternal Starlight is about life eternal," she said with a smile. Hunter knew he was slowly breaking down the walls she had in place for thousands of years. She was finally letting herself feel something besides death and destruction.

"So, what do we do now, Hunter?" Ashley asked. "Do we attempt to rescue Julianna?"

Hunter thought about it for a moment. He tried to concentrate on a hundred different scenarios, attempting to calculate which one was the best route to go. Hunter wished his father were here to advise him. Even he had the spirits of those who previously carried the mantle of Gil-Gamesh to be his counsel. Hunter had no one, but there was one person he could talk to.

"I need to talk to someone first," he said as he took off to talk with an old friend of his father's.

CHAPTER 17
ADVICE FROM AN OLD FRIEND

Hunter raced through Alfheimer until he reached his quarters on the other side of the city. Like any young male bachelor's room, it was quite a mess. Hunter acquired many of his father's old gear, books, and other items. He was so busy, always out and about, he never really bothered to put stuff away or organize it.

A wizard's staff leaned against a stack of crates, a twisted shaft of white birch with a blue gem cradled in branches near the top. It belonged to a friend of his father, Archibald Browbridge, a wizard of extraordinary ability and incredible kindness. He guided his father through much turmoil when he first arrived on Avalon. He had been a family friend ever since.

Morgana le Fey killed Archie during her failed attempt to destroy Avalon with the Dark Tides. He was one of the first victims of that deadly spell. Now, his spirit resided in his staff through the Thaumaturge Effect. Hunter hoped to speak to the old wizard and ask him for advice. He prayed he would not be too angry for ignoring him until now.

Hunter grabbed onto the staff and sat on his bed. He took a deep breath and closed his eyes to clear his mind before thinking about pipe smoke and butter rum—those little familiar smells and tastes quintessential for the old mage—just as his father taught him. He opened his eyes when he could smell the sweet smell of pipe tobacco with the sickly-sweet scent of butter rum.

He stood inside a small cottage in a very sparse room. The room was quite quaint and straightforward: a small bed, a couple of bookcases, a table filled with various bottles and jars, and an oversized chair in front of a roaring fireplace. It was a little dirty and dingy, with a musty smell like an old cellar you walked into for the first time. A couple of other small chairs sat on either side of the big one as if he was expecting company. A smoke ring spiraled up from the big chair and dissipated in the air.

"Well, it's about bloody time you showed up," a voice shouted from the chair. "Do you know how long I've been sitting here, alone, longing for anyone to carry a conversation? Why I have half a mind to—"

When Archie stood up, he saw Hunter instead of his father, Lord Bryan MoonDrake. "Oh, Hunter, it's you. I'm sorry. I was expecting your father."

Hunter stared at the old man in disbelief, and then he realized no one had spoken to Archie before the reclamation. He was unaware that Hunter's father was dead.

"Wizard Browbridge, sir, I'm so sorry I didn't come sooner. I—" he paused momentarily as he saw the confusion on the old wizard's face. "No, I'm not going to make any excuses. I completely forgot that a piece of your spirit resides here. I've been so busy with other things that it has never occurred to me. I'm sorry. I should have come and told you sooner."

"Told me? Told me what? Come now, my boy, spill it out?"

Hunter sighed. "I'm sorry, sir, but my father is dead. He died five years ago at the hands of Abdel Ben Faust. You see—" Hunter stopped when Archie held up his hand. The old wizard was visibly shaken when he heard that Lord MoonDrake was dead.

"Sit down, Hunter, and tell me everything that has happened these last five years," Archie said as he motioned for Hunter to sit in one of the other chairs. He sat down himself as the old wizard listened intently to Hunter. Like he did with King Arthur, Hunter told Archie everything that had happened over the past five years, from the Outlander War to Avalon's Reclamation, Mordred's rise to power, the disappearance of the Lady of the Lake, and the Prometheus Engine.

Archie was dumbfounded and shocked at what Hunter told him. He could not believe everything he had just heard, including the resurrection of Mordred. "How could I be so blind?" Archie chided himself. "I should have considered the possibility of Mordred's rebirth, but we never found his body, so I never considered the possibility.

"And you, my dear boy, going about things on your own for the past five years. You've done a remarkable job. I must say—you and your sisters. Your father would be very proud of you all."

"Thank you, sir. I appreciate it, but I'm at a loss right now. Allain said not to go after Julianna, but I can't leave her there like that. I don't know what to do."

"As much as I hate to say it, my boy, Allain is right. You don't need to concern yourself with Julianna. The moment they captured her, Mordred sealed Julianna's fate."

Hunter was lost and confused by what Archie was saying. "I don't understand, sir. How can you say that?"

"Tell me something, Hunter. Do you know how the Prometheus Engine destroyed Atlantis?" Archie asked as he leaned back in his big, comfy chair and puffed on his pipe.

"Just what I've heard in the stories from other alchemists. The engine exploded because of miscalculation, causing Atlantis to sink into the ocean."

"That's not entirely correct, my boy," Archie interjected. "The engine exploded because of crust buildup within the engine caused by the formula. The buildup clogged the pipes, like the arteries to the heart, and—"

"The engine had a heart attack," Hunter exclaimed. "And since this happened after the fact, they never wrote it down. Mordred doesn't know that running the engine can cause it to go critical and explode."

"But Julianna does," Archie added. "I do not doubt for an instant that she agreed to complete the formula because she knew that running the engine would cause it to explode, and by chance, it could destroy Mordred and any plans or writings referring to that infernal machine."

"So Allain was right. It's useless to try and rescue her. We'd just be putting others at risk unnecessarily."

"Sometimes in chess, dear fellow, you must sacrifice a few pieces to win the match," Archie summarized.

"Yes, but in this game, the pieces are real people. How did my Dad do this?" Hunter queried. "He made it look so easy, ordering others to do something that could kill them. I don't know how to do that?"

"Your father once told me something about a man from the outside world. Lee, I believe he said his name was... Robert E. Lee. He said, 'To be a good soldier, you must love the army. To be a good commander, you must be willing to order the death of the thing you love.'"

Hunter laughed at that quote. "Dad always did love military history," Hunter replied. "Thank you, Wizard Browbridge. I appreciate all your advice, and I'm sorry it took me so long to talk to you."

"In the first place, my boy, stop with all this Wizard Browbridge crap. You can call me Archibald or Archie like your father did. There doesn't need to be any formalities between us. And if you want to make it up to me, you can drop me off at Madam Sonjay's for a few months."

"Sorry, Archie, but Mom wouldn't allow her to open an establishment in Alfheimer," Hunter interjected. "But I could have Rose drop you off at *Mad Mollies* in Barbarossa. I've heard the girls there are quite adventurous."

That brought a smile to Archie's face. "Well, I guess I could use a little adventure," he said with a sly smile. "That'll be just fine, my boy."

Hunter stood up to leave, grateful for Archie's advice. He understood now why his father always turned to the wizard for help. "Oh, and Hunter," Archie said, interrupting his train of thought. "I wouldn't worry too much about Sarafina. I think you'll find she will have all the help she needs to rescue the Lady of the Lake."

Hunter shook his head in utter confusion, but if there was one thing his father taught him, it was never to doubt the word of a wizard. He closed his eyes and thought of home as his spirit faded from the wizard's room. When he opened his eyes, he was back in his room, but something was off.

Somebody had lit his fireplace, and judging by the logs, it had been burning for a few hours. The room had been "tidied up" as if someone had cleaned it with a purpose. When he turned to look around, he saw Eileanora lying on the bed beside him. She seemed uncharacteristically quiet and subdued as she rested so serenely. Even when they were out in the field together, she always slept with one eye open, alert to what was happening around her, while getting very little sleep.

He touched her shoulder gently so as not to startle her. Just as his hand touched her, she rolled over to attack him—a dagger clutched in her hand. Hunter anticipated this reaction after working closely with her for five years. He dropped Archie's staff, rolled over on top of her, and pinned her down with his full weight. Even though she was stronger than Hunter and could easily toss him aside, Eileanora lay quietly beneath him.

They stared at each other, neither one saying a single word. The two were flustered, caught off guard by this rather compromising situation, but neither knew what to do. It's not that they had never been intimate with someone before. They were confused as to what they felt toward each other.

"Hunter," she said breathlessly, "Can I ask you a favor?"

"What? Yeah—I mean, yes, of course!" He stammered his words, still trying to collect himself. "What is it?"

"Would you please remove your hand from my breast?"

Hunter looked down, and then he realized that he was pinning her dagger hand with his left hand, but he had his right hand pressed against her chest—a normal when fighting someone in armor, but quite risqué at a time like this.

"Whoa, oh God, I'm sorry, Elle! I am sorry," he yelled as he jumped back, hitting his head against the bedpost. "Ow! Dammit!" Hunter held the back of his head momentarily as it stung from the impact.

Eileanora sat up and sheathed her dagger. She acted relatively calm under pressure, but her heart was racing a mile a minute. "What? What are you doing here?" Hunter asked her, still rubbing his head.

"You were gone for a couple of hours," she explained while spinning around to sit beside him. "When I found you like that, I decided to wait until you came out of the trance. I must have dozed off while I waited."

Hunter was surprised to hear how long he had been there with Archie, but he remembered the same thing that had happened to his father once before. In the Thaumaturge Effect, minutes can seem like hours. He looked outside to see darkness fill the night sky, so he knew he had been there for several hours.

"And you suddenly had the urge to clean my room?" he asked.

"Well, I wasn't going to just sit in this filth while I waited for you," she said. "I tidied things up a bit, then laid down to rest. I must have dozed off."

"And do you always sleep with a dagger under your pillow?"

Eileanora smiled quite wickedly. "Always!"

Hunter laughed, and even Eileanora smiled as they shared a moment. He rarely saw her laugh, but he loved her smile. Silence hung in the air again as they stared at each other awkwardly.

"Hunter, I just—"

"Look, Elle—" the two said simultaneously, fumbling over their words, but Eileanora put her hand up to Hunter's mouth to stop him from talking.

"Hunter, I know there are some things we need to talk about," she began to say softly. "I sense that your feelings toward me are like mine toward you, but perhaps this isn't the right time to—"

Without warning, Hunter did something bold and impulsive. He reached out with his hands, took Eileanora by her face, and kissed her passionately. Hunter had never felt this way since his relationship with Queen Cadhla. Between duties and protocol, he tried to ignore any feelings he might have toward Eileanora, but not anymore. His heart, which had been closed for so long, was now open to the possibility of love again.

He enveloped her in his arms, drawing her close. Eileanora, in turn, offered no resistance as she reached out to him. In a wordless understanding, the two lovers fell back on the bed, their passionate embrace continuing. No words were spoken; no need for them. Their unspoken desires were the only language they needed.

For hours, the two were lost in each other, never leaving the bed or each other's side. The years of emotional suppression, the pent-up feelings that had been building inside both of them, were finally released. The lovers found solace in each other's arms, a dream they had only dared to imagine. When they finally finished, they lay there, wrapped in a loving embrace, catching their breath and basking in the freedom of their emotions.

"I've wanted to do this for a long time," Hunter said, breathing quite heavily.

"Really? Then why did you wait?"

"Well, I wasn't sure how you felt about me, and I guess I was a little uncertain myself," Hunter explained. "It's been a long time since I felt this way about another woman. After Cadhla, I never thought I would fall in love again."

Eileanora looked up at Hunter, dumbfounded. "You love me?" she asked tepidly.

Hunter saw that he caught her off guard with his proclamation. "I'm sorry, Elle, I guess I thought I made that clear, I mean—" he paused momentarily. Talking to Eileanora was always so easy for him. She was one of his closest friends, but now, she was much more than that.

"Yes... Yes, I do. I love you, Eileanora," he started to say as he brushed the hair away from her face. "I don't know how long we'll have together, but I want to spend every moment with you. You mean the world to me, Elle. I would do anything for you. I—"

Eileanora put her finger up to his mouth and smiled as tears welled up in her eyes. Like Hunter, it has been a long time since someone told her they loved her. "Not much of a talker, are you?" she joked, poking fun at his "Casanova" persona.

Hunter couldn't help but laugh. "Yeah, I'm a better lover than a talker."

"Oh, I can attest to that," Eileanora bemused. "But I must admit, this is all new to me too."

"What do you mean?" Hunter asked.

"In more than 2,000 years, only one held my heart captive. My affair with Eonis went on for more than a thousand years," she explained. "I didn't fall in love with him for at least 200 years, but it took less than five with you. I can't explain why."

"You think it might have to do with the fact that you're no longer the *Dubh Bhean*?" Hunter inquired. "I mean, before the reclamation, your only focus was on killing and death. Now, your focus is on saving people and protecting Alfheimer."

"That may be, I don't know," she answered, gently caressing his face. "All I do know is that I love you too. Your strength, your courage, everything about you tells me what kind of a man you are, and for a human, you are quite exceptional."

The two lovers, lost in their feelings, failed to hear a knock at the door. Without warning, the door opened, and Lady Stephanie entered the room carrying a food tray.

"Hunter, we haven't heard from you for hours, so I thought you might be hungry."

She froze at the door. Seeing the two naked and in bed together caught Stephanie off guard, causing her to turn bright red. She stood there silently in her embarrassment. Instead, she set the tray down, turned away, and left the room as quickly as she entered.

Hunter and Eileanora were equally embarrassed, being caught in such a compromising position by Lady Stephanie. "I don't know who's in worse trouble, you or me?" Hunter stated.

"Oh, I think it's me, definitely me," Eileanora replied. "According to your sisters, your mother would never hold anything against 'her baby'—their words, not mine."

"Yeah, you're probably right. You're dead for sure," Hunter joked. "I'll talk to Mom. She can be a bit of a 'mama bear' at times, you know, over-protective of her children. You might want to wait a bit before you approach her alone."

"Well, in that case, I better enjoy this moment for as long as I can," Eileanora said as she kissed him again. Though she knew she would have to talk to Lady Stephanie sooner rather than later, she did not want to think about that right now.

Right now, she was in the arms of the man she loved, and that's all that mattered. This may be a moment for them to be together forever or perhaps their last time before death. Under Mordred's reign, no one knew their fate until it was too late.

CHAPTER 18
THE END OF THE PROMETHEUS ENGINE

After weeks of frustration, Edwyn Broadfoot was a happy little gnome. Years of hard work toiling under Mordred's thumb had finally paid off. The Prometheus Engine ran efficiently, producing large amounts of Promethium for King Mordred. Even the alchemist was doing her job without any coercion or outside influence. It was all going smoothly.

Edwyn walked over to the engine's control area. He watched as one of his assistants carefully poured the solution into the engine's fill spout. The viscous red liquid bubbled as it spilled out of the glass beaker into the funnel.

"How much more do we have to pour in this time?" Edwyn asked.

"Another five milliliters," he ascertained. "It's averaging that increase in the amount of liquid every other run."

Edwyn looked over the gauges and saw that the input, output, and pressure were all within the proper levels. "Hmm ... It may just be the engine adjusting to the constant running, or something could be blocking the intake to the main chamber. We'll take a look after this run."

"I don't think so, boss. Minister Blackstone said he needs ten more Promethium ingots by the week's end. It'll take several more runs to make that quota."

Edwyn grimaced in frustration. He tried to keep the engine running smoothly but had to do so at a breakneck pace to satisfy his majesty's needs and wants. "OK, tell Miss Julianna to adjust the formula to account for the increased runs."

"I was going to, but it seems she already knew what to do," the assistant said, motioning toward the alchemist's workbench. Edwyn nodded his head as he started walking over to the bench. Julianna looked haggard—dirty and exhausted—wearing the same clothes since they kidnapped her from Alfheimer. She worked tirelessly with very little sleep, barely enough to eat, or been given a chance to clean up. Her hands shook as she measured the ingredients, a sign of her utter exhaustion.

"I understand you've been increasing the volume of formula we needed without being told," Edwyn asked her. "Is there something you're not telling me, Miss Julianna?"

"No, Master Tinker, I just made incremental increases to the formula per the instructions on the parchment," she answered, her voice steady and robust compared to the shaking in her hands. "But I desperately need a bath, a good meal, and several hours of sleep. If I keep going at this pace, I may make a mistake, and neither of us wants that."

"I can't do anything about that, Miss Julianna. Minister Blackstone wants another ten ingots by the end of the week."

"Ten?" Julianna exclaimed. "It takes two runs of the machine just to make one ingot. We're making Promethium here, not distilling whiskey."

Edwyn knew she was right. He sympathized with her predicament. She had done everything that they asked her to do without question. Maybe this time, he could do something for her as a reward for her cooperation. Deep down, Edwyn knew that King Mordred would never let her go.

"Very well, Miss Julianna. When you finish the next batch of the formula, I will see you get a well-needed break," he said with compassion. We'll see where that takes us and go from there."

"Master Tinker!" shouted Edwyn's assistant from the control area. "We've got a problem!"

Edwyn rushed back to the Prometheus Engine while Julianna smiled and breathed a sigh of relief. It had finally reached critical overload, and she knew her freedom was imminent.

"What's the matter?" Edwyn inquired, sensing the panic in his assistant.

"The pressure's building up! I can't get the relief valve open!"

"Shut it down!" Edwyn screamed. "Just shut it down!"

"You can't," Julianna exclaimed. "The engine is on its way to critical mass! Any minute now, it will explode!"

"Insufferable bitch!" Edwyn shouted. "You did this!"

"No, Master Tinker, I didn't do anything but what you asked. You seem to forget what happened to Atlantis. The same thing that's going to happen here."

When Edwyn heard that, he was frightened to his core. Everyone knew Atlantis had been destroyed and sank into the sea, but he never knew how or why it had happened—until now.

"Why do you think no one ever tried to rebuild the Prometheus Engine before now?" she continued. "The ingredients needed to make Promethium cause a build-up on every surface inside the engine. Pretty soon, that residue has nowhere left to go, and it seizes the engine, and then... Boom!"

"You... You knew this, and yet you still helped us? You're going to die down here with us!"

"That's right, I am, and the explosion will destroy the secret of the Prometheus Engine, once and for all. It's a shame Mordred isn't here to die with us, but taking you and your fellow Tinkers out will slow down his wheel of chaos. My death will have a purpose, and I will be with my God. How about you, Master Tinker?"

Edwyn never had a chance to answer. The engine exploded with such force it lifted the castle a few feet higher before settling back into the earth. The ground rumbled across every part of New Camelot, shaking everything from dishes and furniture to walls and building foundations. The force of the blast caused massive tidal waves that radiated out from New Camelot. The waves swamped smaller islands while large islands dealt with a sudden surge of water that washed away crops, buildings, animals, humans, and demi-humans alike. Even though it only lasted a few minutes, the devastation caused by the exploding engine was unimaginable.

Mordred lay on the ground inside the throne room, covered in dust and rubble. Looking up, he saw Minister Blackstone standing over him, casting a protection spell that saved them from the falling debris. Across the room, Magister Ocwyn was doing the same to protect himself, Lady Mavis, and one of the servant girls. However, several members of the *Cosc Fháil* were not as lucky. The large chunks of debris that crashed down from the walls and the ceiling crushed them beneath the rubble.

As soon as the shaking stopped, both casters pushed the debris away from them. As Ocwyn helped Lady Mavis stand, she immediately rushed to the King's side. Ocwyn helped the servant girl up before checking on the King.

"What the hell was that?" Mordred screamed.

"It came from under the castle, Your Majesty. It must be the Prometheus Engine," Ocwyn exclaimed. "I recommend sending someone down to ascertain what happened and inspect the damages, Your Highness. I will send men out across the city to assess the damage to New Camelot."

"I don't give a damn about the witless mortals in New Camelot, Magister," Mordred shrieked. "I care about the Promethium! Blackstone, go down and find out what happened!"

Blackstone was hesitant as fear of being trapped underground swelled up inside him. "Your Majesty, perhaps one of the *Cosc Fháil* can go first to discover if it's safe to go down into the lower levels," he stuttered out as his voice quivered with apprehension.

"In case you didn't notice, Minister Blackstone, the *Cosc Fháil* are lying about us, either dead or injured," Mordred chastised him. "You are a sniveling coward!"

"I will go down to the lower dungeon, Your Majesty," Ocwyn interjected. "Minister Blackstone can inspect the rest of the castle to ensure we are no longer in danger of collapse."

Mordred scowled as he begrudgingly nodded his head to approve Ocwyn's plan. Ocwyn bowed before he departed the throne room, leaving Blackstone to grovel to the King some more. As he descended the steps, he carefully stepped over the scattered debris. The explosion cracked the walls and stairs but seemed to have settled down after the blast.

Why didn't they collapse inward? He wondered as he slowly stepped down further. He then spotted metal within the cracks, a testament to the resilience of Promethium, forming a bond that held the broken pieces together. Walking down a little further, he found the magic door to the room with the Prometheus Engine lying on its side. The metal door was bent and distorted as the explosion blew it halfway up the stairs. Ocwyn had to step around it as he continued down the steps carefully. When he reached the bottom, the Magister was shocked to his very soul.

The room that once held the Prometheus Engine was gone. All that remained was a giant ball of Promethium. Etched into the metal were the gnomes' faces, their death masks forged into the indestructible metal by the explosion, pressing them into the metal. Their faces showed the pain and terror they experienced at the end of their lives. However, one was different.

Ocwyn recognized the face of Julianna Bonapat. Instead of pain and suffering, her death mask showed peace and quiet serenity, a stark contrast to the others. Her beauty shone through as if she had died content, happy that no one could ever build the Prometheus Engine again. He touched her face as a tear ran down his cheek. Here was a woman he had known almost all his life, and she died confident in her faith. He saw the tranquility that her face exuded. He knew it was something he would never know himself. Because of his decision, he would never know peace in this life or the next.

Be that as it may, a giant ball of indestructible metal now encased the secret of the Prometheus Engine. King Mordred still had some precious metal to work with, but he could never get his hands on it anymore.

Sarafina braced herself against the fierce gale blowing across the barren plains of the Wretched Wasteland of Purgatory. The burning winds stung like thousands of bees on her face and hands as they whipped across Purgatory's desolate landscape. As much as it pained her to continue, Sarafina trudged on.

She would pause occasionally and draw her sword from its scabbard. The light from the *Gilded Queen* would flow out from the blade like a beacon, pointing her in the right direction toward the Sainted Lady. Sarafina avoided releasing the holy light for long because she feared exposing her presence.

Sarafina had to be careful with every step she took across the desert. She had to evade both demons and wraiths, hiding instead of fighting. She knew that any confrontation would alert others to her presence there. She did not want Faust to get wind of it, fearing he might move the Lady of the Lake from her captivity before she reached her.

Her throat was dry, and her lips cracked. She was dehydrated and nearly blinded with red and burning eyes, but she soldiered across the wasteland. She pulled the cloak across her nose and mouth, protecting her from the blowing sand as best as possible. She squinted her eyes tightly, trying to keep a sense of her surroundings while protecting them from the unnatural weather.

Through the scorching winds, Sarafina heard a demon's howl. It was a low, guttural cry that was quite distinctive. She quickly scoured for a place to hide. She spotted an outcropping of rocks and rushed over as she crouched down low, peeking around just enough to keep a lookout for the demon she heard howling.

After a few minutes, the demon revealed its presence. The creature was a soldier demon, only about five feet tall, with a lean, muscular frame. Its reddish-brown skin, reminiscent of a reptile's hide, was covered with bony spikes from head to toe. Its misshapen head resembled an obscene goat with razor-sharp teeth and horns wrapped in coarse, black hair. The lower torso flowed with the same black fur, but its tail was also reptilian. The demon appeared to have been in a fierce battle. The beast was bleeding profusely from various cuts and piercing wounds. The monster panted, out of breath, as it struggled to escape from its pursuers.

Sarafina looked up and saw two wraiths closing in on the demon. They carried spears that glowed with the same ghostly aura that surrounded them. As they thrust their phantom blades into the creature, it shrieked a cry so horrible that Sarafina had to cover her ears. She watched as the phantom blades turned the demon into dust. Its remains mixed with the blowing sands of the Wretched Wasteland.

Before the wraiths could leave, a large group of fiends jumped out of nowhere and ambushed them. These soldier demons were different. They were well-trained, attacking with the precision of a warrior overpowering the wraiths before breaking their heartstones. The ghostly knights disappeared, fading into nothingness as their ghostly essence scattered on the breeze.

The demons howled and roared in their victory when a giant commander stepped forward. His appearance resembled the demon soldiers' but was much larger and more muscular. The monster stood over seven feet tall. His face was grotesque and ferocious—withdrawn and desiccated, like a dead animal skull sitting in the desert for years. He carried a large cleaver as a weapon, resting it across his shoulders as he strolled up to his demon soldiers.

"Well done, well done," he complimented. "We'll slowly whittle the wraiths down to nothing, just like General Faust said we would."

"Yes, yes—indeed, he had. For a half-demon, he has proven a boon in our war against the human world," one of the demon soldiers rattled off.

"Oh my, yes! Faust keeps the wraiths busy on Avalon while we pick away at their numbers here," another soldier repeated. "Soon, we will be free of the legion and march to Avalon and the world. Demons will rule over all the earth and the heavens!"

Sarafina was shocked but not surprised that Faust would take advantage of his arrangement with Mordred. He always had a reputation for his disdain for humans, but to help his demon brethren in their conquest of Purgatory was beyond the pale.

Before long, one of the demon soldiers raised its nose and started sniffing the air. It smelled something out of place on the Wretched Wasteland of Purgatory. Sarafina was afraid they had discovered her presence. She grasped the hilt of her sword, ready to draw and strike if necessary.

She readied herself, and not a moment too soon. The demon commander lifted the stone she was crouched behind, exposing her hiding place. "A human, here? Kill her, my demons! Kill her now!"

The demon soldiers swarmed in, but instead of fighting a wraith, they were fighting the Headmistress of the Holy Order of Shield Maidens of Avalon. Sarafina, a fierce and skilled warrior, was something these demons had never fought before, nor had they prepared for.

She drew her sword and sliced through the demons that charged at her. The Gilded Queen blinded them, allowing Sarafina to cut them down swiftly. Her blade cleaved the demon's flesh with relative ease as the monsters fell into the sands. Then, she quickly spun on her heels, and before the demon commander could throw the rock at her, Sarafina charged and sliced into his left knee. The creature's leg buckled under the weight of the stone, causing him to fall backward. The massive boulder dropped on its head, crushing his skull and killing him instantly.

Sarafina looked around to ensure all the demons were dead before she sheathed her sword. Once she was confident the danger had passed, she did not hesitate to leave as she continued her journey across the wasteland. She did not want to linger about, given the chance that more demons or wraiths would appear. Sarafina continued her search for the Sainted Lady, but now she had even more resolve to see it through.

Faust's machinations must be stopped once and for all. Mordred entrusted him with all that power—the control of the Wraith Legion—without even thinking of the possibilities of what he would do with it. Faust may be following Mordred's orders, but he acted on his own plans behind the scenes. For someone so ancient and intelligent, Mordred had a habit of causing more problems with his selfish actions.

Sarafina bore down and moved on as quickly as she could. She focused on her mission but never stopped thinking of her children, Thomas and Meriel: the smiles on their faces, their laughter, tears, and the simple sound of their voices. She wanted to see them again, which drove her as much as, if not more, on her mission.

Her children had already lost their father and grandfather. Losing her would be devastating to them, and Sarafina would never want to put that burden on them. She knew she must succeed for the sake of her children and their future on Avalon.

CHAPTER 19
THE LADY AND THE ELF

The explosion from deep within Castle Pendragon in New Camelot had repercussions across Avalon, especially on Alfheimer. Fierce waves battered the outer rock walls that protected the city while the island shook from the violent earthquakes emanating from New Camelot. People ran for cover, trying to get away from falling debris. Parts of the city that survived the reclamation came apart this time from the tremors caused by the Prometheus Engine's destruction.

Once everything died down, the challenge of picking up, helping people, and rebuilding began again. People around Alfheimer did as they always did—they helped if anyone needed it.

As the people recovered, Eileanora patiently walked around the city to assess the damage. She had lived in Alfheimer for over four millennia and knew every inch of the ancient city. She tried to focus on the task, but her mind was elsewhere.

She couldn't stop thinking about what had happened between her and Hunter the night before. She had been alone for thousands of years, performing her duties as the *Dubh Bhean*. Even when she shared her life with her first love, Eonis, their time together was far and few. That was completely different from her time now with Hunter.

She'd spent the last five years fighting and living at his side every waking moment. She wasn't alone anymore, and that made her happy. She grew closer to him with each passing day, and to finally be able to express her feelings was such a relief. Eileanora knew that many people thought it was wrong for them to be together, but she didn't care. She was in love. Nothing and no one could change that.

Except, of course, for the one person she had been avoiding for days. It chilled her as it never had before. As Eileanora entered Vanir Hall, she spotted Lady Stephanie leading the clean-up effort there. Hunter asked her to let him talk to his mother first—after she had walked in on them—but unfortunately, Eileanora had no choice.

The hall was once a place of conference and deep thought, where the elves came together to discuss their views on philosophy, politics, and poetry. Today, Vanir Hall was more like a meeting hall and mercantile, where the people discussed political strategy, cooperative living arrangements, and bartered for goods and supplies.

Lady Stephanie was coordinating the rescue efforts needed around the city. Eileanora saw that she was occupied, which relieved her. Perhaps she could avoid talking to her after all.

"Eileanora, do you have a moment?" Lady Stephanie called out. Eileanora cringed. She thought she'd gotten away, but unfortunately, she wasn't that lucky.

"Yes, of course, milady. What can I do for you?" Eileanora replied with a courteous bow.

"Have you checked the lower levels near the tombs yet?"

"No, milady. I was concentrating on the living quarters," Eileanora said plainly. "Captain Hawke is checking into the port and warehouses while General McLoughlin inspects our defenses."

"Good, but in any case, I would like to check on them. Would you mind accompanying me?"

Eileanora swallowed hard. She knew this moment would be when she and Lady Stephanie would be alone together. Although Eileanora was apprehensive about it, she had no choice. The elf could not believe how nervous she felt. Here was the *Dubh Bhean*, the Assassin of Alfheimer, anxious about being alone with the mother of the man she loved. She would prefer to face off against a legion of Brood Goblins instead of being alone with Lady Stephanie.

Her reputation preceded her, and she was to be revered and feared. Eileanora experienced that firsthand during the Outlander War when, after insulting Lord MoonDrake's family, Lady Stephanie plunged a dagger through her hair, pinning her head to the table.

"Of course, milady. I'd be happy too," Eileanora said with her best poker face, hoping this encounter would not end like the last one.

Eileanora walked with Stephanie down to the lower levels of Alfheimer. There, they entered the Tomb of the *Ljósálfar*, the ancient necropolis of Alfheimer. Here, the elves' honored dead were buried, including the men and women who died protecting Alfheimer during the *Øriĕntŭr*.

At the center of the tomb, in a place of honor, were the marble caskets of Lord Bryan MoonDrake and his shield maiden, Amelia Pomodoro. They carved the stone covers with lifesize images of these two heroes. Debris scattered around the floor and cracked cover stones along the walls, but the necropolis survived the earthquake.

While Eileanora inspected the mausoleum cover stones, Lady Stephanie looked over her husband's grave. She carefully brushed the dust and debris away as if brushing it off his face and clothes. She touched his visage gently, caressing it like she did in real life.

"Eileanora, what are your intentions toward my son?" Stephanie asked out of nowhere. Eileanora was dumbfounded by her blurting out the question like that.

"I'm sorry, milady?"

"I asked, what are your intentions toward my son? I mean, you don't walk in on two people in bed together without wondering about the consequences of their actions. Especially someone with a sordid past like you. So, I must ask you again, what are your intentions toward my son?"

Eileanora didn't care for Lady Stephanie's tone or insinuations about her past life as the *Dubh Bhean*. "With respect, Lady MoonDrake, my intentions are my own," she stated plainly. "What happens between Hunter and I is, well... A private matter."

"Anything involving my children is not private," Stephanie retorted. Her voice was calm, but Eileanora could sense the anger underneath it.

"I think you're a little over-protective, milady. Hunter is a grown man who—"

"Don't you dare tell me how I should feel about my son!" Stephanie roared back. "You, of all people, have no right to lecture me on my feelings!"

"And you have no right to judge me on who I was, nor who I am now," Eileanora snapped back. "Have I not proved that in these last few years? I stood and fought alongside Hunter, Ashley, Rose, Dame Sarafina, and the others. I endeavor to move past my sordid history—past the monster known as the *Dubh Bhean*—and it was Hunter who helped me through that.

"He doesn't see me as the 'Assassin of Alfheimer' just as Eileanora, which made me fall in love with him." Her declaration of love took Stephanie by surprise. She stood silent. Instead, she decided to listen further to what Eileanora had to say.

"His courage, his determination, and his heart... It's something I never experienced in a human before," she added. "All my life, during the countless missions Lord Baldrid sent me on, I was surrounded by hate, injustice, and death. Your family experienced all that, yet you continue struggling to fight with love, grit, and grace under pressure.

"Most humans I've met would crumble under such intense pain, but not Hunter. He can still crack a joke to make me smile, even after he lost his first love, Queen Cadhla, his friend and mentor, Eonis, and then his father. He still has a wonderful smile for me every day. It's utterly amazing to me, making me love him even more. I can't explain it and can't help feeling the way I do."

Eileanora stepped toward Lady Stephanie and stood firm on her convictions. "I love your son with all my heart, Lady Stephanie, and I would never do anything to hurt him. I would give my life for him from now until *Vídbláin* brings me home," she concluded as a tear gently rolled down her cheek.

Stephanie saw the truth in her words and her heart. She knew then that she had let her emotions get the best of her. She reached out, wiped the tear from her cheek, and hugged Eileanora tightly like she would one of her daughters. "That's all I wanted to hear, Eileanora," Stephanie said. "Perhaps I was slightly over-protective, but that's a mother's prerogative, especially regarding her only son."

"Just slightly?" Eileanora joked. The two shared a laugh as they hugged again until they were suddenly interrupted by Hunter. He rushed in, out of breath, hoping he would not walk in on the two of them at each other's throats. He felt relieved but slightly confused when he saw them laughing and hugging.

"Uh, is everything OK in here?" Hunter asked.

They laughed again, making Hunter feel even more uncomfortable. Lady Stephanie walked over to her son and kissed him on the cheek. "Everything is just fine, Hunter," she extolled. "Eileanora and I were just having a chat while we were inspecting the necropolis."

Stephanie left the two of them alone to return to her duties. Hunter just stood there, confused. "I'm sorry, Elle. I meant to talk to her before she could corner you, but the earthquake prevented that," Hunter explained. Eileanora smiled as she walked over and kissed him.

"It's fine, Hunter. Your mother is quite an understanding woman."

"Really? So, it's all good?"

"Between her and me, yes," she answered. "Between you and her? You'll have to find out for yourself."

Hunter was glad to see and hear that there was no animosity between the woman he loved and his mother, but now he was worried. He still had to talk to Lady Stephanie, and soon. He knew that was never easy. It reminded him of taking a bad report card to her. Hunter would have no problem smoothing things over with his mother. After all, he was her baby boy.

The people of King's Crossing were well known for coming together in times of crisis, and this was no exception. Cleaning up after the recent earthquake was not the same as fending off goblins from Blackbriar Forest, but it still demonstrated how much the people of this community took the term "neighbors" to heart. They spent most of the day trying to clean up after the explosion of the Prometheus Engine shook the land and sea, even out to them.

Some slate roofing tiles cracked, a few fallen, toppled fences, collapsed buildings, and some broken windows amounted to the damage around the small community. Everyone came together to help, including the newly arrived Swann sisters and young Peter McMillan.

Peter was no longer the little boy who worked in the stable at the *Weathered Wren* for extra money. He was a seasoned warrior who fought many battles with the Gil-Gamesh. He learned from the best about leadership and discipline.

To the Swann sisters, Astrid and Sigrid, King's Crossing had become their new home, and they were trying to make the best of it.

The sisters worked together to repair the fence, keeping the livestock corralled. They lived and worked on Peter's family farm, helping his mother as best as possible. Peter was so busy tending to the security and safety of King's Crossing as the resistance's contact that he had little time to help on his family farm. The Swann sisters were a blessing in disguise for Peter. They helped around the farm and continued with his training, as there was no one better than a shield maiden to give combat instruction.

As the sisters diligently worked together to repair the fence, Peter hastily approached them with something urgent on his mind.

"Pardon me, milady's, but I could use some advice!"

"Peter, we told you not to call us that," Astrid said. "We're shield maidens, not ladies in waiting!"

"Yes, of course, sorry," he apologized. "I was just trying to be polite."

"Oh, don't listen to her, Peter," Sigrid snapped back. "I don't mind it as much as Astrid does. Now, what do you need?"

"The town well has collapsed in on itself. I'm unsure if we should try to clear it or seal it and dig a new one."

"Your well still uses the old rope and bucket, doesn't it?" Astrid asked. Peter nodded his head, confused by their question. "We brought a pump-handle water pump with us from Eldonshire. If we can get a long enough pipe to reach the bottom of the well, all we need to do is clear enough debris to pass the pipe through."

"We can shore up the sides near the collapsed section and work to clear the debris," Sigrid interrupted. "Start getting some people, tools, and materials together, Peter. Once we finish this, we'll meet you at the well with the pump."

Peter smiled and nodded, happy to have the sisters here to give him the advice and help he needed. Sir Hunter, his mother, siblings, and the people of King's Crossing counted on him. Suddenly, something caught his eye as he was about to leave.

"What's that?" Peter asked, getting the Swann sisters' attention. Out across the field, toward the edge of Blackbriar Forest, he noticed something coming toward them. As their eyes focused on the growing force, it became clear that they were not friendly.

A combination of Brood, goblins, and *Dökkalfar* or dark elves—hundreds of vile, dark monsters headed toward them. These were the combined malevolence from the deepest recesses of Blackbriar Forest. Only King Mordred could have commanded such a force to march together against them.

The Brood looked like the smaller goblins, except they were twice their size with a blackish-green hue to their skin. Their teeth were sharp and protruded from their mouths, causing them to drool constantly.

By contrast, the *Dökkalfar* were well-groomed weapons of war. Black adamantine armor hid their stark white hair and light blue skin. You could barely distinguish the blood-red eyes staring back at you from underneath their helms. The only distinguishing feature that marked them as Dark Elves was their long, pointed ears that extended more than six inches from their head.

"Peter, sound the alarm!" Sigrid said. "Hurry!"

"Should I contact the Gil-Gamesh?" he asked.

"There's no time!" Astrid warned. "Get the women and children to safety, now! Hurry!"

Peter ran off as the Swann sisters stood fast. What they saw scared them to the depths of their soul, but they never ran in the face of danger. After all, they were still shield maidens.

Astrid stepped over to their cart, carrying their assorted tools and farming implements, and opened a secret panel in the side of the cart. She pulled out two broad swords and handed one to her sister.

"Well, sister, we get to die as warriors, and what a glorious death it will be," Astrid said.

"I must confess, Astrid, I never thought we would die like this," Sigrid said. "I thought we'd be two old maids lying in bed, dying of old age. Instead, I'll die with a sword in my hand next to the one I love!"

Astrid smiled at her sister as a tear welled up in her eye. "Think you can swing that with just one arm?" she joked about her sister's disability.

"Think you can swing yours without falling on your ass?" Sigrid jabbed back at her sister, standing on one leg.

Not another word passed between them as they awaited their fate. The two women did the shield maidens proud that day. They took down more than thirty of the monsters before they fell. They died as they lived, side-by-side.

The Brood and the goblins killed the people without volition, tearing their victims apart while gorging themselves on their innards and entrails, eating them while they were still alive and screaming. The *Dökkalfar* cut the people down with an inhuman glee. Unlike the Brood and the goblins, the Dark Elves never cannibalized their prey. Instead, they enjoyed the thrill of the kill. Each blood-soaked death was like a sonnet to them, a glorious ode to their sick and twisted ways.

In one fell swoop, they wiped King's Crossing off the map of Avalon. While most women and children escaped through magic portals—special teleport channels set up by Ashley when they freed the town from Mordred—more than a hundred townspeople were killed protecting the transportation portals until everyone made it through. Afterward, a few dozen were kept alive in the town square while the buildings burned around them.

They were bloodied and beaten, sitting on the ground as they awaited their fate. Peter sat next to Sam Perrywinkle. He tried to help his old friend as much as he could, bandaging his wounds with his shirt, but Sam was fading fast. "Hang on, Sam! Please, hang on!" he pleaded.

"Don't bother with this old man, Peter lad," Sam whispered in a raspy voice. "I don't want to hurt anymore. Life is just not worth living with Mordred as King."

"We must have hope, Sam. We have to believe the Gil-Gamesh will save us!"

Before he could answer him, the crowd of Brood, goblins, and *Dökkalfar* separated as a small group stepped forward. It was D'Legg, the goblin leader, and Ailbe Dufaigh, Queen of the *Dökkalfar*. For a Brood, D'Legg was massive, standing nearly seven feet tall. He wore spiked pauldrons and gauntlets with a chainmail kilt, all forged from goblin iron. Across his shoulder rested a massive single-bladed ax that no one but him could wield.

His face was grotesque, with an iron plate covering half of it and spikes running across his head like a mohawk. The only predominant feature was his sharp fangs with large incisors protruding from his mouth.

Ailbe Dufaigh epitomized her role as the Dark Queen of the *Dökkalfar*. She wore the same black adamantine armor as her warriors but was covered from head to toe in chainmail with a few plate armor accessories. Even her head had a veil of chainmail that allowed her flowing white hair and long ears to protrude, framing her beautiful, slim face. A red cape flowed off her shoulders, and an ornate adamantine staff clutched in her hands, completing her look like the Dark Elf Queen.

Ailbe looked down on the beaten and bloodied humans with a continued look of disdain, yet a slight smile came to her face as she gazed across at her defeated foes.

"King's Crossing decided to forgo the rule of King Mordred and joined up with the Gil-Gamesh and his little resistance. Now, you pay the price for your disloyalty. Your homes, your land, and your lives are now forfeited. The only chance you have to save your miserable, pathetic lives is to give me the Gil-Gamesh's contact here in King's Crossing. Give them up to me, and we will spare your lives."

They all sat there, unmoving. It wasn't just out of loyalty to the Gil-Gamesh but also to Peter, who came home to help them. It was because of Peter and the MoonDrake siblings that the women and children escaped. They stayed silent, which irritated Ailbe to no end.

But Peter stood up, even as others struggled to pull him back down. He knew the meaning of self-sacrifice, something Lord MoonDrake taught him. He would not stay there when there was a chance that some of these brave men would live.

"I'm Peter McMillan, a loyal friend of Sir Hunter MoonDrake, the Gil-Gamesh of Avalon, and the true King of Avalon, His Majesty King Bowen Pendragon," he said proudly.

Ailbe frowned at Peter's defiant statement. D'Legg just snarled back at him. Peter stood his ground, awaiting whatever death they wanted to throw at him.

"Are you now?" came a voice from behind the multitude of goblins and *Dökkalfar*. Ailbe and D'Legg grinned a twisted, wicked smile as they parted to let someone through. Baroness Brigida Olafdotter stepped past the scourge of monsters, escorted by scores of her Northmen. They were covered in fur, armor, and weapons—Vikings ready for war.

"I remember you, Peter McMillan. You were the Gil-Gamesh's *valp* aboard his old flagship, the *Morningstar*. You followed him around like a dog on a lease."

Peter stared at Brigida, never looking away, just like the Gil-Gamesh had taught him. "And I remember you, Baroness Brigida Olafdotter," Peter said with conviction. "I remember the first time you came aboard the *Morningstar* with your father, how he doted over you as you skipped around the deck. I could tell how much he loved you. It must have been hard for you to kill him as you did."

Brigida gritted her teeth, angered that this boy would dare to bring up her father. She looked over to her men and signaled them with a nod. Two of them grabbed Peter by his arms, forcing him to his knees before Brigida. Through all this, Peter showed no fear. He kept his back straight and his head up.

"You do the Gil-Gamesh proud, Peter McMillan," she said. "You show no fear in the face of death. We Northmen appreciate that in our enemies. Normally, this would grant you a swift and painless death."

In one swift motion, Brigida drew her sword and sliced it across Peter's throat. Blood spurted out as Peter struggled against his captors, but they refused to let him go. They held him in place as he slowly bled out. Brigida stepped forward and leaned in close to the dying man.

"But I won't give you that... Not today," Brigida whispered as Peter choked on his blood. "You will be an example to the Gil-Gamesh of what happens to those who rebel against King Mordred."

Peter gathered all his strength and spat blood in her face defiantly. She stood up and stepped back, not bothering to wipe the blood away. She spun around and, in one swift stroke, beheaded Peter. His head rolled across the ground until it stopped at her feet.

"Put their heads on pikes," she commanded. "That will demonstrate our resolve to the Gil-Gamesh and his family." Brigida turned around and left it to the masses to complete the task. The Brood, goblins, and

Dökkalfar relished in the task at hand, and like Peter, the men stood firm, without fear. They would not give these villains satisfaction by showing fear in the face of death.

CHAPTER 20
MURDER AT KING'S CROSSING

As dawn broke over King's Crossing, the Gil-Gamesh and his forces finally arrived. Hunter had heard about the attack only a few hours ago. Per the protocols established with those under his protection, the women and children teleported to another village. Unfortunately, the earthquake struck these towns hard. It took hours for them to get any word back to Alfheimer.

Three airships landed just outside the smoldering ruins of the border town. As soon as they were down, Hunter led Eileanora, Rhona, a company of shield maidens, and the *Hîldrägo Boquè* into the village. They spread out, searching for survivors. When Hunter and his group reached the town square, these seasoned warriors were horrified by what they saw. Mordred's forces had culled the entire town. The dead bodies lay where they fell, whether man, woman, or child. They disemboweled some while they butchered others to pieces.

What shocked them most were the dozens of decapitated heads on pikes that lined the town square. Hunter recognized some of the men, like Sam Perrywinkle from the *Weathered Wren,* but one stood out to Hunter. At the center of the row was Peter McMillan's head. Underneath his head was a sign with the word "*NÍÞ*" inscribed. Hunter stared at it as his hands trembled. He knew exactly who had ordered this massacre.

"What does that mean?" Eileanora asked.

"It's written in the Old Norse tongue. It means 'traitor,'" Hunter said as his anger overwhelmed him. "It was Bree... Baroness Brigida Olafdotter. She did this!" Hunter screamed in rage, a loud guttural bellow that came from the pain he was feeling. He dropped to his knees and began to cry uncontrollably.

"I promised them! I promised to protect them! I promised Sam! I promised Peter! I promised all of them!" Eileanora tried to comfort him, wrapping her arms around him and holding him close, but even she could not sway his grief.

"Hunter, it's not your fault," she consoled him. "Sooner or later, Mordred would have told them to do this."

"You don't understand, Elle. This massacre looks exactly like Benzir. I told Bree the story about how Sarafina's home was destroyed by goblins, killing everyone in her village except for her. My Dad and Sarafina both told me that story as a warning about the evils of Blackbriar Forest. She recreated that massacre here to remind me that she knows how to hurt me."

Eileanora remembered the story of the town of Benzir. While on his "Grand Tour" across Avalon, Hunter's father, Lord MoonDrake, came across a small village on the edge of Blackbriar Forest. A goblin raiding party had slaughtered the entire town. Only Sarafina survived the attack, hiding under her floorboards while the goblins murdered family and friends in front of her.

"Baroness Olafdotter is a spiteful woman who thinks you spurned her affections and turned against her after the reclamation," Eileanora said as she tried to comfort him. "She probably did this as retaliation for taking Eldonshire and Lord Tomas' death."

While she comforted Hunter, Eileanora watched as Rhona and the shield maidens carried the Swann sisters' bodies and laid them on the ground next to Hunter and Eileanora.

"They went down as warriors," Rhona said. "They took nearly thirty Brood, goblins, and *Dökkalfar* with them."

"Did you find anyone else?" Eileanora asked.

"No, they left nothing alive, not even the livestock. There was no honor in this," Rhona added. "Baroness Olafdotter has fallen back into her heritage of plunder, murder, and pillaging that we knew her Viking ancestors for."

"This wasn't just Bree," Hunter interrupted as he slowly got to his feet. "Mordred did this. The Brood goblins and the *Dökkalfar* would never join forces on their own. They hate each other. They especially wouldn't take orders from a human, like Bree. He's stepping up his game, planning something big."

"But with the Prometheus Engine destroyed, he can't make any more Promethium," Eileanora interjected.

"Yes, but we don't know how much they made before the engine exploded," Rhona added to punctuate the argument. They all stood there silently, not knowing what to do, so they all turned to their leader. "What are your orders, Gil-Gamesh?"

Hunter looked around one more time, staring at the sea of death surrounding him, resolving his course of action before making his orders clear. "General, shore up the defenses with all our allies and make sure they have ready escape plans so this doesn't happen again. Keep a rapid response force at Alfheimer prepared to go at a moment's notice. We should hear from Sarafina soon, and when we do, we will invade Purgatory and rescue the Lady of the Lake. Once we get her back and my father's swords, we will attack Mordred in New Camelot and end his reign."

This was why these warriors followed a young knight like Hunter. He was decisive and forthright, always thinking ahead. It made him the leader they needed in this time of war. "But first, let's give these people a proper burial," Hunter concluded. "They at least deserve that."

"Should we have Ashley check all the gates to ensure they function properly?" Eileanora wondered.

"No, get some of the Magus to help with that instead," Hunter countered. "Ashley started having labor pains just as we were leaving. I think the babies are coming a little sooner than expected."

The sound of war raged from within the depths of Castle Pendragon. Weeks had passed since the explosion damaged most of the castle, but the stout foundation contained the blast beneath the earth. The blacksmith's forge was quickly put back together for an unusual project.

The hammer and the anvil droned on from the blazing heat of the forge as blacksmiths beat out raw metal into swords, and these were no ordinary blacksmiths. These were Iron Mount Dwarves, recognized as the best weaponsmiths in Avalon. While the rest of the dwarves continued to dig their way back into the Gilded Halls, these craftsmen worked tirelessly for King Mordred.

They made weapons, armor, and anything else the immortal king needed, but today, they worked tirelessly on a particular project. They were forging a special sword for Mordred using the Promethium he provided. The metal was hard to mold, even for these master smiths. They had to maintain a constant heat to keep it malleable. If it cooled down, even for an instant, they would have to start the process all over again.

It took three of them to do the work. While one steadied the metal on the anvil, two others would hammer it relentlessly, drawing it out and forming the blade's fuller and beveled edge. It took days to complete, even with the dwarves swapping in and out to give each other the time to rest while the others toiled away. Then came the hardening and the tempering, quenching the blade to rapidly cool the metal, allowing it to remain solid yet flexible.

The sword was ground down, sharpened, and polished before it fit snugly into a gilded hilt of gold and jewels. As they neared completion,

King Mordred and Magister Ocwyn entered the forge to inspect their work. The blacksmith held out the hilt to the king.

"It's finished, Your Majesty," the dwarf blacksmith announced proudly. "No one will be able to tell the difference."

Mordred reached out and held the sword in his hand. "Magnificent!" he boasted as he gripped the blade tightly, admiring the beauty of their work as he swung the sword around effortlessly. "It doesn't have the same enchantments as the original, but it will do." Ocwyn looked on, worried about the repercussions of Mordred's plan.

"Is everything ready to go, Magister?" Mordred asked.

"Yes, Your Majesty, everything has been prepared per your instructions."

"And what about the rest of the Promethium? Is the other weapon ready to deploy?" Mordred inquired.

"Duke Nottingham has it aboard the *Hood's Revenge* and is on his way to Strongürd Keep as we speak."

"Very good, Magister, very good," he proclaimed. "So, let us begin then. It's time to put on a show for the feeble-minded masses of Avalon!"

Shortly after sunrise the next day, people were pulled out of their homes and workplaces and ordered to gather around the square outside Castle Pendragon. The Adalwulf Guard moved them into place, corralling the citizens so they could witness the spectacle.

The people mumbled amongst themselves, complaining in the softest voice possible to avoid the Adalwulf Guard's wrath. They forced them close to a stage set up near the entrance to the castle. In the middle of the stage was a small, raised object covered with a red silk cloth.

Trumpets blared to announce the arrival of King Mordred. The assembled audience, most under duress, dropped to their knees as Mordred stepped out on stage. Magister Ocwyn, Lady Mavis, and Minister Blackstone followed close behind. The *Cosc Fháil* surrounded the stage front, ensuring no one would try to harm the King.

Mordred stood next to the cloth-covered object and looked out over the crowd. He saw nothing but peasants who were not worthy of gazing upon his beauty but realized he needed their support. After Bowen's proclamation, people started to rebel even more against his rule. Mordred needed to end the Gil-Gamesh and his resistance once and for all.

He motioned for the people to stand up before he stepped up to address the gathered crowd. "Citizens of Avalon! I speak to you today as your King, the rightful ruler of this sacred land. The boy-king, Bowen Pendragon, had his chance to speak. Now I will have mine. I do not deny any charges he leveled against me—kidnapping the Lady of the Lake and building the Prometheus Engine. They are all true."

The assembled crowd mumbled and grumbled, surprised that King Mordred admitted to these charges. Mordred held up his hand to quiet them down before he continued to speak.

"But I did those things to secure my rightful place as the King of Avalon," he continued. "You must understand that I only did this to defend my birthright. As the shield maidens' patron saint, the Lady of the Lake would never grant me what was rightfully mine. I cannot say if her absence destroyed Avalon, but if it was my fault, I apologize to all of you for the pain and suffering I caused you."

The crowd mumbled in shock, hearing the King apologize the way he did. It was rather humbling, especially to hear it from an usurper like Mordred.

"As for the Prometheus Engine, I ordered it built in secret, deep within the dungeon of Castle Pendragon, to create the legendary metal Promethium. It was a necessity of war to give us something to end the ongoing rebellion by the Gil-Gamesh and his allies. We were on the verge of finishing the project when a saboteur infiltrated the castle and destroyed the engine, causing a massive explosion that shook the ground beneath our feet again. Only through the combined magical prowess of myself and my loyal council could we prevent another catastrophe like the sinking of Atlantis."

Everyone was impressed with Mordred's lies. He twisted the truth to suit his needs, and the people bought it. Ocwyn stood there, stone-faced, even though he knew the truth. His gaze never left the crowd, stoic and emotionless.

"With what little Promethium we managed to manufacture, we will be using it very soon to end the rebellion so that we may forge the future we all desire. For now, I will demonstrate to you, once and for all, that I am the rightful King of Avalon," he concluded as he motioned to two of the *Cosc Fháil* to step forward. They pulled the covering off to reveal the sword in the stone.

Although it resembled *Excalibur* in the King's Stone, it was far from it. The sword was the duplicate Mordred had the dwarves forge from the

Promethium. It was placed into the stone to double as the real thing. The crowd was in awe of the legendary sword in the stone, but many refused to believe it was real. Some even began to place bets on whether Mordred could perform the feat.

He stepped up to the stone and placed his hand on the hilt. Like a brilliant stage actor, Mordred put on quite the show for the crowd. He tensed up, tugging on it with all his might until the sword came free from the stone. Mordred raised it high over his head for all the assembled to see. The people stared in disbelief when he pulled it out. They broke out in sudden applause, praising the King as never before.

Mordred's plan unfolded with a deceptive brilliance that left the people spellbound. The crowd, believing the copy to be the real *Excalibur*, erupted in awe as Mordred swung the sword into the stone, a dramatic gesture of his power. The rock shattered from the force of Promethium, a testament to the illusion he had woven.

"Behold *Excalibur*, the Sword of the King! Do you believe me now? I am Mordred the Immortal! I am Your King!" he shouted across the crowd. The people started cheering louder, chanting his name—"Mordred! Mordred!"—repeatedly. Mordred relished in the glory and soaked in the adoration thrust upon him. He finally had what he wanted... The love of the people of Avalon.

Blackstone stepped up behind the King to relay a message to him. "Sire, the *Hood's Revenge* has reached its destination. General Faust requests permission to attack."

"By all means, my dear Artūras. Tell him to proceed," he said, a smile playing on his lips as he waved to the crowd. The air crackled with anticipation as he declared, "Let loose the dogs of war!"

Blackstone bowed before leaving to relay the king's command to his general. Ocwyn grimaced, whispering a silent prayer for what was about to happen.

Standing on the deck of the *Hood's Revenge*, General Faust smirked when he received the confirmation from Minister Blackstone via magic message as he swaggered up to Duke Nottingham.

"Jaeger, King Mordred commands us to begin our attack," he relayed. "You may start your barrage. It is time to unleash Hell!"

Jaeger's smile was a cruel twist of fate. He had been waiting for this moment since his defeat by the Gil-Gamesh. Finally, he could exact his revenge. "With pleasure, General," he sneered as Jaeger stormed off the bridge and down to the gunnery deck. "All right, you dogs, open fire!"

The men cheered as they loaded their guns, but this was not standard ammunition nor spellshot. These were Promethium rounds—forty-two-pound cannonballs packed with enough alchemical explosive power to level a city block. They needed these precise rounds to penetrate the magical shields protecting the keep and, ultimately, destroy the structure.

The *Hood's Revenge* quickly moved into range and turned to fire a broadside. Like earlier, the Magus flew out to defend the keep, but they were too late to act. The guns fired over the approaching Magus directly at the base of the keep. Typically, the shells would bounce off the magic shielding the tower, but not this time.

Not only did Promethium allow the shells to penetrate the magic shields, but it also accentuated the explosive power within the armaments. Once they hit the tower, the explosives traveled through the building, following the magical energy flow. They kept up their fire as the ironclad airship circled Strongürd Keep while maintaining the barrage.

The base began to crumble within minutes and cracked under the tower's weight. Like a precision building demolition, Storngürd Keep collapsed under its weight, falling in on itself. You could hear the screams of the mages, wizards, and other magic casters inside, unable to escape.

The dust cloud dispersed outward, blinding everyone who was there. When the dust finally cleared, the damage was apparent. Strongürd Keep was gone. The blast wiped out the tower with all of Avalon's magical knowledge and power in one fell swoop.

The Magus quickly returned, hoping to find some survivors, but it was doubtful. Due to the tower's structure, explosions resonated up the interior columns, shattering the support structures from floor to ceiling. There was no escape for anyone from this disaster.

Faust and Jaeger looked on and laughed in glee. "It's begun!" Faust chortled, his fangs glistening behind his evil grin. "Get ready to send in your men to clean things up. Capture those who surrender but kill anyone who resists, Duke Nottingham. The King does not require prisoners except those willing to pledge their loyalty to him."

Jaeger saluted the general as he headed up to the bridge to make preparations. Faust just looked at the destruction and smiled. "It's your move, Gil-Gamesh! Time to die!"

EPILOGUE
THE RUMBLING OF WAR

The island of Togo was quiet, except for the constant drumming deep within the forest. Since they first inhabited the island centuries ago, the sound echoed across the water between Togo and Avalon. Several wraiths hovered above and around the island. They never go near the shores of Togo. They stayed far enough away to keep anyone from going in or out of the island, per General Faust's instructions.

Faust knew that the mystical Shaman of Togo could use their magic to hurt the wraiths. Their powers were closely related to necromancy, which could be fatal to the ghostly legion. They kept their distance but made their presence known to the people of Togo. The fact that Togo made no aggressive moves toward the wraiths showed they did not want to leave their little island.

A vast cityscape like nothing ever seen on Avalon existed inside the small island. The stone buildings and thatch roofs resembled African villages from the outside world, but never on a scale like this. The buildings rose high above the streets, nearly two to four stories tall in some places, with bridges of stone and wood connecting them. The people filled the streets, shopped at fresh markets, traded goods, and bought beautifully woven cloth and fancy jewelry. It had all the looks of a modern city with the down-to-earth appeal of a small village, all rolled into one.

Togo was a self-contained society, something they thrived on for centuries. When a slave ship crashed through the barrier and ran aground on Avalon's shores, the formerly enslaved people formed a separate society on Togo, apart from the rest of Avalon. They became a closer part of Avalon society within the past decade, thanks to the previous Gil-Gamesh, Lord MoonDrake.

After saving the Chieftain's daughter from death, he became known as one of the *Irunmole*, the *Orisa*. The *Irunmole* were primordial beings, given specific tasks to complete by God, known to Togo as *Oludmare*. As beings of pure energy, the *Irunmole* would sometimes take physical form. In that form, they were called *Orisa*. These legends were crafted to fit the miracles he crafted during his time on Togo.

After learning of his death, Togo found themselves lost. Not only did they lose a friend and an ally, but they also lost their spiritual contact with *Oludmare*. When the wraiths showed up and trapped them on Togo, the people thought this was their punishment for letting the *Orisa* die. They had no desire to leave their island home. Even after King Bowen's announcement, laying the blame on Avalon's destruction and Lord MoonDrake's death at the feet of Mordred, the people of Togo still felt uneasy. They wanted to help and join forces with the Gil-Gamesh, but the wraiths kept them prisoners in their homes. Besides, not all the Togo wanted to get involved in this internal conflict between Avalon's kings.

Sitting in his home, T'Ronga, the Great Chief of Togo, drank some sweet palm wine. He drank more often than usual, as he felt pretty impudent as the Chieftan of Togo. His people were as divided as his mind. He sat alone, staring out at the sky above the trees. He could see the wraiths, even deep within his home in the forest. Their ghostly forms glowed brightly against the night sky. They were there, day and night, a constant reminder of Mordred's control over them.

T'Ronga dressed in a simple loincloth of white leopard fur. He rarely wore his vestments as the Great Chief of Togo, except for the occasional council meeting or prayers and sacrifice within the Gathering Mount—their central hub on Togo. At the heart of the city, the Gathering Mount was a giant domed structure, more than five hundred feet tall, where Togo gathered to meet, adjudicate, and celebrate. It was built over an ancient magical site of unknown origin, making it a source of powerful magic.

As T'Ronga sat and drank, his wife Kendi entered the room. Kendi was a beautiful woman wearing flowing red and white silks, with her head wrapped in a traditional gele. She wore jewelry from gold, set with precious gems. She looked the part of the Chieftain's wife, more so than the Chief himself most days.

"T'Ronga, we will be late to the Gathering Mount," she said. "The children are already there, waiting for us."

"You go, Kendi. I do not feel like celebrating tonight."

"It doesn't matter how you feel, T'Ronga; you are the Great Chief of Togo and have an example to set for your people," she scolded him. "Did you learn anything from *Orisa*?"

"Bringing Bryan into the conversation will not sway me, *mke*... I will not be going to the mount tonight."

"*Laana kwa mpumbavu!*" she cursed him, calling him a reckless fool. "If you will not perform your duties as Chief, give to someone who will! You are ignoring your responsibilities, T'Ronga... To your people and your allies!"

"You think I don't know that? You think I don't want to help *Orisa's* children?" T'Ronga screamed back at her as he threw his cup of wine and stormed toward her. "We have tried everything to get past the wraiths, but nothing works. Our shaman cannot break them, and we cannot contact anyone outside of Togo. We are alone!"

"Then keep trying, again and again, until we get through! Bryan didn't give up on you, your people, or your daughter. Don't you give up on his son!"

T'Ronga took Kendi's words to heart. He knew she was right, but a servant walked in before he could say something. The young woman bowed to the two of them, breathless.

"Forgive me, Great Chief, but you are needed at the arena immediately!"

"The arena? What is it?" T'Ronga asked, confused.

"A great rumbling is coming from the gateway of *Aide Hwedo*!"

Aide Hwedo was the Rainbow Serpent. Togo believed *Aido Hwedo* created the mountains and rivers as the beast moved across the Earth at the dawn of creation. It now lived underground, causing earthquakes whenever it traveled. *Aide Hwedo* came to Togo, visiting it in the giant arena, to punish the wicked from their island.

Like any ancient coliseum, the arena was carved out of the stone itself, from the descending oval shape and the spectator seating to the arena floor. It was the shape and size of a football stadium but carved into solid bedrock.

T'Ronga arrived at the arena wrapped in his Chiefly vestiges: a cloak of various animal furs sewn together, clasped around his neck by an ornate broach of gold and jewels; a headdress made from the feathers of many different birds with a small skull inset with precious gems in the center; and the Staff of Kings in his hand, adorned with metal rings representing each of the Great Chiefs of Togo and a human skull at the top of the staff.

As he stepped onto the arena floor, the Togo warriors gathered at the entrance, weapons ready. These fierce warriors wore simple armor pieces, leather, and loin clothes for protection. Togo pointed their spears and swords toward the arena entrance. T'Ronga could sense their fear but knew his warriors would steel themselves and not run from danger.

"What is going on?" T'Ronga asked.

Before answering, one of the warriors bowed to their Chieftan, saluting with his fist over his heart. "Great Chief, one of the sentries heard rumbling from the gate of *Aide Hwedo*," he explained. "But this does not sound like the Rainbow Serpent. It sounds like an army running toward us."

T'Ronga listened carefully. He agreed with the warrior's assessment. It sounded like the running feet of an army coming toward them, not the usual sound that *Aide Hwedo* made when it came to the surface.

"Women and children, back away from the arena!" T'Ronga ordered. "Kendi, go now!" He handed his staff to his wife and drew his sword. Kendi reluctantly followed her husband's orders and left the arena floor. "Warriors, ready yourselves for whatever comes out of the tunnel! *Ushindi!*"

"*Ushindi!*" they shouted in unison, their war cry for victory. The noise got louder and louder, coming closer to them. The warriors stood firm, waiting for whatever came out.

Then, they appeared at the tunnel entrance. Hundreds of dwarves came running straight at them. They were all clad in massive armor, making them look bigger and bulkier than usual. They carried axes, swords, hammers, and polearms. It was an army ready for war.

They stopped short of running into them, waiting for the other to attack. The two forces leveled their weapons toward the other, ready to strike. "Now, wait a damn minute!" a voice cried out behind the dwarves. Dinius Oddbottom, Lord and Master of the Gilded Halls, stepped forward through the ranks. Unlike the others, his armor gleamed bright with a golden hue. In his hand, he carried a giant golden ax with a hammerhead on the other side. It was *Steinknuse*, Stone Smasher, the weapon of the Dwarf Lord.

T'Ronga recognized him immediately. "*Kupunguza silaha zako!*" he shouted, telling his warriors to lower their weapons. They did as their Chief commanded as T'Ronga stepped forward to greet Dinius.

"Lord Dinius? Is it you?" he asked. Dinius looked at him, momentarily confused, before finally recognizing him.

"Chief T'Ronga?" Dinius asked. T'Ronga sheathed his sword and reached out to his fellow Lord of Avalon.

"Lord Dinius, it is wonderful to see you!" he said as they shook hands. "We thought you and the dwarves were all dead!"

"It takes a lot more to kill this old dwarf, laddie," Dinius exclaimed as he returned the handshake. It signaled to the other dwarves to lower their weapons. "Sorry to surprise you like this, but we came across your tunnels on our way up here from *Nidavellir*. We thought it might be a shortcut back to the Fenris Mountains."

"You must have connected your tunnels with that of the great serpent. Praise be to *Orisa* that you found your way here."

"Never mind that chief. I need to contact the Gil-Gamesh," Dinius said with urgency. "I must let Lord MoonDrake know that the dwarves are back and ready for Ragnarök!"

T'Ronga stood silent, refusing to answer him. He realized that Dinius and his dwarves had disappeared before Avalon's Reclamation. "I'm afraid it's too late for that, Lord Dinius. Lord MoonDrake was killed just as Mordred took the throne of Avalon."

"What the devil, you say? Bryan's dead, and Mordred is alive, and King?"

T'Ronga nodded, saddened that he was the one who had to tell Dinius the news about his friend. The old dwarf stood there, confused, but his anger quickly turned into resolve. He knew what he had to do.

"Well, Chief T'Ronga, you better break out some libations and tell me everything we've missed," Dinius confirmed. "It seems like we've arrived just in time."

"In time? In time for what, Master Dinius?" T'Ronga asked.

"Ragnarök, Chief. The end of the world is coming, and it will destroy Avalon. The Dwarves of *Marglóð Hallargólf* are here to stop it!"

THE END

THE PROMETHEUS ENGINE · MARK PIGGOTT

The final chapter of the Avalon saga concludes in

ARCADIA DAWN:
BOOK FIVE OF THE FOREVER AVALON SERIES.

ALSO BY MARK PIGGOTT:

CORSAIR AND THE SKY PIRATES

A brilliant inventor... A prolific writer... A chance meeting between Nikola Tesla and Jules Verne created a world powered by steam generated, not from any fuel, but a meteor fragment. A comet named Uriel rained pieces of these powerful meteorites across the globe. That led to an industrial revolution years ahead of its time—
a steampunk revolution.

While Tesla made his inventions to ease people's day-to-day burden, Thomas Edison's ERP Corporation used their power and influence to ensure people paid for their modern miracles.

One man brought hope to the people as he pursued Tesla's dream. His exploits were legendary, his crew infamous, and his airship a vision of the future . . . Corsair and the Sky Pirates!

PROLOGUE

A Chance Meeting

1887, in the city of Amiens, France

At a small café in Quartier Saint-Leu, Jules Verne sipped quietly on his coffee as he sifted through the Paris newspaper. Verne enjoyed quiet moments like this. They helped clear his mind and organize his thoughts for the next adventure he would bring to life. The writer appreciated the quiet, little community on the Somme River. The sound of seagulls, steamship whistles, and church bells was as much noise as he could manage.

By looking at this ordinary man, you wouldn't know that he was such a renowned author. His white hair and beard matched the wrinkles on his face. He rubbed his left leg regularly, hoping to relieve the pain. It still ached where his nephew, Gaston, had once shot him. The poor boy was locked away in an asylum with little to no explanation of why he'd done it. All that remained was the ache in his leg.

The pain was a constant reminder to Verne, a reminder of his mortality, and it scared him. He would leave behind a legacy in his science, fantasy, and adventure stories, but was it enough, he wondered? Did these "flights of fancy" mean anything beyond the pages he wrote?

"*Pardon moi, monsieur,*" said a voice, startling the author. "Are you Jules Verne?"

He looked up from his newspaper to see a tall, skinny young man standing by the table. He bowed slightly at the waist with a bowler hat resting in his hand over his heart. Verne knew the young man had to be from Eastern Europe by his burly mustache and thick accent. His dark clothes reminded Verne of an undertaker. He hoped that was not the case.

"*Oui*, may I help you?" Verne asked.

"I am Nikola Tesla," the stranger said. "I am a great admirer of your work, *Monsieur* Verne. I apologize for interrupting you, but your housekeeper told me I might find you here. I was hoping I could have a moment of your time."

Verne thought for a second before nodding and motioning for him to sit down. Although he hated engaging with admirers, Verne knew it was part of the fame of being an author. Tesla seemed giddy as a schoolboy as he sat in the chair across from Verne. Before he could say anything, the waiter approached the two men.

"*Voulez-vous un café, monsieur?*" he asked, inquiring if Tesla would like a cup of coffee.

"*Oui, merci, et un verre d'eau s'il vous plait,*" he replied, asking for a glass of water as well. Tesla waited patiently for the waiter to depart before saying anything, but Verne spoke first.

"From your accent, I assume you are from Eastern Europe, *Monsieur* Tesla. Austria or Hungary, am I correct?" Verne inquired.

"Serbia, *Monsieur* Verne, but it is part of the Austro-Hungarian Empire, so you are quite correct."

"And what brings you to Amiens? Surely you did not come here to get an autograph?" Verne quipped.

"*Non, monsieur,*" Tesla answered. "I work for the Continental Edison Company. I came to Amiens to work on the electrical system. I thought I might get the chance to speak with you before I return to Paris."

"Edison . . . Well, well, I must thank you for the electric lights," Verne commented. "It is better to light the night with your electric light bulb than to try to write by fading candlelight at three o'clock in the morning."

Tesla smiled in appreciation of the compliment. "Thank you, *Monsieur* Verne, but perhaps I can inspire you another way," Tesla remarked as he pulled out a folded piece of paper from his coat and handed it to Verne.

"*Qu'est-ce que c'est?*" he curiously asked. "I thought you weren't looking for my autograph."

"No, *non*. It is something that your writings inspired me to create."

He piqued Verne's curiosity as he carefully unfolded the paper. When Verne saw what was inside, his eyes grew as large as hen's eggs. It was an engine so complicated in design that Verne could not understand the intricacies of what he was seeing. Around the machine was a crude drawing of a ship, a submersible ship that resembled his *Nautilus* description.

"*Incroyable*," Verne whispered, amazed at what he saw. "What is it?"

"A steam-powered oscillating electrical generator," Tesla explained. "It can generate twenty times the electrical power of anything produced today, maybe more. My machine could power a ship like your *Nautilus*, don't you think?"

"*En effet*. Indeed it could, but it would take a ton of coal to generate the amount of steam you would need to power such an engine, would you not agree?"

"Under normal circumstances, yes, but not with this," Tesla said as he looked around first to see if anyone was watching him before he reached into his pocket and pulled out a small, corked vial. A few small blue stones glowed dimly in the morning light and were nestled inside the glass. He handed it to Verne, who stared at them in awe.

"What on earth are they?" Verne asked.

"They're from a meteor that fell near my home in Serbia, near the Balkans," Tesla began to explain, but he abruptly stopped when the waiter returned with his coffee and a glass of water, as he had requested. He waited until the waiter departed to continue his explanation. "It generates a constant heat that never seems to die out. Here, please observe!"

Tesla took the cork off the vial and poured out one of the small meteorite fragments into the glass of water. The blue rock began to bubble and burn, rapidly raising the water's temperature. Soon, the water was boiling as steam arose from the glass. Tesla took a spoon and pulled out the tiny rock before dropping it carefully on the tabletop.

"You can pick it up, *Monsieur*. It won't burn you."

Verne reached down and tentatively touched it with his fingertips until he realized how relatively cool the rock was, then he picked it up and held it in his hand. "*Monsieur* Tesla, this is quite, well, *remarquable!*"

"It expends energy without reducing its size or mass," Tesla boasted. "It could change the world as we know it."

"Is there any more of this meteor?" Verne asked. "Where does it come from?"

"I have a colleague at the Royal Astronomical Society in England who discovered a comet he named Uriel, after the archangel," Tesla said. "As the comet passed by our planet, Uriel's fragments impacted Earth from the Urals to the Alps and even into North America. I am working on a precise method to detect the meteorite fragments because others are beginning to search for them. So far, I've collected nearly five hundred kilograms."

"You are an incredibly talented young man, *Monsieur* Tesla," Verne said as he handed him the meteor before Tesla dropped it in the tube. Verne then folded the paper and gave it back. "But what does this have to do with an old man like me? I am a writer of flights of fancy, not a scientist."

"Your stories have inspired me to pursue new avenues of science. You have dared to dream the impossible, but this," Tesla said as he held up the test tube, "makes it possible. I would like to collaborate with you on some ideas that I have. I have the scientific knowledge, and you have an incredible imagination. Perhaps, together, we can bring about a new age of science and technology, which benefits all of humanity."

"Will that not interfere with your work at the Edison Company?" Verne asked.

"I have already put in my notice to leave my position with Edison. I plan to go to the United States and pursue my dreams there, but I want to work with you on my designs before I go.

"Besides," Tesla continued, "I don't want my ideas to come under an Edison patent instead of my own. He is a brilliant man, but his ambitions are to pursue science for wealth. I cannot be a part of that.

"Something like this"—he shook his design at Verne as he picked it up—"could change the course of human history. It needs a little imagination to make it come true. You, *Monsieur* Verne, are a master of imagination. Think of what we could accomplish together!"

Verne sat quietly, intrigued by the young man's offer. He saw how his novels could influence humanity's future for the first time. "Very well, *Monsieur* Tesla. Where do we begin?"

CHAPTER ONE

HEIST ON THE VALIANT

1907, somewhere over the English Channel

A storm raged over the rolling sea, fierce winds creating a pounding surf as thunder and lightning roared in the overcast sky. It took a skilled pilot to navigate a storm like this.

Murky fog usually shrouded any visibility, a potential hazard for any ship daring to sail these waters, but not this ship. Above the waves and crashing seas, floating effortlessly above it all, the zeppelin Valiant sailed toward Great Britain.

The Valiant was the pinnacle of first-class accommodations for passengers traveling throughout the British Empire. With an Edison Counter-Oscillation Engine, the majestic zeppelin could stay airborne indefinitely, providing its guests with every luxury. At nearly twelve hundred feet in length, the Valiant was the pride of the White Star fleet of airships. It could carry more than twenty passengers with a complement of thirty officers, crew, and staff to tend to their every need.

Thanks to the genius and unparalleled visions of people like Tesla, Edison, Bell, McCoy, and others, steam-powered machines utilized the fragments of Uriel as a power source. The discovery of the comet and its power brought about a new Industrial Revolution, an age where these devices made life easier and more reliable for everyday people. Machines no longer operated only on the ground or on the seas. They moved into the sky. The Valiant was an example of this unprecedented new age.

"Tonight, the sky is quite clear," one crew member said to his companion while taking off his hat. They were climbing down the ladder from their watch station now that their shift was over.

"Maybe for once, the pirates are getting airsick." His companion chuckled.

A prize like the Valiant was also a tempting target. The rigid frame was adorned with gold and brass fittings, emulating its rich beginnings. It tended to attract unwelcomed guests.

"You know my father was a sailor, right?" the first crew member continued. "He always joked about how these new engines brought everything about the sea into the air as if nothing had changed."

The second crew member snickered. "Pirates fight for the 'booty,' and the treasure doesn't have to be on an island."

While the two sailors laughed, they failed to notice another airship above the cloud line, moving in over the *Valiant*. This one was smaller but relatively well armed. Dual-barrel cannons adorned the top, sides, and underneath, rotating around the dirigible frame on a track. The airship's rigid structure was covered in sectioned armor plating to protect it from harm. The blimp was painted to resemble a rainbow-striped serpent, with sharp teeth and an intimidating grin, flowing aft as its body wrapped around it. On the tail fin was the traditional skull and crossbones, denoting its pirate allegiance.

The blimp was the *Galeru*, and it belonged to one of the most infamous pirates of the age, Corsair. The daring deeds of this sky pirate made him a villain to the authorities and a celebrity to the people. In an age of modern marvels, the wealthy grew richer off the workers who toiled in the factories worldwide to produce these wondrous inventions for people, but at the cost of human lives. Corsair was a new age Robin Hood, robbing from the wealthy and affluent and giving to the poor and those in need, but there was more to him than being a thief and pirate. He kept his secrets close, and only those he trusted most knew what they were.

On the bridge of the *Galeru*, first officer Francesca "Kiki" Mori peered out at the *Valiant* through her spyglass. Her long, black hair was pulled back in a traditional Japanese bun called a *shimada*, held up with ornate oriental combs and hairpins. Her appearance and style showed off her adoptive homeland's Japanese heritage with a modern take on samurai armor layered over Victorian sensibilities. She considered herself a *ronin* or a samurai without a master. With a katana around her waist and a Colt M1895 strapped to her hip, Kiki was an intimidating figure. Her skill as a swordswoman was one of many hidden talents that made her an asset to Corsair.

"Keep her steady, Eager! We want to stay right in her blind spot!" she ordered.

Behind her, at the helm, Gelar "Eager" Kingsman kept a tight grip on the ship's wheel. The old Australian Aboriginal didn't look anything like a modern navigator. His baggy clothes, consisting of a short-sleeved shirt and shorts, covered his thin, bony frame. He said he needed his skin exposed like that to feel the slightest shift in the air around him and the ship's movement under his feet. His white hair and beard were quite long, stringy, and somewhat unkempt. The goggles he wore over his eyes had white lenses to hide that he was blind. Although he couldn't see the world around him, Eager had an unnatural ability to pilot the *Galeru*, so Corsair kept him on board. His other senses were so sensitive that he could "see" the world better than the rest of them.

"Don't you worry none, Lady Kiki, we're right where we want to be," he replied in a thick accent, exuding confidence. "Their radio wave detector is focused forward, keeping an eye on the storm. Back aft, they're as blind as I am."

She looked at the *Valiant* again with her spyglass, peering along the top for any lookout or guards keeping watch. These first-class zeppelins had lookout towers and guard posts along the top centerline. The domed viewing posts were visible along the dirigible spine, raised and lowered in inclement weather. Kiki could see that they were all closed and locked down.

"It looks like their top deck lookout posts are down, but why would they do that?" Kiki asked. "Even in this weather, they always keep one operational; it's standard procedure. Why on earth would they risk it?"

"They wouldn't," said a voice behind her. He stepped on the bridge of the *Galeru* with the confidence of a commander. His long, leather waistcoat covered a bronze-metal-inlaid vest that hugged his body tight. He had twin modified Colt M1895s strapped around his waist and a cutlass at his side. The sword's guard wrapped around the hilt in moving gears, leaving one to imagine what power it held within. A flowing red scarf wrapped around his neck, fluttering as he walked. His shoulder-length black hair was pushed back off his face by a large pair of optics. His handsome face gleamed with a devilish grin that made most women swoon. No one knew his real name, only the name he went by: Corsair!

"No guards or lookouts means only one thing, Kiki," he said as he stepped up next to her. "They're guarding something so valuable they can't afford to spare anyone for lookout duty."

"Private security? Pinkertons, maybe?" she asked. "Do you think they're transporting some pieces of the comet?"

"According to my sources, yes, absolutely," Corsair responded as he lowered his optics down over his eyes. He turned some dials to extend the lenses outward, giving him a better view of the *Valiant*.

"And it's not that, Kiki. Our spies saw John Kreusi getting on board in Paris."

"Edison's right hand? What's he doing on this side of the Atlantic?"

"That's what we're here to find out," Corsair said as he continued to look out over the *Valiant*.

"More security means we'll need bigger guns," Kiki replied. "This one could get messy, Captain."

"No doubt, but every world government is trying to find as much of that meteorite as they can for ERP, and they'll stop at nothing to get their hands on it."

ERP, the Edison/Röntgen/Parsons Corporation, was the leading designer for many of the most fantastic machines and engines the world had ever seen. From motion pictures to phonographs, electrical power generators, and weapons of war, ERP supplied them all. Their hands reached deep into the pockets of all the major world powers, from America and Great Britain to Germany and Russia.

"Just so they can keep their factories running without interruption, running the poor and destitute into the ground while they relax in luxury," Kiki said. "Bastards!"

"Go get the crew ready; we drop in twenty!" Corsair ordered. Kiki ran off the bridge to get the rest of the crew ready to board the *Valiant*. "Eager, bring us down to fifteen feet above the *Valiant*, past the tail fin, when I give the signal."

"Roger, oy, *gubba!*" Eager cajoled, calling Corsair his "little boy," as he always did.

Even though more than two-thirds of the *Galeru* was open space for helium bladders, the lower two decks were crew areas. The largest of them was the hangar bay. It held two small aircraft called *aero-wings* designed by two bicycle shop owners in Ohio using a Tesla engine, retractable gun mounts, and a bomb rack. It also contained several drop tubes—hydraulic cylinders that forced their way into the superstructure of another airship—allowing for quick boarding and an equally fast escape.

Corsair's crew gathered around the hangar, checking their weapons for the upcoming raid. According to their criminal records, these men and women were assorted lowlifes, scoundrels, and thieves from the four corners of the globe. Those records didn't reflect the deep commitment to the people who needed their help and fully supported Corsair's cause. Many of them lived for the thrill of the hunt, the adventure, and the payoff after a good heist. The saying might be "no honor among thieves," but this group was the exception.

"Knox, why the Hell are you taking that cannon? They are a bunch of snotty, fancy-pants *stronzo* down there, not the Kaiser's *Eisenwand*, no?" said Eddie "Dash" Castello, trimming his wispy, thin mustache as he gazed into a small hand mirror. The little Italian didn't look it, but he was the weapons and demolitions expert aboard the *Galeru*. He was a regular deadeye for his accuracy with anything from a long gun to a pea shooter. Aboard the airship, they called him Dash because he picked up on things fast. He started using explosives in the Carbosulcis Coal Mine at age ten. Dash's experiences and hardships made him eager to take to the skies when he met Corsair.

He always looked overburdened with various weapons and explosives strapped to his belt, thighs, and back, with bandoliers across his chest. To him, it was like wearing his favorite sweater. Next to Corsair, Dash was the best shot in the crew.

"The captain said to expect the worst, and I always come prepared," replied Heinrich "Knox" Romig as the armored soldier carefully loaded the ammunition feeder into his .58-caliber Gatling gun. He kept the massive weapon slung over his shoulder with the ammunition fed from a huge backpack. Knox was a former member of the Kaiser's elite *Eisenwand*, or Iron Wall, German special forces that wore steam-powered armor under long coats, making them practically invincible. His head was cleanly shaven, but a thick, burly beard covered his jawline. He towered over Dash and most of the crew and looked like he could easily toss a bear. They called him Knox after Fort Knox because he was impregnable in body and spirit.

Knox was one of the most decorated soldiers in the *Eisenwand* until his superiors ordered him to lead an attack against insurgents in an abandoned factory in Poland. However, that factory turned out to be an orphanage full of children. After that slaughter, he left his chest full of medals behind and joined Corsair.

"I have to protect everyone, even you, Dash," Knox said as he hoisted his gun across his shoulder.

"That is always refreshing to hear, my dear Heinrich," Felicia Scarlett "Fox" Bertrand cooed in her quaint British accent as she carefully filed her fingernails. Fox sat comfortably, her legs crossed while she continued with her manicure. Her form-fitting dress underneath a button-down coat didn't seem appropriate for a raid. Her red hair was pulled up tight into a bun under a fascinator, and her makeup immaculately done.

In most circles, Fox—better known as the "Scarlett Fox"—was a shade, an expert on infiltration and information collection. Her beauty and charm, combined with her innate ability to blend into any environment, made her an asset in more ways than one. Her skills were once the pride of the British Secret Intelligence Service, but she left shortly after discovering how deep ERP was into the British government. After British Intelligence framed her for murder, Fox met Corsair and found a new purpose in life.

"You know I will always have your back, *mia adorabile signora!*" Dash swooned as he leaned into her and twirled his mustache. "And what a lovely backside it is!"

In a blur, Fox pulled out a dagger hidden in her belt and spun it around her fingertips until she placed the blade's tip under his chin. "Comment about my backside again, Dash, and your front side will get my full attention." Dash ignored her threats until a strong hand grabbed him by the scruff of his neck and pulled him back.

"Dash, you're one second away from Fox giving you a butcher's Sunday special," said Henry "Bronx" Jones. "When are you gonna learn to leave that woman alone?" Bronx, a Black garage mechanic from New York City, was the chief engineer on the *Galeru*. Bronx was a natural for engines, especially the complex Tesla Oscillating Electric Engines. He was known by many as a Vernian. He studied mechanical engineering, but he also read Jules Verne's novels and—like Tesla—put his ideas to practice. For a Black man in America, that was a hard-fought education he had learned from behind the scenes. He worked as a mechanic by day and a janitor at a major university by night. He would study the textbooks and chalkboards as he cleaned the rooms, getting a free college education on his own time.

"Never, *mia amico*," Dash replied. "She has the key to my heart."

"She's going to shove that key up your backside one of these days," Bronx snapped back. "Besides, Captain's on his way down."

As Bronx spoke up, Corsair and Kiki stepped down the spiral staircase leading from the bridge into the hangar with the team's final member. Nathaniel "Moon Crow" Porter was no exception to Corsair's mismatched crew of infamy. He was a proud Apache warrior from the plains of the American Southwest. The sole survivor of the massacre of his village by American soldiers, Moon Crow was rescued by a frontier family heading west. Although they gave him an

American name, he never lost sight of his Apache roots. He took the name Moon Crow from a story his adopted family had told him. They had found him on a moonlit night, holding on to a dead crow. He saw that as a sign—a vision quest. His destiny lay beyond his tribe.

He dressed like any other man of his time—a button-down shirt, vest, and pants—with a few exceptions that exhibited his heritage. Centered on a bolo tie around his collar was a large turquoise stone, a piece of his homeland he carried. On his wide-brimmed hat, crow feathers with white tips protruded on the side, held in place by a band of multicolored beads that he had woven himself. The white tips represented the moon in the night sky. A pair of tomahawks dangled from his belt, and an 1894 Winchester repeating rifle was slung across his back.

"All right, you knockers, gather round and listen up," Kiki shouted to get their attention. Everyone moved in around Corsair to get their debriefing before the drop. They were always excited when a new job approached, but they never strayed from Corsair's orders. His word was absolute.

"So, what's the plan, *mia amico*? Burn it down or smash and grab?" Dash joked. Bronx slapped him on the back of the head for his lack of decorum in front of the captain.

"Smash and grab, Dash, but with a purpose," Corsair said. "We've got two targets, and we need to get in and out as quickly as possible with the least amount of collateral damage. That means leaving the passengers alone this time. We don't have the time for our normal Robin Hood routine."

"You sound worried, *Kapitän*," Knox observed.

"Not worried, Knox, cautious. I have faith in my crew to do the job." He smirked as he looked around at everyone. "But this is no ordinary heist. There are more than your normal White Star security guards this time around. With Kreusi aboard, there's probably Pinkerton's on his private security detail. So, you know what that means?"

"Shoot to kill," Fox interjected. "Those bastards don't play around." The Pinkertons were the best security money could buy. They were well trained, better than most armies, and equally well equipped. Call them what you will—mercenaries or soldiers-for-hire—they were a force to be reckoned with.

"Exactly, so let's split up into two teams and hit them hard and fast. Kiki—you, Knox, and Dash will head aft. The piece of Uriel's comet is yours. Find it and get it back to the *Galeru*. Bronx, you and Moon Crow are with me. We're going after Kreusi."

"And what about *signora* Scarlett? Why can't she be on my team?" Dash asked with a wink toward Fox. She shook her head, not even bothering to look at him when she spoke.

"I have a mission, Eddie darling, that does not include you!"

"All right then, lock and load, charge up your gear and get ready to drop. Five minutes!" Corsair ordered as everyone made their final preps and geared up for the drop. Kiki didn't like what she heard from Fox and confided in the captain.

"Why is the Fox going solo? I thought we discussed this and decided it was a bad idea?" she asked.

"We did, but then Scarlett convinced me it was a good idea," Corsair snipped back while he loaded his Colt revolver, not even looking up at her, making Kiki scowl.

"Yeah, I bet she convinced you!"

"Kiki," he disrupted her scathing retort. "Fox is familiar with the *Valiant* class of airship. She knows all the hiding places the first-class passengers use to tuck away their secrets. If there's someone or something else aboard, I want to know about it, and Scarlett has the best assets to discover them for us."

"It's not her assets that I'm worried about," Kiki argued. "I don't like it when one of the team goes solo. I may not like that ginger fox, but I don't want her dead or captured."

"Why, Kiki, you do care?" Fox surprised her from behind, her wicked smile and fluttering eyelashes professing her sarcasm. "I knew that deep down you loved me!"

"Love, no. Loath, yes!" Kiki groaned as she stormed away in a huff. Corsair wanted to laugh, but he kept it inside.

"Now, Scarlett, that wasn't very nice," he scolded her. "But Kiki does have a point. It would be best if you didn't take any unnecessary risks. If it gets hairy, you get out of there, understand?"

"Things never get hairy with me, my darling Corsair," Fox retorted as she slowly and seductively dragged her finger under Corsair's chin. "That's why I shave my legs, to get out of those tight situations."

Dash watched her with his eyes wide open as she walked away toward her drop tube. "*Buon Dio, sono innamorato!*" he exclaimed, professing his love for the femme fatale. Knox lifted him by his collar and carried him over to their drop tube; he dangled in the air as he tried to get away from the brute.

Corsair chuckled aloud this time. He loved his team; he would do anything for them. He would die for them. He went over to the internal communication pod next to his drop tube and flicked the switch to talk. "OK, Eager, move us into position and drop when ready."

"Roger, oy, *gubba!* Two minutes to drop!" Eager shouted through the speaker box. Everyone stepped into their drop tubes. About the size of a typical elevator, the metal cylinders could comfortably fit three to four people. Their size was one of the reasons Corsair always put Dash with Knox. Between the two of them, they equaled three people. Even with Kiki, it was still going to be a tight fit.

Once everyone got situated inside their cylinders, the doors closed. A sheath of canvas threaded with metal rings extended down and around the tube. The trapdoors beneath them slid open, and a hiss of steam escaped as the iris unfurled, allowing the wind and rain to rush in from the outside.

"Hold on to your lunches, ladies and gents," Eager yelled out from the bridge. "Dropping in three . . . two . . . and one!" Eager sent the tubes down into the airship below with the flick of a switch. Hydraulic springs forced them through the superstructure and canvas covering the top of the zeppelin, driving them onto the airship's upper platform.

All of the world's airships were similarly designed with an upper catwalk right along the centerline, so the crew could inspect the top of the superstructure, check for leaks in the hydrogen bladders, and man lookout positions, among other responsibilities. Once in place, the cylinders hooked onto the catwalks, keeping them steady and locked in for an easy entry and exit as the canvas retracted to the top of the superstructure. They also self-sealed to keep the elements out, so the targets would be unaware that they had been boarded.

Once the drop process finished, the cylinder doors opened, and everyone jumped out, looking for trouble.

"Pirates!" a voice shouted from down the catwalk. Everyone looked to see a maintenance man running away, shouting out the warning. Moon Crow took out a tomahawk and threw it at the frightened crew member without even thinking. His aim was perfect, hitting the maintenance man squarely in the back of the head. He was dead before he hit the ground.

Corsair and his crew knew that a stray bullet could set off the hydrogen inside this part of the zeppelin, which was why edged weapons were best in the upper reaches of the airship. Corsair motioned for the two groups to take off without saying a word. At this point, no one knew if anyone had heard the dead man's warning. Kiki and her team headed aft while Corsair and his group headed forward. Fox found the first available ladder off the catwalk and started descending independently.

Moon Crow pulled out the tomahawk and wiped off the blood in the dead man's hair. He didn't say a word; he never did in battle. In his opinion, words wasted energy. As they continued forward, Bronx looked around in awe at the mechanics of a zeppelin like the *Valiant*. "Geez, Captain, you sure you can't do this without me? I'd like to get my hands on one of these Röntgen Inertia Stabilizers. It might help to keep the *Galeru* flying straight."

"That's why we've got Eager. Sorry, Bronx, but I need you to focus your 'Vernian' mind on something new," Corsair explained. "Kreusi is said to have one of those new Hollerith Thinking Machines. I need you to tell me whether or not this is something worth stealing."

"Oh, I've been dying to get a look at one of those," Bronx said with childlike glee.

"OK, for now, tap into the communications grid and find that bastard for me."

Find this book everywhere books are sold or on
www.curiouscorvidpublishing.com